ALSO BY SEYMOUR WINTERS

A PIECE
England, 1964 - a flu pand(
but spared Sam and Ra(
in a desperate bid to survi
their lives, they are chall
trying to destroy ...ally.
Fate leads Sam to Claire, blind and abandoned, and their
growing relationship starts to fracture the bond between him
and Rachel and threaten everything they have had together.
Sam struggles to make the right choices for himself and
their community as the odds stack against them,
until help arrives from an unexpected source.
Will they all turn away from the offer of salvation
and choose to strive on alone?
Live or die, the consequences could be no less stark.

EXHIBIT 51
"A tantalising portrait of life, blending humour and mystery;
a slant on a modern day love story,
Seymour creates a tableau of interesting characters
trying to run a museum in which normality
and the unexplained constantly overlap
and become entwined."
"I was dumped by my girlfriend as I lay comatose in a hospital bed."
Lenny settles into a new life in South Devon.
His work at the museum brings challenges; one becomes
the bane of his life ~ an elusive steel ball that arrived
with the founding curator, now sought by a
manipulative American, Hogan King.
Only Flinty Stone, Lenny's unconventional assistant,
can help Lenny keep one step ahead in the
cat and mouse games with the American.
Out of the blue, Lenny's past catches up with him.
Perhaps the reason was always obvious ~
the answer was in the name: Exhibit 51

SEYMOUR WINTERS ~ wintersseymour@gmail.com

A GRACE OF DANDELIONS

SEYMOUR WINTERS

*'Happy reading',
Best wishes
Seymour*

Published in the United Kingdom in 2021

Copyright © Seymour Winters 2021

This novel is a work of fiction. Names and characters are the product of the author's imagination and any resemblance to actual persons, living or dead, is entirely coincidental

No part of this publication may be reproduced, stored in a retrieval system, or transmitted, in any form or by any means, without the prior permission of the author

Typeset in Book Antiqua

ISBN: 979-8-6922-6183-0

For Elliott, Amalthea, Lindsay, Keira, Scott and Imogen – the future of our planet is yours to cherish

ACKNOWLEDGEMENTS

My thanks go to Caralyn Tottle and Pete Day
for their valuable contributions in reading the final proof.
Great work, guys!
Also my eternal thanks to my
agent and editor, Jane Canvin.

CHAPTER 1
I BLAME IT ON MY NAME

My name is Grace. My surname doesn't matter. I like my name, though not the expectation that comes with it. After bearing two sons, my mother invested great hope in the daughter who arrived last. Already in her forties, there would be no more children to follow me and she chose my name with immense pride and anticipation.

But you can't become something you're not, no matter how much you may want to please those you love. Slight in stature, by the time I was five I already felt stereotyped, my true feelings disregarded, without a voice to be heard so early in my life. No matter that I had role models with the same name, Grace Darling not least in my list of heroines.

As the years passed my teachers labelled me as stubborn and argumentative; my brothers as headstrong, muleheaded. Words like 'obstinate', 'outspoken' and 'selfopinionated' seemed to roll off every tongue around me. My parents tried their best, hiding their disappointment, offering advice and counsel aimed to make my life easier. After all, they had named me in anticipation that my name would mould and create my character, not the other way around.

I love the term 'trying to square the circle'. It described the expectations imposed on me to perfection. Not that behaving the way I did was a simple impulsive act; the need to just be 'bloody minded' for the sheer hell of it. Things were never that simple.

You see, from my earliest memories, I had dreams, of great detail and colour, looking at a world I knew I recognised in crystal precision, as though almost transcendental through a clear glass window. Nothing especially odd about that, you might think.

Except …

My dreams came true; exactly as I dreamt them.

CHAPTER 2
GIRL IN THE WIRE

In the dark, witching hours of the night, when fable holds that demons are afoot, an owl passed overhead on silent wings of feather velvet. It was answered by a plaintive distant cry.

Suddenly alert, Homer cocked his head, straining ears to confirm what he thought he had just heard. Beside him stood Joss, stock still, ears pricked, eyes bright with starlight, her posture confirming that she, too, had heard the cry.

"Easy, Joss," he whispered, his hand stroking the crown of her head. Her reaction would be confirmation enough as the seconds ticked by.

Homer had almost convinced himself that they must have both imagined the cry, when it came again. This time Joss disappeared before the sound had even registered on Homer's brain, homing like a canine exocet missile on the plaintive call, leaving Homer silently protesting in her wake.

And the reason for this impulsive reaction?

The cry was made by a human voice.

Homer came upon many things during his nightly excursions through the surrounding fields and woodlands, from courting couples to even an escaped parrot, but he had never discovered a snare containing human prey.

Breathless by the time he caught up with Joss, he found the dog frantically scoring the ground beneath a scene that defied belief. Hanging several feet above the ground, ensnared in an enclosed hammock of barbed and razor wires, was a human figure, writhing and twisting in a vain attempt to break free.

Homer could name most things that inhabit the woods and fields of the night, but a spider capable of spinning a web big enough to catch a man, or a woman for that matter, would be a first. If one such existed, Homer would be out of the woods faster than you can say 'arachnophobia' and back to a boring desk job.

Frozen in surprise, he instinctively dropped to a knee, backing warily into the inky darkness of a clump of wild rhododendron. Every poacher is at heart a hunter; why else would a sane man spend cheerless nights wandering the woods and fields when he could be tucked up in a warm bed? More of an opportunist than a stalker, road kill and wild rabbits that happen to wander into his nets were more Homer's style. So the presence of another person, one that definitely shouldn't be here, presented him with a problem, not least because he had no right to be there either.

Homer knelt, contemplating his quandary. Joss (at least she had no problem with her name; just a love of 'sticks'!) grumbled to remind him that from her perspective something was definitely wrong in the world. He hushed her more sharply than intended. The sound carried; the figure writhed and twisted; a frightened voice called out.

"Who's there?"

It was an anguished gasp that blended pain and fear in equal measure.

Racked by uncertainty, he chose silence. Unfair? Especially when observing a fellow human in obvious distress. But this night-time world, always full of hidden challenges, was far from straightforward.

Less than half a mile away was a fracking site, drilling and extracting oil and gas, where security was overseen by an unpleasant character called Bremer. Since the government had passed legislation to embrace fracking within the Anti-Terrorism Act, ex-criminals like Bremer had enjoyed a field day. Rumours abounded about the tactics Bremer and his guards employed. Granted they were admittedly largely hearsay, but having encountered Bremer's men before, Homer was more than prepared to give such rumours the benefit of doubt.

Which all colluded to aggravate his dilemma. Legally, he had no right to be in the woods; they were owned by the same company that farmed the land on which the fracking site was operating. This brought the area into the orbit of Bremer's jurisdiction.

Homer wasn't the most perceptive of people, but it didn't take an Einstein to join the dots. The trap that had ensnared the writhing figure in front of him had been fashioned with deliberate intent, a fact that more than likely led straight to Bremer, someone he had no wish to encounter on land he considered his 'fiefdom' in the early hours of the morning.

Homer had long decided it was safest to avoid crossing Bremer at all costs. And now, the consequence of being caught helping someone snared in one of his traps would hardly bear thinking about. It would be far easier to throw a pair of wire cutters to the trapped woman (the sound of the voice was definitely female) and disappear before anyone came looking for prey in their trap.

Homer was searching through his rucksack when two things happened simultaneously. The woman emitted a primeval groan of pain and Joss ran to her rescue. Even if Homer was prepared to abandon the woman to her fate, valiant Joss was made of sterner stuff. Reluctantly, he made a grab for the dog, uttering colourful expletives under his breath, before Joss became tangled in the mesh of wires. Only Bremer could be so malicious as to dream up something so vindictive.

"Can you hurry?" the plaintive voice called. "I'm bleeding. Badly."

At first, Homer didn't answer, unmoved by the woman's frightened appeal. This would teach her to go snooping around at the dead of night in close proximity to a fracking site. Bremer was bound to have covered an area of the woods which offered the best camouflage and where the higher ground overlooked the site, especially if you climbed high enough into the tree canopy.

Joss yelped with excitement, as if to offer reassurance to their entrapped victim. Paramount in his mind was a suspicion that Bremer might have alarmed the trap. If such fears were founded, then long before he could release the woman, the guards with their dogs would be upon them.

Homer sighed; there were times when 'man's best friend' got him into more scrapes than he would ever choose.

"Stop struggling; you're making things worse by trying to disentangle yourself."

Homer spoke in low tones, checking for hidden cameras. A smart scanner, provided by his friend, Cosmo, showed no evidence of cameras but a concealed microphone was always a possibility.

Almost unheard, Homer whispered a soft command. Keeping low, as if in search of wayward sheep, Joss moved away to describe a wide circle around him while Homer watched for any movement in the darkness. Beside him, the woman groaned again.

"Quiet," he hissed, easing the shotgun from his shoulder and in so doing realised both chambers were empty. Great! Still, the gun felt reassuring.

"Stay still, you're only making matters worse," he repeated.

Donning a pair of night-sights, he could just make out the matrix of wires that held her. From the tangle of the mesh, he was certain there was little chance of release without his help. Yet still he hesitated. Homer needed to be certain the woman wasn't bait in a second trap designed to ensnare him as well; two for the price of one.

Tentatively searching the woodland underneath, Homer found a primitive pressure plate that had triggered the trap. A single footfall had been sufficient to release concealed fibreglass poles that resembled a fishing rod, sprung upright by hazel whips, ensnaring the unwitting victim in a lattice of barbed and razor wires. Amongst this hammock of wire the imprisoned woman now hung. He tested the tension, drawing a muffled groan as the wires pulled against her body.

"Who are you? Do you work for Bremer?" The voice came, challenging and afraid, in the same breath.

"No names. I don't work for Bremer."

So the woman knew of Bremer. That wasn't surprising; he had a powerful profile in the area. Almost single handed, Bremer had quelled all local opposition to the unpopular extraction operation, employing harsh tactics in his interpretation of government legislation. Even the police were reluctant to intervene, and complaints against Bremer and his methods, no matter how serious, went largely ignored.

Homer carefully examined the construction of the trap, fearing a secondary one that would enmesh him as well. In the pale glow of his night-sights, he could see an ungloved hand, bleeding from dozens of cuts inflicted as the woman struggled to release herself. If she knew about Bremer and what he might be capable of, it was no surprise she would try so hard to free herself, irrespective of the physical cost.

Panting, Joss returned, satisfied that no one lurked amid the trees and undergrowth around them. With a soft command, Homer bid her stay.

"One of these days, dog, you're going to get both of us into serious trouble."

He set about releasing the ensnared woman.

"Do you have cutters?" she said.

"Yes. But only as a last resort. If I cut the wires it will tell Bremer or his men someone has been here and he'll start an immediate manhunt. Best we get you free without cutting any wires, then it suggests that the trap could have been triggered by an animal."

The stories of Bremer's manhunts were notorious. Few, if any, local people would risk harbouring a protestor or activist intent on exposing what was happening inside the fracking compound. If the police couldn't lift a finger to protect you, it was safer just to turn away and keep your head down.

"I'll try to lift the wires away from you to make an opening. It'll be painful, but if I create a gap you should be able to roll sideways and fall clear to the ground. It's not a big drop."

With gloved hands, Homer gathered together several wires, trying to stretch them to make a space for the woman to roll through. The trouble was, given the tension in the wire, even that simple action was easier said than done as unseen barbs and razor edges lacerated his gloves and hands. This was going to hurt them both.

She lay partly on her side and back, and dozens of barbs had hooked into her clothing. Homer swore loudly, using every profanity he could think of. Even if he created an opening, her own body weight kept her hooked and snagged. He pushed harder, squeezing the strands tighter together and heard her sound a deep gasp as the metal points dug into her flesh. Poacher he might be, but the deliberate cruelty of the design of the trap made him seethe with anger. This was designed to both snare and hurt in equal measure, and one day Bremer would have to be called to account. That moment couldn't come too soon.

"Listen, you'll have to loosen your jacket and trousers and leave them behind. We can retrieve them once you're free," he added encouragingly.

A great idea in principle, but suspended on a hammock of barbed wire made the application far harder. Every time the trapped woman moved, her captive net flexed like a trampoline, forcing a painful gasp from her lips. In his head, a silent internal clock ticked remorselessly forward. It was all taking far too long, a fact supported by the normally patient Joss who stamped her paws on the spot as if to emphasise the obvious. Try as he might to help the woman, there were too many strands and too much tension in the wire. After several minutes, she had only managed to unfasten her jacket; getting her out of her trousers would take even longer.

The sudden intervention of an owl, watching the spectacle from a hollow oak tree nearby, changed everything. Its screech of alarm, clear amidst the stilled darkness of the surrounding woods rasped like chalk drawn across a blackboard.

A barb had just stabbed Homer through the glove, the owl's stark warning instantly silencing his curses. Before his brain could register the significance, his hand was tearing open his rucksack, groping for wire cutters. Time had run out. Bremer's men were on their way, which the owl had sensed only too clearly. Now, there were no easy options; the wire had to be cut.

Without any warning, the man abruptly changed his mind; he started cutting the wires, leaving me to tumble to the ground like a sack of potatoes.
    Until today I had never been especially fond of dogs. That changed very quickly; if the dog hadn't come to my rescue, I sensed the man would have abandoned me to my fate. You couldn't really blame him; in his situation I might have acted in the same way. Fortunately for me, his dog thought otherwise.
    "Follow me if you want to stay alive," he fired the words gruffly in my direction, not waiting for a reply, leaving me, bruised and bleeding, to stumble into the darkness in his wake, shepherded by the black and white dog.
    The man, though large of frame, seemed to move with a fluid ease, following trails and pathways as if he would know them with his eyes closed. On reflection, he probably did. The darkness didn't hinder him and the pale glow of starlight even made his night glasses redundant. He didn't run, but made swift progress, relying on the dog, Joss, to make sure I kept up with his pace.
    Very soon I lost all sense of direction; the man turned right and left when my instinct was the opposite, leaving the dog to nudge me onto the correct path. After a short distance, we slithered down a bank, briars tearing at my clothes and hands, into a fast running stream at the bottom. The man turned right to head downstream. Alarmed, I stopped dead.
    "Isn't that the wrong way?"
    My voice challenged him, nerves frayed. The sound of baying hounds carried clear on the night, seeming to come from directly ahead.
    Reluctantly, he halted.

"Downstream. The water flow will carry our scent away from the dogs." He turned and moved on without waiting for an answer.

"And don't question me again," he threw the words over his shoulder. "There'll be time for that if we get away."

He was gone in a second, leaving me to follow in the wake of his angry words, tripping and sliding in the icy stream.

We plunged downhill for what felt like miles, soaked through from the stream. Ahead, the man never once turned to help me, relying on Joss, the dog, to nuzzle and encourage me upright every time I fell. I could sense I was bleeding from the dozens of cuts inflicted by the wire but, soaked through by the stream, at least I couldn't tell how bad the bleeding was.

The sound of barking dogs seemed to pass behind us, their voices excited, angry and hungry at the same time. The man was probably right; if the dogs were loose and found our scent, we would never be able to outrun them. Lurid tales abounded of the fate of those tracked down by hunting packs such as these. I could only hope that my nameless saviour knew what he was doing.

Numbed by the cold, we eventually climbed out of the deepening water on a bend where the stream had laid a gravel bank. For the first time he offered me a hand, my arms and legs stiff from my cold, sodden clothes, despite the exertion. The sound of dogs had drifted away, but that could have been a trick of the night wind, swirling beneath the canopy of the trees. We were moving again in seconds, without so much as a pause to gather breath until soon we broke through a clump of bracken and onto a stone track.

If he had moved quickly before, he now began to jog, pressing on at a remorseless pace, never stopping to ask if I was alright. But then, if your life depends on haste, you don't pause to pass the time of day, or night, for that matter. Time seemed to have no measure. Only exhaustion peeked over the horizon.

I would have run straight past the Landrover, camouflaged in the night shadows of a low, overhanging tree had not Joss, moving effortlessly beside me, pressed her head against my leg. In the darkness, her master was nowhere to be seen until his profile was lit by the glow of instrument lights.

"Don't slam the door," he hissed as I wearily clambered into the cab. "Sound travels."

I hesitated, allowing Joss to leap in behind me, taking sentry duty with her head on my shoulder. It was the closest I had ever been to the wet muzzle of a panting dog.

"I'm soaked to the core," I garbled, by way of explaining the deafening clatter of teeth as I shivered violently.

"Probably shock. The heater will warm up in a few minutes," he said dismissively.

If you've ever travelled in an open top Landrover you might think that was optimistic. But though it appeared battered and worn, the engine started with the first turn. Beside me the stranger donned night-sights and eased the vehicle forward onto the track. Without lights and the merest suggestion of revs, we set off down a rutted and potholed track, in search of a road in total darkness.

I had no idea of our route but the stranger knew his enemy and where road blocks might be encountered, so chose to lead us through a maze of unpaved tracks and lanes. Cold air leaked badly through an ill-fitting canvas top but, as promised, the heater was soon good enough to ease my shivering, helped by the contents of a pewter hip flask. It contained a fierce brandy I think, forging a burning path as it tracked through my insides.

We drove in silence; I half expected him to push me out every time he eased the Landrover to a halt. Instead, warmth and tiredness lulled me into a semi-comatose state until I woke abruptly as the Landrover began to bump *violently along another rutted drive, lined either side with silhouetted trees on sombre sentry duty, eventually jerking to a creaking halt in front of an unlit cottage, barely visible against the stars.*

"Get out," was all he said as he climbed from the cab. It was left to the dog to make a proper invitation.

CHAPTER 3
A CARTOON OF ANTIQUITY

Homer felt agitated. The presence of this strange woman disturbed the equilibrium of his life. It was always the way with things that were 'firsts', and someone in his house was definitely that. It came before considering who she might be and what on earth possessed her to roam alone in the woods at this forsaken hour of the night. The more he thought about it, it only added to his feelings of distraction, in which the figure of Bremer loomed ever larger. Cutting the wires had been a last resort, one that would eventually lead a suspicious bastard like Bremer to his door. Yet despite his misgivings, Joss had obviously taken to the woman and he held great store by the judgement of the dog.

He lit an oil lamp; the batteries were low until the sun rose to charge the photovoltaic panels he relied upon. As usual, he felt awkward in the presence of a woman. In the yellow light of the flame her age and appearance were hard to discern; perhaps early thirties, with small features and dark hair layered and cut short to chin level. Her wet clothes, hardly suitable for snooping around in the dark woods at night, were stained with blood and covered in mud. Turning away, Homer riddled the Aga, adding another log and opening the draught vent to encourage the flames.

Joss gave him a questioning look that you could interpret as, 'Where are your manners?' Uncertainly, Homer fumbled in a cupboard and discovered a half empty bottle of antiseptic. Unannounced, he tossed it to the woman. Unsurprisingly, she dropped it.

"I kept the Aga going, there's warm water in the tank. Fill the bath and add what's in that bottle to bathe your cuts."

Homer hesitated, staring at the ceiling, discomforted by the personal nature of what he had suggested.

"You've got to clean those wounds, stop infection."

He found himself nodding vigorously, always a reaction to an awkward situation, a habit he recognised and particularly disliked.

For a moment, the woman regarded him with surprise. She hadn't expected a kind gesture.

"Thank you."

She half turned, feeling blood wet and sticky on her clothes, waiting to be told where the bathroom was. "But first, shouldn't we be introduced. I've already met the dog but …"

"No names, it's dangerous," Homer blurted, rapidly shaking his head again.

"But we've already seen one another's faces, what difference can a name make?"

She watched him wring his hands together. His previously forthright manner became curiously anxious in her presence.

"Most CCTV cameras are linked to facial recognition. Now it's our features and DNA that identify us; no one seems interested in our names anymore."

Her words seemed to calm him and the hand wringing and rapid eye movement stopped.

"My name's Grace, Grace of the dandelions," she added with an encouraging smile, holding out a hand stained brown with dried blood.

"I'm Homer," he blurted, almost involuntarily, keen to get through the social tripwire of identity.

"What like 'Homer' from the 'Simpsons'?" She chuckled at this immediate conclusion.

He shrugged. "Well that too," he said, slowly relaxing at the thought.

"The real 'Homer' wrote my mother's favourite book, *The Odyssey*. She always claimed it was the best adventure story you could ever read and, bizarrely, named me after the author," he added with an expression you could only describe as bemused. At least his face held the glimmer of a smile.

Despite the pain of her wounds, Grace still stood in front of him, her hand extended, a smile of encouragement on her face. Surmounting the barrier to trust was difficult, but with no way to avoid her, Homer awkwardly reached out to take the offered hand in his. In that one simple gesture, Homer allowed Grace into his world.

In a hot bath, the contents of the bottle Homer had given me cauterised the dozens of punctures in my body. Stretched out full-length, it felt like some exquisite form of torture that had to be endured for its healing qualities. I had left my wet clothes outside the bathroom door. Homer had offered to dry them on the Aga while I soaked in the bath, a strangely intimate gesture from someone so obviously awkward in my presence. As I lay amidst the steam of the hot water, I took a brief moment to take stock of the night's failure and the personality of the curious man who had intervened to release me from the man-trap.

I was working for a secret organisation which held the fracking site, Site 17, as a high priority on the list of gas extraction installations, more for what we didn't know about what went inside the compound than our issues with the extraction process itself. Under new laws, a no-fly zone had been imposed for a half-mile radius around all fracking operations across the country, leaving the sites to appear as simple black rectangles on all satellite mapping platforms.

So what were they trying to hide? I had been preceded by two earlier activists, determined to uncover the truth. Both had disappeared without a trace. Any enquiries the police might have made drew a blank. Nothing remained to show that they had ever existed or had even got close to Site 17.

I winced as I turned in the bath; judging by the wounds from the razor wire, I'd been lucky to escape a similar fate. For a moment, I slid beneath the bath water, trying to erode imagined fears of what might have become of me if Joss and her rather awkward owner hadn't appeared out of the darkness. His, and the dog's, knowledge of the woods had probably saved my life.

Homer appeared to live alone in this isolated cottage, eking out an existence as a woodsman and poacher. On the face of it, he led a simple life, yet beneath the surface, I sensed Homer knew more about Bremer than just his reputation. He seemed more cautious and wary than afraid, not showing the outright fear of other men living locally.

The cottage, isolated and self-sufficient, appeared well maintained in a careworn sort of way. His mannerisms seemed to imply a form of damage or psychosis, the sort that led to becoming withdrawn, choosing the life of a hermit. He appeared enigmatic from the start, not that it mattered; I would soon be long gone. But, my curiosity was aroused, just the same.

Outside the door a board creaked, followed by a paw scratching at the door. Obviously, my newfound friend wanted to come into the bathroom. I grabbed a towel and abandoned the bath, opening the door to find the dog and my clothes, both now dry, the latter neatly folded on the floor.

A contradiction indeed, I decided, as I towel dried in the waxy yellow light of a candle. Homer undoubtedly wanted to be rid of me, yet seemed in no hurry to make me go. Donning my now warm and dry clothes, I smiled as a pair of liquid eyes regarded me from where she lay on the floor. Perhaps the dry clothes showed the influence of the dog in Homer's solitary life.

Homer led Grace to a ladder that climbed to the attic.

"They'll have found the cut wires of the trap and be hunting high and low for whoever escaped from it. Bremer is a persistent man; he never gives up until he finds who has meddled in his territory. He'll hunt you down if you run. It's better for both of us that you stay here and rest until the hue and cry dies down."

Homer pointed to the only furnishings in the attic; a small bed, a table and chair.

"No lights, and keep away from the window, especially if you hear someone arrive outside."

He turned abruptly and started to descend the ladder.

"When I've gone, turn the key on the loft hatch and remove it. I'll bring you something to eat in a short while."

His tone had recovered the edge he had shown earlier, perhaps making it quite plain that he didn't appreciate the intrusion into his private world. Yet, as he descended the ladder he paused, holding the hatch midway between open and closed.

"There's a salve in the tub I've left on the table. Smear it onto your wounds; it will help them heal."

The hatch closed abruptly without another word and the contradictions witnessed in Homer cast a wistful smile across Grace's face.

I must have dozed off on the bed, only to awake when the hatch door unlocked and opened, and daylight came flooding up. The top half of Homer appeared in the opening, holding a steaming bowl, uncertain whether he intended to climb any further.

"Here's something for you to eat. It's only porridge, but I've added honey and dried fruit," he said, slightly apologetically.

I thanked him as I leaned forward, collecting the bowl from where he had left it on the floor. His eyes wandered away, uncomfortable to meet my gaze.

I stirred the hot contents of the bowl, waiting for Homer to climb the last rungs of the ladder and join me in the loft. Instead, he seemed transfixed, half-in, half-out, part incensed by my presence, part driven by the need to help, as though locked in some schizophrenic dance.

"I need to explain …," I started to say.

Homer held up his hand. "I don't want to know. You've exposed me to enough trouble already." Though his tone had an edge sharp enough to cut itself, his face betrayed concern.

"Look, whatever you're up to, I offer one piece of advice; if you want to stay alive, find another way to achieve your aims and stay well away from the fracking compound of Site 17, especially from Bremer and his men."

He clearly wasn't in the mood to listen to my side of the story. The situation was far more complex and dangerous than Homer could know but I could only shrug. Gratitude costs nothing.

"Thanks for saving my life then."

Homer nodded, the merest glimmer of a smile creasing his face. I wondered if he had guessed that I wouldn't, couldn't, heed his warning.

"I'll lock the hatch again. Just in case we have an unwanted visit from Bremer's men. If that happens, and they force their way into the house, you'll have about thirty seconds to escape through the rooflight."

Homer gestured to the sloping ceiling behind me. "It's on the rear flank so keep below the ridgeline and you won't be seen."

He took two steps back down the ladder. "For now, I suggest you rest and sleep. No lights and don't forget, keep away from the windows, especially if you hear voices. We'll see about getting you away once it gets dark again tonight."

Closing the hatch, Homer didn't wait for a reply. Perhaps he could already guess the future.

CHAPTER 4
JOSS HAS THE FINAL WORD

They arrived earlier than Homer expected. A Landrover disgorged four of Bremer's hired 'enforcers'.

"Something of an overkill," he muttered as the four men filled the drive in front of his cottage.

Two peeled off to inspect his Landrover; a hot engine and tyres tell their own story. The remaining two men approached the cottage door. Homer offered a silent prayer, hoping the woman in the attic had heard their arrival. He opened the door before they knocked, rubbish bag in his hand and pushed past them as if they were invisible.

"A word, Homer," the taller of the two men called to his departing back.

Homer made them wait until he returned from the bin.

"You wanted me?"

The clock in his head was ticking. How long did the woman need to climb on to the roof if they entered the house?

"Have you seen anyone new, a stranger in the woods, around here?" the tall man asked without any preamble.

Homer appeared to think for a moment.

"Can't say I have," he said, deliberately bending to pick up a log they had knocked from the wood pile.

In so doing, he cast a furtive glance towards the two men who had moved from inspecting his Landrover and had entered the barn in which he hung the proceeds of his night's work. Fortunately, rabbits and pheasants don't have their owners' names stamped on them.

"You're the first person I've spoken to in almost a week."

"Ah, always the hermit. I often wonder what you're hiding away from," Miller replied provocatively.

In a flash Homer thought, 'People like you' and only narrowly avoided saying it. The moment was interrupted when the other two men arrived from their search of the barn. One carried a dead pheasant.

"Half a dozen rabbits, two brace of pheasant and a dead hind," he reported. "My, my, you have been busy."

"Road kill," Homer stated; at least none of them had been shot to prove otherwise.

"And there was me thinking you might have been poaching on our land," Miller responded, not bothering to disguise a cynical grin. "Because if you had, you might have encountered the person we're looking for?"

Homer shrugged. "I wasn't, so I haven't."

Miller took a moment to consider his reply. "Mind if we look over your house?"

"Of course I mind," Homer answered with a note of resignation.

"But you'll let us go ahead anyway," Miller smiled at his statement.

Homer handed a ring of keys to Miller and turned away, gesturing inside his cottage. He could refuse to give them access, but within the hour they would return with a rubber-stamped warrant and trash the house, as they searched, for the inconvenience he had caused them. He could only hope the woman had made good her escape already.

Miller directed two of his men to enter the cottage while he and a fourth man followed Homer into the kitchen, blocking the doorway, just in case he tried to make an escape. None of them wiped their boots on the mat.

"Aren't you going to offer us coffee?" A bear of a man now standing beside Miller said in fake, pained tones, flexing the knuckles of his right hand as they both waited in anticipation for the search to be completed.

"It's like a trip to the dentist; all over before you know it. Unless you're hiding something, that is, in which case, well, I don't have to tell you how much Mr Bremer hates it when people lie to him."

Homer feigned an indifference he certainly didn't feel. It was expecting a lot for the woman to have made an escape through the rooflight before the men searched the attic. If she hadn't, there was still the blinking red light of the camera discretely recessed into the ceiling cornice behind him, live streaming video onto his blog site since the moment they had had entered the kitchen. It wasn't much of an insurance policy, but it might just make them think twice before approaching him.

Above, Homer heard floorboards creak, the bang of an opening hatch flap, the rattle of a descending ladder. He held his breath, imagining the men climbing into the attic, anticipating exultant shouts of discovery. Miller watched his face, waiting for the look that would incriminate Homer. From above them came the sounds of moving furniture, the whump of an overturned mattress. Endless seconds ticked by without the full stop of a gleeful shout of discovery. Homer fixed his eyes on the tiny red light of the camera, listening to the sounds above them, anything to avoid the unspoken accusation in Miller's eyes.

After what felt like eternity, there came the clatter of descending boots.

"Nothing, boss," a man with a pockmarked complexion said with more than a hint of disappointment. "The place is clean."

So the woman had made her escape. The sense of relief that came with the realisation almost gave Homer away as his left knee began to tremble.

Miller walked past him and picked up a used mug from the sink, carefully examining the rim. What was he looking for? Lipstick? Homer watched him count; plates in the rack, knives and forks. Hell, the man was determined to find something to pin him.

"Clever," he muttered softly. "Very clever."

Miller nodded to the men in the kitchen, his signal to leave. Homer felt the knee tremble slowing down.

"Just one thing," Miller said, picking up the pot containing coffee and removing the lid. He sniffed the contents and wrinkled his nose.

"Next time we call, be a decent host and make us coffee."

With that, he upturned the pot and tipped the contents across the floor.

They left without a backward glance; which was a mistake. Everyone had forgotten the dog. Joss had hidden in the barn the moment the Landrover had drawn up. She hadn't needed to see what transpired to sense the threatening mood that arrived with the four men.

But, keen to see them depart, Joss couldn't resist surrendering to her instincts, racing around the group of men in a manner she would treat a flock of wayward sheep. With an amused look of contempt, the large man who had accompanied Miller in the kitchen lashed out with his boot. The kick, aimed at the dog's ribs, hit nothing but fresh air, the mistimed lunge leaving him momentarily unbalanced. Not enough to fall, but sufficient for Joss to duck beneath the arching leg and bite him hard in the buttocks.

Homer watched the scene with amusement. The whole unpleasant visit had been almost worth it to watch his bullying antagonist scurry painfully into the back of the hastily departing SUV. As they disappeared down the track, spraying dust and gravel in their wake, Joss returned, panting, and gently nudged the side of his leg. Homer raised an eye in her direction.

"Impressive," he said, fondling the velvet hairs on the back of her head. "But I can't help thinking they'll be back for the final word on the matter."

Although his house hadn't been exactly turned over by their search, everything had been left where it fell and would take some time to restore to order. The attic was the final room Homer came to and as he climbed the creaking ladder he felt a distinct feeling of trepidation, unable to guess what he might find.

The room expressed the contempt the searchers had left it in; mattress and sheets lay scattered on the floor along with the contents of a small overturned table and chair. That apart, the room was empty. A feeling of overwhelming relief swept over him. If they had discovered Grace, the dozens of puncture marks on her body would have been impossible to explain away, incriminating both of them and leading to Bremer's idea of summary justice. But they hadn't, and nothing amongst the debris of the room suggested her presence.

Homer checked the rooflight through which he had instructed Grace to escape if needed. Had the men found it open, it could have posed awkward questions, difficult to explain away to Miller's suspicious mind. He checked the handle, expecting at best to find it on the latch. But it wasn't. To his surprise, it was firmly closed, something you could only do from inside the room.

Puzzled, he carefully checked the room, imagining the woman still hidden in some secret place where no one had thought to look. Twice he called her name.

"Grace, are you here?"

But only silence replied. She had simply disappeared, almost as if her presence had been no more than an illusory dream.

Except one thing.

Amongst the knot of a tousled sheet, Homer found a leaving gift; a delicately folded origami flower, its petals frilled to delicate flower spikes; a perfectly formed paper dandelion.

CHAPTER 5
HORSE TRADE WITH A TRAVELLER

There was nothing about his appearance to betray Cosmo's true identity. Despite his rich skin tone and jet black hair he dressed inconspicuously; in matters of business, no one would suspect his Romany heritage. Two full pint glasses were sitting on the table in front of him when Homer slid into the opposite seat, his back to the light, casting his face into shadow.

"I wasn't sure I'd see you tonight after that interlude this morning," Cosmo said with a raised eyebrow. "Trouble with your neighbours?"

"Nothing I can't handle."

They touched glasses and drank in silence.

"One of these days you'll have to let my sons pay them a visit."

Cosmo regularly offered the support of his family 'protection' squad, more out of concern for his supply chain than the personal safety of Homer.

"Thanks for the offer. I'll let you know if things get that bad."

A turf war was the last thing Homer needed. So far, he had woven a path to avoid the worst of Bremer's powers, but like all tightropes there was always a danger you might fall off.

"Anyway, we're here to talk business."

Cosmo nodded, temporarily parking his concern for his friend. He knew all about Bremer's reputation and had watched the live stream of the events from the cottage that morning. It left him wondering what had provoked the visit by the four men.

"So, what have you brought me?" Cosmo said.

Homer cast his gaze around the bar. Two couples stood chatting as their drinks arrived, a noisy group of young lads played an animated game of pool in an adjacent alcove. Just an average mid-week night. The only person that stood out was a man drinking alone at the end of the bar counter. Homer made a note to keep an eye on him, just in case. You could never be too careful.

"Two brace, half a dozen rabbits and a hind." Homer eased himself back in his chair. "What are you offering?"

"No fish?" Cosmo sounded disappointed.

"Depends what you're prepared to pay."

Cosmo spread his palms with a pained expression on his face.

"Money's tight; the metal market is at rock bottom at the moment."

"As ever," Homer said with a smile. "But you always seem to have a bulging wallet."

"You overestimate things my friend. Tell you what; throw in some wild trout or carp and I'll offer you a pony."

"What good is a horse to me," Homer replied with a note of feigned exasperation, knowing full well what his friend meant. "I wouldn't get out of bed for less than a hundred and fifty pounds."

"I suppose I could run to seventy-five if you include the fish."

"Sounds like I wasted my time coming here then; a hundred and twenty-five is my bottom price. I could get double elsewhere."

"Shylock!" Cosmo said in a hissed tone. "You'll clean me out."

Homer shook his head. "I'm a poacher; a hundred and twenty-five and I'll buy you another pint."

Cosmo smiled and stretched out his hand. This was a charade that played out every time they met. Both men had to feel they had got the upper hand. Whatever the outcome, they always parted as friends.

True to his word, Homer bought the next round, while Cosmo collected the ice box and the contents he had just purchased from the back of Homer's Landrover. There were four brown trout in a separate box that Homer wouldn't reveal until he had his money. He held considerable affection for the older man, but many years of trade with the 'traveller community' had taught him to always hold something in reserve.

"No fish?" Cosmo returned with a note of disappointment in his voice.

"Later."

Homer pushed the pint glass across the table, holding out his upturned palm for a roll of bank notes as he looked over his friend's shoulder, carefully scrutinising the man standing at the end of the bar. He showed no interest in anyone else in the pub, intent on studying the screen on his phone. But you could never tell if that was genuine, and it was possible that he had trailed them to the pub. If he seemed to be contacting someone with his phone, Homer would end their meeting immediately.

Ignoring the outstretched palm, Cosmo slid a tight roll of bank notes into Homer's other hand beneath the table, before leaning back in his chair, drinking deeply from his glass.

"Heard from the family?" Cosmo asked, white beer foam lining his top lip.

"Not for six months."

Homer's answer was always the same. He seldom heard from his ex-wife and children and then only by post from an undisclosed address possibly somewhere in Australia. He wasn't even certain that was where they now lived; it was safer that way. Lisara had stayed true to her word and disappeared off the face of the planet. Occasionally she sent photos, always through a third party. Homer memorised every detail before destroying them, leaving no evidence or trace of their existence. Others hadn't been so careful and had paid the price.

"It must be, what, five years now?" Cosmo asked with a note of concern in his voice.

He and Homer had met when sharing a prison cell; Cosmo had served two years for handling stolen goods, Homer almost the same term for assaulting a policeman. Thrown together in a small space, it was plainly obvious that prison was the last place Homer should have been sent. The man was obviously damaged and the only 'therapy' he received came in Cosmo, a small-time villain who inhabited the top bunk of their shared cell. In the months they spent together, Homer never revealed the real cause of his traumas. He withdrew every time Cosmo tried to explore the nightmares that came most nights, often attacking Cosmo when he tried to wake or comfort his cellmate.

"Five years, four months, two weeks and three days," Homer broke into his reverie with a finality in his words that brooked no further discussion.

"You could always come and live with us. We could easily find you a van."

"What, and be ripped off in the process," Homer replied with a half smile.

"At least you'd be safe."

"Perhaps I don't need to be."

Cosmo studied his hands before responding with concern. "We would at least make sure you stay alive."

He felt the same bubble of anxiety well up inside him every time their conversation came back to this.

"And if you don't, I might well end up losing the best source of pheasants and wild fish in the county."

Later, the two men parted in the car park. Homer waited until his gypsy friend had left, watching to see if the mystery man at the bar followed, but he remained, now seated, drinking alone at the bar.

As Homer drove home, he looked at the paper slip Cosmo had given him as he bid farewell. All it carried was a mobile number.

"Memorise that or put it in your phone," he had said. "Call the moment you're in trouble. Ten minutes and my boys will be with you."

Homer had thanked his friend, omitting to add that his kind offer would never be enough.

As he had departed, from an open window Cosmo called out,

"And one of these days, you'll have to tell me what causes you so much grief."

How many times did he try asking that question and never receive an answer? With an exuberant wave, Cosmo drove off into the night, leaving Homer alone with his demons. As sure as night followed day, the moment would arrive when 'they' finally caught up with him and no one, neither Cosmo nor God on high, could spare Homer from that ultimate conclusion.

CHAPTER 6
SMOKE SIGNALS PORTEND

Despite the command, 'stay', Joss inched forward whenever she thought Homer wasn't looking. The temptation to gather the flocks of silly sheep was almost too much to resist; after all it was exactly what she had been instructed to do for the previous hour in the company of another more experienced sheepdog.

With the sheep penned in separate groups, the two men gazed at a distant, northern skyline, now dominated by a tall, seemingly motionless pall of smoke that ascended high into the stratosphere.

"Three days now it's burned. They say it's out of control," the shorter of the two men said while he chewed the end of an unlit pipe.

Further conversation was drowned out as a helicopter clattered noisily overhead, the gondola, suspended on cables beneath, streaming water.

"Seawater; they've had to resort to it; not enough fresh water in the lakes and reservoirs to waste on wild fires," Eustace chuntered on, pointing at the departing helicopter with the stem of his pipe.

"Think what that's going to do to their precious countryside. But some say if they don't stop it, it'll spread all the way to Heathrow airport."

For a minute, both men were silent. It had really come to something when they had to use seawater to fight fires in the tinder dry countryside. Homer counted back; it was almost four months since there had been anything close to decent rainfall and wild fires were erupting everywhere. Most could be dealt with before they got out of hand, but the one in the distance had overwhelmed the already stretched resources.

"Stay, Joss."

Homer had seen her move from the corner of his eye, eager to get amongst the sheep again. She had been trained as a sheepdog in her younger years, a skill Homer occasionally practised with her when the local flocks needed separating for market. This year, all the farmers he knew were complaining. A lack of grass, caused by sweltering drought, had led to a drastic decline in the quality of lambs. They now all faced a brutal slump in prices.

"Can't understand it," Eustace said, reading his thoughts.

"Even the lambs I've finished in the field watered by that new spring higher up seem sickly little things. The better grass didn't make any difference."

Instinctively, Homer turned in the direction of the vivid green scar that slashed the straw coloured hillside, marking the stream path fed from a new spring now issuing from higher up.

"Never seen a spring there in all my years on this farm," Eustace grumbled as another helicopter approached, heading towards the sea to fill its deflated water bowser.

They were flying in a constant convey. A round trip must be taking at least an hour, so things must be desperate.

"Waste of time if you ask me," Eustace said, watching the helicopter as if flew over.

"Ain't no point in putting out these fires until the temperature drops and we get some decent rain."

Homer had heard the forecast on the radio before he left the cottage earlier that morning; late September and yet predicted to be a cloudless day with the thermometer in the eighties.

"Strange thing, the appearance of that new spring don't you think?" Homer floated the question.

Eustace shrugged. "They say it's all because of these mini earthquakes that fracking business causes. Permissible limits? Ground round here never used to shake and wobble 'til they started practising their 'dark arts'."

Homer nodded in agreement. Even at his cottage, a few miles away, the cups and plates regularly rattled as the ground moved beneath his feet.

"The fracturing could explain the appearance of a fresh spring I suppose."

Eustace made a noise of disdain.

"My arse it does. I tried going up there to see for myself. Never used to be a problem walking over them fields. The farmer, Robinson, who owns the land, used to share a pint with me in the local pub until he became a snooty politician and set up some fancy contract with this fracking company. Bunch of thugs I call them. Stopped me halfway across that top field and threatened to set the dogs on me if I didn't bugger off. Me! A neighbouring farmer."

Eustace gave Homer a look of utter exasperation. They were interrupted as two large lorries clattered down the track beside the field, spiralling clouds of parched dust in their wake.

For the next hour, Joss was busy herding flighty lambs onto the loading ramps and into the lorries. Packed tight together, Eustace claimed it was safer.

"It prevents them falling over," Eustace explained, though with margins so tight, Homer suspected it was more about saving the cost of a third lorry.

Once loaded, they filled the water feeders on the trailers and left the lorries to journey to the abattoir. Eustace mopped his brow as they disappeared, now hidden behind the cloud of dust that hung, unmoving, in the still air.

"Glad to see the back of them to be honest," Eustace said, mopping a sweaty brow. "No meat on any of them to speak of, they were costing me money just being here. This is the third year in a row we've lost our grass crop. Don't think the bank will let me go on much longer," he added morosely.

"Perhaps the weather will break," Homer ventured for want of something more encouraging to say, gazing at the smoke pall filling the distant horizon.

Eustace shook his head. "What do you think the average temperature was here on the farm in February?" He paused, then continued.

"Nineteen degrees. Nineteen bloody degrees in the middle of winter. I ask you. I just wish that monster," he gestured towards the column of smoke, "burns its way to London. Then these complacent bastards that govern us might wake up before it's too late and we're all screwed."

Eustace walked away, his mood a mixture of disgust and despair, leaving Homer and Joss alone in the empty stubble field. Perplexed, Joss nudged his leg for reassurance, sparking a memory of the mystery woman they had met a few weeks before.

Grace had been her name, and she had seemed intent on a mission that threatened to drastically shorten her life expectancy. As Joss nudged him again, he wondered what had become of her.

CHAPTER 7
CONSEQUENCE OF A CATCH

Homer was well camouflaged; even his fishing rod resembled a bent bulrush. The darkness of early morning slowly disappeared with the arrival of the sun and another hot day forecast. Above him, the tranquillity of a pale sky was ruptured by the continual flow of helicopters, ferrying ever increasing quantities of seawater to douse the flames on the inferno that lit the northern horizon, still burning its path towards London.

A few days before, when he had watched the conveyor of helicopters with Eustace, you could have counted their numbers on two hands. Now, it was seldom silent; what seemed like every machine in the country had been conscripted in an increasingly desperate bid to douse the flames. Yet still the anger of 'mother earth' seemed to hold no bounds. While every moment of the live news streams dealt with tackling the voracious blaze approaching the capital from the south, a confluence of extraordinary events in the North Sea the previous night had driven a tidal surge against the east coast, breaching sea defences for a hundred miles or more. Scores of inland towns and villages had been inundated by the highest tide in living memory, driven onshore by a surprise unseasonal easterly gale.

Some claimed the wind had been induced by the power of the flames, sucking in air across a wide frontier. But while all the attention had been drawn to the advancing inferno, a wall of water had filled the Thames and overwhelmed the barrage defences. If fear of the flames advancing ever closer wasn't enough, huge areas of London were now in a brown lake miles in diameter. By the time the warning sirens had wailed, belatedly, across the city, parliament was already under a metre of filthy water, all adding to the national state of anxiety. Eustace's prediction of a wake-up call for the politicians had come true on a scale he could never have imagined.

With the first suggestion of daylight, 'Mr Trout' paid Homer a call. Joss had just returned from foraging, spooking a roosting pheasant who had clattered away with a metallic alarm call in the process.

Homer fished without a float, relying instead on the sensitivity of his fingertips. In the dark pools of shady alcoves, where the water remained coolest, he knew the fish would be hungry, open mouths kissing the mirrored surface in hope of breakfast as a host of insects began their dance across the surface of the pond.

It was now a waiting game as the fish balanced hunger against the suspicion of a lure. Tentatively, Homer played his line gently across the surface. Camouflaged amongst the reeds he hid, motionless, aware of the watchful stare of a fish he couldn't see, but knew was there. The line brushed his fingers, trembling as the trout sucked gently on the feathered lure, testing the trap he had cast. As the pressure increased, Homer flicked the line, mimicking a startled fly. In a flash of silver, green and red, the trout, unable to resist the temptation of hunger, lunged for his breakfast. Homer had his dinner for the evening.

He left the shadowy pool before the sun rose above the tree line. There was no reason to suspect that Bremer's men would be up with the cock crow, but it paid not to linger too long. Already, three trout had surrendered to his ruse; one for his pot; the rest for his friend Cosmo when they met later in the day.

Above the shadows of the woods, the helicopters continued their shuttle to douse the fires. Homer had a feeling that all the effort was delusional; only nature could provide the answer, and rain wasn't forecast for at least the coming week. It felt as though 'mother earth', angered by their endless abuse, was hell-bent on using the advancing flames to make her point. From the beginning of time, fire had been as much a part of the world as all the seas and oceans, and she was determined not to release her tap until the lesson had been well learnt.

I hadn't intended to fall asleep at the table, my hands still clasped around a cold mug of tea. It was Joss who woke me with a firm push of her muzzle as if to announce the presence of Homer in the kitchen, hands on hips, his shadowed face hard to read.

"Who invited you back?" His tone was far from encouraging.

Startled, I managed to garble, "It was a warm night. You left the rooflight open for ventilation," I said, feeling defensive.

Given my condition, I probably didn't need to say anything else. I had been on the run for days in which sleep had been almost impossible, and my clothes were filthy and stank of pond slime and ditch water. The security guards at a distant fracking site must have been trained by Bremer's men. Their persistence in hunting me down had tested everything I had been taught. Moving night and day, it had taken scores of miles to escape.

Ignoring me, Homer tipped fish from a canvas bag into the sink and began to wash them.

"Are you planning to make a habit of this?" he said over his shoulder. "I only ask because with your last visit, Bremer's men paid a call. It's not something I want to repeat, so if you're running from his gang of thugs you'd better leave now. They'll probably be here within the hour."

"It's not Bremer, though he has probably been alerted to what happened."

"Which is? Don't tell me, it's best I don't know?" Homer said sarcastically.

It was too late to hide things. I was exhausted and urgently needed to rest in a place where I couldn't be found. Also, though I was loath to admit it, I needed Homer's help to complete the part of my mission that had just gone so disastrously wrong.

"We tried to get access to another fracking site."

"Another of your clever break-ins," he replied sceptically, gutting and cleaning the fish at the same time. "And who are 'we'?"

For a moment I felt tempted to point out the contradiction in his question; the last time I had been here he had angrily refused to listen to any explanations for my presence here.

"The 'we' are a group hell-bent on finding out what 'Blue Horizon', that extreme right party who now share power with our feeble government, are up to behind the fences of the fracking sites. And I'd like refuge for as short a time as possible to try again here. I have one thing to do and I'll be gone; out of your hair for good."

"Don't tell me," I noticed his nervous stutter had returned, "but I guess this involves another trip to the fracking site where you got caught last time," Homer said bluntly. Hands stained red with blood, he hung the fish on hooks to drain, leaving Joss to stare longingly at their iridescent, shiny bodies.

"I'm not planning to break in if that's what you're worrying about."

Homer didn't comment; he just cast a sceptical glance in my direction.

"I just need to take some samples from around the site."

"What? Around as in, not within five miles of the place. Snooping any closer than that is a recipe for suicide in my experience." I noticed the nervous hand wringing had returned.

I was getting tired of this game. I was exhausted, I needed a bed and his help.

"No one knows I've come here so let me rest for today. Tonight I can take my samples and be on my way."

"I take it getting samples involves being up close and personal with fracking Site 17." Homer stuttered twice in the one sentence.

"If I have to, yes. I need to fill some test tubes with water." Well, that wasn't exactly true, but it would have to do for now.

"Which means you'll be caught and incriminate me when they interrogate you."

I found it interesting that he used the word 'interrogate' rather than 'questioned'. "If I am caught, that won't happen."

"Trust me, you will, when Bremer hands you over to his 'gestapo' for a nice friendly chat."

Homer turned to look out of the window and I couldn't read his expression. There was more going on here than just the matter of a fracking site. "And you intend to carry out this hair-brained scheme, irrespective of whether I let you stay or not?"

I shrugged. "It's no longer a matter of choice."

Homer was lost in thought for a few seconds. "How close to the site do you need to get?"

"Close enough to take samples from the waste water outlets. Both the official piped systems and the groundwater. In this drought, groundwater should be easy to find; everywhere else is burnt to straw."

Before Homer replied, the memory of his conversation with Eustace a few days before barrelled to the forefront of his mind. "I know where there is an outlet. Everyone claims it's a natural spring, but it wasn't issuing six months ago."

"Can you show me on a map?"

He shook his head. "The chances of you finding it in the dark, on your own, without being caught are less than zero."

"I have to. Let me rest for today. I'll go and find it tonight."

"No. For a start, tonight there'll be a clear sky and a full moon from shortly after sunset; tomorrow will cloud in soon after dark. And secondly, if you go snooping around trying to find nothing more than a small stream on your own, I guarantee you'll be caught inside five minutes." He sighed. "So there's no option. I'll have to show you. My rules apply, understand? If not ..." He didn't elaborate on the consequences.

Though he didn't admit to it, Homer must have anticipated I might return. He had cleaned the chimney. Not an earth-shaking matter in itself, but actually as somewhere for me to hide. He beckoned me to stick my head in the fireplace. Looking up, all I could see was blackness.
"So what am I supposed to do?"
"Start by wearing this." Homer tossed me a thin paper coverall. "You're small enough to fit inside the flue."
"Er, I can't see any daylight," I said with more than a small degree of uncertainty.
"About a metre up the flue shunts across towards the centre of the house where it joins the flue from the Aga. That's why you can't see daylight."
"But won't the smoke asphyxiate me from the stove?" Uncertainty had turned to alarm.
"The Aga has a sealed flue liner. And the flue shunt will provide somewhere for you to brace yourself out of sight in the unlikely event that someone peers up the chimney." Homer paused, handing me a nose clip. "That's to stop you sneezing." He'd really thought about this.
"Why not use the rooflight again?" I ventured.
Homer shook his head. "I don't think Bremer's men were totally convinced last time they visited. Next time, they'll more than likely come mob-handed and surround the place, expecting you to make a run for it when you're flushed out."
He leaned against the wall, a thin smile on his lips. The stammer seemed to have disappeared for the moment.
"So you think they'll come back?"
Homer shrugged. "Who knows. But if they have a suspicion you're on the run and have come this way or our

next visit triggers one of their alarms, the first place Bremer will come looking will be my front door. When they arrive," he said with a note of certainty, "you've got three minutes tops to clear every shred of evidence from this room and climb that chimney. Three minutes is all I can give you; after that …" Homer left the rest to my imagination.

Resigned, he turned to leave.

"I'll fix you something to eat; you look half starved," he looked over his shoulder, almost as an afterthought, adding, "and take a bath; you stink," in tones that again blended annoyance at my presence with concern for my welfare.

I was fast coming to the conclusion that Homer was haunted by far darker demons than those I had brought with me.

My dreams started with conscious memory. At first, my parents dismissed them as no more than childhood fantasy, the product of an over-active imagination, only to be expected in someone they affectionately dismissed as profoundly egocentric.

I was vaguely aware that Dad travelled to his office every day in London by train, though I had no idea at the time where London was. One morning, when I must have been about four years old, things happened that would dramatically change how I saw my dreams.

Awoken in the middle of the night, I struggled to describe what I had dreamt, causing a great deal of fuss, continually shouting about 'Daddy' and 'trains'. I had refused to be comforted, probably because no one was listening to me. For several hours, my 'wild imaginings' tormented my tired parents. As a consequence, Dad overslept and, much to his frustration, missed his usual morning train.

Just over an hour later, the Clapham rail crash happened and thirty-five people lost their lives. Most were in the carriage Dad always chose for his morning commute.

Though I was too young to understand the implications, from that moment onwards I learnt to pay attention to my dreams. Even if no one else was listening to me.

CHAPTER 8
A STUDENT OF THE DARK ARTS

I saw little of my reluctant host during the next day. Homer disappeared after bring me food, leaving me with a pair of wood pigeons on the roof for company, and the dog.

I spent much of the day sleeping, and then uploaded my report of the earlier, abortive operation at another fracking site some thirty miles away. I had no idea what had become of my three accomplices. Once our presence had been exposed, we had hit the panic button and split up, hastily disappearing to opposite points of the compass. No one knew our names or where we had gone, leaving each person alone with just their instincts and training to rely upon.

Later that evening, Homer invited me down to eat in the kitchen. He seemed distracted (nothing new there) and went to considerable lengths to explain the rules for the coming night.

"Once we find what you're looking for, I'm assuming you won't need long to take whatever samples you need."

"Once we find what I'm looking for I need to do some initial tests so I don't have to return again."

"So, how long then?"

I shrugged. "Ten, fifteen minutes. It depends on the conditions."

"Too long. You'll have to be quicker," he replied, his brow furrowed in concentration.

"It can't be rushed, otherwise it could turn out to be a pointless visit."

He bit his lip. "We have to assume that we'll trigger some sort of alarm," he muttered. "Five minutes is the maximum. More than that and you'll be explaining what you were doing to Bremer in person. By yourself."

While dinner was cooking, Homer collected a dish containing several pieces of burnt cork and gestured to me to lift my hair clear of my face and neck. Without asking, he rubbed one of the blackened stubs around my face and neck and began smearing the ash to remove all signs of my pale skin. His fingers were surprisingly delicate.

"What, no camouflage make-up?" I asked, trying to lighten the mood.

Homer grunted dismissively, adding a tiny amount of olive oil to the cork charcoal, rubbing it on my cheeks and chin, his gesture a stark contrast to the anger that so often coloured his words.

"This is better; there's no reflection if you get caught by a light."

Wiping his fingers, Homer opened a box and tossed me a pair of thin silk gloves. But it was a hot night.

"And wear these all the time so you leave no prints."

The gloves were followed by a pair of old trainers with smooth soles glued over their worn ribs.

"No footprints either."

I blew a light whistle between my teeth. Was this rather strange guy for real? He must have read my thoughts.

"This is Bremer we're dealing with. Never underestimate him; Bremer will test a hair for DNA if he finds one."

Things didn't end there either. Hanging in a tall cupboard were two old, cut down sheets, completely overlaid with hanks of straw, grass and reed, stitched through slits in the fabric to form a carpet of natural vegetation. In the centre was a hole, barely the size of a human head. Homer carefully draped it over me so that it hung like a cape over my shoulders, leaving my arms free underneath it. The outfit was surmounted by what I can only describe as a 'coolie' hat, wide brimmed with an elastic chin strap and similarly camouflaged with grass and reeds.

"If I tell you to go to ground in an open field, lay flat and star-shaped; don't ask questions, just stay perfectly still," he said brusquely. "In the woods, squat down and draw in your neck so that the hat virtually sits on the cape."

Homer stood back to admire his handiwork.

"This way there's a chance we might be able to pull off this hair-brained scheme of yours."

Fine words, but he didn't sound convinced. Fashion parade complete, Homer removed my uniform and served dinner.

"We'll eat now. Then we'll sleep until after midnight by which time it should be completely dark. Dawn starts before six; we won't have a lot of time, so whatever you do, keep things tight and don't hang around unnecessarily. And count every item you take with you," he added. "Leave nothing behind. If you do, you can be certain Bremer's men will find it."

Again, he bit his lip, searching for anything he might have forgotten.

"I've got the message," I quipped. "Remember, I have done this sort of thing before."

He turned his back to my words.

"Really? And what has that achieved, apart from almost being caught on every failed attempt."

For a moment there was a look of hostility on his face when he turned around.

"You're no more than a bunch of amateurs playing Russian roulette with thugs who have been given powers they should never have been granted. Don't you people understand that? None of us like fracking, but leave them in peace to get on with it. Argue about climate change some other way."

I hesitated. He had begun to stammer as the words spilled out and I was aware that the wrong reply might well inflame his anxiety at a time when I most needed his help.

"If it was only fracking they were up to I might just agree with you."

"What? But they are fracking; taking gas and oil from the ground. I know you people don't like that but ..."

"That's not what's causing the problem," I said more sharply than I intended.

Homer gave me a puzzled expression, one that posed a bigger question than I was prepared to answer.

"That's why I'm here; to find the proof, the evidence they hide away under the Official Secrets Act. And it's costing lives to get it." I paused for a moment.

"Come on, Homer, you're not stupid. What's going on in there that's so scary that they're prepared to kill to keep it secret?"

I think he had to admit that I had a point.

We left together just after midnight, travelling on a scramble bike guided by the light of a waxy, crescent moon setting just above the horizon.

I sat on the pillion behind Homer, my arms around his waist. Joss was balanced in front, my fingers full of her soft fur as she braced her front paws against the fuel tank. Having chosen an off-road route, Homer had avoided using the Landrover in favour of the bike. Wearing night-sights and with the orange glow of the fires still raging to the north-west, he rode without the lights.

My experience with motorbikes is limited to loud, raucous contraptions that would usually awaken the dead, but this machine was something else; stripped down to the barest essentials, painted dull grey, and as silent as a ghost. We whispered along the tracks and paths, deliberately avoiding roads and lanes that meandered for miles through the woodland. I was left to wonder where Homer had acquired such a bike; and for what purpose.

From my rear seat, my calves hooked around the panniers that contained our paraphernalia for the night, I took a moment to absorb the surprising activity of the darkness. Homer rode slowly on a soft throttle, occasionally shadowed by the white sceptre of a gliding owl and the provocative red-eyed stare of a dog fox. Spooked at the last moment, a young roe deer sprang from our path with the grace of an antelope. It laid out a tapestry of night very different from the harsh reality of daylight.

We must have been riding for around half an hour when Homer turned from the track and stopped amongst a dense clump of rhododendrons. As we halted, Joss slid from her vantage point on the front and, with barely an audible word from Homer, disappeared into the thicket. Within minutes, the scramble bike was invisible amidst a cocoon of fallen branches, Homer conscientiously leaving nothing to chance. Panting, Joss returned, a rabbit in her jaws and dropped it at his feet. With a word of thanks, Homer picked up the dead animal and placed it in the poacher's bag hung across his chest.

Reading my thoughts, he said, "If we're stopped, we try to argue that we're just out hunting."

Given the elaborate nature of our camouflage clothing, it didn't sound a particularly convincing excuse.

We moved off in a generally northern direction by my reckoning. Joss disappeared for most of the time, scouting ahead of us. Clear of the woods, Homer kept to the shadows of hedgerows, following the course of ditches made dry by long months of a summer drought. This man was impressive when it came to the art of concealment; only a few yards in front of me I often found it difficult to see him. If Homer was a mere poacher, then some university ought to start a degree course teaching his skills. He moved with effortless skill in the shadows, slowing to a languid gait, taking on a slow grace that seemed to make him all but invisible. Carelessly blundering along behind him, I quickly realised I had much to learn.

We must have walked for at least a mile, circling the perimeter of stubble fields grazed barren by hungry flocks of sheep, before coming to a halt at a patch of bare earth with a salt lick in a bucket.

"The farmer used this for his sheep until recently," Homer whispered. The rank odour of their droppings was strong. "A spring has appeared higher up the hillside and collects as a drinking pond just here. The local farmer used it for his sheep in the drought, but they didn't seem to thrive on it."

"The spring only recently appeared?"

"In the last year or two."

"Since the fracking site started?"

"The farmer thinks the earth tremors must have caused it. The green grass along the stream path has marked its course all summer, despite the lack of rain. A haven for wild life in this drought. Odd though; I've seen a lot of dead birds around here."

I looked at Homer inquisitively from under my coolie hat and stooped to fill a number of test tubes from residual puddles, collected in the hoofprints of sheep. Wherever the spring issued from, it dispersed in this field at the bottom of the hill, providing a grass meadow, an oasis amidst straw coloured fields. I didn't need a torch to tell me that the samples were merely diluted mud. We would need to follow the spring path towards its source to get closer to what I needed.

"You must be out of your mind," had been his comment when I had asked him earlier to lead me higher up to the source of the spring. From what he had told me, I realised that the issue was only a few hundred metres from the perimeter to the fracking site and the final approach had to be made across wide, open fields.

"I wondered why you prepared all of this," I had replied, trying to lighten his mood by flapping my arms to imitate some ghostly Ku Klux Klan member.

I stood back waiting for Homer to make a decision, aware that Joss had fixed me with her bright eyes. As we both waited, I swear the dog actually rolled her eyes. Despite her obvious devotion to Homer, at times he obviously tried even her limitless patience.

I didn't catch the next instruction Homer whispered to the dog. He suddenly turned and barked his next command at me. Hadn't he got that the wrong way around? Or was it simply because he held a higher opinion of the dog than me?

"Keep in the ditch and stay low. When I stop, go flat. No questions. You've got no more than five minutes from when we approach the spring issue that you're so bothered about."

With that, Homer turned and moved away, leaving his black mood to fill the space between. Joss trailed faithfully in my footsteps.

Following the spring path, the ditch seemed packed by more nettles and briars than you could imagine growing in a single space. The night was warm; beneath our hats and capes we were wearing only vests and shorts, so our arms and legs were stung and scratched remorselessly. Only Joss, behind, seemed immune. Added to that, the climb was steep, creating something like a sauna beneath the hat and cape. Sweat stung my eyes, Homer having removed my glasses (he claimed they might reflect any light), which left me with opaque vision at best.

"You don't need to be able to see to fill a test tube," had been his answer to my plea for the return of my glasses. Well, perhaps not, but I certainly needed to be able to see him and to know when we were approaching the fracking site perimeter.

Most of the night noise from the site was contained within high fencing, infilled with sound absorbing panels and topped with dense spirals of razor wire. Even the world pole vault champion would be challenged to clear the top of that.

As we drew closer, the rumble of pumps and whine of generators became more audible. They had reduced the lighting and cloaked the outside perimeter in quick growing vines, adding to the pretence of the site's claimed 'eco' credentials.

For the last hundred metres, the bottom of the ditch became progressively wetter and we were soon in a fast flowing stream mid-calf deep. As I flopped against the bank of the ditch to gather breath, a nettle stung me through the fabric of the cape.

Homer leaned back and pressed his mouth against my ear.

"This is as close as we can get. Where the ground flattens out, the ditch swings towards the perimeter fence and there's no cover. Beyond here, we're in the range of their CCTV system."

He left the rest to my imagination.

"Where's the main drainage system?"

"The supposedly legal system you mean? It's another hundred yards farther round to our right. It's a large black pipe that carries all their waste to an underground cistern for collection by tankers to take away for disposal."

For someone who claimed no interest in this particular site or process, Homer certainly knew plenty about it.

"We'll cross the pipe as we move around towards the cover of the trees," he added in a whisper, tapping his watch and showing a hand of spread fingers to remind me I had five minutes; not a second more.

I filled six small test tubes, labelling and numbering them before inserting them in the pouch I carried around my waist. Homer was tugging my arm before I had finished.

Climbing from the ditch we set off in the direction of the woods; the very same in which I had been ensnared by one of Bremer's man-traps several weeks earlier. We had covered only a short distance when lights came on; one minute total darkness, the next a world of bright white light, illuminating the main entrance gate to the site, just as an electric powered tug came into view hauling a string of sealed containers on trailers.

Homer instantly went to ground in the newly cast shadows beneath a dense clump of gorse demarking a rocky outcrop in an otherwise straw stubble field. With a firm tug, he pulled me into the shadow beside him.

"I had almost forgotten; there's an access track that follows the drain line," he said in a whisper. "They told local residents they would only use it for night-time deliveries to avoid traffic congestion during the day."

"How considerate of them," I said with a note of cynicism.

"It's why they use electric tugs; it reduces the noise."

Panting, Joss arrived, squirming into the narrow space between us, as the soft whine of an electric motor approached, underscored by the sound of tyres on gravel.

It was all very 'eco'; unless, of course, your real agenda was to do things you didn't want others to see. As the tug approached, the gates swung open automatically and the rig disappeared inside the compound in a matter of seconds. The gates closed and the lights were extinguished. It resembled a scene from a James Bond movie, leaving me with the feeling that I really had to know what was in the containers to make it necessary to deliver them at the dead of night.

"We need to get clear of the track before they return with empty containers." Homer was already moving as he spoke, leaving me to scuttle along behind to keep up with him. "Their main drain is in a culvert the other side," he added as if I needed an inducement.

As we approached the track, he dropped flat to the ground. I was amused to see Joss, now in front of me, mimic his posture, using her paws to drag along on her belly.

"They have a camera watching the track. We need to crawl from here."

That made sense, again suggesting that Homer knew far more about the site than he was prepared to admit. We must have crawled for the best part of a hundred yards; a hundred yards that cut into our gloves and lacerated our hands and knees as we slithered along.

When fracking had started, public access was supposed to be freely available by law. But so much had changed and the task of finding out what they were up to was proving far harder than we had ever imagined.

After what felt like an eternity we were across, and tumbled into what must have been a man-made ditch, partially filled with a large, ribbed black plastic pipe.

"No time for samples," Homer hissed through gulps to breathe. "They'll be back soon."

I ignored him. I hadn't come this far to leave with only a partial picture of what was happening in the site. With a small electric drill I made a hole in the wall of the pipe. Liquid squirted out under surprising pressure.

"Hurry," he hissed in annoyance. "They turn around the containers quickly, they'll return back down this track before we can get to those trees."

Homer wasn't being melodramatic. As I hastily filled test tubes and sealed the leak with a rubber grommet, a light snapped back on and the gates began to re-open. I had delayed us just a few minutes too long and we were now trapped in the limited cover of the ditch, with only open ground around us. We could go nowhere and I would have to lie next to the pipe while Homer called me every idiotic name he could. With alarm, I noticed his stutter had returned.

Pressed against the sloping flank of the ditch, I drew my neck as far into the cape as possible, lowering the rim of the coolie hat so low that it left the merest slit for my eyes. This was going to put Homer's attempts at camouflage to the *ultimate test. The rig and its guards would pass only a few feet above us. As I lay listening to the approaching sound of rubber tyres on gravel, the hem of the cape lifted up and Joss squirmed underneath to join me. I'm not sure if this was for her reassurance or mine. Either way, it was as though she was fully aware that her black and white markings were a dead give-away in the lights of the advancing tug. What a difference a circumstance can make; only a short time ago, I would have had a distinct aversion to the close presence of a dog. Now, the feeling of soft fur pressed against my side was amazingly comforting.*

Why is it at moments of greatest tension we naturally hold our breath? As if, with everything else going on around us, the sound of our own breathing was going to make any difference.

"*There are two men walking behind the container.*" *Homer urgently murmured his warning, peering over the rim of the ditch.*

If the approaching tug wasn't enough of a challenge, the sound of voices now floated over the whine of electric motors. Apprehensively, I strained my ears to catch what was being said. Had they seen us on the CCTV system and were sending guards to haul us out of the ditch for questioning? If they were, then stealth wasn't one of their tactics; the two approaching men were calling loudly to one another. Occasional phrases drifted above the metallic sounds of the containers, words that weren't in any European language I could identify. Arabic or some middle Eastern dialect? I hadn't a clue, but the implications were disturbing.

I could almost feel the presence of the large rubber tyres just inches above our heads. The absence of noise, after years of the sound of engines, felt weird. The passing of huge containers was almost silent. Empty or full, the ground still vibrated beneath the load. Homer described the nightly arrival of the containers as consideration for local people. Instead, they were using the pretext to hide some dark practice.

I felt Joss tremble against my leg; did the absence of the noise spook her? Within a minute, the threat had passed, now leaving us with the problem of guards trailing in its wake.

The track was narrow, barely wide enough for one vehicle to pass. If anyone on our side of the track looked into the ditch it would test Homer's home-made camouflage outfits to their limits. The best you could say for our situation was that the moon had set and clouds had obscured the stars.

Words suddenly echoed into the ditch, interrupted by an abrupt spike of protest as a radio demanded response.

"Speak English."

"Sorry. Nothing so far."

The words were thick and deliberate, English definitely not the first language.

"Must have been a rabbit or fox that triggered the alarm."

"I'm not convinced," barked the metallic voice on the radio. "Keep looking. Search thoroughly between here and the outer gates. If someone's inside, no more alarms have been triggered, so they're more than likely still here, hiding. Don't miss anything. You know what's on the line if you do." The message finished curtly.

There was silence for a moment. The men exchanged words in Arabic, laughed briefly, followed by the sound of running liquid; one of the men had stopped to pee. I just hoped it wasn't being aimed in our direction.

Still holding our breath, we lay stock still, waiting. The whine of the tug had all but disappeared and I was desperate for one of the men to speak again before daring to exhale. In front of me, Homer's foot jerked abruptly beneath his cape. I discovered later that he was lying on an ants' nest. Joss made a soft whimper as ants bit her too. Fortunately, the man above us was too intent on complaining robustly about their orders as he relieved himself. Miraculously, no one heard or saw Homer move, and within a minute the men had moved away.

Sliding backwards along the ditch beside me, Homer was holding a thin, reed-like tube, one end turned to hold against his eye. He slowly turned the tube through the arc of a circle, scanning the area around us. A periscope; ingeniously little more than another stalk hidden by a sea of dry grasses. Clever.

"Okay. We'll make our move towards the trees as soon as they disappear around the turn lower down in case the lights come on again. Be ready to move quickly," Homer hissed, scratching at the biting ants.

Below our feet I think I heard a rat scurry past in the ditch. Ants and men weren't the only thing we had disturbed. Eventually satisfied, Homer whispered.

"Time to go. There could be more containers waiting at the lower gates. Move fast and watch where you step. We haven't got a lot of time to make for the cover of the trees." He paused.

"And don't forget the trap you fell into last time. Concentrate this time."

His words were a poignant reminder of where this had all begun. With my cuts barely healed, it would be some while before I forgot that particular experience.

Ghost white in night's black cloak, we were shadowed by a pale barn owl, keen to chase us away from its territory. The owl skimmed low above our heads, screeching an angry warning as he departed.

The return to Homer's scramble bike was uneventful. It was still concealed where we had hidden it beneath its covering of bracken and branches. As we approached, Homer gave a soft command and sent Joss on a wide circuit *through the trees to flush out anyone who might be hiding in wait for us. Panting, she returned, five minutes later. Despite all the hidden listening devices, no one seemed to have detected our presence.*

Homer donned night glasses and wheeled the silent bike through the trees to the track. Flicking the starter, we sped off faster than we had arrived, whispering through the trees like a spectre in the night. By the time we approached Homer's cottage the first pale light of dawn was already staining the eastern sky, a counterbalance to the orange glow, ominous along the entire northern horizon, burning its path through village and countryside on its unstoppable march towards London.

Joss and I waited patiently while Homer cooled the bike's engine with damp sacks, haunted by the memory of the previous visit of Bremer's enforcers. The silence felt ominous; defeated, the helicopters had ceased their continuous shuttle from the sea, re-directed to the emergency caused by the tidal surge. The fire had taken on the appearance of a living creature which would only be extinguished by 'mother earth', when, and if, she finally decided to release rain to douse the flames.

The lightening sky, now indigo blue with paling stars as dawn approached, foretold no relief from the previous hundred days of drought. The only visible clouds to stain the sky were made of carbon, smoke veined arteries spiralling right up to the stratosphere. I could only hope nature's anger with our abuse of her world would abate soon and come to our rescue.

"Wishful thinking won't put out the flames," Homer said, reading my thoughts as he passed on his way to the house.

I shook my head. "If more people had listened to the messages when there was still time, we might not have that scene to haunt us now."

"There are many who think the earth is quite capable of saving itself," Homer replied with a dismissive note in his voice.

"As well it might. But will that be enough to save us too? We need the earth for our very existence; the planet can well survive without us."

Homer made no response, pretending to be distracted by the recording made by his hidden camera above the door.

"Your camouflage trick saved us," I said, trying to counterbalance the negativity of the moment. "Where did you learn that?"

The look he gave made it clear that he didn't appreciate even that simple question. But then, asking Homer anything was seldom well received. I guess it added to the enigma surrounding my reluctant host.

CHAPTER 9
H_2O TELLS A TALE

Homer took a bowl of porridge to Grace in her refuge in the roof. Both were tired from their night of exertion, as much from nervous stress as the distance they had covered. While Grace had been distracted by the low pass of the barn owl, Homer had been more concerned by the presence of a ghost drone, its rotors silenced, hunting in the darkness for them. Bremer was cunning, his instincts would have told him someone was inside the boundaries of his fiefdom. Only a combination of a hot night and the camouflage cloaks had saved them from the drones prying infra-red eyes. Keeping one step ahead of Bremer's Machiavellian tactics had stretched Homer to the limits. So far he had kept them safe, aware that his guard could never be allowed to relax. A single slip would offer Bremer the excuse he needed.

"If anyone arrives, go straight to the hide in the chimney flue," Homer reminded Grace. "Sleep on the bed, not in it, and don't leave as much as a hair behind. You'll have five minutes, not a second more."

Homer frowned. Grace had transferred her collection of test tubes into a small case lined with foam. Each tube contained liquid, displaying varying degrees of discolouration and were secured in sockets in the foam to prevent damage. One was held in Grace's gloved hand, against which she held an instrument.

"What are you doing?" he asked. "And don't tell me its best I don't know; just hiding you in my house is enough to land me in serious trouble."

Grace flicked a glance at Homer. "Just preliminary tests on the samples we took."

"At great personal risk I would remind you. I hope they're worth it."

'Was he perpetually grumpy', she thought, or just like this when he's stressed? Grace held the instrument against the test tube and pressed a small button. The needle on the dial flew into a red quadrant and a sound resembling a strangled parrot filled the room.

"What …?"

"It's hot."

"What, 'hot' like geothermal?" Homer gestured for her to stop. The noise grated in his ears like chalk on a blackboard.

Grace was quiet for a moment, considering her answer.

"I'm not a specialist, but this piece of kit," she held up the instrument in her hand, "combines scintillation and geiger counter in one. A reading like this," Grace showed him the dial, "means it's radioactive, far higher than occurs naturally in the ground."

To say her statement was a conversation stopper was an understatement.

"Radioactive?" Homer shaped the word incredulously. "Like background radiation, radon gas?"

"Highly radioactive," she confirmed. "Many, many times higher than anything natural would yield."

Homer's instinct was to doubt, suspecting she might exaggerate to make her point. But his farming friend, Eustace, had referred to ailing sheep that had grazed on the lush grass around the spring outfall. It stopped Homer before his retort could form. If the two were connected …?

"Dangerously high?" That was the question that came instead.

"That's for others to decide," Grace replied, returning the test tube to its socket and closing the lid.

"This box is lined, so we're safe enough from these hot boys at the moment, but I wouldn't go near that spring if I were you until we find out more. It might explain why our friend Bremer is so anxious to stop us from finding out what's going on in that compound."

Homer should have known better before opening the door. They had changed tactics, arriving on soft tyres and a barely audible throttle. In fact, he wouldn't have known they were there at all if Joss hadn't given a whimper of warning.

The punch must have been thrown as he opened the door. Perhaps the merest suggestion of a shadow forewarned him. Enough to turn his head to the right before the fist, armed with a knuckle-duster, grazed the side of his scalp, tearing between his ear and head and carrying sufficient force to send Homer spinning across the room, his backwards fall only broken by the kitchen table.

Stunned, lying on the floor, he was sufficiently conscious to expect worse to follow. But they were savvy, suspecting the presence of a hidden camera. Only words came in the wake of the blow.

"The boss says that's 'just in case'."

Delivered in a thickly accented voice, Homer had just enough awareness to command 'stay' as Joss moved towards his attacker. He recognised the voice; the man had been part of the team from the previous visit and probably still carried the scars of his departure. This time he would be ready for the dog.

"Boss says you won't be so lucky next time," the departing voice promised with a shout.

Groggily, Homer struggled to his feet and heard tyres spraying gravel as they departed. At least there was no encore to follow, suggesting they still held uncertainties, enough to prevent a forced entry. Bremer knew someone had been probing his defences and was annoyed that he had no evidence to confirm exactly who.

Grace waited until the Landrover had left. Alerted by a bark from Joss, and when Homer failed to appear, she cautiously climbed down from her chimney roost. Stained by soot smuts, she stood stock still for a further five minutes before daring to leave the attic. The house was silent. She had heard the Landrover accelerate away in haste, leaving an air of foreboding permeating the house in its wake.

The door to the kitchen was open. Using her hand mirror, she cautiously surveyed the room from behind the door before entering. A chair lay overturned. Beyond, bent over the sink, slumped Homer, a towel pressed against the left side of his head, his shirt collar and shoulder stained red with blood. As if to confirm the room was safe to enter, Joss grabbed her trouser leg and gave a hefty tug of encouragement.

"No. No ambulance," Homer said firmly for the second time, waving Grace away, his words thick with pain, slightly slurred by concussion.

"Well, I can't prevent the bleeding. We'll have to find help to stop it," Grace said, her words a blend of anxiety and frustration.

Resigned to placating her concern, Homer fumbled for his phone, tossing it in frustration to Grace.

"Find Angela in my contacts. Ring her and ask her to come. Tell her I need stitching."

"And she is?"

"The local herbalist. Everyone around here thinks she's mad, most just ignore or dismiss her. Years ago, she'd have been drowned as a witch," Homer added with an edge so sharp it could cut itself.

Angela arrived on a battered motorbike, wearing a helmet bearing the 'rising sun' emblem of the once Japanese national flag. Stick thin, grey haired, she cut a striking figure of an indeterminate age. She had an eye patch covering her left eye, ringed with livid scar tissue. On a leather strap across her chest hung a wicker poacher's basket (courtesy of Homer?) containing her 'witch's potions' in a miscellaneous variety of leather and velvet pouches.

Angela threw a fleeting hawk-eye glance at Grace that saw everything in an instant. She removed the blood soaked towel from the side of Homer's head, probing the wound with pencil thin fingers. She didn't ask what had happened, but Grace caught words whispered in a thin voice.

"Bremer, I suppose."

Homer didn't reply.

With the wound cleaned, Grace watched Angela remove a sickle-shaped needle from a tin, thread it, wipe it in a liquid that smelt of iodine and begin stitching the wound.

"This will sting," she said in a voice that implied that it would.

The manner in which she handled Homer made Grace think that they had shared a history, though she couldn't imagine where their lives might have crossed.

Needlework complete, Angela swabbed the wound and produced a mat of fibrous material which she taped in place.

"It will stop infection," she said. "Bremer's goons aren't known for their hygiene."

With an experienced hand, Angela packed everything into her basket.

"And you are?" It was more accusation than question.

"My name is Grace." She held out a hand that was ignored.

"Are you staying around for long?"

Homer interrupted, answering for her. "She's a friend; just leaving."

"Friend? That's a first." Angela squinted with her one good eye in Grace's direction, measuring the scope of the term 'friend'.

"Well, whoever you are, make sure you stay out of trouble. Bremer's storming around like a mad hornet and he's not tolerant with people, particularly strangers, who get in his way."

As if to emphasise her point, she shot a sideways glance at Homer.

"I'll be back in a week to remove the stitches. Don't touch the wound until then. The moss poultice will do the rest."

Angela left in a thin veil of exhaust smoke. Within seconds it felt as if she had been no more than an apparition.

"Interesting woman," Grace mused as the note of the motorbike faded away. "Do you know her well?"

"Let's say our paths have crossed." Homer didn't intend to say anything more, but couldn't resist adding, "Like many people who are different, they're misunderstood. Not that anyone bothers to find out why."

He left the room in search of a clean shirt.

"I'll be off just as soon as it's dark."

Homer showed no sign of having heard what I had said.

"You'll go when it's safe, not before," he said with his back to me. "Bremer's mad he can't find you; that makes him more than dangerous."

"I can look out for myself," I replied, annoyed by his lack of regard for my own seditious skills.

"As well you might; I just don't trust you with my life as well. You'll go when I say; I'm making arrangements," he said with a sudden, pronounced stutter, leaving the room to force an end to the conversation.

For the rest of the day, he left me to fume in the attic. The day was hot for late September and the room felt airless, even with the rooflight open. I yearned to fling open the door and walk in the cool shade of the surrounding woods. But Homer would only disagree for fear of revealing my presence.

Despite my frustrations, I held back my feelings. After all, I had drawn Homer into my life, undoubtedly against his better judgement. So far he had protected me, though reluctantly, but the least I could do was comply with his wishes.

Homer left at some point the following morning without saying where he was going or when he would return. I slept fitfully with Joss on my bed for company. The dog never ceased to surprise me and had worked out a technique to climb the access ladder to the loft. We both seemed to take comfort from the presence of the other. Around mid-afternoon, Homer returned and brought a late lunch up to the attic.

"The town seems to be in a state of lockdown," he said, standing in the shadow to the side of the dormer from where he could see the access track below without being seen.

"Bremer has got the local police to carry out a house to house enquiry on the pretext that someone tried to sabotage one of his night-time deliveries." He smiled thinly.

"Seems he suspects his defences have been breached, but doesn't know by who or why. His authority has been affronted and he'll be like a bear with a sore head until he finds someone to blame."

Distractedly, his finger stroked the wound to the side of his head. "Almost makes this knock on the head worth the pain just to see our local warlord seethe with rage and frustration."

"Doesn't that make him dangerous?"

Homer thought for a second or two. "More predictable than dangerous. Anger spoils the judgement. It will pass, but we need to get you out of here before Bremer restores his perspective."

Homer turned to face me.

"You leave tonight."

I paused eating, with fork midway between plate and mouth.

"I thought you said it wasn't safe?"

"I've arranged for someone to collect you. You'll be safe with them. Even Bremer will be cautious about messing with my friend and his family."

"How can you be so sure?"

Almost for the first time since we had met, Homer laughed generously.

"Because most of Bremer's enforcers are terrified of the curses gypsy women would cast put upon them and their families."

From the conviction in his words, I could tell he wasn't joking.

CHAPTER 10
JOURNEY BY CARAVAN

I got the distinct impression that Homer's friend, Cosmo, had organised the route of the horse-drawn caravan especially for me. In the darkness, we met them on an isolated lane an hour's hike from Homer's cottage. It felt like, and probably was, the middle of nowhere; only the orange glow of the fire to the north-west, now long out of control, gave me any sense of bearing. Even the stars were obscured in a smoke fogged atmosphere, where the smell of burning jostled with pine, warm resin and horse.

Homer and Cosmo spoke briefly in subdued tones as he passed over a bag of dead rabbits and a leg of lamb; presumably my fare for passage in the night. No one lingered or offered a farewell; Homer just disappeared like an apparition into the night.

A teenage boy sat holding the reigns beside Cosmo on the driving bench. Inside the caravan were two women, one slightly younger than me and a much older woman with a lined, drawn face, her crevasses exaggerated by the orange light of a tilley lamp.

"So," I mused. "My escape has been arranged."

Homer was definitely taking no chances, leaving one of his mysterious network of friends to spirit me away.

"If we're stopped, say nothing," Cosmo said. "Just stare ahead, don't blink. Hold eye contact to make them feel uncomfortable. Grandma will do the rest."

The elderly woman smiled thinly at the sound of her name, leaving me with the thought that Homer's earlier descriptions weren't far from the truth.

No one asked any questions and the slow, rocking gait of the horse-drawn caravan soon lulled me into a doze. I must have slept for a while when bright lights and the sound of raised voices stirred me. The horse had come to a halt and someone was interrogating Cosmo who seemed to answer in a slow laconic voice.

"Where do you think you're going this time of night?" More an accusation than a question.

"To join family."

"At two in the morning?" The interrogator made his disbelief quite plain.

Cosmo shrugged, unconcerned. "It's kinder on the horse. The days are hot and there is little roadside fodder about in this dry weather."

"As if scum like you are bothered about a horse," the voice said in a tone of provocative incredulity.

"Suit yourself. The horse knows the truth."

"Skinny runt." A hand slapped the horse's flank, making her shy.

Beside Cosmo, the boy fired a soft word of reassurance to steady the horse, leaving it to stare at the man with a distinct glare that promised she would stamp on his foot if she got half a chance.

"Who's in the back?"

"Family," Cosmo replied evenly, still watching the horse.

The questioner said something, not Arabic, perhaps east European. From the darkness, the voice that answered sounded uncertain. Perhaps Homer had been right.

"Just do as you're told. Search the back." The reply came in English, drenched in impatience. "Or else."

The two voices muttered unhappily to one another as they moved to the rear of the caravan, reluctantly pulling open the canvas covers. A flashlight illuminated the space inside with a dazzling brightness. Homer's plans were about to be put to the test. Behind the light, I could just make out the bearded faces of two men. The light shone upon the younger girl first. There was a comment that I didn't understand, though the sexual innuendo was quite obvious. I was pretty certain the words were Slavic, not

Arabic. Several snide comments passed between the men as the light turned on me.

"Are you a boy?"

A heavily accented voice asked the question; my hair, cropped short for convenience, became a gender neutral appearance aimed at anonymity. Remembering my instructions, I answered with a hard, silent stare, squinting against the light. For a moment, they slipped back into Slavic, laughing at each other's comments, before the one with the light made a grab for my trouser leg.

"Let's find out shall we," he said with a smirk.

Without thinking, I kicked out with my foot and hit him in the arm.

He swore in response. "Bitch."

He tossed the light to his friend and made a grab for me with both hands.

"You need to learn some manners."

They didn't need much of an excuse to get rough and I had just given them one. I twisted and writhed as the man pulled against me with his weight, grabbing my other leg. I fell hard onto the wooden floor, lashing out with my fists as I slid towards him. Heaving forward, his hand moved from my leg and rammed hard against the underside of my chin, forcing my head painfully backwards.

Suddenly, he stopped. A thin, almost whining voice, spoke raucous Slavic from the darkness. I felt the pressure under my chin ease as a caricature of a human appeared, ghoul-like, in the darkness, a pronounced hooked nose, lines and fissures in a face fringed in black lace. She spoke rapidly, unpunctuated, without pausing, descending into a continuous monotone, almost a chant. 'Grandma' was playing her hand.

Within seconds the hands released me and I scurried back to my seat. My assailant withdrew, vigorously crossing himself as he retreated out of the caravan. His friend laughed at his embarrassment, the two men exchanging course, angry words before hurling, "Gypsy pigs," as they disappeared into the darkness, leaving the canvas to flap in the breeze.

I eased myself back onto my seat, feeling for bruises and grazes. The girl opposite handed me a slim leather flask.

"Drink," she instructed. "You did well."

Coarse brandy bit the back of my throat, the type heavy in alcohol that surges to the brain in seconds. Replacing the cork, I wiped my mouth on the back of my hand.

"What did she say?" I nodded in Grandma's direction. Whatever it was, the effect had been pretty dramatic.

The girl handed the flask to the older woman beside her.

"She told him she could see the devil sitting on his shoulder. If he continued to attack us, she would issue a curse that would release Satan to torment his family for eternity."

Beside her, the older woman took a heavy swig and cackled in amusement.

"Well, whatever she said, it worked, and saved me having to fight him off."

The girl looked at the flask, a smile on her lips.

"She wasn't joking. People such as him," she gestured beyond the flapping canvas, "are born into a folklore of good and evil. It holds a powerful place in their lives, even if they try not to admit it. A part of his primeval brain will always wonder if she did release an evil spirit to haunt him."

The smile she gave as she finished speaking chilled my bones to the very core. There was much I had doubts about, but crossing these people was not one I would wish to experiment with.

"So you and Homer are close friends?" I cast a line to see how Cosmo would react.

I was aware of him giving me a squinty look in the darkness. The boy and I had swapped places at some point *around midnight and it was my turn to keep Cosmo awake as we swished the horse gently on her way.*

I heard Cosmo chuckle. "So, that's the name you call him?"

"What do you call him then?"

"We tend not to do names. I recognise voices. That's good enough."

"How long have you known each other?"

"Long enough." Cosmo was giving little away.

"He often seems troubled."

"And you're surprised. Seems your presence brings its own problems, otherwise we wouldn't be trying to secrete you away tonight would we."

He sounded matter of fact, without resentment for the obvious inconvenience.

"I'm grateful for your trouble. Someone has to find out what these people are up to."

"You think so? I thought we had a government to do that?" He snorted with derision.

"As they do with your people?"

I referred to the recent inclusion of 'travellers' as people of suspicion in the updated subtext of the Anti-Terrorism Act.

"The world goes around," Cosmo said without rancour.

I let silence run its course for several minutes.

"So where does Homer fit into all this? Or his friend, Angela, for that matter."

"Ah, so you've met the witchy-woman," he said with a smile in his words. "If he hasn't told you yet, he won't until he's good and ready."

It was strange to see how this nebulous world turned, where troubled, misunderstood people coalesced together in a realm without names. Cosmo must have read my thoughts.

"You don't need names to judge if a person is decent. You can tell by their aura if you can be bothered to look."

"So, what, you can see mine to judge me?"

I tried to make my words laugh but the attempt fell flat. The thought made me feel uncomfortable, exposed.

"Let's just say you wouldn't be sitting here now if I couldn't."

Cosmo's words finished our conversation. A short time later he slowed the plodding mare and dropped me off well away from the searching eyes of any snooping surveillance cameras.

CHAPTER 11
THE PRICE OF DELIVERANCE

Less than twelve hours after Grace had left, the rain came, without warning. It was the first in four months, falling unannounced through a smoke filled sky. To the north, Heathrow airport had already been closed for several days to anything other than emergency traffic as the country struggled to cope with the double crisis of fire and tidal surge.

Homer had been forensically searching the attic to remove any trace of the woman when fat, bloated raindrops smacked against the tiles above him. He had just discovered another delicate origami flower, hidden within a pillowcase. The detail of the folded flower, subtly different from her previous offering, fascinated Homer both for its intricacy and intention.

Later, Homer sat watching a live newsfeed. The tired and exhausted reporter, her once immaculate hair now streaked with soot, stood against the background of a rising column of smoke.

"The rain will be a godsend in dealing with the out-of-control fires, but in the short term increased smoke will only make matters worse."

No one had thought to bring an umbrella and as the woman delivered her report, sooty rivulets ran down her face. Valiantly, as the rain increased, she soldiered on.

"Already one heavy transport plane, bringing emergency equipment for the flooded capital, has made a crash landing on the main runway at Heathrow. It is thought that poor visibility, caused by smoke, was responsible. The crew escaped unhurt, but the runway will be closed for some considerable time."

She paused to cast an eye skywards. The rain seemed to intensify, adding to her bedraggled appearance. Even the fluffy cover to her microphone had slumped into a wet slick. Around her, technicians scurried for cover.

Professional to the end, the reporter signed off as her support team abandoned her, leaving her as a solitary figure in a monsoon downpour.

Homer had reduced the use of electrical equipment. The combination of smoke and rain clouds had restricted the charge from his photovoltaic panels. If this was the future, he would have to severely ration his usage to only what was necessary.

Head between paws, Joss watched Homer with alert eyes from her floor rug. Since Grace had warned him of the possibility of radioactive poisoning from the spring water, Homer had watched the dog with concern for any sign of loss of appetite or sickness. When she had been rounding up the sheep for Eustace a few days before, many of the sheep had been reluctant to leave the lush grass of the spring outfall. As a consequence, Joss had spent considerable time in the mud and reed grass, flushing out the sheep. So far she seemed alright but, feeling a pang of anxiety about something so invisible, he had given the dog extra rations with all her meals. Of the future, time alone would tell.

It rained all day without a break, grey light bringing an early dusk. Homer had only ventured out to collect wood for the Aga and let Joss empty herself, and found the ground, leached and hardened by the long summer drought, running in rivers of water that were slow to absorb. He had just hung his cape on the drying rack when his mobile rang several times in quick succession. Someone was being insistent.

"I need help," Angela said with concern. "Something's blocking the brook above my cottage and it will flood me out if it bursts its banks. The brook has been dry all summer and I can't see what's causing the problem now."

Homer peered through the window past the rivulets veining the glass. The prospect of digging through a raging torrent in the dark didn't appeal. But if Angela was asking for help, it would need his attention. He collected waders and a cape while Joss obstinately refused to wear her waterproof coat.

Angela met him as he drew up outside her cottage, clad head to foot in waterproofs against the deluge.

"It's backing up quickly," she shouted above the roar of the downpour. "The problem is up there in that thicket. It must have been a branch come down that I hadn't noticed."

Angela pointed with her arm towards a cluster of dark trees and brambles a short distance upstream.

"If it overspills its banks, the stream will run straight through my cottage."

Homer nodded. He returned to the cab of the Landrover where Joss sat, paws braced on the dashboard, reluctant to join him for a soaking. He drove the short distance with difficulty and managed to position the Landrover near to the source of the problem. From here, he could use his front winch to haul clear any obstruction. Angela arrived as he climbed the rising ground with his flashlight.

"How did you see that it was blocked?" he shouted in her ear.

"I went to fill some drinking water bottles from a spring higher up a few hours ago and noticed the brook was running slower and deeper than I remembered in the past. It was already too dark to see what was causing the problem."

Rain streamed like a waterfall from her cape. There seemed little promise of it easing anytime soon. Homer handed Angela the flashlight and unwound the tow hook and cable from the winch. It would be the easiest method to clear the problem. Scrambling against the slope, he pulled her up with him, her stick thin fingers curled in his hand. There was no weight to her and he made a mental note to check her eating habits when this was over.

From the crest, the location of the blockage was clear to see. Saddled on each side by a cluster of trunks and overhanging bushes, roots had grown into the brook and were causing the problem.

"If you shine the light there," Homer shouted as he pointed into the brown swirling water, "I'll climb down and hook this around the fallen debris. We can haul it clear with the winch."

Angela flicked the 'on' switch of the powerful beam and Homer sidled along the bank top. The drought had lulled him to forget how quickly water levels rise once the rains return, and now the dry brook was waist deep in surging water.

Sliding on the muddy flank, he eased his way down to the problem. In the flashlight, it seemed a tangle of briars had caught a basket of small branches, forming a 'beaver dam' of debris, swept down by a monsoon strength downpour. If he cut the thick briars at the sides, the winch would make short work of hauling everything clear.

"Come a bit closer; give me more light," Homer shouted.

Angela tentatively followed him, trying to avoid overbalancing into the cold water below. After a few seconds, with the light in a better position, Homer could feed the hook and cable through the tangle and drag it clear. As he stretched to clasp the end, something caught his eye beneath the surface of the swirling water. Homer eased back to allow the water to clear from the mud he was churning with his feet at the side.

"Get the light a bit higher."

He leaned back so as not to block the beam. Slowly the surging torrent cleared. Just beneath the surface of the water, the face of a bearded man stared back at him.

Back in her kitchen, Angela and Homer moved around each other in thoughtful silence. On the gas stove, a kettle sang a discordant note; an epitaph to the dead man they had found. They had removed the body from the brook and placed it on a sheet of plastic. Angela was certain he had been dead for some time.

"How on earth did he get here?" had been foremost in her mind, a question exaggerated by the clear evidence of a substantial blow to the back of his head.

"I doubt he's floated downstream. Even full of water, the brook's too narrow and contorted for that to be possible."

"We must contact the police, report what we've found," she replied in a pensive voice.

Angela was no fan of the local constabulary, but the death and removal of the body needed to proceed in the correct order.

Homer shook his head. "Not until we work out what's going on." His stutter, usually barely perceptible, was back. "If the body couldn't float down the brook, someone, presumably the killer, must have planted it. So the question is why here?"

For a moment, Angela's face twisted with anxiety at the thought of a murderer disposing of the victim in close proximity to her home.

"Perhaps there's another reason," she said searching for a better alternative. "Perhaps he was out walking, got lost, struck his head in the darkness and fell into the brook. It's possible."

"But unlikely. Something hard, metallic, would be needed to deliver a wound like the one on the back of his head. We have to work on the probability that it's not an accident."

Angela frowned. "But why bring the body to my doorstep? Blocking the stream makes it inevitable that the body will be found."

"Because that is exactly what the murderer intended. The question is, why?"

"Surely you don't kill a man just to block a stream?"

"No, but you might to incriminate someone else."

Angela gasped in surprise, her hand pressed over her mouth as the implications of Homer's words sank in.

"Me? Surely not?"

"I don't know, but if I was a betting man, the police will turn up here at first light on the pretext of a tip off. With your reputation, finding a murdered body not fifty yards from your cottage is not going to go down well in the court of local public opinion," Homer said bluntly.

Indomitable spirit she may be, but his words left Angela horrified at the prospect.

"What do I do, Homer? Surely calling the police to report finding the body will prove my innocence."

"No. We can't do that. I'll move the body immediately. If the police turn up in the morning, they'll find nothing. Later, I'll leave an anonymous call saying I've found a body. But their visit could prove you've been set up."

"Where?" she asked anxiously. "Where will you leave him? The poor man needs to be laid to rest."

"He will be," Homer said, placing his hand over hers for reassurance. "He just needs to be found in his employers' backyard."

Puzzled, Angela shook her head. "Where?"

"Somewhere that will give cause for Bremer to answer a lot of very awkward questions."

Homer was right and wrong with his predictions in equal measure. Sergeant Wailes, in the company of two young constables, arrived in the first grey light of morning. They were even earlier than Homer had anticipated.

Angela had left a gap in her bedroom curtains so that she could see into the courtyard below. The police four-by-four made a noisy approach through the lagoon sized puddles in the drive, its wiper blades blinking at maximum speed in the continuing downpour. Twenty-four hours of unremitting monsoon force rainfall were rapidly chasing the problems of drought away from a cliché driven media; 'It never rains but it pours' trailed every bannerline.

Three policemen presented themselves at Angela's front door. She kept them waiting while she attached the bodycam Homer had given her to the mobile phone in her pocket. Connected to Homer's phone, he would see in real time everything that transpired.

"Can we come in, Angela? We need to ask you a few questions," Sergeant Wailes stated, stepping forwards without waiting for a reply.

Angela extended an arm across the threshold, blocking his path. She detested Wailes, the author of many of the lies that circulated about her, tempered only in part by the departing advice Homer had given her. "Don't roll over the moment they arrive, but don't provoke them either. Stand your ground, remember you're innocent. The bodycam will protect you; even Wailes isn't that stupid." 'All well and good,' she thought, but three against one didn't feel like comfortable odds.

Wailes gave her arm a dismissive stare, contemplating moving it out of his way until his eyes caught sight of the tiny blinking light on the camera.

"Clever," he said, hesitating.

"Come to the kitchen door," Angela said with a stony glare. "Best you drip on my tiled floor."

She closed the door in their faces. The back door was opened before they arrived.

"You can keep your boots on. There's a mop for the floor as you leave."

She turned her back on them, staring out of the window while they entered, the camera focusing on their reflections in the glass pane. "Act normal," Homer had insisted. "Offer them tea or coffee. It won't alter Wailes," (who he had predicted they would send), "but you may gain the support of anyone accompanying him."

As they lowered their hoods, Angela could see a young female PC she had not previously met. Perhaps whatever Wailes was here for would be tempered by her presence? The kettle sang on the stove so Angela took the initiative.

"It's a wet morning to come all the way out here. Would you like tea or coffee."

Wailes shook his head; drinking one of this witch's concoctions was definitely against his principles. The other tall young male PC followed his lead, but the woman nodded her thanks.

"Milk, no sugar, please."

Wailes gave the PC a glance that clearly signalled, 'Idiot; on your head be it.'

Angela reached stiffly for mugs, exaggerating her frailty for the benefit of the woman.

"To what do I owe the pleasure of this early morning visit?" she asked in as balanced a voice as possible, silently praying that Homer had removed every scrap of evidence of the dead man from the brook.

Removing the heavy, water filled body without causing extensive damage to the banks had been difficult. On Angela's insistence, they had laid the corpse in the back of the Landrover with as much dignity as possible. Homer had spent a further hour carefully restoring the scene, using night-sights to avoid drawing attention with the flashlight. He had left some of the debris behind to block the channel, using fallen branches to conceal much of where they had trodden.

While her back was turned, Angela caught a reflection of the silent signals passing between the three of them. Turning to face them with a steaming mug for the female PC, she asked her question again.

"So, Sergeant, what did you say was the purpose of this early, unrequested visit?"

Wailes glared at the tiny camera clipped to Angela's jumper.

"I didn't. We've had reports of a commotion; raised, angry threatening voices and shouting in this area of the woods, close to this cottage. We've been sent to investigate; out of concern for you of course, an elderly woman living alone."

Wailes spoke with a distinctly supercilious tone to his voice.

Angela affected a bewildered expression.

"If I had heard anything, I would have called you," she said with a bemused expression.

"There's nothing wrong with my hearing. It would seem you've had a wasted visit."

She gave a measured look to each of them in turn.

"Sending three police officers looks a bit over the top don't you think?"

Wailes sensed he was losing the initiative. This woman might well have a reputation for being mad, but she wasn't stupid.

"In our line of work, you never know what you might find."

"May I ask who made this exaggerated report?" Angela replied. "It would seem they've wasted your time."

Wailes smiled; it wasn't pleasant. "I'll be the judge of that, Angela. Mind if we look around?"

Of course Angela minded, but she wasn't about to say so. She shrugged. "It's you who will get soaked in this rain."

Wailes made the smirked expression of someone who has possession of facts that lead their victim into a hidden trap.

"PC James and I will make an inspection of the grounds," he said for the benefit of the camera.

He drew the hood over his head. "PC Markham will remain here, to drink her coffee."

His tone was sarcastic, though it was obvious the real reason to leave PC Markham behind was to watch Angela.

As they left, Angela turned to the young female PC.

"I'll just use the bathroom while they have a look around. You stay in the warmth of the kitchen and finish your coffee."

From the bathroom she would be able to see the brook in which they had found the dead body, and convey the scene to Homer watching on his link to her camera. How they behaved might confirm what the two policemen expected to find.

With no more than a nod, the PC smiled and sipped her coffee. At the top of the stairs Angela hesitated, watching the reflection in the landing mirror. Still drinking her coffee, PC Markham had quietly followed her to the bottom of the stairs, blocking any means of her escape.

"So much for empathy," Angela muttered to the camera with a note of disappointment.

One of the many things you could say about Sergeant Wailes was that subtlety was not his strong suit. Having slammed the back door closed, he and PC James chose the direct path towards the brook. Even with heads bent against the driving rain, they took an unwavering line directly towards the thicket where the brook had concealed the body.

With their backs turned to the cottage, Angela stood in full view of the window, her camera filming their actions. It was enough to confirm that they were involved and the body had been left to implicate her, though why was a matter beyond her guess. Pure, simple prejudice wasn't enough to explain it. Labelled as a mad witch because she chose to live alone was burden enough; why add a dead body to her litany of imagined crimes?

While Angela watched the two men approach the trees, PC Markham silently appeared on the landing behind her, looking at her through the open door. Sensing her presence, Angela saw answers to her questions on the woman's face reflected in the window. The rumour-mongers had been busy well before a body had been found.

CHAPTER 12
COSMO CAUSES COMMOTION

Olwyn Wright-Smith stared through the opaque, uncleaned window in anticipation of a long, boring day. She was the first to arrive at the dowdy office she shared with her boss, Jerry Houseman, above a tired launderette in Croydon High Street. Hidden behind a fading company sign, purporting to import 'West African Cocoa and other luxury products', the windows hadn't seen a cloth in years, the dimmed light reflecting a job that had turned out to be similarly disappointingly dull.

Punctual, unlike her boss Jerry, Olwyn boiled a kettle and made a mug of indifferent instant coffee. Adding powdered milk (Jerry was supposed to bring fresh with him every morning and usually forgot), she sighed at the thought of the backwater into which her once 'glittering' life had descended.

A disastrous affair with her university professor in her final year had all but destroyed her degree. What was it with men that the moment a woman uttered the words, 'I've got something to tell you,' they just move on with their life and abandon you to your fate? "But I thought you were on the pill," angrily followed by accusations of 'obsessive behaviour', 'stalking' and a lonely abortion.

Two more unsuitable relationships repeated themselves, each time progressively more traumatic in their fallout, culminating in estrangement from her long suffering parents, desperate to preserve some measure of dignity for the family name.

For the moment, at least she was safe from Jerry. Openly gay, his equally privileged upbringing had rejected him for reasons that were never totally clear.

Olwyn stared morosely at the rivulets of rain streaming down the filthy window, distorting the queue of static traffic in the High Street below her. No doubt Jerry would enter with the excuse, 'Sorry I'm late; bloody traffic,' when everyone knew he only ever travelled by underground.

Olwyn had been initially excited when he contacted her on some unnamed recommendation, suggesting she apply for a position in his newly created office. The prospect of any job, especially one in MI5 had appealed to the romantic side of her nature, though, with hindsight, what she had expected it to involve was now far from clear.

Under the cover of a faded sign, their 'Import Company' did actually import some products from Ghana, protecting the real purpose for its existence. Encrypted on the hard drive of their server were hundreds of files, links to a narrow selection of informers or 'sleepers' in the diaspora of communities in London and other major towns and cities throughout the country and beyond. No glittering office on the banks of the Thames for Olwyn; just a tired, dog-eared few rooms with second-hand desks and computers, perfumed by the smell of washing from the laundry below. Even their files fulfilled their description. Most, if not all, were 'sleeping' and seldom woke up.

The traffic chugged at a snail's pace in a cloud of stationary exhaust fumes. Relegated to the boondocks of life, Olwyn longed for something to change and for a few moments allowed her mind to daydream of the world that could have been before disappointment clamped its vice-like grip on her.

Inconsiderately, the phone rang, unfairly interrupting her reverie. She tried to ignore it. They would call again if it was urgent. They did, five seconds later.

"Good morning, West African Cocoa, how may I help you," Olwyn announced in a flat, uninviting voice.

"The code is albatross, the colour is turquoise; hang on a minute I need to put in more change."

The sound of coins rattling interrupted the call.

"Good, better. I'm in a call box; bloody hard to find I can tell you," the voice continued with a note of exasperation.

"Is this line secure?"

The voice didn't wait for Olwyn to answer.

"Well, it will have to be, I'm getting soaked in this bloody box. I've a message for you and I'm not going to repeat it, so record it or take it down, whatever you need to do."

Olwyn had barely time to press 'record' on the phone before her caller rattled off a ten-digit grid coordinate.

"You'll find a body, a man. Cause of death, a blow to the head and drowning."

Olwyn decided the voice on the phone held a rather quaint, rural accent she couldn't place, in sharp contrast to the London accents she was most accustomed to. He continued after a pause for breath. It sounded as though he was reading a prepared script.

"The victim appears of middle Eastern extraction, a tattoo has been removed with acid from the left wrist, possibly post mortem. There are other signs of violence, before death."

The caller hesitated, allowing Olwyn to catch up with her scribbled back up notes as he cussed colourfully about the rain dripping down his neck through a hole in the roof.

"Are you getting this?"

"What? Yes. Please continue," she said with a breathless gasp.

Everything seemed to be happening at high speed. This was far from the usual calls they received.

The man grunted, blurting something Olwyn didn't catch before continuing.

"You'll see the body in a clearing, north-east of the fracking Site 17. It's probably where he was employed. That's important, because you'll find there are no records about him. He's got no ID on him, probably entered the country illegally. If you move quickly, you'll find real time evidence of who they're employing in Site 17, but you'll have to move fast before his employers find the body."

Olwyn could hear the sound of rain drumming on the roof of the phone box as the caller fumbled against the warning bleeps of the phone demanding more money. The voice cursed loudly as coins fell to the floor.

"Bloody useless piece of rubbish," he cussed, forcing a pound coin into the box. "Listen, I've got no more money. Have you got down what I've told you?"

"Every word I think. I just need to …"

"No time. You need to move fast. Whoever killed this man will be urgently searching for the body." He didn't explain why.

"You need to get there first before the evidence is removed. Your idiot of a boss will know why, so get your satellite images and tell him to get his lazy arse down to the site before it's too late."

The phone started bleeping frantically and the voice was gone before Olwyn could ask the question on the tip of her tongue. 'Why don't the people who killed this man know where the body is?' Only the monotone of disconnection answered her.

Though they were only just visible from the window, Angela could see two luminous jackets thrashing around the area of the brook in which the man's body had been discovered. She could only guess what they had expected to find and mentally held her breath at what might still be there to discover. The larger of the two figures slipped in the soft mud at the top of the bank, sliding knee deep into the torrent racing through the brook. Angela smiled to herself, though it would only add to the sergeant's frustration at being thwarted.

Behind Angela, the policewoman continued to stare at her, silent and motionless. Did she have handcuffs ready to restrain her? Had Wailes briefed her to expect a call as soon as they discovered the body? Angela shuddered at the thought. If Homer hadn't acted on his intuitions when they had found the poor man's body blocking the ditch, she could have been arrested within the next five minutes. It might well have been what Wailes planned, bringing dark and distant memories flooding back to her.

In the hallway below, a clock marked the passage of time with the swing of its pendulum. Angela felt her phone, switched to silent mode, vibrate as a message arrived from Homer. Fabric brushed fabric as an arm moved. Through the window, two figures, one stained brown, glistening in liquid mud, were returning towards the police car.

Angela heard a sound, somewhere between a half laugh and a sigh; then the movement of an arm, the policewoman turned. To approach her or descend the stairs?

"Lucky, very lucky. You'd better take care," the policewoman whispered.

The words floated between them. A threat or a warning? Angela rubbed away condensation from her breath that had formed on the window. Behind her, PC Markham had disappeared.

"A thousand apologies, dear girl. You wouldn't believe the traffic out there."

Jerry Houseman burst into their cramped office, showering raindrops from a shaking umbrella.

"Try getting up earlier, Jerry. You're late as usual," Olwyn grumbled, ignoring his excuses.

Jerry pulled a disappointed face, twirling a fresh pink carnation.

"But he was such a divine boy. So … hard to leave."

He placed a bottle of fresh organic milk on her desk.

"What, if any, earth-shattering events have arisen to shape our dull and boring lives?" Jerry dropped his umbrella into a bucket, flopping into a rickety leather chair.

"What do you know about 'albatross'?"

Against her better judgement, Olwyn flipped the switch on the kettle, deciding it would be petty to ignore his need for coffee; he had remembered the milk.

"Albatross? Large brown sea bird, enormous wingspan, flies around the globe without beating its wings." Distracted, with only half an ear, Jerry sifted through the pile of supposedly urgent messages Olwyn had printed out and left on his desk.

"Not the bird, dimwit." There was only so much of Jerry's oblique attention a girl could tolerate.

"We've had a call; not your usual disgruntled neighbour or hysterical wife. This was a man from a phone box; do they still exist nowadays? Said he was a turquoise albatross, or some such nonsense. Mentioned something about a Site 17, whatever that is. Probably some mental retard who found our number in a …"

Olwyn stopped. She had Jerry's attention, which was unusual and for once he had a serious expression on his face.

"What?"

"Albatross; colour turquoise?" Jerry said.

"Something like that. It's on the transcript in front of you. Voice recording is on the tape."

Olwyn turned away to hide her irritation from continually having to repeat herself.

Jerry speed read her written notes, simultaneously scanning his security pass and pressing keys on his computer keyboard. The screen flickered as he donned headphones and pressed the play button on the recorder. Puzzled, Olwyn decided coffee was the priority and left him to his musings, but watched his reflection intently in the window.

"My, my." Jerry removed the headphones, partially turning the screen for her to view as she returned with steaming mugs.

"What have we here?" He pointed to a shape in the corner of the screen, scrolling the cursor to magnify the image. "Unless I'm very mistaken we have a 'John Doe' as our American friends would call him.

Olwyn peered at the screen. In a clearing amongst trees lay a spreadeagled body, positioned to be clearly visible from an overhead search.

Jerry saved the image, zooming out to get a better context of the location. Several hundred metres to the left was the fenced boundary of a fracking compound, though the detail within its perimeter was almost totally obscured by camouflage netting. Hastily, Jerry switched back to the larger frame of the body. Whether by satellite or drone, the quality was crystal clear. He beat a monotone on his pad with a pencil, momentarily lost in thought.

"Nip down to M&S, old girl," he said abruptly, opening his wallet, handing Olwyn a roll of bank notes. "Buy yourself a grey suit and some heels; I don't think the 'Corbyn for PM' tee-shirt and that charity shop skirt are going to cut it where you're going."

"Me?" she said confused.

"Absolutely, deary," he said, connecting his mobile to some obscure, dust covered gizmo she had never seen before.

"They eat people like me for breakfast where you're going," he added with a camp, affronted shudder.

"Now be a good girl and pop along to the shops; the next bit is strictly off-limits for your ears."

Homer spent almost an hour waiting for Cosmo to return. Improvising, he had found a truck drivers stopover where no one would question two men talking inconsequentially over a pot of tea. On such a rain soaked day, the lorry park was full as a constant stream of drivers pulled over for their mandatory breaks.

Cosmo wasn't in the best frame of mind when he returned.

"Bloody useless pile of crap," he grumbled. "Leaked rain on me the entire time and ate money like a fish."

"But you got the message through?" Homer asked with a raised eyebrow.

Cosmo rolled his eyes.

"Well, I'm hardly going to get a drenching for no good reason. I got some half asleep office girl with a posh voice, but she said she had got down all I told her before all my change ran out. Can't think what would be wrong with a mobile call or an email," he continued, grumbling, pushing a rain smudged message slip across the table.

His gloom was lifted when a huge 'truckers all-day breakfast' arrived courtesy of Homer.

"You got the woman away alright in the end?" Homer asked.

It already seemed like an eternity ago that he had called upon his friend to smuggle Grace out of the hornets' nest their visit to Bremer's site had stirred up, another favour added to the list he owed his friend, which continued to stack up.

"Feisty woman," Cosmo said through a mouthful of sausage.

"Gave one of Bremer's men a few nasty bruises." He raised an eyebrow at Homer.

"He might well remember her face. It won't go well if they ever catch her." Cosmo looked pointedly at the dressing above Homer's ear.

Homer nodded. "The trick is not to get caught."

Cosmo shrugged in agreement and for a few minutes they sat in mutual silence while he finished his breakfast.

"Just one thing," Cosmo said, chasing sauce around his plate with a piece of toast. "This came for you a few days ago."

He searched in his pocket, handing Homer a creased and water-stained envelope. There was no good moment to do this.

For several moments Homer just stared at the writing on the front. It bore Cosmos's name and address, but he recognised the handwriting.

It was written in the hand of his son, Marius.

CHAPTER 13
DISTURBING A NEST OF HORNETS

Less than two hours after she had taken the phone call, Olwyn found herself heading south. The traffic moved slowly, challenged by rain that showed no intention of easing. It was frustrating, but it gave the benefit of space to reflect on Jerry's instructions; or more to the point, lack of instructions.

"Get down to sunny Sussex," he had said as the rain lashed against their filthy window panes, "and put the fear of death into the local PC Plod to make sure we get the whole story. If you're quick, you should get there before they find the body and start the usual cover up."

"Do we know anyone there?" she had asked rather forlornly, the role of an active field worker as obscure to Olwyn as most of the job she was employed to do.

"Just use your feminine charms. Flash your boobs at them and use this to make them behave themselves."

Jerry handed Olwyn a freshly printed security pass, complete with the Home Office crest and a job title that classified her as Field Agent.

"Jerry," she had said impatiently. "I'm a secretary."

He gave her a wolf-like grin.

"You've just been promoted. Now nip down to Sussex and earn your increase in salary. And while you're there, make sure everyone knows we're watching their every move."

He slid a photo of the body lying in the clearing across his desk to Olwyn.

"It will do PC Plod the world of good to know he's trapped between a rock and a hard place for once."

Olwyn pulled a face. "Won't that upset the powers that be above us? We know that security at these fracking sites always hits a raw nerve whenever we bring it up."

Provoking senior secretaries and their ultimate boss, the Home Secretary, didn't sound like a move to enhance their careers.

"Just do as you're told, dear girl," Jerry said rather dismissively. "Leave me to worry about who we upset. For once this just might give us a head start to take the initiative and shake their cage," he said in a forthright tone, before adding, "though be careful if you have any direct dealings with fracking site security. They can play hard ball sometimes," he said with a measure of understatement."

Unconvinced, Olwyn had left, taking Jerry's rather aged Jaguar that constituted their office car, and also the name of the female police constable, Allison Markham, she could call upon if she got into difficulties.

Homer propped the envelope against a vase on the kitchen table, contemplating what lay inside. Rather like 'Pandora's box', it was only when opened that the contents were released. If it remained sealed, he could ignore what waited inside the creased and folded envelope.

It was five years since he had last spoken to his son Marius. Five years of self-imposed exile in which he only received the odd photograph and scribbled note from his ex-wife, and that only via a carefully concealed route guaranteed by his contact in the Home Office. Cosmo provided his 'drop-box', the final leg in a journey created to protect his family. For five years it had succeeded in its task to keep them safe, but every letter, photograph, or trace of an address increased the risk.

Now, for some reason, Marius had written directly; a letter that had been posted from within the UK when the boy should have been living a concealed life in Australia. That was the deal, an arrangement struck at great personal cost to keep his family safe.

In the many dark hours during those five years, Homer had just managed to convince himself that their separation had been a price worth paying for their protection. Then out of the blue, something must have happened to change that. The only way he could find out was by slitting the sealed flap on the back of the envelope.

Homer's thoughts were interrupted by the impatient buzz of an app on his phone. Despite the persistent rainfall, someone, or something, had triggered the movement sensor on the camera he had concealed overlooking the body that he had left to draw attention.

He watched the timelapse images as they arrived on the screen. It gave an erratic picture of what was happening, but enough to tell him that the figure, clad in oversized boots and struggling to support an umbrella, definitely wasn't an employee of Bremer's. At one point, the woman looked directly into the hidden camera, revealing long, blonde hair and an attractive face creased by a frown of distaste for the job she was trying to do. She moved cautiously, as though ill at ease with the environment around her.

"Obviously a townie," Homer muttered to himself as she started taking a series of photos and measurements.

He checked his watch. It had taken almost six hours since Cosmo had made the call; more than enough time for his MI5 contact to put things into motion.

"Amateurs," he muttered.

Somehow Homer had expected a team to be sent. The presence of a single, apparently inexperienced woman didn't bode well.

"Only time will tell," he said, sharing his concern with Joss, asleep on her rug in front of the Aga. The dog slowly opened one eye, making sure all in their world was well, and continued sleeping.

Once or twice, the woman glanced skywards from which heavy, leaden clouds continued to disgorge an incessant downpour. You would need a sophisticated satellite to get a picture through those dense layers but at least the low ceiling would protect her from Bremer's silent, stalking drones.

Homer watched the scene for some time. No one came to join or interrupt the woman and he was left to wonder what her next move might be. One image showed her examining the body, checking the acid removed tattoo and for any obvious means of identification. There was none;

Homer had already made a thorough search. More photos followed, along with notes dictated onto her phone, before the woman retraced her footsteps away from the body to avoid disturbing any more evidence than necessary. A townie she might be, but at least she had some commonsense. Not that there would be any clues to find; the dead man had been stripped clean before his body had been left in the brook above Angela's cottage.

Eventually, the woman moved out of view of his camera. For a while, Homer sat tapping the edge of the envelope against the table top like a metronome, distracted, lost in thought. In moving the body, he had thrown the spotlight away from Angela, a fact that wouldn't be lost on whoever had planted the dead man's body.

But why had they sought to incriminate her? They might guess that he had moved the body. No one would believe a woman in her late seventies could lift the wet, inert corpse, or that it resurrected and walked the several miles to its new resting place of its own accord. So why take the risk in the first place simply to incriminate an elderly woman, especially if the man was an employee of the fracking site?

Beside the Aga, Joss stretched and yawned. Despite the rain, they would soon need to venture outside to check the traps he had set the previous night. Calling upon Cosmo's help had been a necessity, but his friendship came with a price, leaving Homer with a need to gather his woodland harvest to repay his debts. Neither man nor dog looked particularly enthusiastic about the prospect.

From the warmth of his office, Jerry Houseman watched his protégé slide and stumble around in the mud, displaying a yawning gap in her field training. It had been an unfair decision to send Olwyn alone on this particular assignment, but the combination of fracking security, combined with the local police force in their pocket, offered a closed book, even to MI5. It was a gamble but alone, a woman might just make more progress, provided she could handle the misogynous, sexist enclave into which he had thrown her.

"Sink or swim, dear girl," had been his parting words. "Imagine yourself in the role of one of your amateur dramatic productions. It's all an act, but no one else need know. And we get to record everything if you leave your phone camera switched on."

So far, all he had been able to do was direct Olwyn as she stumbled around the crime scene. Avoiding disturbing too much of the evidence, Jerry had instructed Olwyn through her earpiece, a camera clipped to the lapel of her coat, as together they collected sufficient information to prevent the local police from sweeping the case of potential murder 'under the carpet' of death by misadventure.

Against the advice of all the security agencies, the government had included fracking sites within the protection of the Anti- Terrorism Act. To make matters worse, the companies running the sites had been allowed to form and train their own staff for operations and security, with special visas accredited to specialists from wherever in the world they choose, without accountability. Rumours abounded of men from drug cartels and middle Eastern warlords quite happy to exercise lethal force against anyone foolish enough to try to expose what went on behind the high fences of the sites. After all, most of it now came within the Official Secrets Act. Some even muttered treason for those who broke the law, 'Beware to any meddling MP' who tried to speak against them.

Because of the threat to 'energy security' caused by political instability in Saudi Arabia and the middle East, fracking had been massively increased throughout the UK, with special powers delegated to the protection of the well sites. Anyone opposing or questioning the secrets of production and operation could be considered a threat to national security and dealt with accordingly. With alarming regularity, very few of those caught came to trial, evaporating their passing as little more than hearsay or rumour.

Into such a viper pit, Jerry had inserted Olwyn Wright-Smith, a young woman rejected by her family and abandoned by every man who enjoyed her conspicuous charms. As he drank his coffee, it occurred to Jerry Houseman that if the girl disappeared, there was probably no one who would ask after her.

CHAPTER 14
A POACHER'S HARVEST

The traps were little more rewarding than the weather. Nearly all were empty; most of his prey preferred the dry security of nests or burrows to the soaking rain.

For once, Homer toured the woodland paths in a distracted mood, on several occasions needing Joss to correct his route. Despite his resolution not to open the letter, it had become too much to resist. Still clad in parka and boots, he had turned back on impulse and torn open the crumpled envelope.

Marius was nineteen, old enough to know the protocols; no address, no name, just succinct, basic details. The letter had been written in haste.

I need to see you. I've left home. Mum intends to re-marry and he hates me; the feeling is mutual. I won't live with them. I need to see you; at least you owe me that. Contact me. You'll know where I am when you receive this letter. For once try and do the decent thing.

Homer stared long and hard at the words. Despite the sacrifice, the care taken to create new identities and cover all traces to make his family invisible, the human factor always intervened. He had spared his ex-wife the continued trauma of his fears for their safety; she was leaving him regardless, unable to bear the continual years of separation, never knowing where Homer was or when he would return. A marriage fed only on occasional letters and visits, haunted by nightmares, inevitably shrivels and dies. Parting was the easy bit; living with the shadow of her ex-husband's legacy far harder.

And now this letter. The stamp on the front of the envelope confirmed that Marius must be in the UK. It was probably no more dangerous than Australia, only the proximity of geography made the threat feel more real.

Having checked the final trap, Homer hunkered down beneath the tent of his cape and brewed tea on a portable stove. In the dark shadows beneath the branches of a pine tree, he felt safe, invisible. It was only at times like this that he felt truly at peace, hidden, in the illusion of camouflage from the world.

Joss disturbed his reverie, squirming into the narrow space under his cape, and within seconds her damp fur was steaming in the warm bubble created by the stove. From time immemorial, brewing tea had been the prerogative of every squaddie to grace the British army. Today was no exception; all that was needed was a tea bag and a spoonful of dried milk for the world to be restored.

Encamped beneath the spreading branches of the pine tree, Homer removed the letter from his pocket. Wracked by indecision, he scanned the lines for a hidden message. If he replied, it would be through Cosmo, to a solitary post office box where a faceless intermediary would collect his letter for forwarding to another anonymous locked box for collection by the clergyman, along with the usual basket of mail for many of his homeless parishioners. A tortuous route, but a secure lifeline for the past five years.

Homer sipped his tea, a treat when cold hands were wrapped around a hot tin mug. He cared little about the downpour, it helped to make him invisible, harder to track by scent and with markings washed away in the rain. The tea lifted his mood. Despite the risk, turning away his son's request was not an option. It complicated things; another layer of problems that Homer hadn't sought, but at least he had rid himself of the irritating eco-nut who had intruded, uninvited, into his life. Besides, meeting Marius again after more than five years was something for which a part of him yearned. The risk would have to be taken. His note would give a call box number and a time. Land lines were safer than mobiles, especially if you didn't leave fingerprints, virtually impossible to trace.

Decision made, Homer finished his tea, climbed from his hide beneath the tree to find the rain had eased leaving a pale, white sun to shine through thinning clouds. He took that as an omen; even Joss looked happy. He used a stiff branch as a rake to hide any evidence of their presence. Old habits die hard.

Homer decided he must be getting older. It was almost a repeat of the incident of the woman caught in the snare and he would have passed the stationary car without seeing it had Joss not barked in alarm. Dark olive green, it blended well with chin high bracken that surrounded it, but that was no excuse. Mistakes ultimately led to only one conclusion.

Homer backed into the shadows of the woodland. Beyond, thin tendrils of steam rose from the raised bonnet, and a figure in a raincoat stood peering in bewilderment at the mechanical monster of an engine. Despite the mistake of his lapse of attention, he hadn't been seen, but the figure had heard Joss's warning bark and now looked anxiously around her.

"Is anyone there?" she called out into the dripping silence of the woods.

Homer made no reply. He didn't need to; Joss answered for him, eliminating any chance to slip stealthily away. For a moment he glowered at the dog, making a shape of a gun with his hand, then saying with a smile, "Next time, dog, next time."

What was it with the woods that his sanctuary washed up so many waifs and strays to disturb his peace and quiet? Cradling the open shotgun, Homer pushed through the bracken and briars. On the rear of the car, the chrome lettering displayed the Jaguar name, and 3.8 Mk 2. It was a vintage model, at least fifty years old; the owner had taste.

"From my experience, just standing looking doesn't usually fix the problem."

The figure turned and glanced up, her face concealed beneath the hood of her coat.

"Blasted thing just burnt me," she replied, offering a hand marked with a livid red weal.

"Overheated engines have a habit of doing that," Homer continued, showing little sympathy. He came to the front of the car just as Olwyn folded back her hood.

'My, my,' he thought. 'The world is full of the strangest coincidences.' He had seen the same face only a short time before on the motion camera he had concealed overlooking the body he had re-located.

"Unusual car to find in these parts," Homer said, peering at the engine beneath the bonnet.

A thin, pressurised jet of steam issued from a rubber hose at the top of the radiator. The Jaguar had burst its top hose.

"You won't get very far until you get that repaired," he said pointing at the leaking rubber tube.

Olwyn held out her phone. "No signal. I was hoping to get to ..." She hesitated, unsure of the figure who had suddenly appeared out of the woods. "Is there a local garage I could walk to who might be able to repair the ... hose, did you call it?"

Homer eyed her sceptically. He still wasn't certain what she was doing prying around the crime scene.

"Posh car like this; you must work for Bremer?"

"Bremer?" Olwyn shook her head. "No, whoever that is. I work for an import agency. West African Cocoa."

She held out her card to Homer, narrowly avoiding showing him her Home Office pass, only recently printed by Jerry.

"The car belongs to my boss, Jerry Houseman. I don't know any Bremer.

The word 'amateur' immediately flashed through Homer's mind. She had already divulged too much detail. He relaxed and stood back to study her face; the eyes always exposed a lie. He felt slightly amused; after all, he had watched the woman only a short time earlier on his hidden camera. It was obvious she had no idea who he was, so for the moment he held the advantage.

Close up, she was slightly thinner than the camera had made her out to be. A pretty face, dark blonde hair with the features and colouring of what was once called 'a typical English rose'. There were signs of facial piercings and a grey business suit under her coat, contradicted by a pair of worn trainers. Homer could see a pair of high heels on the passenger seat. He looked at the wet muddy trainers she wore. She appeared to have travelled in haste and forgotten to bring any wellies.

"There's a garage, 'Hargraves', in the next town. But that's a four-mile walk. You won't get there before they close and I doubt they'd have a spare for one of these just sitting on the shelf."

His tone implied he thought she was foolish, driving a car of this vintage without spares and travelling dressed like this.

Olwyn had a pained, deflated expression. "There's no mobile signal. Is there a phone box nearby I could call from?"

"No," he replied with certainty. Joss flashed him a sideways look that seemed to say, 'Now what's wrong with you?'

Homer relented. "I could tape the hose. It might be enough to get you a few miles to the garage. Have you got a water bottle in the boot to refill the radiator?"

The woman looked confused. "No, I don't think so. But I've got this." She held out a half empty bottle that held at most a cup of water."

Despite a look from the dog, Homer rolled his eyes.

"We won't get far with that." He paused. "Have you got a spare pair of tights?"

Confused, Olwyn blurted, "Only the pair I'm wearing."

"Take them off if you want to get out of here," he said, searching for a roll of adhesive tape in his rucksack for binding around the leaking hose.

The radiator was still hot. Donning gloves, Homer slowly released the pressure cap. There was very little inside except steam.

"It must have been leaking for some time. Don't you look at the gauges while you're driving?"

Despite another look from Joss, he couldn't avoid a reprimanding tone to his words. Sensing the dog was on her side, Olwyn shrugged; there seemed little point in replying to a question that already had its answer.

With the hose binding complete, Homer tore out a piece of stiff card from the back of his notebook. It took several attempts to roll it into a funnel-shaped cone while Olwyn removed her tights. With a matter of fact expression, Homer held out his hands. Her tights were still warm. He carefully lined the inside of the improvised funnel to form a filter before inserting his ad hoc arrangement into the top of the radiator. Olwyn handed Homer her water bottle with its meagre contents. He up-ended it into the funnel.

"Refill the bottle from the drainage ditch beside the lane. Take the water from the surface and try to avoid any sediment. And don't fall in."

It took more than a dozen refills before Homer seemed satisfied and removed the funnel and replaced the cap.

"Start the engine. Let's see if the repair will hold," adding "and don't rev the engine too hard," in a tone that underscored the low opinion he held of her mechanical prowess.

For a while at least, Homer's temporary repair held.

"Hargraves," he shouted, as Olwyn reversed onto the lane. "Think you can remember that?"

She gave him a sardonic smile. "Thanks for your help. I don't think I caught your name."

"No need. Just tell your boss he's an idiot."

Olwyn frowned. The way he spoke gave the impression he knew Jerry Houseman. As she started to drive away her mysterious helper had already disappeared. It was left to the dog to watch her drive off.

CHAPTER 15
UNEXPECTED ROLE PLAY

Homer wrote the reply to his son. Through a restless night he had waxed and waned between meeting Marius and ignoring his request. Ultimately, the opportunity to see the boy and discover what had changed in his life to alter the ground rules had provoked the risk.

He wrote down the phone number at a public call box, and a time; the rest was up to Marius.

When Olwyn arrived at the police station, she was still rehearsing the part Jerry had given her to play out.

At the garage, a man in oil stained red overalls had promised to repair the Jaguar for the following day, but without a car to loan her, it meant spending a night in a small hotel on the outskirts of town. She decided not to stint herself, and selected a room complete with four-poster bed and a jacuzzi; the bill could be added to Jerry's account.

Olwyn had told Jerry about the mysterious woodsman who had appeared seemingly from nowhere and made a temporary repair to the Jaguar. She had described the nameless man and Jerry had laughed when she told him he had been called an idiot.

"My, my, what a small world," had been his unexplained reply.

As Olwyn entered the police station, she found a tall constable at the front desk looking bored and disinterested. She was about to give his day a nasty surprise. An elderly couple were in front of her, explaining that a lorry from the fracking site had struck their garden wall and run over part of their garden.

"When I complained at the site office they spoke to me in words I haven't heard since I was in the army," the man said in exasperation. "Not a hint of an apology. The man said it must have been the wind and rain what knocked it over. When I said the lorry left tyre tracks right across our lawn, he accused me of making things up. Told me to prove it was one of his lorries. What else could it have been; there's nothing else that size ever travels through the village."

While the old man paused to regain his breath, the constable looked over his head at Olwyn, smiled, and rolled his eyes.

"Did you get a photograph?" he said sceptically to the elderly couple.

"Photograph? It was the middle of the bloody night. But it was one of those big things with a huge ribbed container on its back. I saw it with my own eyes. Crashed through our wall and crossed the garden without stopping. The walls are stone; it'll cost thousands of pounds to rebuild it. Who's going to pay for that then?"

The constable made no comment, just continued making notes in the record book in front of him with a distinctly bored expression.

"I'll pass this on. It's your word against theirs. Without any evidence I can't hold out much hope of anything happening. You could always try suing them privately."

"Sue the fracking company," the older man said incredulously. "Where would I find the money to do that?" His face had a mixed look of frustration and anxiety. "And what about the threats?"

Suddenly, his wife squeezed his arm.

"George, let it go. There's nothing they can do here. This policeman is far too busy to do anything about this and we don't want them coming around the bungalow do we?"

Olwyn sensed the fear in her words tug at her heart as the constable made a smirk and a wink at her while they were distracted. She smiled in reply.

Olwyn braced her shoulders and stepped forward as the elderly couple were shepherded aside like unwanted flotsam.

"Yes, miss, what can I do you for?" The tall policeman at the desk rolled his eyes in complicit humour, having dealt with what he considered were a pair of time wasters.

"Let's start with ma'am," Olwyn replied with a brusque voice that surprised even her. With a flourish, she flashed the pass that Jerry had given her in its embossed Home Office leather wallet.

"I'm here to find out what action you're taking on the matter of a dead body lying less than five miles from this station."

The smirk on PC James face evaporated into an expression of bewilderment. "Come again?"

Being asked to repeat herself irritated Olwyn. The flash of annoyance she signalled in return was genuine.

"There's a male dead body." She formed the words deliberately, as though explaining an obvious fact to a rather dull child. "It's lying in the woods two hundred metres from a fracking site not far from here. From the preliminary examination I've made, the man was struck with a sharp object and left to drown in a ditch. My suspicions are that he worked and lived locally, so I want to see your report of any missing persons and what action you're taking to investigate them."

She slid a copy of the satellite photo Jerry had given her across the counter towards the bemused policeman.

"The grid reference for the location is printed on the top," Olwyn said in a hard, questioning tone.

"I don't …"

"No you don't, do you. I think I had better speak to your boss. Now."

PC James gave a hapless nod. "Sarge," he called over his shoulder.

A large, rather dishevelled man slowly appeared through a door behind him, polystyrene cup in hand. He obviously had a poor taste in coffee as well as his appearance. PC James moved aside without a word as Sergeant Wailes approached beside him.

"Yes, miss," he said in a condescending voice, sipping the coffee while giving Olwyn a look that implied he held a typically misogynist view of a woman's role in the workplace.

Which was fortunate; it made Olwyn angry, evaporating any qualms she may have had with the task Jerry had instructed her to undertake.

"Ma'am, when you address me, Sergeant," Olwyn paused having placed emphasis on his rank. "As I have explained to … PC James," her look underscored his insignificance, "I'm here to find out what procedures you're following in the matter of a dead body lying in the immediate vicinity of this police station?"

It wasn't often that Sergeant Wailes was disconcerted, especially by women. In his experience, the only women he tolerated held the rank of constable and did as they were told. Now he was confronted by a situation that wasn't part of the script. This obnoxious slip of a woman now standing in front of him had control of a script he didn't recognise.

His paymaster, Miller, had given him a totally different agenda to act upon. Wailes urgently needed time to think. He was supposed to have found the body in the ditch above that mad Angela's cottage in sufficient time to make sure that he could plant incriminating evidence on the body.

"Wait here please, miss," Wailes instructed, ignoring the rank on Olwyn's pass. "I'll make a call and find out what has been happening."

"If you must. I'll come with you to save you having to repeat yourself." Olwyn walked around the counter without waiting for an invitation.

"You can't …"

Her steely glare cut Wailes short. "I think you'll find I can, Sergeant."

Olwyn waited for him to lead her on, pointing to the photograph on the counter.

"The Home Office take a great deal of interest when illegal immigrants are given employment." She paused. "Especially on fracking sites."

Homer took a sharp intake of breath as Angela probed his wound with tiny scissors.

"Keep still," she instructed, snipping the looped ends of the stitches to his head wound.

It was healing, but still red and sore. He winced as Angela began to withdraw the twine.

"Baby," she teased.

"Hurts," he replied through clenched teeth.

Angela moved with a deft touch, withdrawing the stitches almost as fast as she had inserted them.

"I've had contact from my son, Marius," he said spontaneously, without thinking. He felt Angela hesitate, a silent breath staying her hand.

"How old is he now?"

"Nineteen. It sounds as though he's left home. I think he's here, somewhere in the UK."

In the silence that followed, Angela swabbed the wound with antiseptic. Homer winced at the burning sensation.

"That should heal alright," she said. "Just keep out of any more fights for a few days."

He smiled weakly. "I'll do my best. Trouble is our 'friends' tend to pick the time and place."

Angela nodded. "How much does he know?"

"Marius? I think his mother told the children I had been sent to prison to put them off asking too many awkward questions. Trouble is …"

"Children grow up and work out answers for themselves." Angela paused for a moment. "Will you see him?"

"I've agreed to. Though it will only happen if he complies with my instructions."

Angela looked thoughtful for a moment. "Can I help? If it hadn't been for me you wouldn't be in this dreadful situation."

Homer waved a dismissive hand. They had had this conversation on countless occasions. The past couldn't be re-written. Nothing that could be said would ever change it.

Seven years before, Angela had led a privately funded aid operation in western Iraq in the path of the storm clouds of an evolving organisation called ISIS. Despite the imminent danger, and with reluctance to abandon her local staff to the brutality of the rising caliphate, Angela and her team had delayed their departure. The delay was almost fatal; it had left them trapped and surrounded. In urgent need of rescue, Homer and his squad had been mobilised to evacuate them.

But there was a price for deliverance. A rescue helicopter to carry them all to freedom was conditional and Homer had been given a target; a white SUV believed to contain the regional ISIS commander. Too late, he discovered that a swap had been made and instead of an ISIS jihadi commander, the SUV carried women and children. The intelligence had been flawed, or deliberately misrepresented, but the outcome was the same. Everyone in the SUV had been killed, including the commander's wife and children.

During the years that followed, ISIS had used its considerable influence to seek revenge. One by one, the families of Homer's squad had been sought out by ISIS, their 'sleepers' activated from within the UK. Now, only he and one other member of his eight-man squad remained untouched by the merciless vengeance.

"Perhaps if I met Marius," Angela offered, breaking the silence, "and explained the risks he could be taking. If he's travelling with a false identity might there still be time to return to the safety of his new home."

Homer shook his head. "Just entering the country would have triggered a cypher somewhere in the bowels of MI5. Some activist will already know that Marius is here. It's only a matter of time before they track him down."

"So what, you think he would be safer with you?"

"It's too late to debate that question. If I send Marius back, ISIS would simply follow his trail and be led to his mother and my daughter. It's what they do, Angela, you know that first-hand. The die was cast the moment I targeted that SUV for that American missile. We can never wind the clock back. His only chance is with me."

CHAPTER 16
A FOX IN THE HEN COOP

They stood, tall and slender like soldiers standing to attention in a glass jug. Half a dozen yellow blooms, a gift of announcement. Homer needed no clearer message. The 'dandelion woman', as he had begun to think of her, had returned.

In the bathroom, he found stained trousers, a shirt and underwear steaming gently on the radiator fed from the Aga. Homer cast a jaundiced eye in the direction of Joss.

"Fine guard dog you are."

If a dog could smile, Joss reflected Homer's scepticism with a bright-eyed look. Grace was back; what on earth was there to be grouchy about?

Curious and on soft toes, Homer climbed the loft ladder. Grace lay in bed, her naked back exposed to the loft hatch, the rolled back covers slowly rising and falling with each breath. He wanted to feel irritation yet, perversely, felt a sense of companionship at the surprise return of the woman.

Silently descending, Homer returned to the kitchen. Grace would be hungry. He threw ingredients into a casserole dish, watching rain tumble from a leaden sky. After the drought of the long summer months, several months of rain had fallen in torrents for days, flooding hard, parched ground into deep lagoons.

It was dark when I woke. For a while I luxuriated in the comfort of cotton sheets, listening to the steady beat of rain in the roof tiles above me. It had been almost a week since I had last slept in a bed. The peace of the moment was almost overwhelming. Here, I felt safe and warm, cocooned under blankets knowing Homer, my reluctant host, was the first line of defence.

My feelings were a contrast to the dream I had been woken by, reliving a day over twenty years previously when, as a ten-year-old, I had shaken the family home, raving about the images that had haunted my night. I had dreamt of wreckage, the remains of a minibus, cast like discarded litter across the lanes of a motorway, broken bodies hurled around like dandelion seeds. Amongst the debris lay panels of dark blue wreckage, a crumpled crest in red and gold on what remained of a side panel. They were the colours of the school my brothers attended.

My mother, the eternal pragmatist, paid no attention to my rantings, though my father made no comment. Instead, he made a silent excuse to take my brother to his rugby match by car.

The rest of the team never arrived. Their minibus burst a tyre on the way to the match. Struggling to cross to the hard shoulder, they swerved in the path of a heavily laden lorry. They never made it to safety; their minibus was shattered by the impact, and half the team died.

My shocked father said little, his face pale and stilled. Henceforth, I often found him watching me, a far-away look in his eyes that suggested he found something difficult to understand. Sadly, a silver plane in a crystal blue sky was to prevent him ever sharing his thoughts with me.

My mother sent me to a child psychiatrist.

The smell of hot food rang an alarm bell in my stomach, reminding me that it had been several days since I had last enjoyed anything that resembled a hot meal.

Every joint in my body ached with fatigue. The operation I had been involved with, hastily conceived in the light of the results from testing the samples Homer had helped me to collect, had gone wrong almost before it began.

Gaining access to a fracking site had become an increasingly urgent priority. To draw attention away, it was thought that an operation at a site some forty miles distant offered the best promise of success. Breaking into the site compound was still beyond us, but attaching a motorised camera to the underside of one of the night-time container deliveries offered potential. If you could fly a drone remotely, why not place a camera on wheels; it should be a piece of cake. All we had to do was attach it to the underside of one of the containers, and to achieve that I had the tricks learnt from Homer to help us.

Unfortunately, haste intervened. There were two things we overlooked; the dreaded whisper drones with thermal cameras, and the foil-backed capes Homer had insisted upon beneath our camouflage smocks.

The idea had been for one of the group to roll beneath a tug and container whilst it waited for the security gates to open. The camera could be quickly attached with magnets to the underside. Once inside, the quick flick of a radio controlled switch would drop the camera to the ground and leave it to scurry away into the darkness. If NASA could control a rover on Mars, what could go wrong in a fracking site from only a few miles away?

We never even got close. The silent whisper drone that orbited above the convoy must have seen us long before we even broke cover from a nearby ditch. It was a warm night, and complacent beneath our camouflage smocks no one thought about the heat signature our bodies projected. And so we had blundered into the waiting trap.

It was only a mixture of the dark and the clumsiness of the men in the ambush that saved us from certain capture. Lacking field craft, they spooked a tawny owl and left her screeching in agitation at their invasive presence in her territory. Another tip hard learnt from Homer; use owls as your night sentries, their calls as your eyes in the darkness.

Invisible in a starless night, the owl flew over our heads, sounding the alarm. By chance, glancing upward into the blackness, someone noticed the merest glimmer of a dim light in the sky; a drone, hanging like a bird of prey, observing our every move. Our saviour, the owl, spooked a hunting dog, who howled plaintively in response. The decision to abort took merely seconds and with little more *than an unspoken gesture for good luck, we evaporated into the night to opposite points of the compass.*

I'll say one thing for fracking security; they can be determined bastards when it comes to pursuit. Three wet nights on the run followed, occasionally taking a few minutes sleep in abandoned barns and sheds. The best sleep I managed was in an empty pig sty which smelt so rank even bloodhounds would give it a wide berth. I had no idea if anyone else had escaped as the net closed around us, comforted that only I knew about my distant refuge with Homer. By a large measure of good fortune, I gave my pursuers the slip and now, for the moment, I was safe.

Eventually, the irresistible smell of cooking overwhelmed the comfort of the bed and as I swung my feet to the floor, I realised the price for my meal would be a forensic interrogation by Homer over what had, once again, gone wrong. The failings in my answers would again be highlighted by his questions, and I would have to expect Homer's silent scorn. I could only hope that Joss was still on my side.

Staring at her reflection in the mirror, in the act of removing her make-up, Olwyn paused. The afternoon had been progressively more difficult as she acted out the role Jerry had created for her.

Sergeant Wailes was far from the most intellectual of men, but what he did possess was the feral cunning of a street fighter. Once he had got over the shock of Olwyn's arrival and the evidence she had presented, he had pushed back with increasing vigour. If it had remained as merely sexual bias, Olwyn could have handled things better, but he was too shrewd to fall into that trap. An expert in the art of evasion, Wailes used every trick he knew to block and obstruct her.

She had followed Wailes to his office as he made the phone call, but he had spoken in a monologue of single syllables. With the call finished, Wailes changed tack and started an interrogation about her role, only to be interrupted by the arrival of the senior station officer who Olwyn had been asking to see from the outset. To her surprise, DI Amos seemed to already know what was happening, cutting short her cross-examination with a sharp look of dismissal in Wailes's direction.

Puzzled by his unannounced presence, Olwyn received agreement to all her requests without hesitation or opposition, as though the arrival of an MI5 field officer in their midst was a normal everyday occurrence. Under the stony glare of Wailes, DI Amos escorted her out of the station, the epitome of charm and politeness. Not that she believed a word he had said, but the microphone hidden in her lapel recorded every assurance he gave her in anticipation of the predictable roll-back that would inevitably follow.

From the look on his face, Wailes knew he had lost the first round, but was already scheming how to gain the upper hand. Olwyn stared at herself in the mirror. She had been told the decrepit Jaguar would take at least a further day to repair. The expression on Wailes's face left her with an ominous feeling of trepidation.

For once, Homer made no cryptic comments about her unannounced arrival. It was almost as though he was resigned to Grace arriving with the hounds of a fracking site hard on her heels. Ravaged by hunger, she consumed all that Homer placed in front of her before he made any comment.

"I'm starting to run out of options for hiding you every time Bremer sends his jackals to find you," he said with an undertone of annoyance.

Grace looked at him uncertainly, trying to measure his mood.

"I have to keep trying. There are few enough of us who will, least of all this government who are in league with this faction, 'Blue Horizon'."

"They're just politicians," Homer said dismissively with a shrug of his shoulders.

"Bent politicians," Grace said between mouthfuls. "Obscuring what they're really doing behind a screen of supposed eco-babble. Does anyone know what 'Blue Horizon' truly stands for?"

"Does anyone really care," Homer quipped. "They're just a minority party with a few dozen MPs and extreme populist views that they can't implement. They're only junior members of the government." He spoke with a dismissive stroke of his hand.

"Except that their junior minister is in charge of the government's energy policy which, in case you had forgotten, includes all the fracking sites," Grace replied.

Homer leaned back against the kitchen sink. "With a policy, I would remind you, from the country's point of view, is considered to be highly successful. After all, they've made the country self-sufficient in energy at a time when the oil states in the middle East are far from stable and global oil and gas prices are extremely volatile. It gives the government a lot of power to be free from that ransom note."

Provoked, Grace regarded him sceptically, unsure if he was speaking seriously or simply baiting her.

"What ever happened to the independence of sustainable energy? Instead, you'd prefer to auction our hydrocarbon futures into the hands of a group of corrupt fascists with a hidden agenda."

"But 'Joe-public' couldn't care less who's in charge, so long as the lights stay on and they can heat their homes in the depths of a freezing winter at an affordable price. Better a tacky local politician than a group of autocratic despots, whose names you can't even pronounce, let alone call to account," Homer replied.

Grace was silent for several seconds, staring fixedly at the flowers she had brought as a peace offering, trying hard to ease her temper. It didn't appear to be achieving much success. She hoped Homer wasn't serious, but that didn't make the issue of the people who controlled the country's energy policy any more palatable.

The trouble was, whether Homer believed his own words or not, to the impressionable media hungry public, 'Blue Horizon' and their plain speaking leader, Hugh Littlemore, proved that for once, politicians could make things they held important happen. 'Hell,' she thought, in charge of the transport ministry, they could even make the railways run on time. It was just that no one thought to ask who that slogan had originated from.

The evening had closed on a cold flat note. The futility of the price, paid by my friends in pursuit of the truth, was laid bare by Homer's words.

It was the early hours before sleep eventually overwhelmed frustration, only to be roused while it was still dark by the sound of a crying dog. I'm no expert on dogs, but I can immediately tell the difference between a bark and the cry of primeval fear. Joss slept in the kitchen, preferring the warmth of the Aga to the bottom of Homer's bed. As I raced to my senses from the belated arrival of sleep, the sound of her cries and the pounding of bare feet rang an orchestra of alarm bells.

I grabbed the oversize shirt Homer had loaned me while my clothes dried, and I half fell down the ladder from my attic roost as the entire world began to shake and rumble around me. How I got to the kitchen I can't remember, overwhelmed by fear as the entire world bucked and pitched around me like an untrained bronco in a rodeo.

In the outside doorway, Homer was waiting for me, hugging Joss in his arms as the dog fought panic.

"Here. Now. Outside. Quickly." His words came in gasps as he struggled to restrain Joss, before disappearing into the darkness.

I plunged through the doorway in pursuit, only to be met by the ground rushing up to meet me as I tripped headlong onto the cold wet surface, my disoriented brain unable to compute what was happening around me. In the wet mud beneath me, the transformation of something, always reassuringly solid, now wobbled like a demented jelly. Lying prone on the ground only exaggerated the sensation.

Slowly, the unnerving uproar began to subside and by the time I had managed to struggle to my feet, some sort of normality seemed to have returned. I found Homer in the edge of the woods a short distance from the cottage.

"Is it over?"

I saw him nod silently, lowering Joss to the ground. His arms a maze of cuts and scratches from the frantic paws of the terrified animal.

"It would seem so," he replied, watching Joss, still wide-eyed and trembling in fear.

The fact that she didn't hurtle off into the night seemed to confirm that the ground had stopped shaking.

"What the hell was …?"

"It's a quake. The real deal."

I tried to sound matter of fact, but my voice betrayed me as I began to shiver, clad only in a shirt that was now covered in wet mud from my knees to elbows.

"But we don't get earthquakes in the UK," Homer said.

"Well, we do now," I said tersely, turning my back to return to the house, unable to move on from his scepticism of the previous evening.

"It seems the planet doesn't think much of fracking either."

Back in the cottage, I left Homer in the kitchen and went in search of my drying clothes. Joss came with me. After the shock and discomfort of the past few minutes I needed something that smelt of me and not wet mud. Or Homer for that matter.

While I dressed, a kettle sang its plaintive note in the kitchen below. Homer had applied the eternal solution to every crisis; he was making tea. I returned to the kitchen; Joss gave me a sideways look and resumed her position in front of the Aga, eyes alert, still panting in nervous anticipation, awaiting the after-shocks which would inevitably follow.

Homer had his back to me, warming the pot before adding a scoop of tea. Clad only in his vest, I could see the livid circle of a scar, pin-prick marks of stitching crowning the circumference where the skin had been stretched and folded. Not old, not recent either. It wasn't hard to arrive at the assumption that it was another example of Angela's handiwork. I let the thought drop. It might be best to ask her the next time we met rather than broach the matter with Homer.

"So, you want to blame all of that on fracking?" Homer said over his shoulder, the shadow of a stutter stumbling his words.

"Not all. But it doesn't help."

He turned, carrying two steaming mugs that he placed on the small, scrubbed table that bore the jar of flowers I had arranged earlier. Several of the flowers now stared at the floor, their stems fractured by the shaking. Homer looked in my direction with tired, hooded eyes. Hearing him stutter again made me wonder what demons the quake had unleashed within him.

"Things happen. Change is an eternal event," Homer said, almost anticipating my next words.

"In six months we've had drought, tidal surge, floods and now this." I sipped my tea, watching for his reaction.

"Coincidence. It may be years before the next. You let imagination run away with you."

"Or perhaps the earth has lost patience; decided to have done with us once and for all before we damage her irreversibly." I posed the statement over the rim of my mug. Was I being unfair to provoke him further?

"Ah, the old 'Mother Gaia' fable." He sounded almost dismissive.

"Theory, not a fable."

"Based upon emotion not science."

"It's happened before; mass extinctions of problem species. From the perspective of the planet, mankind has become far more than a defective experiment. If she decides to be rid of us, there is nothing we will be able to do about it."

Homer stared hard across the table. "You can't blame the earth for the meteorite that wiped out the dinosaurs."

That was interesting. His words had seemed to apply a defence on the side of the earth.

"I don't. But she took full advantage of the conditions that followed to totally eliminate an entire species as though they were some failed experiment, to be swept away."

Homer laughed dismissively. "That presumes a planet can have some form of conscious sentience."

"You could argue that is exactly the case. After the death of the dinosaurs, mammals were already waiting in the wings to have their chance in the laboratory."

For a while we sat, each weighing the other's perspective. Homer would argue that he was a pragmatist and I was the emotion fuelled dreamer. My mother's words rang hollow in my ears.

The cottage began to shake again as the first after-shock arrived with the force of a punch. From her bed in front of the Aga, Joss looked at us both in turn. It wasn't hard to read the message in her eyes.

"I think that could be your answer."

She lay her muzzle on the floor and carried on panting.

Even the violent shaking of the hotel didn't wake a deep sleeper like Olwyn. But the cacophony of the hotel alarm system certainly did.

Still half asleep, she was carried on the tide of hotel guests as they swept down the escape stairs, spilling into the cold damp air of the car park. Olwyn's brain was too disorientated to register the trembling ground beneath her feet, even though the excited gossip that swirled around her included the words 'quake' 'tremor' and 'fracking'. She switched off; such talk was ridiculous.

"Earth quakes never happen in Britain," she grumbled dismissively. "It's more than likely just a convoy of large lorries passing nearby."

The wild gabbling of people around her annoyed Olwyn almost as much as the damp drizzle that soaked her white fluffy dressing gown (courtesy of room service) and plastered her hair to her head. It would take at least half an hour to dry out when they were eventually allowed to return to their rooms.

It was another hour before a highly disgruntled Olwyn was back in her room, her mood only partially assuaged by an unperturbed elderly man who had the forethought to bring his umbrella. He stood patiently beside Olwyn the entire time, shielding her from the worst of the rain whilst regaling her with lurid, amusing stories of the Indian monsoon.

Annoyed and irritated, she deliberately rang Jerry and woke him up.

"Do you have any idea what time of night this is?" he hissed into the phone, echoed by a complaining voice beside him.

"Is that the 'divine boy' you spoke of yesterday I can hear?"

"What? Yes. Wait."

She could hear the swishing sound of silk sheets (only the best for Jerry and his lovers) as he left the bed, apologising effusively to whoever was sharing it. A door closed, boards creaked, and she heard the click of a kettle switch.

"My dear girl, I love you to bits, but three-thirty in the morning does test the limits." Jerry sounded exasperated.

"Because of an earthquake, I've had to stand outside in the rain for the past hour," Olwyn ranted, "whilst being entertained by an elderly white haired gallant with colourful stories of his time in the bloody Raj, wherever that is."

Despite the obscene hour of the morning, her gabbled story portrayed an image so ridiculous that it made them both laugh.

"Such trials beset my dear Olwyn," Jerry yawned into the phone.

"And the car won't be fixed in the morning," she complained in reply. "They can't locate a part for that dinosaur you own. When are you going to buy something modern, Jerry?"

"That's not a nice thing to say about 'Gladys', dear girl."

He paused. She heard the rattle of a teapot and the tumble of pouring water.

"Besides, that will give you a few extra days to play the detective and keep PC Plod on his toes."

"Jerry, PC Plod, actually he's a Sergeant, will eat me alive if I stay around here any longer. Besides, he's more 'wily fox' than 'plod' and well you know it."

"All you have to do is visit the area, take the photo I've sent you and ask around; see if anyone recognises our poor deceased victim."

"What photo?"

Jerry sighed, feigning patience. "The likeness I created from the picture of the man's dead body you sent me."

He paused, a teacup rattled in its saucer. "Check your phone, dear thing; I sent it to you last night."

"And what am I supposed to do with said photo? The locals here seem to take offence if I as much as wish them the time of day."

"Accent, dearest. You sound too posh. Time to get into voice, something rural; bit more country bumpkin might do it."

"Piss off, Jerry."

"Now, now." He paused to slurp his tea. "I need you there to rattle the cage and stop PC Plod, or 'Sergeant Fox', if you insist, from conveniently sweeping the matter under the carpet. I'm sure that's what his paymasters will be expecting."

Olwyn listened in silence. She hadn't signed up for this when she had agreed to come here, and her brief seemed to expand by the minute.

"Jerry." Her brow furrowed at a thought that his words had re-awakened. "How did DI Amos know why I was in his police station? Wailes was particularly keen to prevent me from seeing him. So …?"

"Ah, yes. All I can say, darling, is keep the phone I gave you charged and switched on at all times."

"Meaning?"

"Surely you didn't think I would cast you into this vile pit of vipers totally alone?" Jerry laughed softly. "It brings the cavalry galloping over the hill whenever you're in a spot of bother."

Considering the early hour of the morning, he sounded far too pleased with himself.

"Now, must go. Dear Florian awaits in a warm bed. Be good."

"Jerry."

"Hmm."

"One thing." Olwyn paused.

"Do yourself a favour. Make sure Florian is legal. Reading jail is not far from where you live and I'd hate it if you did an 'Oscar Wilde' on me in the middle of all this."

CHAPTER 17
MORE THAN JUST A PHEASANT SHOOT

In his place, Cosmo had sent his son Milo. For reasons he couldn't put his finger on, the alteration to their normal routine disquieted Homer.

"The old man's at a pony sale," was the excuse for Cosmo's absence.

Homer shrugged. "Did the 'vicar' receive my letter?"

There would be many reasons why Cosmo had asked to meet him at short notice but the delivery of the letter to Marius was foremost in his mind. Milo gave him an unsmiling glance. Perhaps he had no wish to be here either.

"I made the drop personally so there is no reason why he couldn't deal with it."

Homer had offered two dates for Marius to call a phone box on the number he had enclosed. The first date was only two days hence.

"There's an alarming increase in 'chatter' between fracking sites," Milo interrupted his thoughts. "Someone is rattling the cage and making certain influential people unnecessarily agitated." Milo stared at Homer, waiting for his response. "Cosmo doesn't see it as a problem but from my perspective it's bad for business."

Was there a note of accusation in his final sentence? Homer gave him a blank look. Though he was never told explicitly, he had a pretty shrewd idea how Cosmo and his family made their money. Cash never seemed to be in short supply and Homer never asked questions.

"The word is, fracking security is employing more people; men with the necessary skills, largely from the Balkans, but recently from Syria and Yemen."

"Is that legal?" Homer asked as he sampled his beer. They had met at a pub he hadn't visited before which added to his feelings of unease.

"Special visas. This new mob, 'Blue Horizon' decide what's legal and what's not when it comes to fracking site security." Milo paused to let his words settle. "The thing is, tighter security makes it harder to trade. We need these eco-nuts you're associated with to calm things down. I've got a big deal going through and we need them to stop rocking the boat; at least until the business is complete."

Homer could guess what they were talking about. If you kept hundreds of men cooped up in the fracking sites for long periods there had to be some inducements. Homer never asked questions. Drugs or prostitution? He had no idea how they got them into the sites, but he doubted Cosmo's son would have any conscience in supplying either if it made money.

Bluntly, Milo continued. "We need you to put a word in. Tell your people to calm it down a bit."

"That supposes I have any influence."

"That woman we got out for you. Contact her and tell her we've called in the favour. We need a bit of peace and quiet; stop poking a hornets' nest with a stick. Once we're done they can do whatever they want, though if you ask me it seems a sure way to get yourself disappeared."

Milo lacked the natural sense of humour of his father. It made the difficult conversations hard work.

"I'm not sure what role she plays, but I'll have a word if I see her again. I can't make promises," Homer replied.

Milo was silent, stony-faced. "We rely on you to make this work," he said stretching out his hand for the pint glass on the table between them.

As he did so, Homer got sight of a tattoo that finished just below his wrist. A snake's head, jaws wide open, created in livid colours. Where had he seen something identical before? Exposing the tattoo had been quite deliberate, the implied threat at the conclusion of their conversation, layering yet another problem to the catalogue that haunted Homer's life.

The double crack of the shotgun brought the pheasant tumbling to the ground.

"My lead is improving," Miller said with a note of satisfaction.

"More impressive if you'd got it with the first shot," jibed Wailes beside him.

As if to prove his point, another pheasant, flushed by the dogs, broke cover. Wailes brought it down with the first shot. Ejected cartridges were followed by wisps of grey smoke from the open barrels.

"This annoying woman. Inconvenient that she appeared before you found the body." The implied criticism was clear in Miller's voice.

"If things had gone to plan and you hadn't misplaced the body in the first place there wouldn't be a mess to clear up now," Wailes retorted.

"We rely on you to prioritise our interests. It's what we pay you for," Miller added a pointed reminder.

"That's as may be. But I might remind you, I've still got a police station to run. All actions leave a trail; I have to cover the tracks or we're all in trouble."

Another pheasant broke cover. Wailes raised his shotgun but the gun beside him beat him to it. They stood in silence as the dead bird followed its predecessors to the ground in a cloud of feathers.

"You need to get rid of this troublemaking woman as soon as possible. If you don't, be sure, we will."

"She's from London; Home Office," Wailes reminded Miller.

It won't be as easy as that."

Miller snorted. "That won't stop Bremer. He'll go over her head and get it sorted. That might not be good news for you."

A driven bird fluttered noisily across their path. Miller shot it first time. His dog bounded forwards into the bracken to collect the fallen bird.

The point wasn't lost on Wailes. "You sponsor me to use the law in your interests, to open doors wherever possible."

Miller gave him a hard stare. "We pay you to avoid problems for us. Trust me, you don't want to fail in that duty to my boss."

Wailes felt his mouth go dry. "You can't expect me to break the law."

He tried to laugh but his voice tightened. Another pheasant broke cover just to his right side. He fired and missed.

Miller shot the bird instead. "Don't let us down. Sort this issue before I have to bring it to Bremer's attention. If it gets that far there will be trouble."

The dog arrived, bird between soft jaws. Miller extracted his prize, turning to hand the bird to Wailes.

"It's simple; just don't disappoint us."

Wailes was silent for a moment. The day had suddenly lost its appeal. He broke his shotgun and removed the cartridges. As he walked away, behind him Miller downed another bird with both barrels.

Homer moved easily through a mist that seemed to cling to his clothes. He completed a circuit around Angela's cottage, checking the obvious locations for hidden cameras, while Joss swept the woods on a wider compass for intruders. The attempt to incriminate Angela by disposing of the dead body in the immediate vicinity of her house had failed but it still left many unanswered questions. He had a strong suspicion things weren't finished.

Satisfied that no one was watching, he approached the cottage, entering by the back door with the use of a large key. Homer made a mental note to improve that.

"You might knock next time," Angela said looking up from her needlework as Homer and Joss stood dripping on the tiled floor. "The mop's behind you."

He removed his jacket and kicked off his boots. "No one seems to be about. I've checked the woods for cameras."

On the stove, a coffee pot warmed. Homer helped himself to a cup.

"Is this just a social call? Or do I need to repair another of your injuries?" Angela said without looking up from her lap.

"Actually, I need a favour."

Her eyes moved, watching Homer over the top of her glasses, waiting.

"I need you to make a kite. It has to resemble a bird, preferably an owl, and be capable of carrying a load of say, a kilogram."

"You don't ask for much then." Her gaze returned to the needlework on her lap.

Homer grinned. "You're the expert. From what you learnt in Afghanistan I would have thought it was a piece of cake," he said flippantly.

"Doesn't sound like a present for a child."

Homer nodded. "My uninvited guest has returned."

"Ah. The eco-terrorist you've thrown in your lot with," Angela said in a matter of fact voice. "You know that no good will come of it."

Homer shrugged. "She'll get herself killed if I don't help her."

Angela stopped working and regarded him with sad eyes. "I've heard you say that before."

"That was different."

"Aren't they all; but it always ends up the same."

They were silent for a moment, fate whispering of the future between them.

"A kite?" she ventured, leaving the question to hang before adding, "depends on three 'Ws'; when, where and wind."

Homer drank his coffee.

"Soon, as soon as possible. You don't need to know where."

"I do if I'm needed to fly it. Let me guess; Site 17."

Homer nodded. "I need the woman away quickly. Do you think it might be possible during the next three nights? It will have to be in darkness."

Angela sat in thought for a minute, scribbling notes on a scrap of paper.

"My shopping list. The faster you get hold of these, the sooner we'll know if your hair-brained scheme will work." She hesitated for a moment. "Have you checked the weather forecast? We'll need wind for at least two nights."

Homer moved to the kitchen window. Outside, rain fell in vertical rods from a windless sky.

"Any news on the poor man we found in my brook?" Angela asked, returning to her needlework.

"Not yet." Homer's words trailed away, remembering the antique Jaguar and city dwelling driver he had come upon the day before. "Nothing so far, but I think the body has been found."

"Do you think our local policemen will pay me a return visit?" There was the faintest hint of concern in Angela's voice.

"To reassure you, I've hidden a camera with a movement sensor to cover the location in which we found the dead man. Just in case anyone tries to play games," Homer said, pulling on boots and his jacket. "I'll leave Joss with you while I collect the items on your list."

The dog was already asleep, wet fur steaming gently in front of the range. Living alone, it was about time Angela found a dog of her own, Homer mused.

"I'll be a couple of hours. Don't feed her if she wakes." He smiled in the dog's direction. "She'll always try to convince you she's hungry and you're too soft by half."

Homer moved to the door, and lifting the latch, he hesitated with his back to her.

"I'm sorry to drag you into this, Angela," he said with genuine concern.

"That journey began seven years ago when you and your team rescued us from the clutches of ISIS." Angela raised her tired eyes to Homer's face.

"Times change but, unfortunately, not the path that fate ordains for us."

I stared at my phone, stunned by the single emoticon on the screen. No message; just the image of a coffin, fired off seconds before the phone had self-destructed. It was a simple precaution; a button fitted to all our phones which released the warning emoticon and a tiny sachet of nitric acid hidden beneath the SIM card.

One of my previous group had been caught. Their final act had been to alert the rest of us and destroy the phones so we couldn't be traced. Simple. The digital equivalent of a suicide capsule. I could only hope that whoever had been arrested was in the hands of the police and not the vigilantes who now protected the fracking sites. If it was the latter, a human equivalent of the digital version might be needed.

I shouldn't have been shocked. We were taking ever increasing risks. It was only a matter of time before our luck ran out and I knew it was only the ingenuity of my reluctant host that had so far spared me from a similar fate.

Feeling a spasm of anxiety, I looked at the clock. Homer and Joss had been gone for longer than I had expected. Normally, that wouldn't have mattered, but losing one of my colleagues made me retreat to my attic refuge and check my bolt-hole in the chimney for the umpteenth time. I'd have to watch myself; this act of checking was becoming impulsively repetitive.

In the corner of the room, my drone blinked with a green light. Now fully charged, what had been intended as a child's toy had been adapted as an improvised spy camera. It should have been carried into the fracking site on the underside of a delivery container. Since that plan had been such a hopeless failure, it was now left to whatever ingenious scheme Homer had dreamt up.

We had taken a toy remote control caterpillar tractor, removed the top casing and fitted a multiple lens ball-shaped camera. A clever chip did the rest. It was neat, small and light and sparked Homer's interest. He wouldn't let on what he was planning but I had the distinct feeling his principle aim was to keep us both safe. Grumpy as ever, he hid behind the excuse that keeping me out of trouble protected him. True to a point, but the healing scar on the side of his head betrayed the risks he was taking. On such unspoken actions, trust evolves.

Alone and anxious, I closed my phone and removed the SIM card, hiding it in the sole of my boot. Waiting for

Homer to return only aggravated the feeling of loneliness at the loss of a friend. On previous trips away Homer had left Joss with me for company. Today the cottage was empty, still and silent, except for the hammering of rain on the roof above me. I had come to miss Joss when she wasn't around. For someone with a profound dislike of dogs, I think that said more about Joss than me.

CHAPTER 18
THOSE THAT FIT

Battling with her umbrella in the wind, Olwyn walked headlong into a man outside the hardware store. Her morning was proving to be almost totally fruitless.

No one recognised the photo-fit of the dead man, or if they did, they weren't prepared to admit to it. A blank shake of the head ended the conversation in every shop she visited. Perhaps the men she questioned had been slightly more forthcoming than the women, but the most she had been given was the probability that the man worked at the fracking site and no one from there ever ventured into town. Some she interviewed had a nervous expression when she showed her ID card and asked her questions, others were downright hostile. The man in the hardware store fitted the latter, evicting Olwyn from his shop on the pretext he was busy as soon as she showed him the photo when his shop was clearly empty.

"Be more careful," the man outside the hardware shop said gruffly as he helped Olwyn with her umbrella, turned inside-out by a vicious gust of wind.

"You," she replied in surprise, recognising the bearded face beneath a rain stained cap.

"No Jaguar?"

"The garage can't find a replacement part. I'm hoping it will be fixed tomorrow." Olwyn's voice carried a hint of weariness. "I'll be glad to get away. I can't say I find the locals particularly friendly."

Homer handed her the umbrella, now folded correctly. "You're obviously not spending enough or don't look Chinese; tourists are welcomed with open arms. Snoopers less so."

Olwyn frowned at what he had just said. "Well, thanks for the repair. At least it got me here without cooking the engine."

Homer offered a smile for the first time. "Did you tell your boss he's an idiot?"

"Why do you say that?"

"Well, you stand out a mile, and a man has been following you for the past twenty minutes, though I doubt you realised that. Your boss would have to be an idiot to send you to a place like this."

Olwyn gave him a cross look. "Oh, that man."

She tossed her hair, an act that failed in the attempt as it was damp from the rain.

"So, describe him."

"With respect, I don't have to answer to you."

"It's up to you. For the avoidance of doubt, he's in jeans and leather jacket with a black cap; stands out almost as ridiculously as you do."

Without another word, Homer turned dismissively and made to walk on.

Olwyn stepped slightly across him, momentarily blocking his path. She stooped to pick up an imaginary item from the pavement.

"I'll be in the café with the blue door at the bottom of the high street in half an hour. I could at least buy you coffee in return for your help," she said.

"Only if you get rid of your sour faced shadow first."

'Curious,' Olwyn thought as he walked away. His final words had been uttered without appearing to move his lips.

The café was busy, its windows streaming with condensation. Olwyn found a small table at the back of the shop and ordered a pot of coffee.

Earlier, she had received a negative reception when approaching the owner with a photo of the dead man's likeness. At least now, with her jacket stained by rain, she merged into the background as 'just another tourist'.

There was no sign of 'Mr Coincidence' as Olwyn had labelled him, her nameless man, who kept appearing out of thin air, fixing broken cars and alerting people to dubious characters who followed them. 'Not someone you expect to meet every day,' she thought with a bemused smile.

Olwyn filled her cup, eyeing a sugar dusted pastry on the counter with a hungry eye. If 'Mr Coincidence' failed to arrive, she could always order the pastry instead.

It had been easy to give her 'tail' the slip. Her coat had a tartan lining and once reversed with the hood raised she had walked past the man in the leather jacket without him showing any hint of recognition. Yet that left the unanswered question as to who was having her followed. Perhaps her mysterious woodsman could throw some light on that and why, in such a rural market town, anyone would want to do that. The obvious culprit was the police sergeant. But the guarded nature of the locals she had questioned left her with the suspicion that dark forces swirled in the shadows in this sleepy rural backwater.

For consolation, Olwyn ordered the pastry and took a generous bite, aware that a dust of fine white sugar had decorated her top lip. She would enjoy the delight of slowly licking it off before indulging in the next bite. Eyes closed, she was still enjoying the first mouthful when the spare chair at her table moved. Olwyn's eyes blinked open in surprise; 'Mr Coincidence' had arrived. Despite the busy cocktail of voices and nameless music, she hadn't heard the chime of the bell above the entrance door.

"I didn't hear …" she said in a puzzled voice.

"I came through the kitchen. Someone had left a crate of milk outside, so I finished the delivery."

Most men would have smiled at their own ingenuity; instead, his face remained expressionless.

"You lost your follower. Not a particularly bright specimen; reversing the coat was too obvious."

"Oh," Olwyn said in a rather deflated voice. "I thought I had been rather clever."

"It worked." For once he smiled. "So I guess it was clever enough."

Suddenly aware of the sugar dust on her top lip, Olwyn hastily licked it clean. She wished she had covered her mouth with a serviette.

"The trick is to learn." He leaned forward and poured himself a coffee from her pot. He didn't offer to refill her cup.

"Work out why you're being followed and plan ahead. Do the unexpected, behave erratically and always have an escape plan."

"But I …"

Homer held up his hand. "I don't want to know. Keep the 'why' to yourself; share with no one." He paused to drink his coffee.

"What's your name? I seem to owe you at least a thank you for helping me the other day."

"Save the thanks for another time," he said with a neutral face, which suddenly lit up with an unexpected smile.

"Don't worry, you're not my type. Just remember, the secret is never get emotionally involved; it obscures your judgement."

Homer drained his cup and stood up.

"Thanks for the coffee; I'll do my best to 'not' see you around." He turned to walk in the direction of the kitchen.

"And tell your boss he's still an idiot."

He was gone before she could reply. 'What the hell was that all about?' Olwyn thought. If he had meant to teach her subterfuge, it was the shortest lesson she had ever received.

Homer recognised the warning signs while he was in the cafe. Towns had that effect upon him; that, and the disturbance caused by others to his life.

He drove in haste as his vision began to blur, barely able to see the road ahead, let alone somewhere to stop. The symptoms accelerated rapidly; by the time he passed a spot to pull over, the fog settling on his brain denied Homer access to any memory of how to self-administer the antidote. Twice he narrowly avoided other vehicles, ploughing randomly along the verge as he fought control of the Landrover. At times like this he was a liability to others; any doctor would have taken away his driving licence. That was partly why Homer never visited doctors.

Perhaps the Landrover drove itself; Homer had no memory of the last few miles. By some miracle the roads were empty, and surviving by the grace of his last few conscious thoughts, Homer gambled that there was just time to get to the one person who could help him.

Angela had been watching the dog for some time. Joss had woken suddenly, her alert eyes darting nervously around the room, panting slightly, as though disturbed by a bad dream. Something felt wrong, or was it just Angela's imagination? She checked the locks on doors and windows and turned the radio to a higher volume. Woman and dog eyed one another, glances asking questions in uncertainty. They didn't have long to wait.

The Landrover would have driven into her barn had it not shuddered and stalled as it swerved wildly into the yard. The driver's door hung open, the figure rolling from the seat and landing face down in the rain filled lagoon that now filled her forecourt. It was Homer.

Dragging his sodden, comatose body into the kitchen was almost beyond Angela, but somehow, with the experience of years, she managed to pull him inside out of the rain. How had he driven to her cottage before the seizure overwhelmed him?

Pausing only to force the tube between Homer's teeth to clear the airway, she dragged his rigid body across the tiled kitchen floor. Angela wasn't surprised; she'd seen him like this several times before.

Retrieving Homer's rucksack from the front of the Landrover, Angela found his medical kit. It contained the magnet she needed to actuate the implant stimulator. Soaked through by the act of dragging his body into the house, Angela remained on the floor beside his inert body, reading the instructions.

Could you use magnets when the body was covered in wet clothing? She had no idea, but set about removing everything that covered his chest and swiped the magnet several times. There was nothing to tell her if it had worked; the implant either worked or it didn't; only time would tell.

Twisting Homer into the recovery position was almost as difficult as dragging his body across the yard. Written in bold capitals on the instructions for the magnet were the words 'NO EMERGENCY SERVICES'. All well and good, but if a second seizure followed she would need help.

Beside Homer's body, Joss paced nervously back and forth, dark liquid eyes searching anxiously from side to side. Snatching a pad from the table, Angela hastily scribbled a note in black biro, wrapped it in a plastic bag and secured it to the dog's collar.

Homer ill. Follow the dog.

That troublesome woman must be at his cottage and Angela would need her help if anything more serious arose. Afterwards, she could drive Homer home when he recovered.

"Home, Joss. Go home." Angela twice repeated the instruction.

It was asking a lot of a dog, but Joss was intelligent and seemed to catch the urgency in her voice. For a moment, Joss hesitated, reluctant to leave Homer's side.

At a loss, Angela said in a sharp voice, "Go get the girl".

Suddenly, the penny seemed to drop. The dog disappeared into the gathering dusk.

CHAPTER 19
LESSONS IN DOG HANDLING

Life never ceases to surprise. Before today, I could never have imagined running in blind pursuit on the trail of a dog in a darkening forest.

Dusk was rapidly replacing twilight as I ran through the trees, my only guide an occasional glimpse of the black and white flash of a small body somewhere out in front of me. Whenever I wandered off the track, Joss returned to nudge me back to the path. Despite her excitement, she had the sense not to give away our presence by barking. If I stopped for breath, she magically reappeared, narrowly resisting the urge to nip my heels like some wayward sheep.

There had been no name with the scribbled note on Joss's collar but I guessed it had to be Angela. The dog had waited barely long enough for me to change my shoes, leading off without a backward glance, certain I would follow; another example of how much my life had changed. Now I was prepared to be recklessly led by my new canine companion without thought or explanation

We must have run together for at least half an hour before I tripped on the wet, muddy surface as I snagged a foot on a briar covered slope, and tumbled downwards, coming to rest beside the dark shape of Homer's Landrover, its doors open wide in front of a darkened cottage.

Joss announced our arrival, scratching furiously at the cottage door with her claws. The door opened as I approached behind her, throwing a yellow bar of warm light across the yard. Once inside the kitchen, I saw Homer lying on his side on a tiled floor and Angela bent over him, intently massaging his chest.

"Help me lift him onto the sofa," she commanded, without looking up. "He's too heavy for me to lift on my own."

"What's happened?" I gasped.

I slipped my hands under Homer's armpits as instructed and lifted as Angela tried to raise his legs.

"What's happened," I repeated in alarm.

"A fit; the second one in less than an hour. Put that cushion under his head," she instructed, drawing up the cuff on his shirt sleeve to expose his arm.

"I've tried using the magnets, but they don't seem to prevent the fits re-occurring, so it has to be this."

Angela held up a syringe and needle, already loaded with a clear liquid. She flicked it several times with her finger, watching for air bubbles.

"Hold his arm while I find a vein."

She worked methodically, without haste or hesitation. It didn't seem the moment for questions, so I turned Homer's ice cold arm and Angela administered the injection with an accomplished hand.

"There," she said. "Let's see if that does the trick."

"Shouldn't we call an ambulance?"

Angela shook her head. "Not yet. This happens quite frequently. It will only attract unwanted attention."

Together we moved Homer onto his side and I noticed the breathing tube clenched between his locked teeth.

"How often is frequently?"

Angela gave me a hard-eyed stare. "Only when he's under too much pressure." *The accusation in her words was unavoidable.*

I cast a worried look at Homer's unconscious form. "What causes this?"

"Trauma, PTSD."

I looked at her questioningly.

"Some of us have to do things no human being should be asked to do. This is the consequence," *she said, closing the medical pack and clearing waste from the floor.*

I had a feeling her words were intended to project the blame onto me. Aware I was considered the uninvited guest, I braced myself for a verbal onslaught. Instead, her shoulders seemed to slump as distant memories shouldered me out of the path of blame.

"It's my fault. It should never have happened," she said.

I wanted to know more but thought it better to wait. Reflectively, Angela reached towards a half-full brandy bottle on her dresser.

"I think we've both earned a stimulant while we wait for the drug to work."

She filled two small glasses with amber liquid and checked Homer's pulse and temperature, placing a cold, wet cloth across his forehead. Angela seemed to know what she was doing, which made me wonder how many times she had repeated this procedure.

"All we can do now is wait".

In a surprise gesture, we touched glasses, Angela fixing me with a stare.

"You know how your story will end if you carry on like this."

'Ah, so now we cut to the heart of the matter,' I thought.

"We have to try to stop them," I said, sipping from the brandy glass, trying to avoid further questions. I stroked the dog's head as she lay protectively at Homer's side.

"We?" Angela was inquisitive.

I continued trying to ignore her, but she wasn't to be put off so easily.

"There are many who think fracking is the answer to all our problems; that you're just a bunch of looney anarchists, hell-bent on causing trouble."

"If fracking was all they were up to it might not be so much of a problem," I said with derision.

"Meaning?"

"We don't know yet. But they're definitely concealing something. Why else would 'Blue Horizon' be so keen to run the Environment and Home security ministries?"

"Ah," she said with a raised eyebrow. "A conspiracy theorist as well as an eco-terrorist."

I shook my head. "I'll accept activist. We're not terrorists."

I sensed Angela was baiting me; time to push back.

"So what did you mean by 'it's my fault'?" I looked deliberately at Homer.

Angela hesitated. "That's not my story to tell."

"I doubt that Homer will tell me," I said provocatively.

"Then you'll have to earn his trust. And be patient. He'll tell you, if and when he's good and ready."

At that moment Homer stirred. His eyes snapped open.

It was gone midnight before Grace left Angela's cottage, grating the gears of the Landrover, with Homer propped in the passenger seat. A thick mist had gathered since the rain had stopped, adding an air of mystery to the dripping darkness.

The only words Homer uttered were directions for the maze of narrow lanes. They drove with the windows wide open to ward off waves of nausea. Homer sat with his eyes closed, his head feeling as though a gorilla was trying to kick its way out of his skull.

Angela had only agreed to them leaving with the promise that Homer would see a doctor in the morning for a check-up, advice she was certain he would ignore. Delayed by the mist, their journey took almost as long as Grace's arrival on foot.

Relieved, Grace slowed the heavy vehicle as they bumped into the ruts that scored the track that led to Homer's cottage. She suspected he deliberately left it that way to discourage visitors.

Homer was always alert for the presence of the bounty hunters who made their living out of tracking down people such as Grace and had used his skills to protect her. Now, he lay slumped in the passenger seat. This time, it would be down to Joss to make sure no unpleasant surprises awaited them further along the mist shrouded track.

Grace hauled the Landrover to a creaking halt on the track amongst the trees.

"Stay here. I'll go ahead with Joss and make sure that there's no one around."

Homer turned to protest, but words wouldn't form. Instead he just sat back, exhausted in his seat.

"Home, Joss," Grace called softly as they left the Landrover behind them.

But who needs a map or compass when you have Joss, she thought with a smile. Twice she lost sight of Joss, only for the dog to return to collect her.

Eventually, the trees thinned out. Ahead of her, Homer's cottage was in darkness, except for the solitary light she had forgotten about in her haste to follow Joss. The track and yard were empty. All seemed as she had left it, but Grace decided she would feel happier if Joss conducted one of her broad, sweeping searches, performed so often at Homer's command.

But what to say? 'Home, Joss,' had been simple and worked almost immediately. But sending the dog in a wide arc around the cottage left Grace conflicted.

"Circle around, Joss," seemed to fit the task.

The dog sat wide-eyed, panting. She didn't move.

"Circle around, Joss," Grace tried again, drawing a wide circle with her arm.

Still the dog sat, waiting expectantly. Grace wished she had paid more attention to Homer's commands. She closed her eyes, thinking hard.

"Joss, away; away to me."

It worked; the dog disappeared in a flash of black and white. Grace stood patiently, suddenly aware she hadn't thought of a plan if someone was there waiting for them. She had left the Landrover without her phone, so had neither torchlight or a means to communicate with anyone, if and when the dog returned.

In the isolation of mist and darkness, the trees around her assumed an ethereal presence, one in which the imagination could run riot if given free reign.

In the silence, Grace resisted the impulse to continually look behind her. Then logic told her no one was likely to be around at this time of night and Joss would be her litmus paper. If she scented nothing then Grace needn't worry.

After five minutes, Joss reappeared, panting, her fur beaded with tiny jewels of moisture from the mist. Grace concluded that the absence of a warning bark meant her long circuit had found nothing out of place, so with renewed confidence, they left the cover of the trees to inspect the house. There was no sign of forced entry; the doors were still locked, no window panes were broken.

Her task completed, Joss moved in front of Grace, blocking her path, a reminder that she had overlooked something of great importance. Grace laughed, fumbling in her pocket, where she found the remains of a cereal bar. She broke it in two and gave half to Joss.

"You're too clever by half."

The dog didn't contradict her.

They returned back down the track to find the Landrover unaware of a fresh coarse chunky tread imprinted into the wet mud, an impression that hadn't been made by the worn tyres of the Landrover. It was something Homer would never have missed.

CHAPTER 20
WANTED DEAD OR ALIVE

Olwyn's mobile woke her from a dreamless sleep. It was still dark, which was an ominous sign. Jerry.

"What time is it?"

"Something with a five in front of it." He sounded disgracefully bright and alert.

Olwyn yawned. "What do you want, Jerry? Can't it wait until morning?"

"Apparently not, dear girl. And by the way, it technically is morning. I'm ringing because clever you have genuinely rattled someone's cage. I had a phone call an hour ago from our boss, or more as I suspect, shortly to become our ex-boss."

To Olwyn's ears, Jerry sounded far too pleased with himself.

"Let's say he was a trifle miffed," he continued. "Fancy, a delicate flower such as you sticking your nose in where it's not wanted," he said with a chuckle.

Olwyn thought it was tinged with foreboding. Momentarily, she felt an ache in the pit of her stomach.

"Am I in trouble?" she asked.

"If you are, darling, you're obviously doing something right. Keep meddling and digging. You seem to be making certain people rather unhappy."

"And that's good?" Olwyn asked with a note of irony in her voice.

"It's what I hoped for when I sent you down to the back of beyond. People get angry and agitated and start to make mistakes. Keep it up."

"Jerry," she whispered, as if she feared someone might be listening. "I'm being followed."

"Splendid."

"What? I could be in danger for all you know. Or seem to care," she said with an air of indignation. "I'd be in an even worse situation if he hadn't tipped me off."

"He?"

She had his attention. "Big, hairy woodsman; throwback to the stone age, judging by his manners. Keeps turning up in my moment of need, just because my boss has thrown me in way above my head. You're such an idiot, Jerry; his words not mine."

"My, my. I do believe this wild Norseman you've met is bringing out a primeval side to you I didn't know existed."

Olwyn sighed with impatience, disinclined to bother contradicting him.

"Listen. That dinosaur of a car of yours will be fixed today, no, tomorrow. As soon as it's driveable, I'm out of this place. Assuming I'm still alive."

"Now, now, no need to be melodramatic."

"Melodramatic? All the locals here treat me as if I've got Ebola, and strange men shadow my every move. I'm only surviving because of this weird guy I keep running into. Misogynist to a fault, he plainly can't stand the sight of me. What's worse is every time our paths cross, he can't resist pointing out the glaring shortcomings in my training."

There was silence for a moment.

"Well, at least it sounds like your virtue isn't under threat. Most Norsemen I heard of were rather big into rape and pillage."

"Not funny, Jerry. What do you want me to do? Or is this call just to poke fun at me?"

"Ah yes, a tiny task to fulfil. In the next hour or so, a courier will arrive at your hotel door with a warrant signed by our 'big man' himself."

"Warrant?"

"Indeed. It will authorise your access to the fracking site we're so interested in. You need to take it to the local police station and insist they accompany and assist you in its execution."

"They won't like that," Olwyn said, her stomach performing a somersault.

"Of course they won't. They will also prevaricate and try to prevent you gaining access. Which is precisely our intention."

"You've lost me." The image of a puppet on a string came into Olwyn's mind, with Jerry as the puppet master.

"It's quite simple," Jerry said with a note of forbearance. "'Blue Horizon' control the fracking sites and how they are operated, and the site security people have the local PC Plod in their pockets. There's no chance they will let you anywhere near one of their precious fracking sites. Far easier to turn nasty and run you out of town. Preventing our dear Olwyn from exercising her duty is an extremely seriously offence. It should open the door for the heavy brigade."

"And what about me?" She suddenly felt like discarded flotsam.

"Simple. Command performance complete, you gather up our precious 'Gladys' and high tail it out of town. QED."

"Put like that, what can possibly go wrong." Her words were heavy with irony.

"The trouble is, Jerry, these people aren't nearly as stupid as you seem happy to make them out to be. They see me coming a mile away."

Exasperated, she was talking to herself. Jerry had closed their call, obviously deciding he had bigger fish to fry elsewhere.

An unfortunate metaphor in the circumstances. It was only after he had gone that Olwyn realised that she hadn't the first idea of what to do if she was granted access to the fracking site.

I woke with a start. Beams of sunlight arced through a gap in the curtains, illuminated by an endless spiral of dust particles. The bed was empty except for the impression made by Homer's body.

I had decided to share the bed with him in case another spasm returned while he slept. Angela had been concerned that he might choke if no one was on hand to supervise. She showed me how to apply the magnets to his implant. If that failed, well, we just had to hope that it wouldn't.

I must have fallen asleep at some point in the early hours. Exhausted, I had stretched out on the bed beside Homer. Even with my back to him, it felt strange to be sharing a bed with another person. He needed a bath and smelt of a mixture of wood shavings and pond water, an odd cocktail which was surprisingly homely.

When I entered the kitchen he was riddling the Aga, his face illuminated by the orange flames from a wigwam of burning kindling just visible through the glass panel in the door.

"How are you feeling?"

The teapot was warm; I poured myself a cup.

"Right as rain. A headache, but that's normal." Homer opened the door, tossing split logs into the flames. "The water will be hot in an hour."

I guessed he knew he needed a bath.

"Thanks for last night." The reluctance in his tone spoke more than words could describe.

"That's okay. Does it happen often?"

Homer shrugged. "I deal with it."

"Are you getting help?"

"What? A chip in my chest? I guess they think that helps."

If I was hoping to open a door, it was obvious from his voice that he intended it would remain very securely shut.

"You have a problem."

Was resentment back in his voice again? He held up his phone displaying a page in social media. My face stared back at me, framed in a poster, surrounded by fake bullet holes and a caption that read,

'Wanted; dead or alive'

like something out of the wild west.

"Seems you've been careless."

Shocked, I was thoughtful for a moment. The phone of my arrested friend would have been destroyed and besides, we never took photos of one another. So where had the picture come from?

"There's no name; it might not be me," I ventured.

"So when Bremer finds you here we're going to tell him it's your twin? Even if that were true, do you think it would make any difference to what will happen to us both?" The note of resentment was back in Homer's voice.

"How long has the picture been posted?"

"A few hours. Long enough to get thousands of hits."

"Who posted it?"

"Irrelevant. It'll be a fake identity. You could make a complaint but, by the time the portal take it down, it will already be too late. Eco-terrorists ..."

"I'm an activist, not a terrorist."

"... are not especially popular in modern Britain. Every bounty hunter in the country will be on the lookout for you. There's big money to be made from catching terrorists."

"So this is what we've become. A nation of informers, duped and bought by the fascists."

Homer leaned forward, his fingers supporting him against the table top.

"You may not have noticed, but people live in fear of the lights going out. Returning to the stone age, which is the narrative our government portrays as the destiny intended by eco-nuts like you, doesn't appeal to the majority of people." He paused.

"You've lost the propaganda war, Grace, and the sooner you wake up to that fact, the more chance that you won't be seen as public enemy number one. Sure, people might hate the thought of being governed by 'Blue Horizon', but they hate the thought of being cold and unemployed far more. Cut off the route to limitless gas and oil and that's where you'll take them."

"It doesn't have to be like that," I barked back, bitterness tinging my words.

"Then how does it have to sound like? People are lost and confused by the science you spout. 'Blue Horizon' keep it simple;

Vote for us and you can turn on the lights and light the gas to keep warm.

"It's dark, cold and a scary place back in the caves." For a moment, his face creased with concern.

I knew he was being deliberately provocative to hammer his message home, but it didn't make being on the receiving end any easier.

"You're right, we blew our chances to win over public support years ago. Too much time spent on infighting and eco-babble; too many options and unpalatable alternatives. Now we've lost all the best people. No one gives us airtime or are prepared to print our side of the story. Fascism rules. True. But that doesn't make the final outcome any easier to bear. We're all going to hell in a handcart and killing the world along the way."

Homer shook his head. "It's the toss of a coin. Without convincing evidence to persuade people, 'Blue Horizon' win heads-up however the coin lands."

"But that's why I'm here. To find that crucial evidence. And to do that, sooner or later, I'm going to have to get inside that fracking compound, whatever the cost."

In the silence that followed, we both suddenly realise that my 'Dead or Alive' poster had disappeared.

It was almost as though someone had been listening to our heated conversation.

CHAPTER 21
AN UNEXPECTED INVITATION

A tall, willowy policewoman was behind the reception desk when Olwyn entered. PC Allison Markham, her face creased with a puzzled frown, appeared to recognise Olwyn before she announced herself at the desk.

"So, what troubles do you bring to our doorstep today?" PC Markham asked, head slightly tilted to emphasize a mildly amused tone of curiosity.

Olwyn held out her latest warrant, delivered less than an hour before.

"I want access to the local fracking site and I don't want a faceless office with a temp who knows nothing about the operation. I need entrance to the site and the chance to interview site workers without the presence of the bosses."

Even to her own ears, her opening gambit sounded optimistic. In her mind's eye, she saw herself turned away, rebuffed, already walking to the exit door.

"Mind if I take a copy?" PC Markham held out her hand for the warrant.

Surprised, Olwyn handed over the document.

"I'll be lucky to see that again," she muttered under her breath, hoping Jerry was listening in on her phone.

The police station had a tired, worn appearance, that of restricted police budgets not able to stretch to a tin of paint. Olwyn suspected it was a malaise that demotivated the staff who worked here to the same degree.

She watched PC Markham disappear into a back room, expecting her to immediately defer to the obstructive Sergeant Wailes who Olwyn had met the day before. To her surprise, PC Markham simply photocopied the warrant and returned to the front desk. She handed it to Olwyn without comment and spent the next few minutes entering its details onto an aged desktop computer.

"There," PC Markham said pertly. "Can't get lost now."

Now with her own puzzled frown, Olwyn slid the folded warrant into the inner pocket of her bag.

"When do you want to visit the site?"

"Er, today I suppose?" Olwyn replied, feeling distinctly optimistic. The other woman's manner had caught her off-balance.

PC Markham gave her a half smile, which somehow reminded Olwyn of a cat sizing up a cornered mouse. After searching for a file on the antique computer, PC Markham made a call without turning away to conceal her conversation.

'Ah, here comes the rebuff,' Olwyn thought, her stomach clenching in anticipation.

The call lasted less than a minute and PC Markham made an entry on the computer before turning back to Olwyn.

"Would ten o'clock be suitable? It's only a twenty minute drive."

"What? Yes. Of course." She could barely suppress a gasp of stunned surprise, adding somewhat feebly, "can I take a bus to get there? My car's …"

"… with Hargreaves being fixed." Continuing her cat impersonation, PC Markham finished the sentence for her.

With a light air of efficiency, she made another call. "I need you to man the front desk. I'm out on a call for an hour or so. What? No. Now."

She reached for her keys and cap, lifted the counter flap and walked past Olwyn .

"We don't want to be late, so are you coming? Or am I driving there alone?" PC Markham didn't wait for an answer.

"Phone." PC Allison Markham held out her hand.

"The only camera in the car park doesn't cover the spaces occupied by police vehicles."

Was she trying to put Olwyn at her ease? With surprising dexterity, Allison Markham switched off Olwyn's phone and removed the SIM card in a seamless movement.

"You can have it back when you've finished your visit." Her tone implied no room for questions.

For the next ten minutes, neither woman spoke, their thoughts conducted by the rhythmic sweep of the wiper blades; old worn blades smearing and fighting to clear the windscreen. Eventually, Olwyn broke the ice.

"Thank you for arranging things and giving me a lift," she ventured.

"I thought it's what you asked for. Though you may get more than you expect, if you're not careful."

At first Olwyn thought Allison Markham was mocking her, but there was a note of concern in her last sentence.

"Meaning?" Olwyn asked directly. "The body I'm here to investigate was found next to a fracking site. Preliminary evidence suggests foul play and these sites have a history of being somewhat obscure with their operations."

"Remember, you'll be overheard and taped, even if you insist on interviewing staff alone," Allison Markham said with a raised eyebrow. "Around fracking sites, busy bodies," she emphasised the term, "have a habit of disappearing, including policemen."

Olwyn didn't answer, her mouth turned dry, converting words into dust.

Allison Markham continued.

"A word of advice; avoid direct questions, cover what you really want to ask within the triviality of ordinary life. Don't write things down, watch for facial signals to answer questions. The men you interview will be too scared to tell you anything much, but their reactions might tell you what you need to know. If the site security goons believe you're harmless or better still, incompetent, well, there's a chance you'll be disregarded and safe."

She didn't elaborate on the alternative.

Homer had been watching the phone box for half an hour. Rain dripped with the beat of a metronome from the brim of his hat; he counted the rate of drips to pass the time.

In an age of mobile phones, no one visited the phone box. He wasn't expecting that anyone would, but as the time for Marius to call approached it brought with it a heightened state of alert. If someone had intercepted his message and had the wherewithal to trace the number, a trap could easily have been set.

In the squat position beneath his cape and without appearing to move, Homer changed legs, easing his cramping muscles. Occasionally, cars passed in tumbrels of spray. He memorised their numbers, partly to pass the time, more importantly to check if anyone made repeat journeys. Predictably, no one stopped or came, leaving the phone box unused, alone with its decoration of cards offering a range of dubious services unvisited.

The wait had eased his mood. Homer felt indebted to Grace for the support she had offered during his seizure, yet frustrated that she had been so careless as to allow her image to be taken in plain sight on some CCTV system. The mock-up of the 'Wanted' poster on social media had serious implications. Bounty hunters were becoming ever more commonplace, some even had the audacity to advertise on mainstream television, encouraging people to download 'wanted' images, *'ring this number if you see anyone who matches this description'*. High rewards were common for information about those labelled by the government as terrorists, the ubiquitous 'enemies of the state'.

A car slowed as it passed the lonely phone box, hesitated, then continued on its way. Homer made particular note of its registration number. If it returned and repeated the slow pass, his ruse had been blown; Marius's call would go unanswered. Homer stretched gently, easing his back, rubbing his hands together for warmth. The rain had brought a distinct chill with it, occasionally swirling into flurries of sleet, a precursor for what was to come.

Before arriving for his stake-out of the phone box he had stopped in a town where he wouldn't be recognised. It was pointless buying hair dye; facial recognition cameras would contour Grace's facial features and only plastic surgery could alter that. Instead, Homer chose a scarf she could use as a hijab when a peaked cap wouldn't work, with glasses and skin toning cream to defect all but the most discerning glances. Eye make-up, which he bought with a degree of embarrassment, would serve to change the shape of her eyes. It didn't amount to very much, but it would be better than nothing. The sooner she was gone the better, this time with a strict instruction not to return.

At ten minutes after the hour, the phone in the box rang. He could just make out its repeated tones above the hiss of tyres from a passing car. Homer waited for it to ring out. Camouflaged in a covert of briars, he scanned a broad radius with a hand held thermal imaging scope. Nothing; even the rabbits ignored their hunger and hid in their burrows.

Another ten minutes passed. The phone began to ring for a second time. This time, Homer was moving before the first tone had completed; a solitary, lonely man with only his wits for protection.

CHAPTER 22
UNWANTED VISITORS

"Beware complacency."

It had been Homer's angry retort just before he left when I had tried, and failed, to explain the source of the photo. As a result, his ingratitude had placed me in a bad, self-absorbed mood, exaggerated by a strong feeling of injustice.

So much so that I almost missed the arrival of a large four-by-four in the driveway. No doors were slammed shut and without Joss to bark a warning (she had gone out with Homer) it was left to a pair of ducks to sound the alarm.

Five men crossed the yard amidst a flurry of feathers. I knew the doors were locked, but without Homer to stop them, my emergency plan kicked in without a second's hesitation. Like a well-rehearsed rat in a drainpipe, I was in my 'priest hole' in the chimney before the first doorlock had been tripped.

With hours to spare, I had cleaned all the loose soot in the flue and practiced the climb to avoid dislodging any evidence. The house had been scoured for anything that might reveal my presence. If they broke in, my efforts to hide would be put to the ultimate test.

For what felt like an age, the house remained silent. I had begun to think it was a false alarm, that they had been thwarted by Homer's locks, when I heard the sounds of opening drawers and cupboards on the floor below the attic. Almost simultaneously, the hatch to my attic hideout sprung open, followed by the metallic rattle of an extending ladder. Heavy boots clumped around the floor below; a chair was knocked over, the fall of a table turned on its side, the thump of a mattress tipped onto the floor.

They were being thorough, and obviously keen to mark their presence. Words floated in intermittent bites; only when they were close to the firehearth could I make out what was being said. Not Arabic this time; something

Slavic; east European? My lack of languages served me poorly but it wasn't a bad guess.

The bag now hanging from my waist contained my mask. In the haste to climb the chimney to my refuge I had forgotten to use it. Now, soot, mortar and dust combined to gather in my nose, portending the inevitable sneeze. I fought it back as though my very life depended on it. It probably did. Absorbed by resisting the sneeze, I missed the ball of paper thrown in the hearth below me, the lighted match thrown with a laugh into its midst. Did they suspect I might be hiding in the chimney or was it just random chance?

Within seconds a stream of white smoke funnelled through the flue around me. Eyes pressed shut, mouth sealed in a grimace, I held my breath. As children, it was a game I used to play with my brothers, to see who could hold their breath the longest, often until we were blue in the face. A pointless game and not one I was very good at, but the practice now stood me in good stead in my moment of need. Desperate not to breathe, I counted seconds until I became confused somewhere in the sixties.

Below, the flames suddenly flared and died; the smoke made a ballooning belch so I could feel its presence around me. Compulsively, I risked a half breath and choked, forcing my eyes open. The voices diminished, the creak of the ladder followed.

It was like drowning; whatever the consequences, I would have to breathe soon, very soon. I tried filtering air through clenched teeth; as if that would somehow filter the smoke. I rubbed my streaming eyes. The smoke passed in thin white veins. I blinked what felt like a hundred times until slowly my vision began to clear as fresh clean air arrived. The fire was out.

Rain hissed on the surface of the pond. The afternoon was windless, and rain continued to fall like stair rods.

Homer fished without a float, relying on the pressure of the slack line draped across his fingers. If the carp as much as kissed the bait, (one of Joss's favourite dog biscuits), he would know. Recent torrential rains had fed the carp ponds in fast running streams, clearing the mud and weed accumulated through long summer months of drought. In a pond filled with clean fresh water, the fish would become more active, their bodies cleaned of ingested mud, making much better eating.

On the back of the seizure the previous evening, the day hadn't started well. Homer had by chance seen the post, the 'Wanted' poster framing Grace's face.

'I think this is one of yours', had been the simple message from an unnamed source.

How could she have been so careless? These people were amateurs, playing a dangerous game, haphazardly implicating others in their myopic pursuit of protecting the environment.

Since the beginning of creation, climate had continually changed, often beyond anything the narrow perspective of our wildest imagination could conceive. Were the present climate variations really beyond man's ability for adaptation?

Homer eased his stiff buttocks on the canvas seat, sending rivulets of water sliding off his cape.

"Careful," he muttered under his breath. "Mr Carp will see you."

The anger he had felt earlier for Grace had dissipated, washed away by the calming influence of rod and line and the elusive fish.

The phone call with Marius, initiating another spike of anxiety, had passed in the rivulets of rain. His friend, 'the Vicar', had tutored him well. Marius had rung from another phone box, given no name, asked no questions, with a voice that sounded deeper than Homer remembered, no longer that of the young boy that he had left behind.

Five, no six years, is a big gap in the life of any child. Even before that, Homer had often been absent for long periods. And now? He couldn't imagine a future that would include Marius. Besides, what of his ex-wife and young daughter? Separation had been essential for their safety, and now Marius had arrived unannounced and turned the entire plan upside down.

Homer could have ignored the request to meet, but he didn't have the heart to and it would have left Marius more exposed. When they met, a new plan would have to be agreed. Would that include the truth? The boy believed his father had spent the last five years in prison. Well, that was partially true, yet hidden in the complete story lurked more dangers than the lies he had already created?

The stroke of a feather disturbed his reverie as he felt the line stroke his fingers, drawn delicately like a hair across his skin. Was Mr Carp hungry and looking for his dinner? Perhaps sensing his sudden awareness, Joss eased her body into the reeds beside him. Homer chuckled.

"Not for you, girl" he whispered. "This one's bound for Cosmo's plate."

A second later, the line disappeared. He whipped the rod upwards and away, easing against the muscular strength of the carp. If he was careful, a down payment on his debt was about to be made.

Olwyn slumped into the seat beside Allison Markham. With a silent gesture she nodded, and Allison Markham swung the car in a U-turn and drove away from the fracking site. They had only travelled half a mile when Olwyn urgently indicated she needed to stop.

"Pull over."

The car had barely halted when she flung open the door and crouched, retching on the grass verge. Several minutes later, she returned, bedraggled by the drizzle, to the car.

"Good as that," Allison Markham said, waiting for Olwyn to gather herself.

"Mainly nerves. I'll be okay. I just need to get away from here."

Allison Markham nodded. "I'll take the forest road. It will be easier to stop if you need me to again." She paused. "Did you get much from your meeting?"

"More by what was unsaid than said," Olwyn replied in a tired voice, gazing out of the window at the sombre passing pine trees, painted black in the grey light of late afternoon.

"Spooky place," she added, though Allison Markham wasn't sure if she meant the fracking site or the forest.

"I'll drop you somewhere in town; you might prefer not to return to the station. We could meet tonight to write a report on your interviews?"

Olwyn gave her a questioning glance.

Allison Markham continued, her face creased in a frown as her eyes glanced several times into the rear view mirror. "To justify my involvement I'll need a copy of a report on what was said," she explained.

She had left Olwyn to enter the site alone while making several local calls. It covered her involvement in identifying the dead man while Olwyn conducted her interviews with individual members of site staff.

"What?" Olwyn saw Allison Markham's eyes grow large, glancing nervously in the mirror again.

"Large SUV; pulled out of a side track as we passed. Check behind us," she said, stepping down a gear and accelerating in the same moment. "Black windows, extra large bars on the front."

Their small car responded with a jerk as she increased in speed.

"I think it's closing on us fast."

Olwyn turned in her seat. The front grille and bars were already looming large in the rear window.

"I hope you've got your high speed pursuit licence," she said in a tight voice.

"I only passed my driving test two years ago, just before I joined the police," Allison Markham replied nervously, white knuckles on the steering wheel as they drifted alarmingly through the next sequence of bends, tyres sliding on the needle strewn surface.

She punched several buttons on the dashboard, repeating her call sign urgently into the radio. Coarse static roared in reply. Allison Markham punched another button, flipping frequencies, but it made no difference.

"I think someone is jamming the radio." Her voice, which had been steady, was now underscored with fear.

For a short distance, the narrow road straightened. The small police car had greater agility through the bends, only for the bulkier SUV to rapidly close the gap as soon as the road unwound its twisting path.

As they swung nose-to-tail into the bend, the SUV struck a sharp blow against the rear of the smaller car. Any thought that the intentions of the pursuing 4-by-4 weren't malevolent had been immediately dispelled.

"Are you armed?" Olwyn gasped through clenched teeth.

She watched the SUV momentarily diminish into the distance behind them. Within seconds, course corrected, it accelerated and grew menacingly large again.

"Nothing more than a truncheon? I don't think that's going to do a lot."

"How far to the main road?"

"Two, maybe three miles."

Allison Markham changed down a gear as the next bend approached, engine screaming high in its rev range. As they rolled violently into the curve, she pulled aggressively on the handbrake for several seconds, releasing it only as the 4-by-4 filled the rear screen, preparing to shunt the small car clean off the road.

"He might be driving on my brake lights," Allison Markham shouted. "It may throw him off if I don't touch the brakes." She didn't sound optimistic.

The impact against their rear was harder this time, the car fishtailed alarmingly, on the limits of Allison Markham's control, but her concealed braking bought precious seconds as the driver of the SUV misjudged his braking.

Some way off, amidst the trees to their right, something flickered, light and dark, moving towards them. It was invisible to Allison Markham, her eyes jumping between the road ahead and the mirror, anticipating another impact at any moment.

Olwyn, face transfixed in terror, just managed to garble, "Ahead; look out."

Barely had the words left her lips than a Landrover appeared out of nowhere, swaying drunkenly across their path, its driver oblivious to their speeding approach.

"Idiot," Allison Markham screamed as the battered, dirty vehicle suddenly blocked their path.

The prospect of becoming sandwiched between the rampaging 4-by-4 and the lumbering Landrover offered a terrifying prospect. The driver of the Landrover was either blind or hadn't seen them, or, he could be in league with the driver behind them.

While the driver struggled to correct the Landrover, for a few brief seconds a narrow gap appeared, just wide enough for another car. Without hesitation, Allison Markham slammed the accelerator to the floor. Olwyn heard a sharp metallic crack as the wing mirror on her side was torn free and the police car rippled down the side of the slower vehicle.

In a second they were through, the road clear and empty in front of them. Unless the Landrover pulled over to allow the SUV to pass, it now blocked the route of their pursuers and once they joined the main road, the safety of the town lay but a few miles distant.

"Who the hell was that moron?" Allison Markham exploded, still driving hard.

Olwyn turned in her seat to stare through the cracked rear window, crazed by a web of fine lines, but just clear enough to reveal the face of the driver behind them.

Coincidence can be strange. She was certain she recognised him as he extended his hand through the side window and defiantly raised his middle finger. As the diminishing image of the Landrover filled the centre of the lane, Olwyn wasn't entirely certain who the gesture was intended for.

CHAPTER 23
FALLOUT

"You can come down now."

Homer's voice echoed up the chimney flue. I was so stiff from bracing myself for the best part of three hours that I more or less fell down the flue when I started to move. Homer threw me a blanket.

"Wrap this around you while I run you a hot bath."

It was amazing how he could distort a kind gesture with a note of irritation. If I had expected praise by avoiding discovery, I would have been sadly disappointed.

In the course of the search, every room had been turned upside down. Nothing was stolen or broken, simply an act performed to make a statement of control.

"Will you report this to the police?" I gazed around at the mayhem of debris.

"What? And invite a return visit? Next time they'll smash everything just to teach me a lesson."

Homer wandered off to make something warm for us both to drink.

"So, this is what your online mug-shot causes. They were obviously suspicious and on the hunt for you."

He handed me a brandy glass filled with something warm and delicious, with the kick of a mule.

"I want you out of here tomorrow."

"Is that a good idea?" I asked, sipping my drink; whatever it contained, it spread like a comforting amoeba through my cold body within seconds. "Given that there is a hunting party out searching for me at the moment."

"There are no good options; just some give a better chance than others, and sitting here waiting for Bremer to catch us out isn't one of them."

"And what of my drone? I can't leave without getting it inside the fracking site, even if I have to go down and crawl under the fence by myself." I added the last bit with a note of defiance I didn't feel.

"What's the range of the camera? How close does the receiver have to be to pick up a signal?"

"Provided the drone can get a signal, distance isn't a problem. We've got to be able to control it to get the pictures we need."

"And you don't think they've thought of that?"

I shrugged. "I'll admit that no one has succeeded yet. But we only need one to work and film the evidence of what they're doing."

I gave Homer an appealing look. "You said you had an idea of how we could get the drone into their compound which didn't involve me actually climbing over the fence."

He looked sheepish. "The events of last night have set things back a bit."

I guessed he was referring to his seizure but thought it best to avoid a direct question. "So how long before we could try to get the drone into the compound?"

"If we include tonight, three nights from now." Homer's face looked strained.

"I've arranged for Angela to make a kite in the shape of a large owl. Just in case someone sees it in the darkness, it will look like a bird out hunting. Your drone will be attached beneath it; it will just have to survive a drop of about fifty feet."

The word 'audacious' came to mind, though I would have preferred the drone to be dropped on a small parachute to have a better chance of landing in one piece. Perhaps that was something to arrange with Angela.

"Won't a replica of an owl be too small to carry the drone?"

"Not if Angela makes it look like an eagle owl. There's word that a pair roost somewhere hereabouts."

"But wouldn't another carrier drone be better?"

Homer shook his head. "Too noisy. They also have a jamming transmitter to prevent drones flying within half a mile of the site. 'Blue Horizon' have thought of every eventuality to protect their operations, including a sophisticated grid of camouflage netting to hide them from satellite surveillance."

I felt suddenly alarmed. "Surely the netting will defeat the object of your scheme? It'll catch anything you drop from above."

Homer had a rare smile. "No. It actually works in your favour. I'm relying on the mesh to break the drone's fall. The gaps between the net cords are wider than the dimensions of your little toy. Even if your drone lands on the netting, you just need to use its tracks to pull it around until it falls through a hole. That way it only needs to survive a drop of eight to ten feet."

"All without anyone noticing?" I said with an unavoidable note of scepticism.

Homer frowned. Perhaps I had burst his bubble. "Well, in the absence of anything better that doesn't risk getting caught …"

He turned his back; Mr Grumpy had just returned.

"You can take it or leave it. Either way, you leave tomorrow," he said as he slammed the door and left the room.

It took a hot bath and several bottles from the minibar in the hotel room to steady Olwyn's shaken nerves.

Allison Markham had dropped her off in a side street some distance from the hotel, and the incessant rain had soaked Olwyn to the skin by the time she had reached her room. Still, it was better than arriving in a police car, especially one with a conspicuously bent rear end.

"Less attention if I drop you here," Allison Markham said, colour slowly returning to her paste white face. "If it hadn't been for that idiot in the Landrover …" She left the unspoken words to answer for themselves.

Olwyn looked at her uncertainly. If she hadn't been so shaken she might have said, 'Actually, I think I know that idiot.' Somehow, it seemed to complicate the situation. So they had parted with an agreement to meet later to discuss what had just happened and for Olwyn to give Allison Markham a statement on her meeting with workers inside the compound.

"I need to keep the records straight if I'm to keep my boss off my back," she had explained.

Olwyn wasn't sure if that was Sergeant Wailes or DI Amos.

"You need to make sure the statement you give to me covers everything you discussed, no speculating on what you may have read between the lines. They will have secretly filmed the entire thing, and be in no doubt that Wailes will have seen it by the morning. He'll give you a hard time if you try to leave things out."

Olwyn nodded as she climbed out of the police car. As it drove away, she noticed that none of the lights were working in the tangle of its rear end.

Feeling restored after her bath, and wrapped in a fluffy white towelling robe, Olwyn took the call on her phone.

It was Jerry. How quickly her peace of mind could be disturbed.

"Darling Olwyn, seems your life has been saved yet again by your wild man from the woods."

"Jerry?"

She presented his name as a question. How the hell did he know what had happened so quickly? Her phone had been switched off at the time and it had taken half an hour to work out how to return the SIM card.

"Despite your assurance to the contrary," she paused, "my request for an interview with some of the workers in the fracking site was granted." Olwyn sounded suitably exasperated.

"Ah, that I didn't know. But good, good. What did you find out? Did anyone identify our dead body?"

"What? No. They had all obviously been told to say nothing before they came into the room."

"That we should have expected. Anyone give away any clues, any clear indications they were lying?"

"A few. Most were just scared witless. I think several didn't even understand English, or at least pretended they didn't."

"Names? Did you get their names and places of origin."

"Beyond all being called 'Mohammed', no. Look, I need to collect my thoughts together and write things down. I had to memorise everything. That was intended to keep me safe," Olwyn said with a slightly incensed tone to her voice. "Fat lot of good that did me."

"At least our hero was there to intervene."

"Random chance. Again."

This time she let anger show. The idiot was laughing at her.

"How do you know?" she challenged.

"There was a call. Phone box again, where does he keep finding them? Though a different voice. I actually think it was our man this time. He said you ought to keep out of the forest if you know what's good for you, especially in a police car."

There was a silence for several seconds while Olwyn digested what Jerry had just said.

"Jerry, after my meeting someone made a pretty determined effort to drive us off the road and into the trees."

"I know. Our caller told me."

She ignored him. "Why? Why would they try to do that?"

"Presumably because they don't like us rattling their cage, or you've been told something they don't want you to share. So good so far, we're achieving what we intended."

"We're achieving?" Olwyn replied incredulously. "From where I'm sitting, I'm the only one putting my neck on the line here. Why don't you come and join me?"

"Now, now, dear girl. Let's not get all uppity. Our wild man from the woods wants to meet you. It's why he rang."

"Oh, really. And there was me thinking he rang to boast about how he had intervened to save us … and to call you an idiot, I hope."

"Well, that too. But he needs to see you, which is different. Seems he wants a favour from you."

"A favour?" Olwyn asked testily. "How can he want a favour from me?"

"Well, arrange a cosy little tête-à-tête with your hero and you'll find out. He said it was urgent, so I gave him your number."

"Well, I'll ignore his call. Besides, I'm busy tonight."

"What, some lovers' tryst already? My, my, you have been working fast."

"Sod off, Jerry. I'm returning a favour to the policewoman who got me into the compound as you instructed. Just to remind you, it was she who was driving the car when we were attacked."

"Well," Jerry paused to affect a sigh, "be careful what you say, dear girl, and don't go walking the streets alone. Seems the natives down there in sunny Sussex aren't particularly friendly."

Why did he always seem to be laughing at her, as though causing annoyance in others was his stock way to get them to do his bidding.

"Olwyn?" His voice was suddenly serious.

"Umm," she responded, feigning profound indifference.

"Be a good girl and speak to our woodland friend. He may turn out to be the only ally you've got." Jerry hesitated.

"And one other thing; 'Gladys' won't be ready in the morning. Seems our friends at the fracking site have paid a visit to the garage man repairing the car."

"How do you know?" she asked, fear suddenly spiking in her voice.

"Seems your woodland friend paid a call on Hargreaves. He said he had received a visit from someone and knows what's good for him."

Jerry left her to consider his words for a moment before adding, "Someone wants to keep you there, Olwyn dear.

Looks like the only way you're going to get out of this vipers' nest you've stirred up is with the help of our mystery man. Be a dear and make sure you answer his call. I would at least like 'Gladys' returned in one piece."

Olwyn filled the air with obscenities, but she was talking to herself. The call had been terminated.

A couple of medium sized carp and trout had placed Cosmo in a generous mood. Homer made no attempt to barter, the fish represented payment in kind for received favours from the gypsy family.

The two men chinked beer glasses, silently reviewing the world from their respective positions. The meeting had been made in haste, partly to transfer the fish while they were still fresh, but importantly to confirm the request that Milo had made at the earlier meeting.

"Trust you had a fruitful meeting with my son." It was a statement not a question.

Homer drank his beer. "Milo drives a hard bargain." He paused to lick the foam from his top lip. "He also assumes I have more influence than I can actually exert."

He stared hard at Cosmo. Friendship with these people, though generously offered, never came before business.

He trusted Cosmo without reservation. You can't share a prison cell with a man for twenty hours a day and not establish a common bond. But his son was a different generation, unencumbered by ties of loyalty beyond what his father requested.

Instinct told him that Milo would be difficult if he thought he wasn't getting his own way. It was hard to trust the younger man, a fact he guessed Cosmo wasn't beyond exploiting if it held a business advantage for him.

"Milo pushes hard. He only sees things in black and white." Cosmo answered the question implicit in Homer's words. "But he's not unreasonable; you're family, just do your best."

Uncharacteristically, Homer laughed. "You make it sound like some mafia heist, you old rogue."

Cosmo shrugged, trying hard not to smile. "Family always comes first; even before business." A soft lie, presented for the value of friendship.

"It seems that Milo believes that matters beyond my control are starting to ruffle feathers. How long do you need to complete this supposed transaction?"

Cosmo gazed into a space somewhere above Homer's head, pretending to look for an answer he already knew. "A month should cover it."

Homer made a derisive snort. "A week will be difficult enough to achieve where our troublemaker's concerned."

Cosmo shook his head. "You've got to do better than that. Three weeks minimum. And even that's tight."

"What? To sell a few packets of white powder?" Homer shook his head. "Ten days would be a stretch."

Cosmo returned his stare. "Try imagining a thousand packets. Takes time to shift that quantity."

"Not if there's only one buyer," Homer quipped back to him.

"Two weeks. Not a day less."

Reluctantly, Homer stretched out his hand. "I'll do my best," was all he could offer as they shook hands on a deal. "But you have to be aware that MI5 have been drawn into the situation. And they are something I definitely can't control."

Homer seldom saw his friend look surprised, but the mention of MI5 caught him unawares and made a rare exception.

Wailes had a man shed. In a metal locker bolted to the floor, he kept his shotgun and cartridges. Cleaning and oiling the gun was a ritual he performed with great reverence. The blue metal barrels gleamed and shone beneath the spotlight, the walnut stock varnished to a sheen, the breech darkened with fresh oil.

He stood back to admire his workmanship with a feeling of pride. In his stress filled life, the relationship with his gun brought Wailes peace, a mood that was abruptly interrupted by the demanding ringtone of his private phone. There was no ID, but he had been waiting for a call ever since PC James had reported what had happened to Allison Markham and one of the station cars. The fact that she was in one piece and still alive confirmed that their attempt to deal with the problem had failed.

Hesitantly, he pressed the green button. The voice was disguised. It had been pre-recorded, reverberating as though it had been recorded in a metal box.

"You have until tomorrow morning to resolve the problem. After that, the matter will pass on to someone who really doesn't want to be involved. If that happens, rest assured, things will work out very badly for you. You have until six tomorrow morning to deal with it once and for all."

The call ended abruptly. Wailes put the phone to one side. There remained one last option to eliminate the problem caused by the annoying Wright-Smith woman.

Distracted, he laid the shotgun in its cabinet, for once forgetting to lock the lid. He donned heavy duty gloves and goggles, grabbed a pair of tongs and walked to the glass aquarium in the corner of the shed. There was one thing that would deal with the troublesome Olwyn Wright-Smith, leaving neither evidence, nor trail, that could possibly lead back to him.

Olwyn stood in the shadows behind the bus shelter. It meant getting wet from the drizzle that had replaced the downpour of earlier in the day but she felt safer in the anonymity of darkness as she waited for Allison Markham. Her day had been turbulent enough without advertising her presence under the light of the shelter.

Despite the flippancy of his words, the warning had been implicit in what Jerry had told her. And now that wretched heap of a car he had given her would maroon Olwyn for an additional day at least. It really was all too much.

A small white car passed slowly on the opposite side of the road; it fitted the description Allison Markham had given Olwyn as she drove away in the battered police car.

Olwyn felt a profound feeling of trepidation as she stepped from the shadows into the light.

The inside of the car was warm. Something inconsequential played on the radio. Out of uniform, with her hair released, Allison Markham looked transformed. It was amazing the difference a peaked cap and a stab-proof jacket could make.

"Hungry?" was the first word that greeted Olwyn as she closed the door against the wet night.

"Starving." Olwyn hadn't eaten since breakfast and the normality of the ordinary world inside the car reminded her of just how empty she felt.

They drove in silence for several minutes during which Allison Markham regularly cast a nervous glance in her driving mirror.

"I've chosen a pub well away from the town, somewhere neither of us are likely to be recognised," she said.

"Amen to that."

"Can you remember most of what happened during your interview?"

"Fairly clearly," Olwyn replied with a note of hesitation.

Jerry's words had aroused her guard and despite their shared experience, she didn't completely trust Allison Markham.

Allison sensed her hesitation.

"Look, I only wanted to know what questions you asked and the answers your interviewees gave. It will have been recorded, so the more accurate the information you can give me, the better for both of us."

Allison paused and glanced sideways at Olwyn. "It doesn't have to be everything you tell your boss, just give me enough to keep my CSI happy and Wailes off my back."

Olwyn nodded and relaxed, her stomach grumbling noisily just as Allison turned from the main road into a sparsely lit pub car park.

Angela had a workroom; her kitchen. Unannounced, Homer let himself into the cottage and found her there, his entry eclipsed by the sound of Beethoven's fifth piano concerto playing on an aged CD player.

Unnoticed, he watched her for several minutes as her blotched and veined hands wove brown fabric around a wire frame in the form of an owl with wings outspread.

"There's coffee in the pot on the hotplate," Angela said without looking up from her work. "You're too early if you want this finished tonight."

Homer grunted. "Actually, don't rush. The weather forecast is awful for several days yet so we can't even test fly it until it improves."

He left the room, instinctively checking window locks as he moved around the house. You could never be too careful.

He had left Joss with Grace and felt somewhat lopsided without her. The continual wet weather played into his hands; with luck he could push back the date at which he next stirred the hornets' nest in the fracking site. Instead, he could concentrate on ridding himself of the ever dangerous presence of his troublemaking eco-warrior.

He returned to the kitchen and poured two mugs of coffee. Beethoven was approaching his finale so he sat in silence admiring the meticulous care with which Angela's hands worked as she hand sewed a fabric seam between the body and a wing.

"Will that carry our package?" he asked as the final cadence of music died away.

She regarded him over the rim of her glasses. "Would I question you on how you tickle trout or lure pheasants with your whistle?" she asked with the merest shadow of a smile on thin, pale lips.

Homer grinned and nodded. "Point taken."

She turned back to her work. "Any news on Marius?"

"We're meeting. A couple of days' time."

"Do you have a plan?"

He shrugged. "He's nineteen. After five years' absence, I doubt I can tell him what to do."

"If there's anything I can do ...?"

"You could try and persuade him to believe I'm not just a convicted criminal. It was the story my wife used to explain why I had to abandon them."

They sat in silence for a few minutes, Angela waiting for the real reason for his visit.

"There's something else."

Something in Homer's voice made Angela look up.

"That cretin, Houseman, who runs the office at '5', has sent us a complete novice to investigate the corpse we found in your ditch. Totally out of her depth, she's stirring things up with our 'friends' at the site, with predictable results."

"Surely she's Houseman's responsibility?"

"Fat lot of good that will do her. Houseman has a history of using people as human bait without regard for the consequences." The inflection in his voice was impossible to miss.

"And you think this woman could be in danger?" Uncharacteristically, Angela pricked her finger with the needle.

"I suspect someone tried to silence her today, and the policewoman she was with. No plates on an SUV but you don't need two guesses to know who they were."

"So?"

"We may need somewhere to hide her until we can get her out of the area."

Angela shot him a worried look.

"I had another 'house visit' while I was out today," Homer continued. "They must have known I wouldn't be there. Nothing smashed or stolen, but they turned over the entire place."

"And the woman, your eco-warrior?"

"She used the 'priest hole' in the chimney. Worked well, but it can't hold the MI5 woman as well."

Angela was thoughtful for a moment. "We have to do what we must do. Do you have a plan?"

"I'm still trying to contact her. Houseman gave me her number but she isn't answering. The woman doesn't seem particularly bright," he grumbled, "and it appears she has no idea of the danger she is in." The grumble had expanded to a tone of annoyance.

Angela smiled; this sounded like the normal Homer. "I'm sure you will work something out. You can hide her here if you have to."

Her simple statement put an end to things. Angela re-angled her worklamp and returned to the job in hand. There was nothing more to be said.

CHAPTER 24
AN APPRENTICE IN MANY GUISES

The pub bar was busy for a mid-week evening, so their conversation would be covered by the babble of conversation and bland music system. At least it guaranteed a measure of privacy.

Allison Markham withdrew a small laptop from her shoulder bag.

"You dictate, I'll type."

"Narrative or bullet points? I prefer the narrative," Olwyn proposed, taking a generous gulp from her wine glass.

"I'll take it down as it would be if you made a police statement. I can't pretend to have been there so it has to be in your own words. Keep it tight, just the questions you asked and the answers you received. I don't need speculation or any reading between the lines."

They waited twenty minutes for their dinner to arrive. In that time Olwyn was able to deliver the bones of her interviews. Twelve men, all of whom gave middle Eastern names, had presented themselves for a strict five-minute interview; twelve interviews that predictably followed exactly the same format.

They were all vague about their country of origin and when, or how, they had arrived in the UK. None could identify the face of the dead man or had noticed any member of staff missing in recent weeks. Most spoke limited English, all answered as if rehearsed from the same script. Which they probably had.

Olwyn had been given paper and a pen by the staff member who had chaperoned her from the gates to the interview room. The only notes she made were the names of the men she had interviewed, to each of which she had given a number. It made it easier to memorise individual mannerisms.

Some were plainly scared out of their wits; others more guarded, avoiding any form of eye contact with her, especially when appraising the photograph she showed them. There was much she didn't tell Allison, much that fell outside the facts or what was recorded on those inevitable hidden cameras.

A natural break arose when a tall, languid waiter arrived with their meals. He showed little interest in either of them, or his job for that matter. Perhaps it was a defence mechanism. He might have sensed the presence of police; on or off duty Allison was always a policewoman, the job creating an aura no one completely ever threw off.

"Are you married?"

Hungry, they started eating, leaving conversation to return to normality. A woman's interest in another's personal life is eternal and Allison was curious to know more about Olwyn who sat opposite her.

Olwyn shook her head, holding up her left hand in contradiction. A gold ring shone on her third finger.

"Professional protection; it's my grandmother's; prevents nuisance attention."

Allison nodded with the smile of an accomplice.

"And you?" Olwyn asked.

Allison shook her head. "My shifts ruin a personal life. And I don't fancy marrying another copper."

"And today? What was that about?" Olwyn asked uncertainly, aware she was drinking more quickly than she intended. "We were in a police car."

"Not that it would make any difference," Allison said with resignation. "All the top police appointments are now made with the collusion of 'Blue Horizon'."

She exercised her frustration on the steak on her plate. "Running the Home Office was one of their conditions when they 'lent' the government their support. Now we cross their 'red lines' at our peril."

"One of which is …?"

"Fracking sites. In practice they're off-limits, even to us," Allison said, chewing aggressively.

"The Landrover that pulled out in front of us?" Olwyn floated the question, curious to see how Allison would react.

"Part of the set-up, aimed at trapping us between them."

"It's just that I thought I had seen the driver before; perhaps someone from around the town."

"Quite possible. Half of the town are in Bremer's pocket one way or another. Most people living here wouldn't trust their own shadow half the time."

Allison leaned back in her chair, watching Olwyn while she sipped from her glass.

"And you? How many people would you trust in this place?"

"Fair comment."

Olwyn reflected silently on the games Jerry played with her, along with the manipulations of many other men who had crossed her path. At least this nameless woodsman she kept running into was consistent, doing nothing to hide his contempt for her abilities.

Allison didn't take her question any further, so Olwyn let it drop. It might be better not to mention that she thought the Landrover may have deliberately blocked the path of the raging SUV or that the crude one-finger gesture hadn't been directed at them.

Together, they concocted her statement into a form that would satisfy Wailes and DI Amos. Olwyn signed it electronically and Allison emailed her a copy.

"Do you think that Wailes knows what happened to us on that forest road?"

"Not before it happened, that was something spontaneous, but it was known about within minutes of our escape from their trap."

Allison stared directly into Olwyn's eyes. "You're probing into a sensitive area here and you seem to have hit a raw nerve."

She leaned forwards, placing her hand over Olwyn's. "If you want my advice, I wouldn't sleep alone tonight."

It was a gesture you could take two ways; either genuine concern or a side to Allison's character Olwyn hadn't expected. She smiled, not immediately removing her hand.

"A nice thought, but I snore loudly and besides, I have to complete my version of the report for my boss before the morning. I'll need to work late."

It was a 'some other time' push-off. A flash of disappointment crossed Allison's face when Olwyn slid her hand from beneath hers.

Homer donned his wax jacket and prepared to leave. They had shared the cottage in mutual silence while he brooded over his plan and Angela glued and stitched the kite to its wire frame.

"Does it ever occur to you that we know next to nothing about this woman?" Angela said without looking up as Homer moved towards the door.

He turned slowly, showing an expression that suggested the thought hadn't occurred to him.

"Grace turns up alone, at random times, usually in some scrape or another; you don't really know who on earth she is or what organisation she's associated with. She could be an under cover agent for Bremer for all you know."

Homer laughed. "I very much doubt that. Anyway, I'm on the side of anyone who is opposed to Bremer. I would remind you, knowledge is a dangerous thing. Sometimes it's safer not to see too much."

Angela carried on stitching. "Reminds me of Syria and Iraq."

"Ours is not to reason why."

"Fine mess that got us into." The irony in Angela's voice couldn't be missed.

"Would the 'knowing' have changed anything?" For once Homer spoke with a soft perceptive tone.

Angela looked up from her needlework. "I might have left earlier if I had realised the full implications of staying."

He turned towards her, a soft smile, or was it resignation, on his face.

"I suspect the outcome would have always been the same. You were too busy trying to save everyone for things to have worked out any differently."

Homer turned away, his hand on the door latch, not wanting Angela to read his emotions.

"All the same, find out more about this cuckoo who keeps intruding into your life. She just might not be who you think she is."

Angela felt the gust of chilled air enter the room as Homer closed the door firmly behind him.

Homer was late. Still, I had Joss for company which eased the passing hours. I re-assembled most of the kitchen and collected scattered books and personal items into piles for Homer to sort out. Nothing appeared damaged but all was chaos, everything scattered as if by a raging wind, and no one to be held to account.

The cameras Homer had installed had recorded the arrival of a four-by-four without a registration number, and five black clothed, masked men, wearing gloves. Not that it mattered; the police wouldn't be interested unless anyone had been hurt, and even then it would amount to no more than files and reports jammed in a legal and judiciary system overwhelmed by cutbacks and closure.

Time hung heavily on my shoulders. It had been dark for some hours when I decided to venture out for some fresh air, taking Joss with me in case anyone was about. Homer's strict instructions had been to remain hidden within the walls of my attic room, but that meant accepting a form of imposed house arrest, like a silent curfew imposed by 'Blue Horizon' on everyone living in proximity to a fracking site.

Homer's cottage was surrounded by woods on all sides, creating pools of deeper night shadow amidst the darkness. There was a time when it would have threatened me. Now it meant camouflage and safety. I had learnt to move in the shadows; from Homer I was learning the art of invisibility in plain sight.

Walking amongst the trees, I had just started my second circuit around the cottage. Joss was nowhere to be seen, but then, she was better camouflage than my eyes could register and was probably out there somewhere, close by, teasing a rabbit or spooking a pheasant.

I wondered if Homer would suspect I had been out here in the woods? He had a number of concealed cameras in the surrounding area, each triggered by movement. He had given specific instructions that I should only release Joss if the need arose and in no circumstances take the risk of venturing outside alone myself. Well, that was all well and good, but I still reserved the right to make my own judgements, with or without his permission.

About halfway around my circuit, I heard a sound, unlike any other in the soft concerto of the night, pitched somewhere between a whine and a whimper.

"Joss?" I called.

Almost in answer, the sound came again, this time underdrawn with … pain … fear?

"Joss? Where are you?"

Where was the dog? Trees played tricks with sound, but it felt as though it came from behind me, deeper amongst the trees.

"Joss?" I repeated, trying to home in on her voice.

The dog responded again, farther off this time. I had turned the wrong way.

I retraced my steps, calling again. After a few seco nds, I heard heragain, closer, more anxious by its pitch. I took a fix on the only light illuminating the cottage and side-stepped deeper into the woods.

With only the sound of her whining, and the dim light of the torch on my phone, it took another five minutes to find her, half standing, twisted, tugging urgently at her front leg.

I had never seen a wire gin trap before, a single noose on a slip knot pulled ever tighter as an animal panicked. Poacher though he might be, I knew instinctively that Homer abhorred such cruelty, using nets or humane traps before despatching his prey painlessly.

Who could possibly have set such a thing? The question surged through my brain as I knelt beside Joss, making instinctive, sympathetic noises to calm her. The dog knew she was trapped and was fighting desperately to free herself, biting furiously at the restricting noose that was already embedded deep into her flesh just above the elbow of her right front leg. Without cutting the wire, there was no way the wire could be drawn over the jutting bone of the joint.

My first priority was to calm Joss, stop her panicking, which was drawing the snare ever tighter. Panting, I could see her bright eyes glimmer expectantly in the light of my torch as I searched urgently through my pockets for the penknife that I already suspected I had left behind in the cottage.

"Idiot," I cursed myself in vain. It was nowhere to be found.

Joss squirmed in pain. The next whimper was heartbreaking. If I had to leave her to find something to cut the snare, how on earth would I convey, 'Don't worry, I'll be back in a few minutes.'

"Bastard."

I threw the word into the night, cursing whoever had set this evil thing. Every time I moved, Joss moved in unison, by her gesture asking me not to leave her. Keeping one hand pinned against her flank, I desperately searched for the other end of the wire. If I could release it, I could carry Joss back to the cottage and cut the snare in the kitchen.

But they had been clever. I found another noose at the opposite end, looped and pulled tight around a sapling, stout enough to need a saw to cut through. It was beginning to look as though leaving Joss might be the only way to release her.

Abstractedly, my spare hand felt its way along my belt. A canvas pouch rested against my right hip, containing the small first aid kit that travelled everywhere with me. Inside, I found scissors. Tiny ones, meant for cutting tape and *gauze, but if I worked carefully I might just saw through the wire, at least enough to break it with my hands.*

It took ten minutes of scouring and rotating the blades around the wire before the scissors snapped. The wire was hardened, not intended for easy cutting. I now needed both hands to try to snap the wire, but the moment I took away the reassurance of my hand, Joss struggled to stand.

I replaced my hand with my knee. Intuitively, Joss seemed to get the message and lay still. It took ten more minutes. In desperation I kept bending the wire at the point I had scored it, until, with a sudden scream of frustration, I snapped it.

CHAPTER 25
A STING IN THE TAIL

"Be sure you leave town tomorrow. It's not safe for you here alone."

They had been Allison's final words as she dropped Olwyn a short distance from her hotel. Whether her words were motivated by genuine concern or disappointment, Olwyn wasn't sure.

Jerry had told her that 'Gladys', the Jaguar, now wouldn't be ready to drive the following day. Someone obviously wanted to keep her in town. The question that loomed large in her mind was 'why'?

She checked her phone. Another missed call, this time from an unidentified mobile number. It seemed that 'mystery man' was still intent on harassing her. If their paths ever crossed again she would be sure to tell him what she thought about that.

The night manager wasn't at the reception desk when Olwyn returned to the hotel. Not that it mattered; she had taken the card lock to her room when she had left earlier. She pressed the lift call button, changed her mind, and opted for the stairs. As she wound her way to the fifth floor, she distractedly began to wonder why she had made that choice.

Her room was as she had left it. She switched off all but the bedside lights and partially opened the curtains to lift the shadow of claustrophobia that sometimes haunted her nights alone. She was tired, but there were things she needed to add to the report that she had not shared with Allison. Just in case.

Why had she thought that? She felt a shudder pass through her. Her mother had often used the term that 'someone had just walked over my grave'. Strange that the idiom had suddenly returned over the passage of the years. For company, she switched on the television. Perhaps flickering images without sound would ward off any demons.

Olwyn spent the next hour adding supplementary notes to the report she had prepared with Allison. As far as it went it had been factually correct, but the devil would be in the detail, for which she slowly trawled her memory.

The interviewees had given her names and places of origin that were undoubtedly fake, all claiming to have been born in Europe. Instead, Olwyn had given them individual numbers, using unique features to identify each one. From their scars and disfigurements, most had experienced a hard life, which they were not prepared to divulge. All wore elastic cuffs around their left wrist. She wondered what they had hidden.

Three of the group appeared in worse physical condition than the others; they had tired eyes and listless, jaundiced faces partially concealed by peaked caps. With dense black beards, little of their facial features were visible, but Olwyn noticed many livid red blotches on their hands.

The obvious question, "Where did you receive those injuries?" was answered with a shrug of the shoulders or a thickly accented, "I don't know."

There had been one exception. Eleven of the twelve men she had interviewed had avoided any form of eye contact, especially when she showed them the photo of the dead man. Frightened, bored or pretending to misunderstand her questions, all feigned a poor command of English. Her hour of interrogation had produced a predictably blank response.

Until the last man was about to leave.

Evasive as all the others, he seemed more alert, with a better command of English. As he stood from the desk, he appeared to accidentally catch his cap, raising the peak, his dark eyes attentive, signalling. What?

On impulse, he held out his hand in a gesture of courtesy. Surprised, without thinking, Olwyn found her hand returning his grasp.

"Is pleasure to meet you."

He looked at their joined hands, nodded and withdrew, leaving the room without a backward glance as Olwyn closed her hand, dropping her arm to her side. There was a post-it note stuck to her palm.

Now, sitting with her laptop open in front of her, she unpeeled the piece of coloured paper. It bore a single line message in English.

We all have radiation sickness. Help us.

Confused, she stared at the words for several minutes. They worked on a fracking site for goodness sake. So what the hell did that mean?

I had never before considered the prospect of hugging a snoring dog. Now, amidst my ever changing world, it seemed a very natural thing to do.

With the snare still caught around her leg, I carried Joss back to the cottage. Though she was a small dog, her coat now soaked by the incessant rain made her much heavier, and I was quite breathless by the time I re-entered the kitchen.

As I nudged open the kitchen door, part of me hoped I would find Homer had returned. It would have been worth enduring his scorn to have the benefit of his expertise with dogs. I guessed my mistimed venture outside would not sit well with him, but at that very moment, my main concern was for Joss.

But the cottage was empty, so the task of trying to remove the wire noose fell to me. As I towelled off her soaked fur Joss immediately began worrying her wounded leg. With the wire embedded in her flesh, it was hard to see how either of us was going to find an easy solution.

Leaving the dog to steam in the warmth of the range, I started hunting through the toolbox Homer kept on the floor in the pantry. Most of the contents were heavy duty, but I found a small tin which contained some delicate instruments. Rust stained by age and time, they might have belonged to a watch or instrument maker at some time in the distant past.

I peered again at the snare. Most of the circumference of the noose was lost in the red flesh of the wound. Cutting the wire would be tricky; how do you rationalise with a distressed animal? 'This is going to hurt you far more than it will hurt me,' is all very well in films. In the real world, I didn't give much for my chances.

The sensible answer was to wait for Homer (who was already very late) to return, and hope he had a friendly vet to call upon. But what if he didn't come back for hours or even the next day? How long would it be before infection set in and Joss ended up losing her leg?

I very soon learnt that dogs can give you a look of great expectation; that look that says, 'You're supposed to be the clever one here; do something about it.'

I rummaged back through the box of instruments, finding tiny files, blades, screwdrivers and lenses; nothing of particular use to cut a wire gin trap. Hidden at the bottom of the box was a tiny pair of snips. Not much use for attacking the wire in her flesh, but a few millimetres of wire lay exposed at the slip knot. It would undoubtedly cause Joss pain, but there might just be enough clearance if I could squeeze a blade of the snips beneath the knot.

I'll say one thing for Joss; she's tough. Several times she snatched her paw away from me, grumbling deep in her throat from the pain of my probing. With her upper leg wedged beneath my arm, we worked together and I managed to twist the snips into position without entering the wound.

My fingers were slippery with her blood, but there could be no holding back. It took a dozen attempts, followed by a gasp of triumph and the broken ends sprang apart, releasing her paw from the rusty noose that might well have killed her.

You get no thanks from a dog. Joss skulked into the darkest corner of the room and spent the next hour licking her damaged leg. I contemplated cleaning and dressing the wound and in the end decided to leave that to the dog, or Homer, when, he finally returned.

Wailes was pleased with himself as he paid off Hansen, the hotel night manager. It was the easiest back-hander Hansen had ever earned.

But then, when the local police sergeant offers you a hundred pounds to turn off the CCTV on the second floor of the hotel, saying, "If you know what's good for you, you'll disappear for half an hour," you don't ask questions. Especially when the involvement of 'others' are concerned.

Hansen didn't need two guesses to know that meant security staff from the fracking site. It was far safer to look the other way to prevent your facial features from becoming permanently re-arranged.

It was easy to track PC Markham; Wailes had cloned the phones of everyone who worked for him and could watch her drive into town. Hansen confirmed the timing coincided with the Wright-Smith woman leaving the hotel and after the events of the afternoon, Wailes was certain the pair would spend the evening together.

It all left ample space for his simple plan; in less than ten minutes it was all set up, leaving plenty of time for a second whisky at *The George* on the other side of town where the compliant publican would vouch that Wailes had spent the entire evening sitting alone at his bar, drinking single malt.

With a tired yawn, Olwyn clicked the send button on her laptop. It had taken longer to complete her report than she had anticipated, but finished, at last, it was now locked away on Jerry's server. In the morning, he could make his own conclusions of what she had discovered, including the attempt to run her off the road as she had returned with Allison Markham.

"Make what you will of that," she muttered to her laptop as the encryption web site finally shut down.

As Olwyn used the bathroom she contemplated the stilled silence of the hotel. Business was slow in mid-week rural Sussex, and the rooms around her were all empty. For a moment she felt a sense of loneliness.

The pass Allison had made had both flattered and surprised her. On another day, with a few more glasses of wine inside her, she might have made a different choice. Now, the only company to share her bed was a fleeting fantasy and the thought for what might have been.

Abstracted, Olwyn set her phone to charge on the table close to the bed. Energised, the phone flashed a missed call; the same unidentified number that had rung earlier in the evening. Obviously it was the 'wild man from the woods' to whom Jerry had said he had given her number.

Her finger hovered above the 'block this number' icon. Yet something made her hesitate. But no; next time it rang, she would continue to leave it unanswered. If he tried enough times he would surely get bored and leave her alone.

Yawning, she slid between fresh Egyptian cotton sheets that crinkled and crackled against her naked body. She preferred sleeping in the nude, especially with the feel of freshly laundered bed linen. Squirming at the sensation, she momentarily regretted not taking up Allison's offer. Olwyn didn't particularly enjoy the prospect of sleeping alone, with only fantasy for company.

Despite her disappointment, sleep arrived quickly. Within seconds she felt the first waves of drowsiness sweep over her. The bed was deliciously comfortable, with or without someone else to share it.

Drowsy, a fleeting, mischievous thought flashed through her mind as she wondered if Allison wore regulation police knickers in bed. It left a smile playing on her lips as she fell into the arms of sleep.

A few moments later, something stroked the back of her thigh. And it wasn't Allison Markham.

CHAPTER 26
THE PRICE OF NAKED FEAR

I'm not sure why I chose to tell my story to the dog. Everyone in my action group had been trained to work in isolation. In the event that we were caught, the true purpose of our missions couldn't be extracted from any one individual. Each group or cell worked like a broken mirror; you needed to join all the pieces together in perfect sequence to obtain a true reflection of what we had planned.

Somehow, telling Joss felt different. It was as though the shared experience of the past hour created a bond of confidence between us that couldn't be shared with others.

Once the trauma of her injury had abated, Joss crept from the corner of the kitchen to warm her wet body in front of the fire I had lit in what Homer used as a living room and study. I felt certain he would be far from pleased when he finally arrived home but I was as soaked through as Joss and for once the need for warmth overwhelmed the need to hide from a surprise visit.

I left my outer clothing to dry over the kitchen range while I joined Joss and sat cross-legged on a rug in front of the fire beside her. She lay with her head between her paws, forehead furrowed, occasionally licking her injured leg.

"So, have you guessed my secrets?"

Large, liquid eyes blinked in response to my words. Still panting slightly, Joss turned her head to one side, as though debating my question in her mind.

"Do I tell him? You know as well as I do that Homer might not believe the truth even if I tried to explain it."

Joss whimpered slightly, the notes floating above the soft sound of her panting. I grinned.

"I'll take that as agreement. I think you've guessed something hangs over me, so shall I share my life story with you?"

As if in response, the dog shuffled closer.

"That sounds positive. I don't think you'll be too surprised."

Joss adjusted her position, resting her chin on my leg, her eyes locked on mine in rapt attention. I threw another log onto the fire and cleared my throat. The story would take a while in the telling. Cathartic? Well, it beats only ever talking to yourself; thereby lies madness.

With my audience of one, I embarked on my story. Some might find it difficult to believe but devoted Joss neither interrupted nor judged me as my journey unfolded. Perhaps I rambled, went on for too long, for eventually we both drifted into sleep on the rug in front of the fire.

Homer yawned, staring at the lagoon that now filled the lane in front of him. After more than a hundred days of the summer drought, it now rained in almost biblical proportions. Bone weary, his thoughts returned to the warning Angela had given him.

At first he had been inclined to dismiss her concerns, but as time passed and tiredness provoked his peace of mind, Homer became irritable and ill at ease. He decided to clear the uncertainty once and for all and demand the truth the moment Grace awoke in the morning.

He had driven halfway through the flooded road when his phone rang. He glanced at the number. It was the annoyingly incompetent woman who Jerry Houseman had sent, who couldn't be bothered to answer his calls when he rang her. Too bad; she would have to wait until the morning.

By the time the Landrover crawled clear of the muddy water, his phone was ringing for the fourth time.

'Persistent,' he grumbled to himself, affronted by her demand for attention at a time that suited her.

"What?" Homer barked into the phone.

There was a pause, accompanied by the sound of heavy breathing.

"There's a scorpion loose in my room. Someone put it in my bed." A tremor in her voice betrayed her attempt to sound matter of fact.

Homer burst out laughing. "You're kidding me. It's likely to be no more than a harvest spider. Go back to sleep and stop bothering me."

"Try four inches long, black, with a sickle tail and huge front pinchers." Olwyn hesitated, gasping for breath.

"It was in my bed. Someone's been in my room while I was out. They've put this disgusting thing in my bed," she repeated, anguish clear in her voice, blending fear and effrontery in equal measure.

"Scorpions aren't native to rural Sussex. Have you been drinking? I suggest …" Sarcasm laced his words only for Olwyn to interrupt him.

"You don't have to be stone cold sober to recognise a scorpion. This one was in my bed with me," she repeated. Was he really so dim he had to be told countless times to accept the point? With a shudder she added, "It stroked the back of my leg."

"Are you sure?" He was still laughing.

"I don't recall that scorpions are particularly touchy-feely. Did you actually see it, or did you just feel what you thought might be a scorpion?" Homer still sounded sceptical.

"I saw it alright. The thing chased me across the bed with its tail extended. I only leapt clear because the vile thing snagged in a fold in the sheet. That was no harvest spider. It must have been put there by the same people who tried to kill me and the policewoman this afternoon."

"Ah, your little disagreement in the forest." He still refused to take her seriously.

"They would have driven us off the road if you hadn't carelessly driven in front of us without looking."

"Serves you right," Homer said reproachfully.

"It may have escaped your notice, but I've been sent here with a job to do."

"So your idiot of a boss tells me."

"Look, are we going to argue all night? There's a scorpion loose in my room and I need help. Besides, you told my boss that you needed to speak to me; something about needing a favour?" Olwyn said.

He ignored her. "You could try ringing the night desk in the hotel. Let them come and deal with your problem."

"I've tried. They're not answering. Besides …"

"You think they might be colluding with whoever planted this supposed scorpion in your room."

Homer was silent for a moment. "Where had you been this afternoon when I interrupted your little drama on the forest road?"

"Interviewing staff at the fracking site. And it wasn't a little drama as you call it. Whoever it was wrote off a police car in the process."

"Were the interviews with Bremer's permission?" Homer asked incredulously.

"I had a warrant. They gave me access. Reluctantly, and only then with the help of Allison Markham."

"So obviously someone didn't intend you to get very far with the information you had been given." Homer sighed in resignation. "Is your door locked?"

"What? Yes, of course it is." Olwyn found it hard to hide her irritation at the continued rudeness of this man.

"And where are you?"

"Me? Sitting on a table holding a shoe in case the evil thing comes after me again."

Homer thought for a moment. "Okay. Don't ring reception again. They'll probably ignore you anyway, waiting for the scorpion to do what scorpions do."

"Which is what, exactly?"

"If your description is accurate, sting you. Fatally." He sounded as though he was enjoying this. "Can you unlock the door when I get there?"

"Not a chance. I'm not getting off this table while that thing is loose," she replied indignantly.

Homer sighed again. "What floor are you on?" he asked tetchily.

"The second. The room with a small balcony on the side gable. It was supposed to be quieter here; no road noise they told me."

"Just scorpions instead," he added mockingly, "Is there an open window?"

"Yes," Olwyn answered, uncertainly. "Why?"

Homer ignored her question. "You haven't got a gun by any chance?"

"Gun? Me? I'm just a clerk, not a spook."

"So it seems. I just needed to check, so you don't shoot me when I climb through the window."

In the background, Olwyn heard the starting rattle of an engine as it suddenly accelerated.

"Stay where you are. If the scorpion comes after you, flick it away with your shoe, don't try to kill it. You won't succeed and, if it's not already, you'll make it really mad. If it's the type of scorpion I think it might be, trust me, you really don't want to do that."

Olwyn was certain she heard Homer laughing as he rang off.

Sitting naked on a table, Olwyn spent an endless half-hour imagining shadows moving in the dark recesses of the room. She was growing colder by the minute; tantalisingly beyond her reach, her gown and vest top lay draped over the back of a chair. It left the prospect of shivering from the cold as the best, worse option.

In the blur of leaping from her bed, Olwyn thought she had seen more than one scorpion. As the minutes ticked by, she was now convinced they were surrounding her, sickle-tails quivering, filled with venom intended for her pale, quivering body.

Amidst the room haunted by shadows, she jumped at the sound of a dull thud. Curtains billowed and torchlight lit the darkened room. Dressed in dark clothing, the 'wild man from the woods' levered himself from the floor. The amusing thought crossed her mind that all he needed was a box of Black Magic chocolates to complete the scene, though he had none of the panache.

Sweeping the room, the torch came to rest on her naked form, one arm protecting her breasts, her other hand imitating a fig leaf. At first glance Olwyn resembled a reclining Renaissance nude as she squinted into the beam of light.

"My, my, I've seen some sights," Homer said, seized by laughter at her circumstance.

"Not funny," she said sulkily. "Pass me my gown from that chair, and make sure there's nothing hiding inside it."

To be fair, before turning on the lights, Homer waited while Olwyn wrapped herself in her gown, an act that precariously rocked the table from side to side. He donned thick gloves, his face holding a lightly amused expression as she struggled to cover herself.

"You could have looked the other way," she said in mock indignation.

"What, and miss the ridiculous sight of you squirming to dress on a table far too small for even a desk lamp." He shook his head, barely concealing his laughter.

Affronted, she gave him a challenging look. "It's huge, and fast. I hope you've brought something to kill it with. It can't have escaped from the room so it must be lurking somewhere in here, perhaps under the bed."

"It's not the scorpion's fault that it ended up sharing your bed. The experience probably gave it the fright of its life."

Homer delved into his rucksack and came out with a pair of long handled tongs and a small plastic bait box that smelt bad when he lifted the lid.

"You intend to catch it? You must be mad. You said it was highly poisonous," Olwyn said incredulously.

"If it's *Androctonus crassicauda* it's lethal, actually. I once shared a foxhole with one. An interesting experience; not one I'd recommended," he said in a reflective voice.

"You can climb off the table if you like and stop looking ridiculous," he said, sweeping the floor with his gaze. The scorpion was nowhere to be seen.

"Why not just kill it and have done with it. Surely any sane person would do that," Olwyn replied, refusing to move from the table top.

"As I said, it's not the scorpion's fault. Besides, I think we should return it to its owner."

His words were either mischievous or malicious, she couldn't be certain which, but his face still held an amused grin.

Homer spent the next five minutes combing every possible hiding place in the room. It looked to be a fruitless search, until,

"Gotcha."

He flicked the window drapes and a large, segmented body scurried into the folds of the fabric, just above head height. Sensing his presence, or alarmed at the shake of the curtain, the scorpion dropped to the floor and ran between Homer's legs, making a direct line towards Olwyn, cowering terrified on the table. They were lucky that most of the hotel rooms were empty; the scream she emitted was so piercing it would have awakened the dead in the graveyard opposite.

Had she wondered what use he had with her towel hanging in his left hand, the purpose arrived with a flourish of a matador. As the scorpion sped past him, Homer spun on his heels and flung the towel in a spiralling arc. Suddenly enclosed under a cotton blanket, the source of Olwyn's worst nightmare stopped dead.

Moving with the ease of the poacher he was, Homer used his long handled tongs to extract the writhing, black body, dropping it expertly into the plastic box before securing the lid. The angry scorpion furiously charged the sides and lid in a vain effort to escape.

Olwyn shuddered when Homer held out the box to her, curiously watching the scorpion barge around in its plastic prison with frantic energy.

"An Arabian fat tail." He cast a raised eyed glance in Olwyn's direction. "I would say you're lucky to still be alive."

Unsurprisingly, his tone brought her little comfort.

CHAPTER 27
IN THE GUISE OF DUNKIRK

It still took a lot of persuasion to entice Olwyn to leave her refuge on the table. Homer placed the box containing the scorpion on the floor and sat cross-legged beside it, withdrawing a battered hip flask from his pocket.

He gestured to Olwyn, still trembling, to join him. Reluctantly, she climbed down from her roost on the table. He removed the cap and passed the flask to her.

"Strictly medicinal purposes only. Take it gently, it has a powerful kick."

Ignoring his warning, Olwyn took a deep swig, coughing and spluttering as the fiery liquid set light to her throat.

"What on earth is that?" she asked, eyes watering in a grimacing face.

"Brandy. Made by a friend." He looked at her mischievously. "There are some who think she's a witch."

Homer took the flask back and took a more cautious sip.

"Recuperative on matters relating to scorpions," he said, nodding towards the box between them.

"Here's to avoiding the third time." Homer took a deeper drag on the flask.

"Third time?"

"Yep. Don't they say something about third time lucky? From where I'm sitting, someone has made two determined efforts to kill you today. Might be wise to avoid their third attempt, just in case."

She knew he was mocking her. She snatched back the flask and took another swig.

"Let's try to set this on a better footing," she said, her voice hoarse from the effects of the brandy.

"My name is Olwyn Wright-Smith. You know who I work for. And your name is?"

Despite his persistent rudeness, something about him was intriguing; maybe he had hidden secrets.

"Homer will do."

He took back the flask before she knocked herself out on the contents. "You sound posh. No wonder you're not having much luck with the local inhabitants."

"And that warrants trying to kill me?"

Homer raised a sceptical eyebrow. "It's best to choose your friends carefully in these parts."

"Murder isn't socially exclusive," Olwyn replied. "Or is it a custom here to kill people merely because of their names?"

He stared at her impassively.

"Trust me, they tend to over-react for far less than that. Especially when people like you start to stick their noses into their business."

As if to emphasise a point, the scorpion vigorously attacked the sides of its box. Disconcerted, Olwyn looked sideways at him.

"Then why are you helping me?"

It was a good question. For a second, a cloud passed across Homer's face. Perhaps her words released a memory from some distant recess.

"You're an amateur playing a lethal game in which the players can make an art form out of being unpleasant. People like you," he continued pointedly, "posh or otherwise, by their haphazard actions, tend to get others hurt as they flounder around in something they don't understand. Helping you, if that's what you think I'm doing, is more self-protection than protecting your skin."

"Nice to know I'm valued," Olwyn said, sarcastically.

"I didn't invite you here," he reminded her.

"No? And there was me, just for one moment, thinking it might have been you who sent us the photo of the dead man I found in the woods. That's what brought me here."

Homer's face remained expressionless but his eyes blinked rapidly for a second as he processed her rebuke. If she expected a rebuttal, it never arrived. Instead, with a softening grin, Homer nudged the plastic prison box of the scorpion.

"We ought to give her a name."

"Who said it's female?" Olwyn retorted.

He continued, smiling, "With a temper like that, it has to be female. Besides, a male would have stung you straight off and saved himself all this trouble."

"Touché," she said retrieving the flask. "We'll christen her 'Scorpio'. But beware, that if my history is correct, she killed Orion the hunter to stop him from killing all the animals in the forest. Perhaps you'd better watch out the next time you open that box."

She raised the flask and drank a toast to 'Scorpio'.

For the benefit of the CCTV cameras, Homer carried Olwyn through the hotel lobby and out into the darkness of the car park.

The intention of planting the scorpion in her bed had been to prevent Olwyn reporting on anything she might have learnt from her interviews, permanently stopping her with a technique practically impossible to trace.

"As they intended to kill you, it's best we continue with that idea. How good are you at playing dead?"

Olwyn gave her first smile in some time. It sounded an easier role than the previous one she had used to try to work her way around the obdurate Sergeant Wailes.

They had to move with haste. Homer had described, in explicit details, the speed with which the scorpion's sting would immobilise the body. The intentions of whoever had planted the scorpion was plainly obvious and they were bound to return to the scene of their crime within minutes.

"They would come for good measure, just to finish you off," Homer stated with a wicked smile on his face.

It took only a few minutes to fashion the bedroom as a scene of high drama; furniture knocked awry, bed clothes leading a path to the bathroom, water glass tipped over, tablets spilled across the floor.

"There's no time for anything more; we'll leave the rest to the imagination."

Olwyn nodded. At this rate, Homer could have a bright future as a set director.

"How much do you weigh?" he asked her.

"About fifty kilos," she fibbed.

Homer raised his eyebrows, mentally adding at least another five.

"Okay. Let the drama begin," he said, pitching Olwyn over his shoulder; the best way to carry a 'limp and lifeless' body was in a fireman's lift.

He heard Olwyn laugh softly as he pitched her over his bony shoulder.

"Quiet," he hissed. "Dead bodies don't make a noise."

If this charade fooled anyone, it would be a miracle.

As he had suspected, the night manager was still absent from his desk. He had probably 'disappeared' the moment he heard the lift start to descend. Despite that, Homer felt hidden eyes follow them as they crossed the lobby, Homer with his cap pulled down tight above his eyes, Olwyn slumped limply over his shoulder, desperately resisting the urge to giggle.

"Our best chance is to convince them the scorpion has done her work," Homer had told her as they were about to leave the hotel room.

"Won't your sudden appearance confuse that impression?" she had reminded him just as they set out. "Remember, no one saw you enter the hotel."

Homer just shrugged. "By the time they find out that I'm not an agent of MI5, you'll be no more than a distant memory."

Olwyn hadn't been sure what he meant by that remark.

It had seemed a good plan, probably the only plan, but he hadn't anticipated the effort required to carry her.

'Fifty kilos,' he thought, drawing breath through clenched teeth. 'Try nearer seventy.'

As the automatic exit doors slid closed behind them, Homer had barely time to whisper, "press the button," before he dropped her legs to the ground in the hope that the jamming device he had handed her would protect their escape.

"Will it work?" Olwyn whispered, while they stood concealed in a patch of deep night shadow, hidden beside the front of the building.

Homer found his night scope and checked the CCTV cameras, one by one, in the car park.

"Judging from the flashing red lights, we've scrambled all of them," he said with a note of satisfaction.

He swung the rucksack containing 'Scorpio' from his back and handed it to Olwyn. He was winded by his journey with her over his shoulder. She could carry his rucksack while he regained his breath. If she was going to make a habit of this, she was going to have to lose weight.

"You take this. Follow me and stay close. Don't try to wander off," he warned.

He left without waiting for her reply, leaving her to trail in his wake with the rucksack held at arm's length, the thought of carrying the scorpion on her back, albeit secured in a box, too much of a reminder of her encounter in her bed.

Homer chose a route that followed the shadows thrown by the orange glow of neon street lights, finally ascending a steep muddy bank into the cover of the surrounding vegetation. In the dense undercover, Olwyn tripped on roots only to find herself lying prone with the rucksack now underneath her. Squashed against her abdomen, she felt disconcerted vibrations caused by 'Scorpio' charging the walls of her plastic prison.

The involuntary shriek she emitted more resembled the call of an overflying owl, and so avoided the worst of Homer's silent, disparaging gesture. He had hissed her to be silent with ill-concealed grace, yet in contradiction, offered a hand to help her to her feet with surprising grace.

"In future, place your feet in my steps. Perhaps that way you won't fall over." As ever, his words spiralled, a hint of annoyance lacing his tone.

"Wait." Whether from fear or insult, the flame of independence had returned to Olwyn.

"I've had more than enough close shaves for one day. I want to know where we're going and what's the plan. I'm not taking a step farther until you tell me."

"What? Now? Here?" he demanded incredulously.

"Yes, now. If not, I'll take my chances on my own."

"You can't be serious? How long do you think you'll last out here alone?"

"I have options," she replied, more precociously than she intended.

"Like you did in your hotel room."

"I'll muddle through. And anyway, I could have dealt with the scorpion if it had tried to attack me," she added, folding her arms, making a clear signal of obstinacy.

"I doubt it," he replied with a snort of derision. "More than likely it would have stung you first."

Frustrated, Homer snatched the rucksack and turned his back, determined to leave her if she carried on like this.

"You're not moving until you answer a question," she said to his departing back.

Reluctantly, he paused.

"Which is?" He half turned in her direction.

"The favour you've wanted from me," she said, sounding decidedly petulant. "Or has your misogyny caused amnesia?" she said with a bite.

Homer was speechless for a moment. Houseman had obviously repeated his request to Olwyn. He had hoped Houseman had told her to cooperate.

"There's a woman staying with me. A complete pain in the backside, like you," Homer grumbled. "She seems driven by some crazy death wish to break in to the fracking site in complete disregard for the danger, not only to herself, but me also. I need you to tell her what you found out from your visit to the fracking site."

"Is that all?" Olwyn replied.

"No. That's just the easy bit. I then need you to spirit her out of here when you leave. Judging by the mess you've both managed to stir up, that's going to be far easier said than done. Satisfied?"

"Yes. Clearly. But be polite in future. I don't do anything by being shouted at."

Homer looked exasperated. As if politeness was going to protect anyone. But …

"Right," Homer said with a reluctant, tired sigh.

"Can we please both leave here now, before someone rumbles our little trick and turns up demanding a very unpleasant conversation."

He turned and started to walk off, muttering quietly, "women," in a tone of exasperation.

Which was just as well. If Olwyn had heard him, she would have probably hurled a rock in his direction.

CHAPTER 28
A LASSO LESSON

It was almost daylight when I woke. The fire was cold and Joss had wriggled away without waking me. My back ached from sleeping on the hard floor. I stretched painfully and headed for the kitchen, following the aroma of fresh coffee.

Homer sat at the table, stroking Joss, examining her injured paw and the remains of the wire snare. His red-ringed eyes looked tired. He looked up and nodded as I entered.

"You were late. Everything okay?"

Homer nodded. "I got back an hour ago. You were asleep."

I poured coffee from the pot warming on the range and pulled out the chair opposite him.

"I hope that's not one of yours." I gestured to the cut wire hoop.

Homer made a sound of derision. "I only use humane traps and despatch quickly and painlessly," he said pointedly.

I nodded. I wasn't accusing him. Perhaps an explanation might help.

"Last night I let Joss out for a pee. When she didn't return I became concerned, only to find her with her paw caught in that snare," I gestured in disgust to the wire noose, "a short distance from the cottage."

I couldn't avoid colouring my words with contempt for whoever had set the trap.

"These things are evil. Animals are not intended to escape from them. You did well to release her." This was praise indeed from Homer.

"Cutting the snare from its fixing was the easy bit. Releasing the noose from her leg was something else. I think I did some damage; you'll need to check the wound."

Homer nodded. "I have already. The snare will be a deliberate act; another warning and, as like as not, the wire will have been coated in dung to guarantee infection."

He paused to fondle Joss's ears. "I've sterilised the damaged leg. She's tough, but I'll have to keep an eye on her."

For some minutes we sat in silence leaving me to wonder where he had been.

"You were away longer than I expected." Much to my surprise, concern coloured my words.

He shrugged. "A woman, who has been stirring up trouble and meddling in the business of our fracking friends, had a problem with an Androctonus crassicauda."

"What the hell is one of those?" I said.

Homer opened his rucksack and dropped a plastic box on the table.

"Holy mother of ..." The expletive burst out of me. "And that is?"

"An Arabian fat tail scorpion. Not considered a native to these parts," Homer said with a note of dry humour. "Someone placed it in her bed."

I shuddered. "Was she hurt? Did it sting her?"

"Miraculously not. A close thing though; I suspect the bedcovers slowed it down."

Homer picked up the box, gazing at the scorpion as it angrily attacked the sides.

"What do you intend to do with it?" I felt myself pull away from the table in horror.

"I'll return her to her owner."

"And how are you going to do that?"

Homer held the box close to his face as though daring the scorpion to attack him through the thin layer of plastic.

"Someone must be buying her food locally. There's only one likely supplier of live bait in the area. I think I need to pay him a friendly visit and ask him who he's supplying.

Tracking down her owner shouldn't be too difficult," he said, as much to the scorpion as to me.

Homer seemed angry. I shuddered a second time, as much at the thought of the surprise visit for the scorpion's owner, as sharing a bed with the black segmented body in the box.

Later that morning, I broke the rules while Homer slept. Taking one of Homer's maps and a compass I headed northwards through the trees, avoiding tracks and paths, heading for the high ground a few miles away from where I thought I might gain an aerial view of the fracking site.

Though most of the compound would be hidden beneath camouflage netting, so created that not even satellite imaging could penetrate, I hoped to gain a picture of what might be happening around the perimeter.

I left my phone behind, suspecting that fracking security could now track mobile phones, even when they were switched off. As I was hoping to get close to the site, avoiding tripping a hidden sensor would be essential. Most fracking sites were ringed by layers of passive security, triggered by body heat, movement or human smell for all I knew.

After an hour of walking, I had reached the highest area where trees still offered a vantage point from which to overlook the site. With luck, I should still be beyond the range of their sensors. Any closer would be pushing my luck. I could see nothing but tall sentinel trees that blocked the view at lower level, but I had anticipated that and brought rope and climbing gear from Homer's kit room.

I made slow progress; grateful for the crude harness I had fashioned as I slipped and grappled my way up the tallest trunk I could find. I don't particularly have a head for heights, so the best trick is never look down, tie yourself securely to the tree and rely on hemp and nylon for your security. I braced myself against the trunk, fumbled for

Homer's binoculars and turned the focus wheel with numb fingers.

Predictably, concealed beneath a dense mat of camouflage netting, the only things within the site that were visible were an array of drill heads, cranes and stack pipes. Like the woods around me, the compound streamed white clouds into the chilly air, further obscuring anything the camouflage failed to hide.

To the north side of the compound, hidden beneath an extended camouflaged roof but visible from my tree top eyrie, were a string of the previous night's delivery containers, high on their springs, empty of their contents. At first glance it offered a poor return for my climbing efforts.

But ... the tops of the empty containers were connected to a system of thick black hoses that ran to a large cistern on a gantry. At ground level, water was cascading into an outlet drain beneath the containers. A simple flush through wash-out; nothing ominous about that.

Except, when the men operating the system came into view, all were wearing olive green rubber suits, complete with face masks carrying enormous breathing filters, with what looked suspiciously like oxygen tanks strapped to their backs. Container valves were opened and sealed as huge quantities of waste water finally drained away. Was this a normal routine of any fracking operation?

I could see that the volume of waste water exceeded the capacity of the cisterns, and was cascading to the ground and left to run into streams and ditches. The tests at the spring and stream with Homer a few weeks earlier had revealed high radioactivity far above the levels normally expected in groundwater.

Fumbling to operate a micro camera and zoom with numb fingers is seldom to be recommended, especially while suspended in a tree top roost. I managed a series of hasty, long distance shots. They would be distant and grainy, but *clearly caught the men in their protective suits working on and around the containers. A breakthrough. I couldn't believe my luck.*

Unfortunately, like so many good things, it all came to an abrupt end. I dropped Homer's binoculars. They fell, clattering through the branches, all the way to the ground.

In her dreams, something stung the back of Olwyn's leg. She screamed, clearing the bed, frantically kicking her legs to throw off her imaginary assailant.

When daylight came, her surroundings were unfamiliar, the smell of pine and lavender further confusing any sense of place and time. The room was small, and threadbare curtains did little to filter the bright sunshine.

All Olwyn could remember was that it had been raining when they arrived in the darkness. An older woman, with long grey hair had greeted her with a kind, impassive face, and a bed was already made for her anticipated arrival. Homer and the woman had spoken briefly before he departed without another word.

Angela; that was her name. Slowly, as Olwyn woke, fragments of the previous night returned. Reluctantly, she slid from a temptingly warm bed, seductive beneath its feather eiderdown. She was surprised when she caught sight of herself in a tall mirror, the edges peeling silver. She was wearing a faded winceyette nightdress, the type her grandmother would have probably worn, complete with an evocative scent of lavender.

A single bed almost filled the small attic bedroom, and a soft mattress, covered with a hand-quilted eiderdown, had seduced Olwyn to sleep more effectively than any sleeping potion. She took her phone from the night stand. Predictably there was no signal. To her amazement it was mid-morning. How could she have slept so long?

She felt the claws of panic rake her insides as a kaleidoscope of memories from the previous day spiralled back to consciousness. Someone had made two attempts to kill her, and now, here she was in the back of beyond with her life in the hands of the woodsman and a strange woman.

The door swung open. It was Angela, dressed in vibrant colours, bearing a mug of tea.

"I left you to sleep," she said without introduction, placing the steaming mug on the night stand.

With two people standing beneath the sloping roof, the small room was decidedly overcrowded.

"Bad dreams? I heard you shouting out."

Olwyn nodded. "Tough day. Not nice."

She reached for the mug of tea, her foot catching the floral pot under the bed, vaguely remembering Angela had told her to use it if she needed to pee as the bathroom was on the ground floor.

"From what little Homer has told me, it sounds like par for the course for the people at the fracking site. When you cross their path beware; never underestimate what they will do."

Angela offered the warning as a matter of fact, the new norm in a fast changing world. Distracted by returning memories, Olwyn didn't at first reply, gratefully sipping her tea.

"I think it's time I left the area. I'm more than unwelcome and terribly out of my depth here," she confessed in a sudden gush of admission.

"Aren't we all, my dear," Angela replied with a surprisingly kind inflection. "Yet, somehow, Homer seems to keep us one step ahead."

"Ah, the mystery man from the woods."

"Perhaps more 'enigma' than 'mystery'. In another world, things might work out differently for all of us. It's a question of accepting the hand we are dealt."

Angela turned to leave, then spoke again.

"Perhaps we must hope there are enough men like Homer to spare us from the aberration that pretends to govern us." She paused.

"I'll leave you to wash and dress. There's still breakfast in the kitchen if you want some."

Angela left without another word, the brief interlude leaving Olwyn with the worrying feeling that the older woman felt almost as insecure as she did.

As I lost my footing I saw two men almost directly below me. Groping to catch the binoculars as they fell away from me, my feet slipped from the narrow branch. I was now hanging from my improvised rope harness.

A stream of obscenities hung, unspoken, from my lips. The sound of the falling binoculars echoed in my ears. My saving grace was the carpet of pine needles which dampened their impact on the woodland floor. By some miracle, searching around for the source of the noise, neither of the men looked up.

I could see them gesticulating, arguing about the direction from which the sound had come. Their words drifted up to my tree top eyrie, voices speaking Arabic or some middle Eastern tongue. Homer's constant warnings had come home to roost. I must have triggered a sensor, and Bremer had despatched this pair to investigate.

Suspended on a single length of nylon rope, the image of the 'Wanted' poster on social media flashed in front of my eyes. Only a few years ago, even 'Blue Horizon' wouldn't have got away with something like that. But now? Under the disguise of the latest version of the Anti-Terrorism Act, it was 'open season' on anyone foolish enough to cross their path.

'Wanted; dead or alive'. It sounded like some joke from a wild west movie, but in a world where jokes of bounty money for the skins of dead eco-terrorists abounded, incitement from dark, secret sources, obscurely conducting 'Blue Horizon' business, was enough to encourage bounty hunters without fear or penalty.

What would the men below get for me? Five thousand, ten thousand perhaps? Or, more likely, the currency would be a British passport for the men below and their families. It offered a temptation that would obscure any thoughts of normal human decency; the pelt of some eco-nut for lifelong security for you and your family? Not really a choice when presented with the opportunity of a lifetime.

All they needed to do was put shots through the rope that held me. Gravity would do the rest. Powerless, I could only hang, swinging gently on a pendulum of fate, like a fly in an invisible web, while my hunters scoured the woodland floor for the source of the sounds they had heard.

CHAPTER 29
CLOSE ENCOUNTERS

Homer bristled, a feeling of latent anger barely suppressed. He had slept far longer than he had intended and woke to find Grace missing from her room and the cottage.

The former made him late, the second broke house rules for their safety, forbidding Grace from wandering outside the cottage, particularly during daylight hours. Homer avoided the Landrover, cutting a path through the woods, forcing the pace, burning energy to cover his anger. He needed to get his focus back before Marius arrived on the train.

It had been five years since they had last met. Arriving at the station in a foul mood didn't bode well for their future relationship. Keeping Marius safe would require his maximum attention and left no room for the indulgence of anger. He would deal with Grace later, provided she didn't fall into Miller's clutches before then.

It was hard to break the habits of a lifetime. As the trees thinned and a road approached, Homer exchanged forest camouflage for something less conspicuous. Changing his jacket and cap as he walked, he had already swapped the old Landrover for the anonymity of public transport. Only the previous day he had found a tracer clipped under the wheel arch on the Landrover. For now, it served his purposes to leave the tracer at the cottage, hoping whoever had planted it would think he was still there and not begin searching for him on CCTV cameras.

Mid-week, Littlehampton railway station was quiet. In five years, Marius would have changed considerably. Homer's ex-wife sent occasional photographs which he memorised and destroyed, hiding all evidence of his children. The last picture of Marius had been two years previously.

Even then, the boy had grown, much changed by a life in the sunshine of rural Australia. In that time, they had lost much of what a family holds in common. Separated by time and events, Marius had been shielded from the past, told only the cover story that his father had been sent to prison.

As the stress caused by Homer's mistake increased, his ex-wife, Lisara, longed for her home in Sri Lanka, eventually finding it impossible to accept the threat his career brought on their family. Yet, as even Sri Lanka became dangerous for her, safe exile to Australia represented her own prison sentence for Lisara. As a consequence, she chose to sever all ties with a husband often absent and invisible for long periods.

Homer couldn't blame her for feeling the way she did. Living with him, nothing could expunge the price they would have to pay. Airbrushing them out of his life, with new identities and a life of anonymity, offered the only chance for their happiness and security.

Homer watched the station from the corner opposite. He could see the main entrance and foyer. When the scheduled train arrived he should have an unobstructed view of the passengers as they spilled out into the street, with time enough to check for anyone following Marius.

The onset of rain brought out a mushroom field of umbrellas. A delivery lorry arrived and parked, partially blocking his view. There were more people on the train than Homer had expected. As the train disgorged its passengers Homer moved, choosing a circuitous path, collar raised, cap pulled down, hands in pockets, his well-ordered plan disrupted amidst the melee of a wet autumn afternoon.

A car horn blared angrily as he crossed the road and entered the throng now jostling for taxis and pick-ups. His head hunched down between his shoulders, yet alert to those around him, Homer hustled his way against the flow. Beneath his cap, his eyes checked every face. Many thought him rude; bumping shoulders and hips as he surged against passers-by, checking, memorising faces, looking for a son he would barely recognise.

Within a minute, the throng thinned and cleared. No one seemed to fit his expectations. Puzzled, Homer stepped to one side, watching the reflection in a plate glass window. Had Marius missed the train, or had second thoughts about meeting his father?

He searched a sea of departing backs. One stood out, almost a head taller than the others. Nothing looked right, but the figure seemed to hesitate, unsure, looking around him for someone who hadn't appeared. It was the hair that confirmed it for Homer; thick, almost blue-black; his mother's hair. But the posture had changed; gangly, awkward in the way of teenagers as they mature. The boy's clothes were typically unkempt, probably caused by days of travelling.

His head turned, a sixth-sense alerting the boy; an olive-skinned face, framed by round, rimless glasses, with the first shadows of unshaved facial hair, carrying a slightly lost frown, disorientated by the bustle around him. His gaze moved beyond Homer without any sign of recognition.

Homer moved quickly, passing his blind side, head turned casually, glancing the boy's shoulder, whispering words only he would hear.

"Café opposite. Don't look round; meet me there."

Homer moved on without a backwards glance, an anonymous messenger on a grey wet morning. People dispersed and Homer shadowed his son from the opposite side of the road.

Marius must have heard his instruction. He paused, looked thoughtfully at the sky and pulled up the hood of his parka before crossing to enter the coffee shop on the opposite side of the road.

When you're hanging on a rope twenty metres from the ground, five minutes can feel like five hours. Fortunately, below me, the two men seemed more intent on bickering with each other than searching thoroughly. I tried to translate the Arabic by the inflections in their words, trying vainly to comfort myself with the illusion they might think it was all a waste of time.

Abruptly one barked in a clipped phrase. 'What's this,' I imagined him saying as he picked up the shattered binoculars. The discovery would inevitably lead their eyes skywards.

A radio squawked, sharp staccato words drifted towards me. Were they summoning help, extra men to net their prey obviously hiding nearby? A gust of wind buffeted me. I tried bracing myself against the trunk but slipped, my boots noisily scuffing for grip against the bark. I swung again like a pendulum. Surely they must see me now?

But instead, they simply moved away. I thought I saw one of them shrug, muttering what sounded like expletives, bored, cold, unimpressed at being sent on a wild goose chase.

Despite being cold to the core, I remained attached to my tree top eyrie for another half an hour, then clumsily lowered myself to the woodland floor. Clear thinking had become a problem; I only just remembered to choose an alternative route to return to Homer's cottage, a different path from the one the two men had left by.

And the binoculars that had started it all? Except for a dent in the casing, they were fine. The only thing that was damaged was my hip, where I had landed on them as, stiff from cold I had tumbled down the last couple of metres of the tree. However, my pride, reluctant though I was to admit it, was severely dented. Homer had been right to be cautious.

I had known for some time that I was riding my luck, like some runaway horse, hanging grimly on to the mane, with little say in where it was taking me. Hidden events were constantly spiralling around me. My luck had long since evaporated, leaving only instinct to shout a warning even before my close shave that morning. The trouble was that my dreams drowned out the message.

It was an old trick; Homer entered the café using the kitchen service door. Before the astonished chef could complain, he slipped a bank note into her hand.

"I'm surprising a friend. She thinks I'll arrive through the front door." With a wink he was gone before she could respond.

The café was busy; half the train seemed to have sought refuge from the rain; wet coats steamed and umbrellas dripped, misting over the large front windows. Homer saw Marius sitting at a small table in the middle of the room, checking his phone, occasionally casting a self-conscious eye at the entrance door.

Homer found a table at the back of the café where the light was less bright, a side door to toilets with windows just behind him. Despite the passage of years, his mind always looked for options, continually making escape plans for an emergency. He had spent five minutes watching the front entrance from across the road, checking who entered, who lingered or waited in parked cars. He was confident that no one had followed Marius, but you could never be totally sure.

A young waitress appeared at his side and gave Homer an expectant look.

"Black coffee, please. And could you ask that young man at the table over there what he wants. Ask him to come and join me?" He nodded towards Marius.

For a brief moment, an uncertain look crossed her face. Had he implied some sort of gay tryst? You could never tell these days. Despite her suspicions, she did what he asked, giving a curious glance in Homer's direction as she moved towards the counter to place the order.

Marius rose slowly. If anything, he was taller than Homer had first thought, with a slight stoop in that way of teenagers unaccustomed to their newfound height. With frameless, round glasses and facial hair sprouting in random tufts perhaps, unfairly, it all contributed to an impression of geekiness. Homer remembered that as a boy, Marius had been absorbed by books, disinterested in sport, instead taking refuge in his studies and not shy of hard work.

Now, his face frowned as he walked towards his father. Homer felt a sharp pang of guilt. The years, and his enforced absence, hadn't been kind on either of them. They both looked at the vacant chair. Still sitting and choosing not to stand and announce his presence, Homer moved the chair opposite with his foot.

"Please join me." It sounded inadequate, but what could you say that wouldn't sound facile.

The boy looked nervously around the room. The decision to contact his father had involved a tenuous route of subterfuge and lies. Here, now, he had too much imagination to miss the clandestine implications of their meeting. Slowly he lowered himself into the chair.

"Are you hungry?" Homer asked.

Marius shook his head.

How do you start to apologise for years of absence and neglect? Anything Homer might say would sound inadequate. Yet Marius had asked to see him, so unless his purpose was to pour bile and anger upon his absent father, he must have had reasons to have come all the way from Australia.

"How long were you planning to stay?" Homer asked directly.

Marius considered the question. It was almost as if it had just occurred to him for the first time.

"Abdul says I can stay as long as I want, at least until I get sorted out. His place is busy, more like the YMCA than a house."

Homer grinned. "For Abdul, mosque might be a better description."

Coffee and a pot of tea arrived. Homer noticed the waitress checked them out, evaluating her suspicions. Never one for small talk, Homer continued.

"You can stay with me if you want. It's quiet, not a lot going on. You might be bored." None of the normal 'why are you here?' or more importantly, 'why have you broken the rules?'

"Have you got decent internet speed?" Marius asked.

Homer nodded, stirring his coffee.

"Then I'll be fine. I'm studying remotely. There's a lot of that in Australia. I do Facetime tutorials, send assignments by email. Usual things."

The boy's voice was deeper than Homer had expected. Like his height, much had changed, much he had missed.

"What are you studying?" The need for the question confirmed his enforced absence.

Marius shot his father a glance, aware of the distance between them. "Geography; climate change. It's one of the reasons I'm here."

The answer hinted that seeing Homer wasn't his only purpose in coming to the UK.

"I got my grades and left school. I've got an Australian passport, so I need to do a year's introductory course before I can apply to university."

It was a simple answer, the words implying 'If you had been a half decent father you would already know that.'

There was an awkward silence for a minute as he poured tea with what seemed like exaggerated care. Homer felt he wasn't managing this well; after years of distance how could you manage any situation well? He tried to smile encouragingly, trying a different tack.

"Any questions you want to ask me? Anything to clear the air? It's good to see you, but you must have reasons to have come this far?"

With his usual, blunt frankness, he was trying to understand what his son wanted, how he had been allowed to disregard the strict protocols put in place to protect him.

Marius sipped his tea, seeming lost in thought for a moment. When it came, his question surprised Homer.

"Why did you lie and abandon us?"

The question was delivered with the sharpness of a stiletto.

CHAPTER 30
A BODY DISAPPEARS IN THE NIGHT

The hotel receptionist had just commenced her morning shift when Wailes arrived. The police sergeant was dressed in plain clothes. The receptionist wasn't entirely convinced he was really on duty, but his curt manner left little room for refusal when he demanded access to the hotel CCTV network. Standing too close, Wailes reeked of last night's stale whisky, and tried to sneak a look down her cleavage each time he leaned forward to study the grainy images in more detail.

Wailes was perplexed. A search of the room belonging to the Wright-Smith woman had revealed all the trappings of a hasty departure; the bed awry, clothes left on the back of a chair and the floor, even her toothbrush was still in the bathroom. But there was no sign of her body.

Almost as disturbing was the complete absence of the scorpion. The thought that it might be loose in the hotel added even more to his worries, as did the lack of any call to the emergency services. In his plan, Wailes had imagined an early morning trip to the morgue to identify her body, including planting a few grams of laced white powder beneath her nails, to further obscure the cause of death.

Wailes had planned carefully. The venom from the scorpion sting was highly toxic and quick acting, but it still needed a time delay to prevent a call for help which might just deliver an anti-venom in time. The night manager had recorded several urgent calls from Olwyn's room to reception. All had been ignored and deleted as instructed.

It was all too much, he thought. A study of the CCTV footage added yet more confusion. Unexpectedly, the corridor cameras on Olwyn's floor had captured the image of a man leaving, not entering, her room sometime after the calls to reception had been placed. The man was carrying a limp form of a female body. Mysterious. There was no camera evidence of him entering the hotel on any of the cameras.

Distracted, Wailes scratched his crotch from a trouser pocket, a habit the receptionist found repulsive. Suspicions aroused, they checked the cameras on the other floors. Nothing. It was almost as though the intruder knew the location of every camera.

Simple things like a peaked cap and high neck scarf obscured his face, and carrying the weight of a lifeless body further distorted his physical appearance, leaving no clue of his identity as he made his way to the lift. Without a working camera in the lift, he next appeared in the ground floor lobby. Without pausing, he carried his burden past the reception desk, not bothering to stop to call for help. It was as if he already knew no one would respond.

"Go to the outside cameras," Wailes instructed on a belch of whisky fumes.

Nothing. Outside the hotel foyer, the cameras showed only a blanket fog of interference.

"Clever," Wailes muttered under his breath, his eyes noticing the timelapse clock in the corner of the screen.

From the moment 'man and body' should have appeared through the main entrance doors, all recordings had ceased. He was watching a professional who knew how to avoid being recorded.

Fast-forwarding fifteen minutes, the screen blinked, the 'fog' had disappeared. The car park was still and silent. Empty, except for half a dozen cars. Time enough to cross the square of open space and disappear into the night.

Wailes counted the number of parked cars before and after the 'white out'. As he already suspected, they were the same; no one appeared to have left during the lost period. A professional disappearing act.

The receptionist could smell the hot body odour of the large man beside her as he deliberately leaned forwards to get a better look at the footage on the screen; Wailes had been up most of the night and needed a shower. There had to be something that would give evidence to what had happened.

Irritability pricked Wailes. He had been certain the scorpion would do its job. On the face of it, the chaos in her room and the figure carrying her body confirmed that. But to satisfy Miller and Bremer, he had to produce a body for identification and disposal. They demanded thoroughness; without physical proof they would assume he had failed again, the consequence of which made his bowels churn uncomfortably.

He had already performed a hasty search of the woodland surrounding the hotel and found nothing. Likewise, a preliminary check through the camera records of the main road passing the hotel showed nothing out of the ordinary either.

Whoever had carried the body from the hotel had disappeared into thin air, a vague statement that wouldn't sit well with his paymasters. Though Wailes doubted they would carry out their threats, his stock was seriously depleted by the arrival of this meddling woman. Even with her dead, it seemed he couldn't control events.

Wailes tried to reassure himself. Experience told him that bodies always turned up. From seemingly nowhere they arrive in morgues, often distant from the scene of death, or are found floating in the river or on rubbish dumps. Provided he didn't panic, an unexpected door would open and allow him to control the evidence and distort the facts.

However it happened there could be no physical evidence linking him to the death of Olwyn Wright-Smith. That was the good thing about scorpions; they didn't carry fingerprints or make incriminating statements. But Wailes still had to find the scorpion before anyone else did.

I suppose I could justifiably claim it was down to the effects of cold that I came precariously close to making a fatal mistake. With my brain free-wheeling, I approached Homer's cottage through what little cover remained from trees stripped of their leaves. I could see the back of his Landrover parked in the barn where I had last seen it. The track in front of the cottage was empty; nothing stood out of place.

Yet the front door to the cottage swung back and forth in the icy north wind that had increased as I walked. Should that have immediately rung an alarm bell? At least it meant I didn't have to knock to rouse Homer.

Just a few more paces and I would have been clearly visible from the house. At such moments, the pendulum of fate swings on a hair's breadth. Or on Joss, as it so happened. She appeared from nowhere, stopping me in my tracks. She whimpered, the blur of her frantically wagging tail the bell-weather of problems. A livid graze above her right shoulder hadn't been there a few hours before when I had slipped out of the back door.

It took a second or two for the implications to sink in. Alarmed, I backtracked deeper into the woods, beckoning Joss to follow me, aiming for a dense clump of wild rhododendron for cover while I tried to muddle out what had happened.

Bright eyed, Joss lay beside me, holding her previously damaged paw outstretched, the new wound in her shoulder staining red her soft black and white fur. The poor dog had certainly been in the wars and I didn't need two guesses as to who was responsible.

Raised voices floated on the breeze, accompanied by the smell of cigarettes. Homer didn't smoke and if he was in the house, I was certain Joss would never have left his side. So that meant …?

"Stay."

Loyal Joss, bright-eyed and gently panting, needed no second telling. Crouching, I left our cover and moved to a fallen tree from where I could get a clear view of the front of the cottage; I focused Homer's dented and battered binoculars.

The outline of two dark figures stood just visible inside the open front door, another in partial profile to the side of a first floor window. In the shadows of another window glowed the red tip of a cigarette. So, at least four by my count. No sign of an SUV or a four-by-four. I could only speculate that they must have hidden it, arriving on foot, surrounding the cottage to prevent anyone from slipping away.

Crouching low, I returned to Joss. The thought occurred to me that her absence might arouse their suspicions, leading to a search of the area around the cottage. Given that we were no more than fifty metres away, the cover of the bushes wouldn't protect us.

"Where's Homer, Joss?"

The dog gave me a puzzled look. She wouldn't easily have left his side, so the odds were that Homer hadn't been home when these men, Bremer's men, had paid their visit.

Leaving felt an act of desertion, but in the event that Homer was still in the house, if discovered, my presence would only make things worse. The only thing to do was leave now while there was still a chance to slip away. Indecision and delay could be fatal for both of us.

"Joss." She gave me a surprised look. "Angela. Find Angela."

I was learning a lot about communicating with the dog but still found it difficult to know if she understood.

"Find Angela," I repeated, keeping things simple.

Within seconds, Joss responded, scoring the ground for a trail, weaving rapidly from side to side in search of a scent labelled 'Angela'. I had no idea where we were heading; I had only taken the route once before and then it had been dark.

There was a time when I would have laughed at the thought of trusting my life to a dog. Now, I followed in Joss's limping wake with total confidence. How times change.

Allison Markham was puzzled. Her boss, Sergeant Wailes, had returned to the station from a visit to Olwyn's hotel, a dark expression clouding his usual inscrutable face.

Without explanation, PC James had been instructed to check CCTV camera recordings from all the roads surrounding the hotel which, coupled with a request to search the grounds of the hotel, rang alarm bells. All Allison knew was that hotel staff had reported a guest was missing, and without another word Wailes had left to start a thorough search.

There was no mention of exactly who they might be looking for. It all added up to a nagging worry for Olwyn's safety as Allison had a clear idea of what Bremer was capable of. If only Olwyn had taken up her offer of a bed for the night. For a moment she stood biting her lip, trying to control her imagination.

There was one person who might know something about Olwyn's whereabouts. During their pursuit through the forest she had caught a fleeting glimpse of a registration plate on the Landrover that had haphazardly barged its way into their drama. Something Olwyn had said had given Allison the impression she knew more about the mysterious driver than she was prepared to admit. A quick DVLA search confirmed that the vehicle had been written off several years before, but a call to a few local garages soon provided a name and an address.

There was one possible way to put her concern to rest. Taking an early lunch break, Allison Markham left the station alone, using an unmarked car, telling no one where she was going. If nothing else, she owed Homer a word of thanks for his timely intervention.

Homer and Marius chose separate seats on the bus. This was partly for security, but mostly to give Homer a moment to take stock.

In five years, his son had changed out of all recognition. Not only a foot taller, but with a mind and personality of his own, able to think and make decisions without the influence and guidance of others. Though Homer realised he shouldn't have been surprised, the change, like the questions Marius challenged his father with, had taken him aback.

Homer should have been more prepared to be immediately confronted for his absence and divorce.

'Why did you lie and abandon us?'

Not a question as it first appeared; more a statement of fact, delivered in a tone feigning indifference, conviction for an act of betrayal.

A distance of half the planet had always held the question at bay, the pain of separation assuaged by the excuse of the need to hide his family from vengeance. In the absence of truth, conclusions are made in the remaining vacuum and Marius had made his own judgement on the actions of his father. He was here now to hold Homer to account.

With a heavy sigh of resignation, Homer realised that there was no longer any means to hide the truth, at least not one he could accept. But that didn't change the facts. Accepting the fiction spun about their father had been crucial to the safety of his children. 'Homer is a bad father who has abandoned his family' was an easy narrative for Lisara to spin without need of explanation.

The killing of ten women and children might well have been an unintentional mistake, one not of Homer's making, but the blame still ended up hung around his neck. How do you explain such a terrible event to your children?

'In self-defence, I targeted the wrong vehicle. It wasn't my fault, the terrorists set up their own families as martyrs, offering them as bait to the brutality of the uncaring west.'

It mattered not that the intelligence Homer had been given had been wrong, that he was no more than the facilitator holding the laser guidance that had targeted the missile, expedited in a desperate effort to rescue a group of innocent aid workers from the capture by a ruthless, barbaric regime.

Self-justification was part of the struggle to save his own sanity. But the conclusion was always the same when Homer's conscience came whispering in his ear. The blood of the innocent was on his hands and could never be washed off.

By different doors, two figures left the bus at the stop in the woods. Homer waited until the bus was out of sight before he drew level with Marius. They hadn't spoken since he had deflected his son's question. A coffee shop wasn't the time or place to try and explain the true reason why the family's lives had been torn apart.

"We'll have to buy you some waterproof boots if you're going to spend time here," Homer said, looking at Marius's soaked trainers. "It's not like the dry, arid outback. The parka looks good, but needs proofing."

Dark, wet patches were already soaking from their shoulders, stained waterfalls to the front and back. As they set off, heads bowed against the rain, Homer noticed a white car pass them, brake lights spearing through tendrils of spray. For a moment, the driver thought of stopping to offer the two men a lift, then thought better of it and drove on.

"Is your place far from here?" Marius asked, shivering.

They had left the road, following the merest suggestion of a path through the woods. His feet were already numb.

"Too far to walk dressed like that. I've a friend who lives closer, about a mile away. We'll stop there to dry you out. We can borrow her van."

Marius nodded in reply, as the first flakes of sleet laced the cold north wind.

Angela looked up as Olwyn entered the kitchen. The room was warmer than the rest of the house; a range glowed in the corner and Angela sat at a large oak table, hand sewing a seam with clawed fingers, on what appeared to be a large bird of prey patterned fabric.

"There's coffee in the pot." Angela nodded towards the hotplate without looking up from her work.

Olwyn found a clean mug at the sink, rolling up the sleeves of a thick, hand-knitted jumper Angela had lent her.

"Nice bird," she said quizzically, raising an eyebrow, leaning back against the sink.

"One of Homer's wilder schemes." Angela looked up from her sewing. "Best not to get involved."

"Too late for that I suspect," Olwyn replied with a wry smile.

"So, what brings you to these parts?" Angela asked.

"My job."

"Which is?"

"Officially? Import and export licenses, but, as it turns out, it currently involves poking my nose into a hornets' nest."

"Ah, the local fracking site."

Olwyn nodded, unsure how much to tell Angela.

"It's not how things started out. My boss plays games. He's thrown me in over my head, to be honest."

For a moment both women were silent, alone with their thoughts.

"I hardly know the man who brought me here. Homer, did you call him? Does he make a habit of getting involved in the lives of others?" Olwyn asked, a note of humour colouring her words.

Angela shrugged, ignoring the thrust of the question. "Homer mentioned something about Jerry Houseman. Is he your boss?" she asked instead.

"You know Jerry?" Olwyn said in astonishment.

"Let's say our paths have crossed." There was a note of caution in Angela's words.

"Take my advice, if it's the Houseman I know who's the man you're working for, you'd do well to let Homer meddle in your affairs until you're clear of this place. Unless you feel like becoming a scorpion handler?"

Angela turned back to her sewing, a faint mischievous smile on her thin, pale lips that said far more than words.

Olwyn was about to respond when further conversation was interrupted by the sound of whining and scratching at the back door.

CHAPTER 31
THE PROVENANCE OF DOORS UNGUARDED

Guided by scent alone, Joss had to backtrack several times to locate the right path. My head felt clammy and sweaty, while the rest of my body seemed to shiver uncontrollably. By the time we arrived at Angela's cottage I was overwhelmed by fatigue, hardly able to place one foot in front of the other.

Alerted by the presence of Joss, Angela opened the door as we approached. From the shocked expression on her face we must have looked a bedraggled pair; the dog limping and battered and me shaking like a jelly in an earthquake.

I stumbled into the kitchen.

"Men, four of them, in Homer's place," I announced, rambling.

In extremis, Angela used few words. Within seconds, she had removed my soaked jacket and led me towards the battered sofa next to the Aga. For a moment she disappeared and I was vaguely aware of the presence of a young, blonde woman who was busy filling kettles to boil on the range.

Without introduction or explanation, she pulled off the thick, shapeless jumper she was wearing. She sat beside me.

"Put your arms around me."

Beneath the discarded jacket I was wet through, so hugging this strange woman didn't make sense, but nothing much did at the moment. I felt her wrap an arm around me, pressing her body tightly against mine.

'What a bizarre thing to do when first meeting a stranger,' I thought, as she used her spare right hand to stretch the over-large jumper over both our heads.

"Hi, I'm Olwyn. We'll have you right as rain in a few minutes," she said with a note of bright optimism.

Feeling as I did, I sure as hell doubted that, but I was grateful for her vote of confidence.

"What's your name?" she asked.

"Grace," I manage to slur, as though drunk.

"Okay, Grace, tell me what's happened. Try to concentrate, don't go to sleep."

She hugged me tight, feeling my grip slacken as the welcome arms of sleep made their approach. I must have rambled for some minutes, tired beyond words, intensely irritated by this annoying woman who insisted on keeping me awake.

I was vaguely aware of Angela returning, arms filled with an eiderdown, blankets and hot-water bottles. The next few minutes went in a blur. Together, both women stripped off my wet clothes and wrapped me in a gown and blankets, placing the hot-water bottles all around my body. For a while, Angela refused to let me lie down or, more importantly from my perspective, let me fall asleep.

"Drink this, slowly."

I was still shaking; Angela helped me hold the mug. It was obviously one of her concoctions laced with something that burned fiercely as I drank it.

Olwyn stuck something in my ear, removed it and showed the reading to Angela.

"Shall I call an ambulance?" I saw her give Angela a questioning look.

Angela shook her head. "Not a good idea. We'll have to manage."

I drifted in and out of sleep, just aware of both women moving around me, replacing hot-water bottles, forcing me to drink, and regularly checking my temperature. At one point, I felt my arm exposed and the prick of a needle.

The two women spoke little to one another, vaguely aware through the haze that surrounded me that Olwyn seemed lost in the kitchen, constantly asking where everything was, as lost as I was in this ever changing world.

Eventually Angela allowed me to lie down on the sofa. I lost track of time. Occasionally, Joss left her place in front of the range, prodding me awake with her nose, an alert look in her eyes that asked unfathomable questions. Angela had cleaned the graze on her shoulder and dried the open wound on her leg. Despite all the injuries men caused Joss, her devotion remained a constant.

Homer's arrival caught even Joss by surprise. The kitchen door swung open without as much as a perfunctory knock and Homer entered, closely followed by a much younger man almost a head taller.
"Damn weather," Homer muttered without greeting. Flakes of sleet peppered his jacket. "We walked from the bus stop; Marius has no sensible shoes."
Angela stepped forward and hugged the boy, standing back to take a better look at Marius.
"Goodness, you've grown."
For a moment he looked at Angela with a lopsided smile, pleased and embarrassed in equal measure.
"It's been five years," he said, an Australian lilt coloured his words.
Despite feeling dreadful, Grace was aware of being surprised. This must be Homer's son, Marius. She had overheard Homer express concern to Angela about the boy's imminent arrival and the circumstances that might have caused it.
But it wasn't his abrupt appearance inside Angela's cottage that caught her off guard, nor his height or thick, blue-black hair, partially concealed by a green beanie. His lips were almost brown and his skin naturally pigmented, the colour of milky coffee, definitely not the result of Australian sunshine.
Amidst the excitement of their arrival, Grace must have drifted into a hazy doze, waking with the rising urge to stumble to the sink, bile rising in her throat. It took a while for the nausea to pass.

As it abated, Angela handed her a glass containing another one of her witch's brews.

"It smells awful but it will help. You've got mild hypothermia, thermal shock."

Mild? She certainly wasn't exaggerating. The drink tasted little better than it smelt. But it worked and Grace soon started to feel human again, over the worst.

Homer made a beeline for Grace.

"How many men?" The usual Homer; he didn't even bother to ask how she was.

"I counted four. There may have been more."

"Vehicle?"

Grace shook her head. "None visible. They must have hidden it in the woods."

"Armed?"

"Possibly. Not that I saw anything conspicuous."

"And you're sure they didn't see you?"

"Joss intercepted me in the woods before anyone could have seen me. She must have escaped the house when they broke in." Grace paused. "One of them must have lashed out at her, there's a wound on her shoulder."

Homer showed no reaction to her words, just gazed somewhere into the middle distance. Looking for support, Grace shot a glance in the dog's direction. Joss had a look that implied, 'Sounds like normal Homer.'

"That's enough interrogation for the moment," Angela said, insinuating herself between them. "Grace has hypothermia."

"That'll teach you a lesson," he replied, her reprimand for ignoring his instructions.

He turned away, looking out of the window into the dying grey light of a winter afternoon. Sympathy was obviously not one of his strong points.

Angela gave him a few minutes. Still tired beyond words and bleary-eyed, Grace noticed that Olwyn had also returned to join their terse discussion.

"You can't go alone," Angela said, standing beside Homer. "Grace can't go with you, neither can Marius, so I'll have to come. We can use my van."

"No, I need you here," Homer replied gruffly.

"Well, you can't go on your own; not until you know who they are and why they broke into your cottage."

The room seemed filled with his anger and frustration. Grace noticed Angela place a hand on his arm, a subtle warning that another fit might erupt if he didn't allow his temper and frustration to cool.

It was Olwyn who intervened.

"If you have to go, I'll join you. Just give me an old coat and a hat. After all, I owe you a favour for 'Scorpio'," she said with an amused grin.

'Scorpio'? Grace thought. 'Who the hell was 'Scorpio'?'

A sharp retort stalled on Homer's lips as Angela squeezed his arm.

"That's it then. You both go; conceal the van and approach cautiously through the woods. Only enter the cottage if you're sure no one is there. Make the place secure and come straight back here. Don't linger."

Homer gave her a brow-beaten look, reluctantly accepting Olwyn's company. There was obviously more to their relationship than Grace had expected, but for the moment, this was one argument she was happy to stay out of.

Within moments, Homer and Olwyn had donned coats and boots. Angela handed him a backpack and what looked like a battered rifle. Homer frowned, only taking the backpack.

"I'm not going to shoot my way into my own home," he grumbled, annoyance flaring once again.

"Besides, an air rifle and half a dozen pellets aren't exactly going to cut things with the likes of Bremer," he added sarcastically.

As they moved through the door, Angela drew Olwyn aside for a final word.

"The rucksack contains his medical kit. He's bound to have forgotten. Slow him down; before you drive off, make him take this."

She handed Olwyn a large tablet from a bottle in her pocket.

"What is it?" she asked with a note of uncertainty.

"Benzodiazepines," Angela told her. "Insist he takes the tablet. It may be the one thing that keeps him from having another seizure."

As they left the cottage, Olwyn wondered if volunteering to join him was the wisest decision she had made that evening.

Her sat-nav was seldom wrong; Allison Markham was certain this was the house. Why anyone would choose to live in such an isolated spot she couldn't imagine, but Homer had a reputation as a cantankerous hermit.

Darkness came early as she left the car, partially concealed to one side of the rutted track. She checked her phone, in two minds to tell the station where she was. Predictably, the phone signal had disappeared.

Allison hadn't seen any other vehicles as she wound her way to Homer's cottage, but as she approached the dark outline of a house, she could just make out the back of a Landrover in the gathering dusk. The registration number, barely visible beneath a layer of mud, was the one she had fleetingly seen the previous day.

She thought for a moment. In the gathering darkness, the cottage had a tired, worn appearance. Although the Landrover was there, no lights shone from the un-curtained windows, suggesting that no one was home. Perhaps her journey had been a waste of time after all. Yet there had been something about Olwyn's words the previous day that posed a question.

Cautiously, she approached the front door, just visible in the deeper shadow of the porch. In torchlight, the path was littered with cigarette butts. All appeared to have been discarded recently. Homer was either a heavy smoker or there had been visitors.

The door was plain, perhaps older than the rest of the house, made of thick, weathered oak boards. As she reached for the ornate knocker, Allison paused. The door was already slightly ajar. Instinct made her take a step back.

"Hello? Anyone home?"

Unanswered, her voice echoed back to her. She shone her torch into the narrow gap between the door and the frame. There was no obvious sign of forced entry.

"Anyone home? This is the police," she added, just in case Homer hid himself from strangers until they identified themselves.

The door was unusual; it was hung to open to give the person on the inside a free right hand.

"Hello," she called again. "I'm from the local police. I would like to talk to Homer. The door's open; can I come in?"

In the silence, a group of crows squabbled noisily above her. Was that an omen? Something felt odd, not quite right about the place. Decision hung in the balance; go forward, or back to the station for help and forget her worries and just wait for Olwyn to turn up.

With hindsight she should have at least left a message of where she was going, even though by the manner of his behaviour, she had started to develop a nagging distrust of Sergeant Wailes. Still, why waste a journey, only to have to do it again? She had much to demand her attention.

Allison Markham stepped forward and pushed open the door. And in one innocent gesture, changed the path of her life.

"So, does 'Scorpio' make us a couple?"

Driving Angela's decrepit van, Homer gave Olwyn a confused glance.

"What?"

He had disappeared into a silent sulk since leaving, brow-beaten by an increasing number of headstrong women who were invading his world.

"Us, a couple. After all, 'Scorpio' brought us together and now she relies on us for everything, locked up as she is in a plastic box. We need to talk about her future," Olwyn said with a serious voice.

"Future for an Arabian fat tail scorpion? The only future I'm prepared to talk about is how to return it to its owner, along with a few interesting questions."

"Her," Olwyn corrected, a teasing grin on her face. "She's our joint responsibility. Granted, people have more romantic reasons to come together, but I just thought …"

She couldn't finish her words for laughing, hiding her fears behind the ridiculous. At last, Homer caught her drift.

"You're crazy," he said with a tight smile. "Besides, I make a lousy husband."

"Beats being terrified."

There was a slightly nervous edge to Olwyn's words. She paused for a moment, to ease her position from Joss panting in her ear.

"So, the tall boy, is he your son? We weren't introduced."

Homer grunted in reply. He had been surprised by the interest in Marius from the waitress in the café and now, from the tone of her voice, Olwyn appeared to feel the same.

What was it with women that even at times of crisis, personal things were still relevant? He quickly glanced at Joss between them. She was probably on Olwyn's side.

The journey was longer than Olwyn had anticipated. She felt an adrenalin surge as they bounced down the rutted track towards the outline of a darkened cottage. She steeled herself; it was probably a trick of the dark, but on either side, tall pine trees seemed to lean over to embrace them.

Approaching with only side lights, the cottage made a sombre manifestation, no trace of a welcoming light. But that wasn't her main distraction. Parked to one side as they passed was a small white car, identical to the one that Allison Markham had driven the previous evening.

"Seems I have a visitor," Homer said in a low voice, flicking a glance in the direction of Joss to measure her reaction. "Unlikely to be the four men Grace saw; not their style."

"I travelled in a similar car only yesterday. It belonged to Allison Markham, the woman driving the police car in the forest when you miraculously appeared in front of us."

Olwyn's words drifted away, the implied question unanswered, suddenly eclipsed by another, more immediate one.

"What would bring her here? There's no …"

A deep, low grumble emanating from Joss stopped her dead.

"Joss?"

Homer stopped the van and stepped aside, making way for the dog to slip from her perch with the grace of a slippery eel. Olwyn followed almost as quickly, her imagination over-ruling her thinking brain as she ran to follow the dog.

Homer hesitated, taking just long enough to turn the van lights to full beam. With lenses masked by mud and grime, they didn't add much, but enough to show in a glance all he needed to see.

With no response to his shout of warning, he brought Olwyn down just as she reached the open door, taking her sideways, full length onto the tiled surface. Arms encircling her waist, he felt her gasp, the wind driven from her lungs by the force of the fall.

"Lie still. Don't move until I tell you to."

Winded, Olwyn nodded, and gasped one word.

"Allison."

Whining softly, Joss scored the threshold where an outstretched leg marked a body partially hidden by the darkness of the hallway.

Using only elbows and knees, Homer crawled over Olwyn, not daring to spare her from his weight, his eyes searching in the dim light from the van. His hand found blood, quite a lot of it.

His first instinct should have been to check the body, but a cord was visible just above them, at waist level, where no cord should be. From the back of the door, tied to the handle, it ran taut, towards the staircase.

Homer eased himself gently past the body of a woman, reassured by a low moan confirming that she was at least still alive. But for the moment, the cord demanded his full attention.

The hallway was almost completely dark, so he searched for a box of matches in his pocket; the match flared brightly, just enough light to show the destination of the cord.

A shotgun.

On the bottom post of the staircase, the gun was blacker than the darkness around it, horizontal, aimed at the door. Homer eased himself across the floor, feeling his way, seeking out a hidden tripwire.

The match singed his fingers, but he had seen enough. At the staircase, he slowly levered himself up, his hands gently following the cord, finding the metal finger-guard protecting double triggers, one yet to be fired.

Working in the dark, he gently eased the cord from the live trigger, and slid a soft hand along the stock searching for the safety catch. At last he could breathe, releasing his tension.

Cautiously, pressed against the wall, Homer groped his way to the light switch. A solitary bulb lit up the scene.

Bound to the staircase post with insulating tape was the shotgun; his shotgun, gleaming bright with oil as he had left it, pointing directly at the front door, its triggers pulled by the tension of the white cord the moment someone swung it open.

Homer looked at his hands now covered in blood. Intended for him, that 'someone' was the unfortunate Allison Markham.

CHAPTER 32
THE MEANING OF CURRENCY

"What was the name of the organisation you said you belonged to?"

Hands coated in flour as she kneaded a bowl of bread dough, Angela threw out the question, loosely disguised as a casual afterthought in their conversation. She continued kneading; she had a need to feed the ever increasing numbers turning up at her cottage.

Her back propped against the side of the sofa, sipping another cup of Angela's bitter herbal recipes, Grace yawned. A warning bell chimed at the back of her brain urging caution.

"I don't think I did. Names are just names," she said in a tired voice.

"Still, you can't be working alone. It would be ... reassuring ... to know exactly who you represent. The media claim that most fracking protests and civil disobedience are organised by dubious anarchist organisations just pretending to be environmentalists. You could belong to one for all we know."

Angela paused in her work with the dough, wiping loose hair back from her forehead, leaving a white smear of flour on her face. When she became serious, it accentuated the way her nose curved into her eye sockets. Grace thought it created more than a passing resemblance to a hawk.

With no reply from Grace, Angela continued.

"You already know Homer has ... vulnerabilities." She chose her word deliberately. "I wouldn't want to see those exploited."

It was impossible to miss the warning note in her last word. Grace shuddered at the bitter taste of her drink; it would be the easiest thing for this witch's brew to be laced with something unpleasant. But somehow, she couldn't see Angela as a 'poisoner'.

"I have no intention to take advantage of Homer," Grace said. "He can turn away at any time without recrimination."

"Ah, but you know he won't do that. Despite the brusque exterior, he's really very easy to read. And manipulate," Angela replied.

Grace chose her words carefully.

"I'm not exploiting him if that's what you're implying. Homer's free to throw me out the moment he wants to. Helping me is his choice. Although he's loath to admit it, perhaps he believes in my quest to uncover what's hidden in the fracking sites. Why else would he go out on a limb to help me?"

Self-justification suddenly got the better of her. "It's not that I expect him to repeat what he has done for you. You can't hold me responsible for his burgeoning need to pay back, as though making penance for past deeds."

Despite her best intentions, Grace knew her retort had become spiteful.

"I think you're talking about atonement," Angela replied without looking up, her mind absorbed in memories of the past.

"Whatever description you want to use. Words alone won't absolve guilt if Homer is always seeking absolution."

"Which we both know he will never find in this life." Angela's tone was defensive, drawing a protective line for the man who had sacrificed much for her and others.

Aware she had gone too far, Grace avoided Angela's sad eyes and was about to apologise when the door opened and Marius entered in search of something to eat.

For the moment, 'hostilities' had to be suspended. Angela turned her attention back to her dough and the room was filled with clumsy noise while Marius hunted through cupboards for something to eat.

"It's called 'Terra Mater'; the organisation I'm involved with," Grace said abruptly, answering the original question in an attempt to offer an olive branch.

"Sounds cool," Marius exclaimed, taking up the conversation, his back to both women. "'Terra Mater'? Isn't that Latin for 'mother earth'? A pagan god. Sounds sinister."

Had he sensed animosity in the room when he entered? When Marius turned around, his face held what could only be described as a look of curious amusement.

"No more so than a number of modern beliefs," Grace replied, countering his word with a complicit smile.

To be fair to Olwyn, she hadn't panicked. Almost before Homer had disarmed the shotgun, she had rolled Allison onto her side, tearing away what remained of the blood soaked tatters of her jacket and shirt. What lay beneath looked an unimaginable mess.

They needed an ambulance. Searching in vain through the pockets of the borrowed coat, Olwyn realised she had left her phone behind at the cottage. Homer arrived at her shoulder; he needed no more than a glance.

"Angela's rucksack; it's in the van. Get it."

Without question, Olwyn ran out into the darkness, and Homer groped for the blanket from Joss's bed. Having lain for some time on the tiled floor, Allison was shivering, a consequence of cold and shock. Blood was seeping from dozens of small pellet wounds from the exposed and torn flesh of Allison's left side. Her eyes, though open, were badly dilated, flitting nervously around her, colourless lips forming unspoken words.

"It looks worse than it is," Homer announced for Allison's benefit to stop her panicking.

"The door has taken the worst of the blast. You were lucky," he said, speaking encouragingly to Allison, spoiling the effect by adding, "They were clumsy. If the second barrel had fired it would probably have killed you."

Olwyn couldn't begin to imagine how that was going to reassure her, but she let it pass, concentrating on swabbing her friend's colourless face and offering water to her lips.

"Get more blankets. Landing cupboard," Homer directed. "She'll need a hospital, but first we need to deal with the shock and stop the bleeding."

He had already covered Allison with his jacket. Olwyn hesitated, reluctant to release her friend's hand.

"Do it. Now," Homer said.

They worked in silence as a team. From the stopped, broken watch on Allison's left arm, she had probably lain injured for almost an hour before they had arrived. Somehow, in the mists of consciousness, she had tried to use her shattered phone to call for help and started to fashion a tourniquet on her upper arm.

Homer looked at the broken phone.

"If she was using it as a torch it probably saved her hand."

Together, they tore bedsheets into strips, binding towels to cover a host of wounds and slow the blood loss.

"That should keep you alive until we can get you proper medical attention," Homer said as he secured the dressings. He really had a poor bedside manner.

Using an old discarded door from Homer's barn as a stretcher, they wrapped Allison in blankets and managed to transfer her to the van.

"Thanks," she managed with a painful grimace.

Homer paused for a moment, searching the remains of the rucksack for Angela's 'magic' flask.

"Drink this. It will help," he said with a smile of encouragement.

"Ughh. Disgusting," she muttered, taking several mouthfuls nevertheless.

"Want to tell me what happened, assuming you don't think I was the one who shot you." Homer deliberately looked in the direction of the shotgun, now lying in the back of the van beside the rucksack.

"Not much to tell," Allison said weakly.

"I was worried when I couldn't contact Olwyn. My sergeant insisted on a search for a missing woman, though no missing person report had been received."

Her brow furrowed, as if suddenly puzzled by that fact. "Then I remembered your registration number from the other day in the forest."

Allison paused for breath and Olwyn squeezed her hand.

"You're not registered at the DVLA," she continued with a weak smile of reproof. "So I enquired at Hargreaves garage and they told me where you were."

"So you came here alone. Did you tell anyone?"

"No," she answered warily.

"And your reason for coming here?" Homer tried not to sound suspicious.

"To see if you knew what had happened to Olwyn. From the way Sergeant Wailes was flapping I knew something was up."

She glanced at Olwyn. Homer was thoughtful for a moment.

"This Wailes; does he keep animals, unusual things, lizards, snakes, insects?"

Allison looked puzzled. "No idea. But he did bring a live tarantula into the station last Christmas as a party joke. Not many of us found it particularly funny when he released it. He sometimes has a strange sense of humour."

Homer nodded, but said nothing. He silently wondered how Wailes might enjoy his re-acquaintance with his scorpion.

It was a slow, uncomfortable journey for Allison Markham. They transferred her from the van to Angela's cottage and while Angela examined her damaged side, Homer took Olwyn and Grace to one side.

"If we take her to hospital, she'll have to make a statement to the police; gunshot wounds, especially caused to police officers, always arouse a robust response. Can you find out how much she intends to tell them?"

He directed his question to Olwyn.

"Allison will have to tell the truth," she replied defensively.

"True. But you don't remember much when you've been shot," he said with a note of personal experience in his voice, "especially when a shotgun is involved. If she can be persuaded to have selective memory, it will help to protect us. That booby trap was meant for one of us, not her."

Homer shot an angry glance at Grace.

"Coupled with the scorpion in your bed, someone has declared war on us," Homer said, turning back to Olwyn. "Whoever is behind this has raised their game. It won't stop here."

"I could tell her about the scorpion, that we're both on the same side, coupled with the attempts to drive us off the road in the forest. It should instinctively warn her to be careful about what she says in her statement."

Olwyn thought for a minute.

"Plus, I think she will go out of her way to protect me."

She didn't explain further, but the thought left the shadow of a wistful smile.

"Well, she must have suspicions about her boss, Wailes, even if she can't prove anything," Grace added with a note of resignation. "'Blue Horizon' seem to own half the country's police force, from what I understand."

The three of them fell in silent thought considering that grim fact.

"Anyway, can you find out what she intends to say?" Homer shot a questioning glance at Olwyn.

"Suggest the dangers if she tells too much about her involvement with us. Don't ask her to lie; just encourage her to have selective memory."

He turned away to find Angela cleaning and re-dressing Allison's wounded arm and shoulder.

"And hope that she's not also in the pay of Bremer and been double-crossing us all along."

Angela interrupted them.

"She will live," she said brightly. "You both made a good job of stabilizing her," she nodded in turn at Homer and Olwyn. "But she needs hospital; sooner rather than later."

"We've just been discussing how she is going to explain her injuries without implicating the rest of us." Grace glanced at Angela, remembering their conversation only a short time before.

Puzzled by the sudden change in atmosphere, Homer interjected.

"We can't risk an ambulance, in case Bremer has someone listening, there's no guarantee it would ever get to the hospital. We'll have to use your van and take her ourselves. I could always claim I found her injured in the woods."

"Well, you can't go," Angela shook her head. "You're bound to be recognised and that would raise too many questions, for both Allison and the rest of us. No, the only way this will work is if I take her and Marius accompanies me."

"Marius?" Homer moved his head in surprise. "He's only a boy."

"Nearly nineteen," Angela reminded him. "He's strong. If he wears his glasses, a peaked cap and hoodie, no one will even notice him. He'll look as inconspicuous as any other teenager. Besides, the three of you are known locally, you daren't show your faces, while I'm thought to be too mad to pull a stunt like this."

From his expression, Homer clearly wasn't convinced, but, out-voted once again by the women, he would have to accept their plan.

Out of concern for Allison, the van departed within ten minutes. Angela drove with Marius beside her. At the last minute, against her wishes, Olwyn accompanied them, and sat in the back holding Allison's hand as she lay in pain on their improvised stretcher. It was partly to keep a check on her condition, but primarily to rehearse the statement she would give to account for her injury.

As the lights of the van disappeared down the track, Grace started preparing supper. She was feeling better; the worst effects of hyperthermia had abated, and neither she nor Homer had eaten all day.

"There's something that I need to tell you."

Grace knew she would need to make her point before Homer took her to task for breaking his house rules earlier that morning.

He looked at her in distraction, only half listening.

"The photo that appeared on social media; the one of me in the 'Wanted' poster?" she said as she slid the loaf Angela had prepared earlier into the oven in the range. "I think I know who took the photo."

Suddenly, she had Homer's attention.

"Your gypsy friends, the ones who smuggled me out a few months ago?"

Homer nodded, slowly coming up to speed.

"After Bremer's security men had stopped the caravan at their road block, when they tried to pull me out of the back," Grace reminded him.

"Well, the younger man sitting on the front bench next to your friend, Cosmo, took a photo of me. He seemed impressed by my reaction and said the picture was to remember me by. It all seemed a bit of fun, no more than a joke. Certainly the other two women in the back of the caravan with me seemed to see the amusing side of it. But that's definitely the same photo; if you enlarge it, you can see the green canvas of the caravan roof behind my head. At the time, I didn't give it another thought. But now? I'm not sure what it means?"

Grace left the question to hang. She knew perfectly well what was going on, but that was best unsaid for Homer to arrive at his own conclusions. He looked at her sideways, unhappy with the implications if she was correct.

"Are you certain?"

Grace nodded. Homer turned away, staring through the window into the darkness. Not Cosmo, he was certain. But his son, Milo, or one of the women? He would have to be careful before he made any allegations.

'It's just business,' Cosmo would dismiss it with a shrug. Loyalty comes in many guises. After all, the bond of friendship was extended to Homer, not Grace.

But, however you wrapped it up, he felt betrayed and worried in equal measure. If they had traded the photo with Bremer, what else might have been used for currency?

CHAPTER 33
A UNIVERSAL KEY

Dusted with snow, three figures entered the cottage several hours later.

"It's come early," Angela pronounced, warming her hands in the glow of the Aga.

Though concern for the injured woman was foremost in my mind, it was interesting to pause for a moment to watch the interplay between Angela and Homer as he fussed around the older woman with his trademark mask of annoyance. Unspoken, he pushed a chair closer to the range and placed a mug containing something hot into her hands.

"Someone should try telling climate change deniers that there shouldn't be a blizzard in October," Marius added, stamping cold feet on the tiled floor.

"It's the opposite extreme where I live in Australia; forty-five degrees for days on end last summer. And the aircon only makes the carbon emissions even worse."

I noted the same abrupt inference in his words; like father, like son. As if to make his point, he stepped forward and pushed another log into the Aga in a deliberate gesture.

Despite the late hour, I laid five places at the table and started serving our meal, setting a basket of slightly over-baked rolls and a pan of soup in the middle of the table. For several minutes, we ate in silence, hunger trumping concern for a few, brief moments.

"How was Allison?" I broke the silence.

"Weak; shock, I expect. And loss of blood." Angela shot a glance at Marius.

In the shadow of his cap and hoodie, he had sat in the hospital corridor while Angela ensured Allison received the care she urgently needed. Anonymously, he had listened to the ebb and flow around him, ears pricked for the inevitable appearance of the police.

"We stayed while they prepped her for surgery. I told them the story we had agreed with Allison, that we had found her beside her car on the road in the woods," Angela continued.

"I was vague on exactly where; the snow conditions made that sound plausible. I told them that she had said something about being shot when she stopped for a comfort break in the woods. We'll have to rely on Allison to explain the rest. I just hope she can be convincing."

She paused to break a roll in half, noting the burnt top without comment.

"We slipped away the moment Marius heard the police arriving."

Her final sentence stilled the room.

"Big chap. Had sergeant stripes. Came in with a tall, gawky policeman in tow," Marius offered between hungry mouthfuls of food.

"That will be Wailes and his shadow," Angela confirmed. "It's as we expected. Allison is one of his team."

"Was Wailes surprised to find the victim of the trap he had helped set up was one of his own?" I asked.

"We didn't stay to find out. Best we left before they started to look for us," Angela said. "We waited in a side corridor. When Wailes appeared and entered the treatment room to see Allison, we made a swift departure."

As she finished speaking, she passed Homer the loaned device he had used to obscure the CCTV cameras at the hotel.

"I hope that worked. I have an aversion to being caught on camera." She gave him an ironic smile.

"So, do we think Wailes was responsible for what happened to Allison at your cottage?" I asked.

Homer shook his head. "Not on his own. He probably knew something was planned and helped Miller with the information to achieve it. The trap was meant for you or me; both of us if they were lucky. Shooting Allison was bad luck; collateral damage. From what she told us they couldn't have known she was going to my cottage."

"The same people who put the scorpion in my bed?" Olwyn asked, trying to join the dots.

"Probably," Homer ventured. "I'm certain that was Wailes, though he most likely did it on Miller's instructions."

We sat around the table, finishing dinner in silence, aware of the dark forces gathering around us.

"So what do we do next?" Olwyn asked the obvious question.

Homer stood up and cleared away his plate.

"First, you two need to talk, share what you know about the fracking site." He nodded towards Olwyn and me before turning to Marius. "Meanwhile, we have a job to do. Do you know how to hot-wire a car?"

Marius looked startled, shaking his head. "I've never had need to. I don't do joy-riding," he added defensively.

"First time for everything. You never know when it will come in useful. We're going to retrieve a Jaguar."

The ambiguity of his words clearly bewildered Marius, but he followed Homer, a reluctance in his step at the thought of leaving the warmth of Angela's kitchen.

A few minutes later, I saw the headlight beam of Angela's bike light up a blizzard of driving snow as they disappeared into the night. Marius was right about one thing; it definitely shouldn't be snowing like that in October.

The snow eased some while later. On leaving Angela's, Homer took the decision to make a diversion to repair the door to his cottage and clear all evidence that Allison had been shot. It no longer fitted with the statement she would make, while at the same time creating confusion for whoever had rigged the shotgun inside his front door.

Despite the conditions, he chose to keep to lanes and tracks, the tyres of the scramble bike leaving a solitary, treaded trail in their wake. He and Marius spoke little, partly a result of the bitter cold, both absorbed by their own thoughts on the events of the evening.

The damage to the front door clearly showed the signs of the shotgun blast. Amazingly, the thick oak planks were still intact, needing little more than sanding and a series of cut nails to re-fix the loosened boards. Homer added additional draw bolts at the top and bottom.

"Safer than a lock," Homer grumbled as he tightened the final screws.

Holding a flashlight while Homer worked, Marius looked at the flayed door. As they cleared away the tools and evidence of the repair, Marius didn't feel especially reassured.

When they rode away, Homer dragged a scouring branch behind the bike, erasing all evidence of their tyre tracks. The forecast was for more snow before morning but you could never be too sure.

Once in town they hid the bike and chose a darkened bus shelter almost opposite Hargreaves garage in which to warm themselves before undertaking the main purpose of their visit.

Huddled together, with Joss sandwiched between them, Homer and Marius sat for some time watching the forecourt of Hargreaves garage. There was no sign of police activity. As their cold, numb hands slowly warmed, Homer decided to address Marius's unasked questions about Grace and Olwyn.

"They're just a pair of amateurs," he started, already sounding exasperated. "Without any plan, they're working separately to expose what's going on in the fracking site not far from here."

Homer placed a note of scorn on the word 'amateurs'.

"It's no surprise that they've upset some very nasty people who don't enjoy others poking their noses into their business."

Homer continued.

"You'll have already guessed that the men responsible for fracking operations apply strict security around what goes on. What they do is supposed to be authorised by emergency temporary laws brought in a year ago by the new coalition government. These people don't play games. It's something those two women seem slow to learn, which is why I need to get both of them away from here."

"Away to where?" Marius asked, a challenging note in his voice.

"Anywhere, out of this area; as far away as possible. And if they're arrested, somewhere that won't lead the police and Bremer's thugs back to us."

From the tone of his voice, Homer made it clear he was keen to be rid of the pair of them.

"Don't you think you could support their cause instead of chasing them away?" Marius replied, rather accusingly.

"Perhaps; if it was a worthwhile cause, backed by a decent plan."

Homer paused, studying his son's face. He had matured a lot in the intervening years.

"The problem with these two is how they go about things. Blundering around like a bull in a china shop against people like Bremer and Miller always ends up with someone getting seriously hurt," Homer said.

"And I don't intend to become collateral damage while they do so."

He turned away, signalling an end to the matter, but Marius had other ideas.

"Surely it's the moral duty of all of us to stand against authority when it's plainly wrong or corrupt." There was bite in his words.

Taken aback by his son's spirited stand Homer hesitated, still watching the dormant buildings opposite.

"I've done some of that." Slowly he turned to face Marius. "Last time I looked, it had ruined my life."

Homer left the ambiguity of his words to hang in the air between them as he left the bus shelter and set off across the road towards the garage and the snow covered Jaguar.

Homer removed a wire coat hanger from his rucksack. They were both wearing white smocks over their parkas with balaclavas to match, creating ghostlike figures in the pre-dawn darkness.

Holding a small flashlight between his teeth, he brushed a covering of snow from the Jaguar's side window and, prising away the rubber seal, managed to create a small gap at the top.

"Watch this, you never know when it might come in handy."

Homer straightened the wire hanger, forming a loop at one end which he fed through the opening at the top of the window before bending it through a right-angle, groping for the release button of the door lock in the cracked leather upholstery.

"Hey presto," he announced a few seconds later as the door swung open.

Homer slid across the red leather of the Jaguar's front seats. Preferring anything to get out of the cold, Marius followed him.

"Hold this, shine it onto the ignition switch." Homer handed him the flashlight. "Now, pay attention; your life might depend on this one day."

He searched behind the aged switch, tugging coloured wires into small balloons. Separating them, he selected two colours, snipped the wires and bared the insulation. Sparks flashed as he touched them together.

Amazingly, the battery still had some life in it as the frigid engine strained to turn over, pistons straining in glutinous, thick oil. On the fourth attempt, 'Gladys' roared into life. Homer allowed himself a smug smile.

"You okay to follow me on the bike? There'll be no traffic so no lights until we're clear of town."

Marius nodded, apprehensive at the prospect of a long, cold ride alone on the scramble bike.

They left separately, Marius wheeling the bike through shadows to an unlit side street while Homer reversed the vintage Jaguar out of the garage forecourt. Hargreaves had no CCTV cameras so with luck he might think a casual theft had taken place.

Ten minutes later, they were travelling in convoy; Marius as close to the pin-prick rear lights of the Jaguar as he dared in the snowy conditions, Homer in the warm comfort of the car's heater, while Joss sat on the rear seat staring out of the rear window, watching the solitary light of the motorbike wobbling in the slushy road behind them.

It took an hour before the Jaguar drew to a halt in the station car park. Homer parked in an unlit corner, well clear of the probing cameras.

Marius, stiff rigid with cold and in need of assistance to even swing his leg over the bike, pulled to a halt in the shadows beside the car. Homer admired his son's pluck and caught him before he and the bike fell over.

"Come on. I'll buy you a hot breakfast so you can thaw out."

"What about the Jag?" Marius mumbled between frozen lips.

"That's for the owner to sort out. Hargreaves doesn't have a working security camera. This will make the police believe whoever took the car brought it to this station and caught the train to London. With luck, they'll be dim enough to think it was merely an opportunist theft. I'll buy a single ticket from the machine and show myself on the platform. Heavily clad against the cold, even if there's a camera they won't be able to tell who bought a ticket."

Car parked and ticket bought, Homer and Marius set off to find an early morning breakfast, opting for an all-night transport café already buzzing with red-eyed, haulage drivers.

Camouflaged behind windows streaming with condensation, Homer located a table at the rear and ordered two full breakfasts and mugs of coffee and then slipped out the kitchen door to ensure there was no one in the car park following them. Even in sub-zero temperatures, it never paid to be complacent.

"Start without me if I'm not back in time. Don't talk to anyone."

Marius could only nod in reply, his jaw still numb and frozen. Homer was back in a few minutes.

"It's all a waste of time if someone is watching us," he said warming his hands on a hot mug.

"You could have used the ticket to go back to London if the cold has got too much and you want to take the return flight back to sunny Australia," he said, teasingly, offering the first sign of humour.

"I had little or no option; either come here or continue living in a house where I'm no longer wanted," Marius replied.

Dejected, he seemed to slump in his chair. For the first time the truth was coming to the surface.

"On balance, your old cottage seems marginally the best option."

Homer looked at his son with concern. "Stepfathers? More often than not they're a problem."

"He loves Lilley; just can't stand me."

"He sees you as competition for your mother's affection. It's not the same with daughters."

"You reckon?" Marius said with a tinge of venom in his words. "The pervert makes a habit of walking into the bathroom or her bedroom uninvited." He stared hard at Homer. "We all know what that's about."

"So why come here? You said your course is mostly online. You could have stayed in Australia to look out for your sister?"

Lilley was thirteen. Homer felt a sharp pang of concern for his estranged daughter. This time Marius regarded his father with an expression close to hostility.

"You surprise me. I thought looking out for her was a father's job? Or does being a convicted criminal exonerate you from that role too?"

The force of his words rocked Homer back in his chair, the harsh condemnation of youth biting into his soul.

"There's nothing I can say to change what's gone. There are reasons …" Homer's words drifted away from him.

"Look, if it's to sit in judgement, you're entitled to, but why come all this way to do that? If you've only come here to vent your spleen, save your breath, my conscience got there first, years ago."

The sad wash of their words was interrupted by the arrival of two heaped plates that masqueraded as full English breakfast. Perhaps it was the gulf between them, or, just simply, the force of cold and hunger; silence reigned while they ate.

With a maturity beyond his years, it was Marius who tried to find a way to bridge the abyss between them. He knew little, but suspected much. But blood is blood, and poison is self-defeating and only leads to sepsis of the soul.

"I came because I care. I wanted to see for myself if you did too. Despite her harsh words, there was something Mum said that hinted this might not be totally of your choosing. Hating you is the easy bit. But that doesn't stop you from being our father. If you want to be, that is?"

What Marius had said a few moments before stunned Homer. Was it simply easier to hide behind guilt and pretend the blame excluded all parental responsibility, even if that one day risked an ISIS operative finding his family?

But time never stands idle. Without replying, Homer stood to leave, searching for money to pay for breakfast. As he did so, two small photos fell from his wallet. Bent and creased, taken years earlier when his children were small, before their family life was shattered by his actions. Marius saw them before Homer could pick them up from the table. He handed them back to his father in silence, a gesture that said far more than words.

As they donned gloves and helmets, Homer paused to offer Marius a hug. It was the first time in years that father and son had embraced. A moment of epiphany amidst the noisy babble of a greasy transport café.

And to further salve his conscience, Homer had saved the streaky bacon for Joss, leaving the dog wondering what had just happened at the table to bring about such generosity.

CHAPTER 34
FORTUNATELY, DOGS AREN'T COMPLACENT

Angela was a late riser. Unseen, Olwyn slipped from the house before it was light. She left a note, *'Back soon'*, and borrowed the keys for Angela's van. In the snowy conditions, traffic was light, which made it easier to find the hospital.

Olwyn arrived before the wards became busy to find a night shift policeman asleep on a hard chair outside Allison's room. Since they had left the previous evening, Sergeant Wailes had obviously taken precautions. The policeman barely acknowledged Olwyn as she passed him. Wearing a borrowed, careworn jacket, her blonde hair wound up and hidden beneath a peaked cap, she didn't fit any descriptions he had been given.

Whether he was there to prevent anyone walking into Allison's room, or to prevent her from leaving, was a debatable point. 'Hide in plain sight,' she told herself; hadn't that been Jerry's advice a lifetime ago? Her disguise wouldn't fool Wailes, but she doubted he would make an appearance so early in the morning.

No one had asked for her name. Breakfast had been cleared away and staff were busy making preparations for the doctors' rounds. Visiting was risky, but she felt somewhat in Allison's debt.

Had it not been for her concern for Olwyn, she wouldn't have walked into the shotgun and come within inches of losing her life. Olwyn couldn't leave without making sure Allison knew she was grateful and that she had put herself at risk in her effort to find her. And there was also the matter of her statement.

Olwyn entered without knocking. The room was semi-dark, blinds half drawn, lit by the ghost green glow of monitors and a pale light over the bed. Allison lay, eyes closed, a drip in the back of her hand, her exposed upper body swaddled in bandages, a large dressing on the side of her head.

She looked at peace. Olwyn guessed her friend had been lucky. If the door had opened a few inches further and the second barrel had fired at the same moment, she would be visiting her in the morgue.

Olwyn drew the only chair to the side of the bed and lay her hand gently over Allison's.

"Hello stranger," Allison smiled weakly, one eye half open.

"What's a scruffy girl like you doing in a place like this?"

Her voice sounded dry and rasping, so Olwyn offered a glass of water from a covered jug.

"I'm your second cousin, Martha, just rushed down from Birmingham to be by your bedside," Olwyn announced in her best impersonation of a Midlands accent. "Sorry, no time for fruit or flowers."

Allison attempted a small laugh and winced.

"Stupid question to ask, but how are you feeling?"

"Woozy. They've removed all the shot." Allison nodded towards a small metal dish at her bedside. "Forty-three pieces at the final count."

"That'll teach you to go poking your nose around someone else's door," Olwyn replied.

"It's what I'm supposed to do; I'm a policewoman," Allison said, pretending justification. "It wouldn't have been necessary if you had accepted my invitation to stay the night. I hear you had a bedtime tryst with a scorpion? You ought to be more careful who you share your bed with."

Somehow, Allison still managed to tease, despite her injuries. She rolled her eyes.

"Scorpions included, I certainly score low points on the popularity stakes." Allison grasped Olwyn's fingers. "So, when do you leave"?

"Soon. It seems our wild woodsman has come up with an ingenious plan."

"The sooner the better. Wailes is cunning. He'll work out soon enough that the scorpion didn't kill you. You've probably not got very long."

"And you? Have you made a statement?"

Olwyn found it hard to keep anxiety out of her voice. Allison was a policewoman and took her role seriously.

"Not a formal statement yet, but when I do, I'll play amnesia. Comes in very useful. The last thing I remember was stopping for a comfort break in the woods just as it started to snow. I can't remember where or when that was and the snow will cover any trace of evidence."

Olwyn frowned. "What about your car? Won't it still be at Homer's cottage?"

"It's been moved already, I hope. The last thing Angela whispered as she left me last night was that Homer would arrange for it to be driven to a spot in the woods where she claimed she had found me. I gave her my car keys so, with luck, the cover story should already be complete." A wan smile barely hid the discomfort of her wounds.

They seemed to have thought of most things, and noises in the corridor confirmed that the doctors' rounds had begun.

"Time for you to go," Allison added reluctantly, her voice attractively husky.

"My guard outside the door is bound to rouse his interest at any moment."

She frowned. "By the way, your fake accent is lousy; best not to put it to the test."

Olwyn found a slip of paper in the side cupboard and wrote down her phone number under the cover name 'Martha'.

"Keep in touch when you get a new phone. The last phone is a complete mess, but at least it spared your hand." With a smile, she slipped it into Allison's hand.

For a moment, Allison seemed reluctant to release her hand.

"Keep safe. No more sharing a bed with scorpions," she said with a note of mischief.

When she finally released Olwyn her sigh held a note of disappointment. Perhaps she had hoped for a kiss of farewell.

The following morning was clear evidence that the years had started to catch up with Angela. Homer and Marius left the previous night, leaving me with the instruction to move Allison's car before daylight.

Walking miles in the snow was obviously beyond Angela, so the task fell to me. Without Joss to act as my faithful guide, and in woods sown with traps and sensors, I had to resist the temptation to use my phone for guidance and resorted to a map and compass instead. At least it had stopped snowing.

Rising before dawn was difficult, my flirt with hypothermia the previous day weighed heavily on my reserves. Despite Homer marking the location of his cottage on the map, it still took an hour to thread my way through the snow covered woods.

The cottage was empty, its doors locked and bolted, and from the condition of the front door, Homer and Marius must have worked late into the night to repair the damage. Only a slight depression in the snow marked their departure along the track to the road; flurries of snow had made a good job of concealment. You had to hand it to Homer; he was thorough.

I found Allison's car, now hidden beneath a pristine white blanket of snow. Feeling the bite of cold in my hands, I hoped the car had a decent heater. Driving the snow filled furrows in the track was no mean feat and it was almost light by the time I reached the road where a few tyre tracks already swept a path. Whilst I couldn't hide my tyre tracks from the cottage, I could at least use these to conceal the rest of my plan. It might also help if it snowed again soon.

When I had awoken, I had discovered that Olwyn had left early, no explanation beyond a scribbled message devoid of any detail. In 'Terra Mater' we worked in isolated groups; I had long learnt to accept the secrecy and unexplained actions of others, and the unfortunate consequences they often caused. It seemed Olwyn had brought enough trouble already and I felt disconcerted by the thought of what another of her private adventures might bring upon us.

The previous evening, before Homer and Marius had left, we had discussed where to leave Allison's car, thinking of somewhere close to a road whilst not immediately visible to passing cars. The options were limited but Homer had identified a spot on the map that might fit the bill.

Without sat-nav, finding that spot, on roads transformed by the snow, took longer than expected. By the time I found the location at which to abandon the car, it was already broad daylight. So far, all well and good, but it worried me that it didn't credibly explain how Allison came to be injured by the shotgun.

I could only hope that her statement would support her claim that she had been followed and attacked the previous day. And that, at least in part, relied upon Olwyn, who I didn't particularly trust. None of it addressed one significant point; whoever had rigged the booby trap in Homer's cottage would be deeply troubled by Allison's version of the events.

I left the car unlocked, churned footprints around a nearby tree, scattered blood stained bandages and the discharged shot pellets that Homer had given me, before re-tracing my tracks back to the road. After that, it was simply a matter of walking in the path ploughed by car tyres until I found a spot where the snow had thinned to a bare covering, and then branching off into the woods in search for a route back to Angela's cottage. With the forecast of more snow, that promised to be easier said than done.

I never expected to miss the companionship of a dog. With Joss's constant loyalty and bright intelligence, I felt a hole inside me into which loneliness intruded. With the rising sun, the air had warmed, creating a veil of thickening mist that cocooned the world. It erased any chance of locating landmarks, adding to my solitary feeling of isolation.

With only a map, I tried to make a fix of the point I had left the road. I needed to avoid passing cars, but once away from the road, I soon lost my location. The prospect of going around in circles quickly ceased to be a cliché and became reality. The mist seemed to erase the passage of time, my attention consumed and eyes locked on an errant compass needle.

'Eyes down'; it was like playing bingo. As a result, I almost walked into them, and I probably would have done had not one of their number stopped to pee against the trunk of a tree. I froze and dropped the compass. Unaware of my presence, the man cursed raucously to someone close by. In the mist, they could be all around me for all I knew.

Transfixed, I registered his camouflage smock, a shoulder slung rifle, words in a foreign tongue. Not Arabic, perhaps something east European, a reminder of wild rumours that 'Blue Horizon' were stiffening their security organisation with mercenaries; anyone offering their services for payment.

If the peeing man in front of me turned around, I was standing barely ten feet behind him. Holding my breath, I side-stepped behind a pine tree which offered a chance of concealment. But time wasn't on my side. I saw the man shake and zip. Intuition must have pricked him and he began to turn, his rifle sliding from his shoulder, sensing that someone was behind him.

He was interrupted by a flash; black and white, moving fast through the snow amongst the trees. Still in half turn, it distracted him, his rifle rising to horizontal in a smooth continuous motion. The crack of a shot rang out, spooking cawing crows into the air as I stumbled behind the alarmingly slender trunk of the tree. The shot reverberated back and forth amongst the trees, chorusing calls and shouts from invisible sources in the mist.

Miraculously, no one else seemed to be aware of my presence. The man moved off, searching for whatever he had shot at, intuition momentarily forgotten. I could breathe again.

I lay hidden in the snow for a long time, then finally set off. Twice I had to stop and listen as ghost voices drifted amongst the trees. At least there were no further shots to send me scurrying for cover. My morale began to improve; even the invasive bite of the cold seemed to be held at bay.

Voices suddenly broke the spell; they were directly behind me. Someone was following my footprints in the snow. The voices called to one another; they must have realised I had heard them and begun to run. Adrenalin surged through me. Throwing everything to the wind, I ran faster; capture was not an option.

Breathless, I fumbled for my phone, pressing the 'on' switch in preparation for a last, desperate act of sending the warning code to 'Terra Mater'; a flashed signal that I had been caught, in that instant before the acid capsule destroyed the SIM card.

I'd been doing so well. Complacency always wins in the end. Behind me, the men were crashing through the undergrowth, fanning out, calling ahead for others to close the net. I fought back a fatalistic pang of the inevitable; I'd fight if they overpowered me but the odds were stacked in their favour.

My lungs were bursting and my vision was greying out, but I caught a brief glimpse of something crossing my path. It was gone in an instant; small, moving fast, the flash of black and white I must have glimpsed earlier, at which shots had obviously been fired. Only now it was coming straight towards me. It could only be one thing. Joss, my faithful, one-dog rescue team.

Scrabbling for her footing as she turned in a tight arc, accelerating past me at full speed, heading only she knew where, back in the direction from which she had just appeared. No bark of greeting, just grace, power and pure speed of a dog at one with her environment, relying that I would have the sense to follow her without question.

I changed direction, hurdled a gorse bush, feet pounding in her paw prints, an adrenalin fuelled boost of hope driving my legs. How long we ran for I had no idea. Without any sense of direction I just drove myself in the wake of the dog, blind faith in Joss knowing where we were going. What else was there to do?

The voices diminished, or was that my imagination. We must have been following a snow covered track for several minutes before I even realised that the way ahead had become clearer.

In a moment, Joss disappeared, replaced by the apparition of a battered Landrover, cocooned in a cloud of exhaust smoke, already moving slowly away down the track, side door open, signalling like a rescue flag, as it slowly accelerated.

"How?" Grace blurted out, chest heaving, gasping for air.

"Blame the dog."

Homer gestured to Joss, panting behind them, bracing herself as they swung into a snow covered lane.

"She's been pacing and moaning for the past hour. Only way to get some peace was to let her run and find you. I think the two of you must have become telepathic," he added with a rare note of humour.

Grace turned in her seat to hug Joss, wet fur and all. Perhaps it had been the empathy of releasing her from the snare. Pay-back time, as though the dog knew she was lost and in danger and in need of her special skills.

"You did well to get this far," Homer offered a rare compliment.

Grace slumped, exhausted, in her seat as Joss climbed over to share the front footwell.

"I moved the policewoman's car as you instructed. I took the map and a compass; no phone. Sat-nav would give away my position."

"I thought Angela said she would move the car?"

Grace shook her head. "Not in this weather."

Homer grunted in agreement. "The Wright-Smith woman has disappeared, taking Angela's van." He didn't sound happy.

"That will be to visit Allison. Angela said she was worried about her."

"As if that's going to make things better," Homer said. Abruptly, Mr Grumpy had returned.

"It's what people do, Homer. A bit like you coming to my rescue with Joss."

Homer gave a derisory snort, an attempt to be dismissive.

"It appears you're worth more alive than dead. Besides," a barely hidden grin had returned, "Joss would have never forgiven me."

They sat in silence for a few minutes. Homer searched the pockets of his poacher's jacket and tossed Grace his battered flask. She felt the contents burn all the way down.

Eventually he slowed the Landrover, turning onto a vague depression of a side track. He stopped, cut a rake-shaped branch from a sapling and tied it to the rear tow hook.

"It'll snow again soon," he said, climbing back into the cab. "If anyone is following us, this will help erase our tyre tracks."

Homer engaged a low gear and set off into the woods.

"I hope you haven't forgotten my drone," Grace eventually reminded him as they bounced and jolted amongst the trees. "It would be a shame to waste Angela's owl."

"In this weather. Forget it."

He swerved to avoid a sapling, copper coloured leaves in a white landscape.

"Besides, you and the Wright-Smith woman leave tonight."

It was interesting in two parts; Angela excepted, Homer pointedly evaded the use of female names, as though they conferred an intimacy he would never address. Secondly, she was being told to leave without being asked.

"But ..."

"No buts," he snapped. "It's safer if you're both out of here. For all our sakes."

He glared pointedly at Joss. "Though I doubt the dog thinks so."

"But I need ..."

"If it's needs you're talking about, try speaking to the Wright-Smith woman, as I told you to. She's been into your precious fracking site and interviewed the staff. That's what has got us into this latest mess. Some people," he didn't need to explain who, "have taken great exception to her snooping around, despite her fancy warrants."

'Exception'. Though he didn't refer to them, the scorpion and the booby trap shotgun were clear examples of what Homer meant.

Fortunately, he omitted to add, 'They could be working on third time lucky.'

CHAPTER 35
TO TRADE WITH THE DEVIL

"Allison says she'll stick to the agreed story when she makes her statement to the police."

The van was back in front of Angela's cottage; Olwyn had returned from her hospital visit. Homer raised a sceptical eyebrow.

"That's going to cause confusion if Bremer's men tell him and Wailes that they set the booby trap inside my front door."

Homer looked pointedly at the clock on the wall. He needed to return to his cottage before the police came snooping for answers.

Angela sat silent in her chair, listening to the conversation wax and wane around her. She looked drawn and tired, reminding Homer of her advancing years. He had always thought of her as invincible, her spare frame seemingly made of iron. On this cold day she looked her age, pale in body and spirit.

"You two need urgently to talk."

Homer changed tack, directing the words at Grace and Olwyn as he gathered a blanket that had slipped to the floor and draped it around Angela's shoulders. Her hand brushed his in thanks.

"But I can't ..."

Grace was interrupted by a shake of Homer's head as Marius lifted a pan of hot porridge from the range.

"I've already told you, it's no longer possible to stay here. Things are well beyond just unsafe. Whether or not you share what you both know, you leave tonight. And you," Homer pointed an accusing finger at Grace, "stop meddling in this area for at least a month."

"Why?"

"Because I need to see the man who gave Bremer your photo for the 'Wanted' poster and I need the promise of your inaction to trade with."

An unhappy frown creased Grace's face.

"A month won't be possible. Plans are forming too quickly. In a month …"

Her words trailed away as she thought of the photos she had taken from her tree top eyrie.

Homer shook his head. "A month is the best I can offer. Break that agreement and you're on your own."

His words were stark and blunt as he pulled his jacket from above the range where it had been drying.

"Where are you going?" Angela asked, the concern in her voice stalling Marius as he ladled porridge into bowls.

"To trade with the devil in the unlikely chance I can keep us safe."

A flurry of snow had the final word, blown in through the door as Homer slammed it shut behind him.

"I still need evidence of a body."

Miller was insistent. Sitting in Wailes's car in a layby, they had been arguing the matter for ten minutes without agreement.

"The cameras show her body being carried from the hotel. She made one untraced call an hour before. There's no record of anyone entering the hotel, or a call for an ambulance. No one could survive that level of toxic sting without immediate medical help. Anyway, your efforts don't seem to have achieved anything beyond getting one of my officers in hospital with shotgun wounds."

Miller frowned. "You said she was found in the trees on the forest road?"

"Yes. A passer-by found her."

"The passer-by who has conveniently disappeared without giving a name or statement and of whom no one at the hospital can offer a description?"

"The hospital was busy. Besides, most people are too scared to get involved with anything near the fracking site because your thugs put the fear of dread in them," Wailes said with a note of exasperation.

"That's not where we set the trap."

"So you keep telling me. But that's where the car was found and there are blood stains in the snow."

Miller wasn't happy with Wailes's tone of accusation. "Mind explaining what happened to the Jaguar in Hargreaves garage? I hear the cameras conveniently weren't working."

"Has the hand of MI5 all over it. Perhaps they removed the woman's body and came back for the car. We still haven't found any trace of it; presumably it's disappeared back to London."

Miller stared through the windscreen with a stony expression on his face. "Far too many loose ends and presumptions for my liking. Bremer has already intervened once. When I present him with this mess, there'll be hell to pay for someone." The inference in his words made it clear it wouldn't be him.

"Don't try threatening me."

Miller shrugged. "More a warning than a threat. You know that Bremer doesn't tolerate failure in any shape or form; his boss even less so. My advice is that you locate the body of the Wright-Smith woman immediately so I have evidence to present and, while you're at it, give me the leads I need to find this other troublesome eco-nut we're still looking for."

Without another word, Miller got out of the car just as a black four-by-four drew up alongside. As the vehicle disappeared in a cloud of snow, Wailes fumbled for his tablets; the chest pains were becoming a regular visitor.

Homer entered the caravan without waiting for an invitation. Cosmo could see that his friend was far from happy.

"We need to talk; me, you, and Milo. Now," Homer said without any formality.

It was obvious to Cosmo it was better not to argue. He didn't need two guesses for the reason of his friend's abrupt arrival.

Homer waited with barely suppressed impatience while Cosmo herded his wife, daughter and noisy grandchildren out of the van.

"Tea or coffee?" Cosmo offered.

Homer shook his head. "This isn't a social call," he said in forewarning.

Cosmo nodded as they waited for Milo to arrive.

"Guess it might be too much to expect that you've brought a couple of fresh rainbows or a nice juicy carp?" he quipped in an effort to dampen Homer's obviously slow burning fuse.

"A couple of live, hungry jack-pike would be more appropriate at the moment," Homer retorted sharply, staring out of the window, refusing to meet Cosmo's eyes. 'He knows why I'm here,' he thought silently to himself. 'Let's see what excuses he has to offer before I confront them.'

"I hope you're not here to confuse business with pleasure?" Cosmo asked, pouring coffee for himself. "It's hard to stay level-headed when that happens."

Locked in a prison cell designed for one, the two men had shared many dark moments. There weren't many bleak places they hadn't visited.

The door opened and Milo entered in a flurry of snow, shadowed by another man almost twice his size. Much to Cosmo's disgust, he didn't wipe his boots.

"What a pleasant surprise," Milo said, almost dismissively. "We don't often receive visitors."

Homer didn't smile. "You don't need the heavy protection." Homer pointed at the tall man standing behind him. "He can leave. It's you I want to talk to."

Milo pressed his lips tightly closed, considering refusal. Cosmo intervened with a slight shake of the head towards the taller man.

"Okay, Mouse, you can leave us."

For the first time since his arrival, a smile cracked Homer's dour expression. Mouse was at least two metres tall and probably weighed well over a hundred kilos. He left without a word, stooping to exit through the narrow caravan door.

"Shall we sit down? My poor legs ..." Cosmo played his hand at diffusing the building confrontation.

Homer shook his head. "There's no need. This won't take long."

Milo folded his arms across his chest, preparing for the imminent outburst.

With a slightly exaggerated gesture, Homer withdrew a small velvet bag from his pocket and threw it to Cosmo.

"Take a look at these," he said, pointedly ignoring Milo.

Cosmo emptied the contents into a cupped hand. He poked it with a finger for a few moments before exhaling with a whistle.

"Nice. If they're not fake."

He returned the contents to the bag and passed it to Milo, frowning at Homer, who waited for Milo to examine the contents before answering.

"They're the real deal; amethyst, agate, garnets, lapis, a few pieces of sapphire; all semi-precious uncut stones."

Milo fired a questioning glance in his direction. "Why? Why show us this?"

Homer leaned forwards and took back the bag.

"Because I want you to stop selling Bremer drugs and giving him information that is intended to … damage certain people I know." He stared hard at Milo who tried to feign indifference.

"So what are you supplying Bremer? Cocaine, heroin?" Homer didn't wait for an answer.

"He'll use you for as long as it takes to root out your suppliers and take control of your sordid ring for himself." He paused to allow his words to sink in.

"How much is he taking off the payment for your deals? A quarter of everything you make? Maybe more?"

Homer looked amused, watching Milo's attempt at an impassive face. He caught a glance of Cosmo making signals to his son with his eyes.

"Still doesn't explain the stones. What are they to us," Milo said with a shrug, an attempt at bravado.

"Because here's the deal. I have a contact in a refugee camp in Syria. He can supply that," Homer pointed to the velvet bag, "and more every month. But you know what these camps are like."

He stared at Cosmo, revisiting memories of men they had both met in prison and the hard life journey that had brought them there.

"He needs someone in the west to process those stones; get them cut and polished and sold into the jewellery markets of Europe and America."

"Sounds like 'blood diamonds'."

Homer smiled. "Not remotely in the same league. Most of these just lie around in the deserts of Iraq and Syria. My contact needs an outlet, something he can't achieve behind the wire in Syria. You think you're some hot-shot business man."

He gave Milo an impassive stare to remind him he knew he had given Grace's photo to Bremer.

"Now's the chance to prove that you really are; build something that's legal and legitimate before Bremer turns on you, snake that he is, and lands you in prison."

It still took a time to agree a deal but in the end the three of them spat on their palms and joined hands.

"And not a word about our deal to anyone. I'll know the moment you start telling tales. If you're asked, the woman in the photo has long since left the area and I'm just a sad, lonely hermit and small-time poacher."

Homer stared unsmiling at Milo.

"They're my terms. I will not forgive you breaking them in any shape or form." Only after they had both nodded in agreement did Homer release their hands.

As Homer left the caravan, Cosmo fell in step beside him.

"Why?" he asked as they walked towards Homer's motorbike.

Homer was silent for a moment.

"Let's say two years sharing a prison cell has to be worth something. I can't do anything with those stones. My contact is a good man. One day in the future he might just get asylum provided Assad's thugs don't kill him first. He needs money for his family and to get them out. Doing a deal with Milo might just make that possible if you can steer him away from drugs and Bremer."

Cosmo sighed. "I'll do my best. Milo's greedy and ambitious, but he's not stupid. You've tweaked his honour, that's always the best card. He won't let you down on that alone."

Cosmo paused. "And your friend in the photo?"

Homer ignored his question while he swung his leg across the fuel tank of the bike. It would be a cold ride back to Angela's cottage.

"Some days I feel as though I'm on a train, racing towards a destination I don't want to arrive at and just hoping that the journey doesn't come to an end too soon."

He donned his helmet, kicked the starter and left without another word.

Marius made coffee hoping that Grace and Olwyn would stop shadow boxing and share what they knew about the fracking site.

Angela had appeared briefly around midday and, though Marius guessed she knew of Homer's plans, she said nothing. Pale and drawn, she had returned to her bedroom.

In Angela's absence Marius felt awkward in the midst of the silence that hung between the two women. He had little idea of their roles in all of this, or for that matter, how it was anything to do with him. But his father had insisted they talk and share information. Marius knew it would be a lost opportunity if they wasted the time while Homer was gone.

He placed mugs and a pot on the scrubbed kitchen table. It was Grace who broke the ice, speaking to Marius.

"The weather must come as quite a shock. What has brought you here to all this?" She nodded to the white glare of snow that lit the cold afternoon.

Marius guessed that 'all this' referred to the turbulence of events ever since he had arrived. It left him in as much of a quandary as the brutally cold weather.

He shrugged. "You know; stepfathers."

Grace nodded. Simple, but it explained a lot.

"Rather a case of out of the frying pan and into the fire," she said with a complicit grin.

"How do you come to know Homer?" He felt uncomfortable using his father's first name, but the other woman, Olwyn, was listening intently to their conversation.

"By chance. I'm an environmental activist and I became snared in a trap in the woods set by the fracking site. Fortunately, Joss found me," she paused to stroke the dog leaning against her leg. "She persuaded Homer to release me."

Both Marius and Olwyn laughed at the thought that it took help from the dog to overcome Homer's reluctance to act.

"That sounds like Homer," Olwyn said as she drew up a chair and joined them at the table, pouring coffee from the pot.

"And you?" Marius said, turning to the younger woman. She may have had an unusual name and a posh accent, but, like most men she came in contact with, he found her attractive. "You and Homer make an unlikely pair."

Olwyn smiled at his words. "We met over an *Androctonus crassicauda*".

Grace and Marius passed a bemused look at her statement.

"Perhaps better known as an Arabian fat tail scorpion," Olwyn continued, enjoying their confusion.

"Someone put her in my bed. By some miracle I managed to escape her sting but, having little experience with scorpions, I became marooned in my hotel room. Given my options, I had to ring Homer, who climbed the outside of the hotel building and captured the lethal arachnid."

Olwyn omitted to mention that she was naked at the time. "Homer just slipped her into one of his boxes," she said as though it was an everyday event. "We've christened her 'Scorpio'. I think Homer intends to return her to her owner."

The image made Grace laugh, that soft laugh that creates common ground between people and breaks the ice.

Marius grasped his moment.

"So, Olwyn, are you an environmentalist too?" It would explain how she had become mixed up in all of this.

She shook her head. "Me? No, I don't like to get my hands dirty. Just a humble desk job in the civil service for me."

"And that warrants someone placing a lethal scorpion in your bed? Who was it; another man's wife?"

Olwyn sighed at the thought.

"Mmm, not so simple. It's most likely to have been Allison's boss. He collects them."

They were silent while they digested the implications.

"Her boss, Sergeant Wailes, has friends who have taken exception to my conducting what on the face of it are only a few pointless interviews with the men who actually work at the fracking site. We suspected that one of them has been found dead in a ditch up in the woods. No one I spoke to at the site owned up to identify the dead man. They were all monosyllabically well-rehearsed to avoid admitting to anything."

The news that she had been in the fracking site immediately pricked Grace's attention.

Olwyn continued.

"But there was one thing that puzzled me? Do either of you know anything about radiation sickness and why it might turn up in sleepy, rural Sussex?"

Homer stopped beside a rare public phone box that he knew still worked. He fumbled for coins, being reminded of a simpler bygone age. The call was answered the second time he rang.

"I've left a piece of your feline property at the station at Petersfield."

Homer paused to allow his description of the Jaguar to sink in.

"You should be more careful in future," he said reprovingly.

"Ah, 'Gladys'," the voice replied, the distinct note of relief in his words.

"And the chauffeur?" he added, very much as an afterthought.

"Alive. No thanks to you. You really need to look after the people you employ; there are laws against this sort of thing."

The voice chuckled. "Fortunately, not ones that we pay much heed too. Are you sending her back?"

"Well she's not safe here, as you well know. Try convincing me she'll be better off if she returns to London?"

"My, my, you never change. Forever his brother's keeper."

Homer ignored the cynicism. "Unlike you who uses people like yesterday's newsprint."

Their words fenced with one another down a telephone wire. Homer knew it was pointless; somehow, the man with the power always got his way.

"I'll send her back tomorrow. Whether that's to continue working for you might be another matter."

The voice laughed. "We'll see. Though I have to say, she's performed far better than I expected."

"Games," Homer muttered. "You treat this all as some sort of puerile game. These men who run the fracking sites are serious about their secrecy, and before very much longer someone is going to get killed while you sit comfortably at your cosy desk in London."

"Bigger fish to fry, dear chap, far bigger fish," the voice said dismissively. "Besides, they've always got you to look out for them."

"Listen, you idiot," Homer exclaimed, feeling riled by the man. "A policewoman got shot yesterday. Someone broke into my cottage and set a booby trap, using my gun, in my house. That's how serious it's got."

"I saw nothing about that on the newsfeed?"

Did he detect a note of defence in the voice?

"You won't. It's what you would call collateral damage. If you recall, a lot of that seems to happen around you."

There was silence for a moment.

"How's your family?" the voice asked.

Not the innocent question it sounded; Homer didn't like the sharp edge to his voice. Behind the phone box, a car passed, travelling too slowly for his liking. It was probably the snow, his paranoiac tendencies were kicking in. This call was taking far too long.

"Fine. But remember one thing. If anything happens to them, I'll come looking for you."

Homer left the receiver hanging. Houseman could talk to himself.

Allison Markham had never thought of herself as an actress. Though still connected to a drip, she was out of bed waiting for Sergeant Wailes to arrive to take her statement. In the hours of waiting, she had ample opportunity to reflect upon her life.

It had seemed all so innocent when, in her second year at university, a woman slightly older had approached her in a night club. They appeared to share the same interests, and Allison, struggling to survive on a university loan, had been offered a small monthly sum by the woman if she undertook a few simple tasks.

It had started with surveillance; listening to the opinions of fellow, outspoken students and summarising them for her new friend. She tried to remain objective, but many had been quite radical, extreme, outside the folly of youth. At times she felt a snitch, informing on friends.

"If you don't do it, we'll have to find someone else. They might not be so … balanced," had been the inducement to ease Allison's conscience, the occasional flash of a Home Office badge underpinning the value of the work she was doing.

And the money helped. That, and the photographs. Taken clandestinely one drunken night, of Allison together in a room with another girl, whose name she couldn't recall, now shared with the suggestion that they could accidentally find their way onto social media sites if she didn't continue; somewhere her father, a parson, might stumble across them.

Allison Markham gave up alcohol from that moment onwards. She became more reclusive, choosing her private contacts with scrupulous care. She carried on with her work, creating a mission to root out homophobic, rather than political, zealots.

Her approach to Olwyn had been uncharacteristically spontaneous. Disappointingly, it seemed to come to nothing, but you never knew how things might work out.

Now, she awaited the arrival of Wailes, a man she knew had barely concealed homophobic opinions, who was capable of using his position to try to harm Olwyn. Only that morning, in an act of kindness, Olwyn had visited her in hospital; a dangerous visit.

Wailes might well be an ignorant man, but he possessed powerful depths of animal cunning. To protect Olwyn, Allison would have to use her only reliable defence. Put on a great act, faking loss of memory, and hope Wailes knew nothing of her secrets with which to blackmail her.

CHAPTER 36
ESCAPE IN PLAIN SIGHT

Before I had seen it, Joss sensed the presence of the whisper drone as it skimmed low over the trees towards the cottage. A few minutes later, in the fading light, I might never have known it was ever there.

I had taken Joss for a run in the woods around Angela's cottage and she must have felt the air vibrate as the drone approached. She whined, something to which I've learnt to pay immediate attention, and gazed skywards, instinctively stepping under the shielding canopy of a pine tree. The whine turned to a warning growl as the drone passed directly above us.

Whisper drones are evil things; small, slender, ghost grey, invisible, the modern assassins' weapon of choice. On this occasion, it moved on without noticing our presence as I squatted in the snow, arms wrapped tight around Joss, as much for my own comfort as hers. Such silent surveillance drones were the prerogative of the military, another clue to the tendrils of power exercised by 'Blue Horizon' in a quest to hide the secrets of their fracking sites.

As we watched, it drifted slowly sideways in the cold evening breeze, imaging cameras and sensors combing the surrounding woods. I had heard they were equipped with facial recognition, intent on tracking anyone in unguarded moments. Armed with a simple compressed air gun that fired high velocity pellets, these silent assassins were rumoured to kill autonomously, leaving no trace or evidence of their passing.

I shuddered, not just from the cold. For several minutes, the machine hovered silently above Angela's cottage like a ghostly sentinel while the cottage slumbered in the gloom, the only light from the kitchen window thankfully obscured by a drawn blind. A thin coil of grey wood smoke drifted from a chimney pot; evidence of human presence.

After a moment, the drone switched its attention to the track leading down to the road. But Homer, being Homer, had obscured his departure with the usual raking arms of a branch. Windblown snow had done the rest. Only my footprints stood out clearly like a hunted animal's spoor, indigo puddles in the growing darkness, awaiting the attention of the drone.

Such was the world into which we had descended, each denuding step taken to strip away personal privacy, leaving opposition no place to hide.

'Joining the dots'. Such a throw-away cliché. Sure, exposing what was happening in the fracking sites was desperately important for the sake of the environment and the planet. But of greater significance was peeling back 'Blue Horizon's remorseless grip on power; a slow, insipient march towards a form of totalitarian control that avoided mistakes of fascist's regimes a century before.

At least they couldn't read our thoughts. Not yet, anyway.

Homer was silent while Grace told him about the drone. With no more than a nod, he deliberately dropped her bag on the floor at her feet.

"All the more reason for you to leave tonight. I went to my cottage to collect your things. You hid them well," he said abruptly. "Now we just have to hope Bremer doesn't spring a surprise visit before you go."

As Homer left the room in search of Angela, Marius frowned, looking around the room with concern. Living on the edge like this was taking some getting used to.

"How?" He asked the question foremost in all their minds.

"No doubt we'll all find out in good time." Olwyn spoke with a note of resignation. Marius shrugged.

He had shown unexpected culinary skills, and prepared dinner which he had kept warming in the Aga. Without prompting, he started serving the meal. It seemed obvious that Homer and Angela wanted to talk in private, so he carried a tray to her bedroom, leaving Olwyn to set the table.

Hopefully, Grace and Olwyn would be able to continue the dialogue he had encouraged earlier, slowly evaporating an air of distrust that seemed to have caused a barrier between them. It also gave Marius the opportunity to sit closer to Olwyn.

Although she was perhaps five years his senior, he had taken an immediate attraction to her. Intrigued by her quirky appearance and pretty, in a casual unaffected sort of way, she displayed an air of confidence that he suspected hid vulnerability. Despite the difference in their ages, he had been aware from their first meeting that she watched him with amused interest, with a slightly puzzled look in her eyes, a half smile greeting him every time their eyes made contact.

For Marius, girlfriends in Australia had frequently come and gone. He had often felt awkward and gawky in their presence, relationships that were regularly estranged by the need to keep moving for reasons never properly explained to him.

Of the two women, Grace was older by some margin. A more distant, remote character, her face was often expressionless with eyes that seldom rested; searching, evaluating, fight or flight imprinted in their signature.

Perhaps it was her aloofness that drew him in the direction of Olwyn, the uninvited stress of their circumstances creating common ground between them. Either way, he was hoping for a contact number from her before she left. Unknowingly, he would have to join the queue behind Allison Markham.

Over dinner, they discussed the mysterious presence of radioactivity at a fossil fuel fracking site. Olwyn told them of the note that her final interviewee had concealed in her hand, and described the red lesions some of the men displayed on their arms and faces.

Grace listened in silence for some while, evaluating whether she trusted Olwyn enough to tell her that she had found radiation present in groundwater leaking from the same site. One way or another, it would soon be common knowledge so there seemed little point in keeping it secret. Decision made, she gave no opinion of the likely cause and held back her suspicion that there was radioactivity in the containers that arrived every night at the site.

"Doesn't radiation sometimes occur naturally in groundwater?" Marius had read that this could be a common occurrence in certain geological conditions.

Grace nodded. "True. But not this form or at this level." She left her statement to hang in the air.

Olwyn shuddered. "Any talk of radiation frightens me. It's up there with scorpions at the moment," she said, nervously.

Marius took the opportunity to place his hand over hers. On the mention of scorpions, they all wondered when Homer would carry out his promise to return 'Scorpio' to her rightful owner.

His gesture didn't pass unnoticed by Grace. Despite his youth, Marius had left adolescence well behind him; his voice deepening and beard already shadowing his chin. Blessed with social skills his father plainly lacked, Grace guessed he must have learnt much from his mother, from whom he had presumably gained the ivory colour of his skin and thick, black hair that held its own natural wave.

Though subtle in acts and gestures, it was obvious he was attracted to Olwyn.

'Curious,' she thought, having noticed a barely concealed interplay between Olwyn and Allison that seemed beyond simple acts of friendship.

She just hoped that Marius wouldn't get his fingers burnt.

"So, when you visited the hospital, did you get the code I asked for from the policewoman?"

Despite Homer's instructions to the contrary, he had guessed Olwyn wouldn't leave without saying farewell to the injured woman. In that event, she might as well obtain something worth taking the risk.

With a puzzled frown, Olwyn wrote a four figure number on a post-it note.

"They call that security?" Homer said with disdain. "I've seen better security on a child's money box."

Shaking his head, he turned to Marius who had just entered the room.

"Do you remember the bus stop we used on the main road when we arrived here from the station? Make sure you guide these two there by five o'clock tomorrow morning."

Homer turned to Grace and Olwyn.

"Pack your bags. Anything left behind will be thrown away," he added gruffly.

"Marius will lead you there and you must all wait behind the shelter where you can't be seen; only show yourselves when I call to you." He added curtly, "And dress warmly, it will be cold."

Grace smiled; again that final, hard won note of concern, as though, no matter how objectionable Homer found their presence, he couldn't help himself.

He was gone without another word, leaving only the muffled note of his bike in his wake.

Angela made an appearance shortly after Homer had left. She looked better for resting, though now clearly bearing the strain of recent events.

Despite what Grace had described of the actions of the drone, Homer hadn't thought it would provoke an immediate reaction from Bremer. Having shot a policewoman in error, he suspected Bremer would act with circumspection for at least a short time until he had more clarity about what had actually happened.

Hopefully, the police would likewise remain confused by Olwyn's disappearance for long enough to get both women out of harm's way. While Homer was out he'd left Joss with everyone at the cottage. Her instincts would give some measure of warning if anyone decided to pay a surprise visit.

Marius added logs to the range.

"Best sleep together in the kitchen tonight," Angela announced. "It will be warmer."

With tired rheumy eyes she looked for their agreement, and made herself comfortable in the chair next to the range.

Olwyn took the battered sofa while Marius stretched out in a sleeping bag on the floor beside her. That left just Grace to curl up with Joss on a mattress on the floor. She was surprised how natural it all felt.

The night was cold. Angela left an oil lamp burning, its pale yellow light adding a warming glow to the room. Joss was asleep in seconds and Grace felt the weight of the dog's chin resting on her leg. In the dim light, through half closed eyes, Grace thought she saw Marius and Olwyn holding hands. It was curious how quickly relationships formed when a group of disparate people were thrown together in difficult circumstances.

She turned over, avoiding disturbing the dog, and saw that Angela was still awake and wondered if she too had noticed the affection that had blossomed between her two younger guests.

There were always veiled depths in Angela; secrets only shared with Homer, concealed behind the direct gaze of sad blue eyes that now held their look, not on the affections of Marius and Olwyn, but on her.

Huddled behind the bus shelter, the bitter cold gave Marius the excuse to rub Olwyn's hands to keep them warm. Grace looked on and smiled to herself, pressing numb legs against Joss's body that leaned against her.

How did the dog manage to stay so warm? Didn't the Australian aboriginals have a saying, describing how cold the night would be, by measuring how many dogs were needed to sleep on your bed to keep you warm? If that were true, it was definitely a 'two or three dog night'.

She reflected that her presence had achieved mixed success. Inserting her caterpillar drone with its camera into the fracking site had so far failed, but she was leaving with a photo of the note Olwyn had been given by the man she had interviewed.

We all have radiation sickness. Help us.

It only confirmed what Grace knew already, but seeing it written down was the first evidence that their suspicions were founded. That still left the question; what was the cause and, more importantly, how to prove it.

For months she had experienced a recurring dream in which she saw herself standing in a tract of the countryside, leafless, empty, sterile, dead. It all increased the pressure to confront 'Blue Horizon' with the truth of what they were so blatantly covering up.

So far her group had threads of evidence, but little that couldn't be denied or re-scripted with plausible lies. If the rumours were true and Hugh Littlemore, 'Blue Horizon's party leader, soon rose to become Home Secretary, then what would be their chances for ever setting the truth before the public?

Grace shuddered from the memory of her dreams and the cold that filled the darkness around her. Marius had moved from rubbing Olwyn's hands to hugging her. Grace looked at her watch; Homer was late. She felt a pang of anxiety; he was never late without a reason. What if Bremer's men had accosted him?

No vehicles had passed in the time they had been waiting behind the shelter. It was a disconcerting possibility that the next vehicle to appear might belong to Bremer, not Homer. If that happened, could they escape into the woods behind them? They hadn't discussed a contingency plan, assuming Homer would be true to his word.

Sensing her unease, Joss pressed harder against her leg. They were going to miss one another when Grace had left. Perhaps it was simply an intuitive reaction, impulsive, the sort you only realise after its taken place; hastily, Grace searched beneath her parka for her scarf. She drew it from her neck and looped it loosely around Joss, a dark blue square, covered by yellow flowers. Grace secured it with a double knot.

"There," she said, her mouth pressed against the soft fur of the dog's ear.

"So you won't forget me and I'll always be able to find you."

She gave Joss a final hug and was thanked by a look from her bright eyes that glinted in the darkness.

With a long sigh, Grace stood up and checked her watch. She wanted the hands to slow down; the longer the wait beyond the agreed time, the greater the chance something had gone wrong. She swallowed hard, forcing down fear, just as pin-prick sidelights appeared, accompanied by the crunch of tyres on frozen snow. Apprehensive, Grace leaned forwards.

"If this goes wrong, we dive back into the woods, run, split up and hide. Try and head north-east when it gets light. It's the direction of Angela's cottage."

The approaching vehicle slowed, lights suddenly flashing twice as it drew alongside the bus shelter. Joss paddled the frozen ground. They peered around the side of the bus shelter and Grace saw with alarm that the slowing vehicle was a police van.

The side door swung open. Grace backed away, tensing to leap the snow filled ditch and make a run for the trees. There came a familiar whistle; Joss's call sign. In a second, the dog bound off, entering the van with a single leap, to greet Homer.

"Grace, Olwyn," Homer's voice shouted. "Quick, into the back where you can't be seen."

Homer gave impatient instructions.

"I need to return this to the police station before the morning shift arrive and find it missing."

They lingered only long enough for Homer and Marius to exchange a few words. The boy looked disappointed; he had hoped to travel with them. Instead, he would have to settle for a cold, lonely walk back to Angela's cottage.

Without time for farewells, the police van drove off, leaving Marius standing alone in the middle of the road. At least he could take comfort from a blown kiss from Olwyn through the van window.

"A police van?" Grace sounded incredulous.

It explained the code that Olwyn had obtained from Allison.

"It's the only feasible way to get you out of the area. There are mobile road blocks on most main routes, and drones patrolling the lanes and side roads," said Homer swerving to avoid a car abandoned in a snow filled ditch beside the road.

"No one seems to be bothering to stop police vehicles; I've been through two checkpoints already and waved straight through on each occasion."

"Can you turn the heater up?" Olwyn asked, hugging herself in her thin coat.

Dressed for London, her wardrobe really wasn't suitable for the conditions. "It's like a fridge in the back here."

Grace smiled in the darkness. Olwyn was obviously already missing the warming attentions of Marius.

"Won't someone notice one of their vans is missing?"

"Not if I get it back before the police station opens," Homer replied.

"Er, CCTV cameras?" Grace reminded him.

"The one in the station car pound has been disabled. They'll think it was the snow. I've picked a route avoiding cameras wherever possible. If no one notices one of their vans has been borrowed, Wailes won't have a reason to go looking for cameras."

"What about the Jaguar?" Olwyn asked unhappily.

Grace wasn't sure if that was because she was missing the comfort of the car or Marius.

"It's at a different railway station to the one I'm taking you. It's dangerous for you to go anywhere near it. And before you ask, your boss knows where to collect the car."

They drove in silence for another half-hour, using main roads, skirting around town centres, until they eventually stopped a short distance from a railway station on the edge of a still sleeping town.

"The first train to London is in fifteen minutes. Mask your faces against the cold and pay cash at the machine for your tickets."

Homer threw them both scarves. Grace thought hers smelt comfortingly of Joss.

"Put your hoods up; speak to no one."

Irritatingly, when he was anxious, he felt the need to explain even the most obvious details.

"Remember to split up. Don't walk together, or sit together on the train."

It was early and brutally cold when Homer parked beneath the low sweep of branches of a roadside tree and waited while his phone checked for cameras. He climbed out first, looked around, and satisfied that no one was about, ushered the two women out of the back of the van.

"Now, off with the pair of you before someone comes," adding as an afterthought, "and don't come back."

As he climbed back into the van, for a moment Grace caught him say, "Just keep safe and take care of yourselves."

He slammed the door and drove away without a backward glance.

"Can anyone explain that to me?" Grace muttered to the wind as the van disappeared into the darkness.

She was thinking more about his final words than the bizarre fact that they had just escaped in a borrowed police van.

CHAPTER 37
BEWARE OF KICKBACKS

Well before London I left the train at a station already thronged with the huddled figures of early morning commuters.

Lost amongst a sea of coats and hats, my small, shapeless figure felt as anonymous as those around me. I made a brief call from a public phone box to summon a nameless supporter of our group. An unmarked van soon arrived, and before long I had disappeared into the busy streets of suburban London. No lonely rural hideout for me; that's far too easy to get picked off by 'Blue Horizon's bounty hunters. Though I didn't know the numbers, there was a price on my head. What had that online poster said?

'Dead or Alive'

The options seemed to matter little to whoever had created the poster. If it was meant to be funny, I didn't get the joke.

At the start of the journey I had sat apart from Olwyn. When no one boarded the train for several stops, it seemed safe enough to sit next to each other and chat, at least until other passengers joined the train.

"So, what do you know about 'Blue Horizon'?" I asked.

I found it difficult to trust people if I knew nothing about their background.

Though Olwyn hadn't disclosed the fact, Angela had said that she worked for some branch of government. That automatically aroused my suspicions. With only Homer's acceptance of her presence, I needed to find out more to make my own assessment. How she reacted to my question would serve as a litmus test.

Olwyn shrugged. "I'm just an admin clerk, but I hear they're a dodgy bunch and not to be trusted. My boss doesn't think much of them."

Do humble admin clerks get attacked by deliberately planted scorpions? That didn't seem likely.

"And your boss would know?" I asked, trying to hide my suspicions.

"Let's say, as an active member of the gay community, he would have good reason to keep an eye on them." She spoke with a meaningful look that said much.

Beyond the windows, the snowy darkness swirled by in a kaleidoscopic blur.

"Marius is a surprise package." I knew I was probing into personal areas without being quite sure why. "In a crowded room you wouldn't pick him out as Homer's son."

Olwyn smiled, though whether at the thought of my question or the languid good looks of Marius, I couldn't guess.

"He must get his looks from his mother. She's Tamil, Sri Lankan," Olwyn said. "She and Homer met in a refugee camp."

"Another of Homer's good deeds?" This story was becoming boringly familiar.

Olwyn shook her head. "Quite the reverse it would seem. Homer, despite his obvious skills, got himself captured by the Tamil Tigers in another of his NGO operations that went wrong. It was her intervention that saved his life."

Well, that was a surprise; from how much Olwyn knew in such a short time, to Homer's unexpected role reversal.

"So, who is, or more accurately, was, our enigmatic Homer?"

Olwyn stared out of the window for a moment.

"I'm not sure, I don't think Marius knows much. Not ex-SAS if that's what you're thinking, though Marius said he had been in the army. I've heard about men like Homer; misfits who leave to join shadowy, security companies who provide protection to NGOs and the like, and work in the many trouble spots of the world. On paper, they're privately run, though often paid for by the government when it suits them," she said with a raised eyebrow.

We sat in silence for a while and I tried to digest what Olwyn had just told me. I felt the train begin to slow; I would get off at the next station. I doubted we would meet again, which perhaps made what I said next something of a surprise.

"Be careful how you treat Marius. He's young and obviously smitten with you, as are certain other people," I added, obliquely.

I had noticed the way the injured Allison Markham had looked at her. I half expected Olwyn to tell me to mind my own business, but I guess she's not wired that way. Perhaps that's why people are attracted to her.

"I had noticed," Olwyn said with a wry smile. "It's nice to meet someone who shows genuine interest in me rather than just how I look. I've had enough experience with the latter to last a lifetime."

I left the train a few minutes later and disappeared into the throng of the early morning commute. I didn't expect our paths to cross any time soon.

Which was unfortunate. If I hadn't been so distracted by my conversation with Olwyn, I would have paid more attention to the nondescript figure that stepped off the train just seconds before it left the station.

Wailes felt irritable. The description 'chewing a wasp' would better describe his mood. Try as he might, he couldn't find fault with Allison Markham's statement. He had interviewed her twice in her hospital bed and both times, almost word for word, it produced the same result.

Her statement was borne out by the evidence in the woods at the scene where she claimed to have been shot. They had found her car, keys still in the ignition, and battery flat from the lights left on. There had been another deep fall of snow before they had discovered her car, filling foot and tyre prints, though there was clear evidence of blood and discarded bandages beneath the new crust. It all tied together.

But Wailes's instincts left him restless. Her reason for being in the woods, though plausible, didn't ring true in his mind.

'I was retracing the route I took yesterday when that SUV appeared and started ramming the back of the car.'

There it was, in black and white, in her statement. But Wailes didn't buy it. There was no reason for it not to be true. It implied that whoever had attacked her the previous day had followed her and taken their chance to finish the job.

The trouble with that line of reasoning was that Wailes knew exactly who had been driving the SUV, and their method of choice wasn't a shotgun beside the road. As he knew, they were far more subtle than that and look where that had got them.

So who, then? The sudden appearance of a rogue Landrover the previous day, conveniently insinuating itself between the car carrying the two women and the SUV still left unexplained the identity of the driver. Wailes could think of a few names, but no one had seen him well enough to give a description or, even more surprisingly, get the registration number.

There were too many loose ends, and Wailes hated loose ends. What about a visit to Angela, the 'mad woman' in the woods? Rumour had it that there was some connection between her and the reclusive hermit, Homer, though Wailes couldn't see how that was very likely. Still, Homer had a Landrover.

Yes, a visit to Angela's lonely cottage, apply a measure of intimidation to rattle her cage, and see if she let slip anything of interest. It might just reveal something he hadn't thought of before.

Back in the peace of his home, Homer gathered the movement cameras he had hidden in the woods and checked their contents. There were the usual culprits; a few hungry deer, a roaming badger and a dog fox, who stopped and stared provocatively into the lens of the camera.

Nothing else of interest, until an armed man, bizarrely dressed in black in a snow covered landscape, crossed the lens, moving in the direction of his cottage. He checked the time of the clip. It was a good half an hour before Grace had said she had arrived and found intruders already there.

Someone had disabled the camera on the barn giving a clear view of the front door, so there was no record of anyone leaving the house. Having detected that camera, they must have taken steps to avoid the others. Homer made an estimate for the time he thought Allison Markham might have arrived and searched the footage for the access drive. Sure enough, just around the time it got dark, her white car appeared briefly. Beyond that he found nothing, but it was enough to provide the shape of a timeline. Enough for Homer to be certain the trick with the shotgun had Miller's style all over it.

The question was, who was the trap intended for? Obviously not Allison Markham; she had called on the off-chance; wrong person, wrong time. It was his shotgun they had used, so it would only carry his fingerprints. But shooting him made no obvious sense; there was nothing to gain by killing Homer.

Unless. What if he found Grace's fingerprints on the gun? Killing, or maiming him with a gun bearing her prints would result in a hunt for Grace with justification far beyond simple eco-terrorism. There were bound to be prints in the attic bedroom she used. If he found prints on the gun that weren't his and they matched Grace's the intention of the trap might become clearer. Kill Homer and blame Grace for his murder.

But why go to that length to simply incriminate her as a murderer? Homer felt disturbed by that conclusion. It implied that someone knew far more about her than he had feared; the disturbing question was, who?

It took half an hour to dust the shotgun for fingerprints. In the light of a UV filter his own prints stood out clearly. Many had been smudged, but on the barrel and stock they were overlaid by something smaller. Distinct, recently applied, fingers and palms overlaid on top of his own. They were prominent, intended to be found.

He had fooled himself into thinking he had kept her presence well hidden, camouflaged by his vaguely tolerated poaching habits. Someone was watching, and knew enough to set a trap for some ulterior motive. Well, if they were looking for Grace they would have to look elsewhere.

Wearily Homer rubbed his forehead; it ached from too many questions, his body suddenly drained by fatigue. He knew he needed sleep to avoid a return of the seizures that hid in the shadows at times of stress.

He checked all the locks and set the alarm sensor on the track, and set off for bed, abruptly pausing, foot raised, on the bottom step. He had missed the obvious. Whilst he might have questions about who had set the booby trap, if it was Grace's fingerprints on the gun, it wasn't so much who had put them there, but where had they got them from?

He had a feeling Cosmo and Milo had a lot to answer for.

It was dark when Homer awoke. A glance at his watch confirmed he had slept most of the night. The cottage was silent. He had left Joss with Angela and Marius and he missed her presence. The house was cold, the Aga dark and unlit.

Hastily, he raked the ash, found embers and fed in kindling. It would take an hour to heat water for a much needed shower. A layer of frost on the inside of the window panes discouraged any idea of having cold water.

Moving through empty rooms, he became unexpectedly conscious of Grace's absence, aware, though he would always pretend otherwise, that she no longer represented just a negative influence in his life. Sending her on her way with the instruction, 'and don't come back', had, he realised, been more from concern for her safety, than a façade of irritation at her uninvited presence.

Begrudgingly, he had grown to admire her stoicism. She seldom complained, determined to expose the operations in the fracking sites with almost obsessive determination. A thought hung heavily upon him; Grace was hell-bent on her task, regardless of the cost.

Would a vase of yellow origami flowers, her inevitable call sign, have been left on Angela's kitchen table? The ghost of inevitability gripped the pit of his stomach. When Bremer inevitably caught her, how far would his own instinct drive him to protect her?

In the beginning, there was always a chance that Grace wouldn't return, that she would write off her quest as a mountain impossible to climb. In the past, he had fervently hoped that would be the case. But now?

Was shared experience eroding the comfort of loneliness? Homer had tried to hide from the world, convinced he was simply bad at relationships. Okay, for many years Angela had been there, a troubled soul so much like himself, tolerating his moods and demons, as faithful as Joss.

Homer grinned at his straggly bearded image in the mirror. His thoughts about Angela might seem like praise but she possibly wouldn't see it as a compliment to be compared with his Joss.

Jerry Houseman was fed up with having to make his own coffee. It had been several days since he had last heard from Olwyn. Her report, sent encrypted to his private server, had been thorough, yet posed more questions than answers.

Matters in politics swirled around him, things change hour by hour; governments seemed to fall in the space of a day and there were rumours that 'Blue Horizon' would be promoted in an imminent emergency re-shuffle.

The government's poor handling of the wild fire and flooding of much of central London had caused a surge of unpopularity for the governing party. Reports of a pending vote of 'No Confidence' abounded. Promoting 'Blue Horizon', popular with a certain swathe of public opinion, would ward off the consequence of such a vote, and place their leader, Hugh Littlemore, in charge at the Home Office.

From Jerry's perspective, placing Littlemore in control was equivalent to placing a fox in charge of the hen house. Even more alarmingly on a personal level, it would promote a suspected homophobe as his ultimate boss.

For almost a year, Jerry and a close coterie of associates had been running a covert operation to discover the source of 'Blue Horizon's party funding. There were wild allegations but nothing could be proven or substantiated. Yet their meteoric rise to power, driven by a cunning, obviously expensive media campaign, had to be financed from somewhere. Such sums couldn't all be achieved by small donations from the average man in the street.

In the course of his forensic search, Jerry had uncovered their financial interests in the fracking industry by accident. 'Blue Horizon's interest in the rapidly expanding operations had been clear from the outset, there was nothing hidden or obstructed, and their support for the country's independent energy source had been one of the primary reasons for their popularity. That, and the espoused views on family values and uncontrolled immigration, had allowed them to rise to their current position of influence in the government.

Since rising to a position of power sharing, their iron grip on fracking site security and the introduction of covert laws on security had aroused Jerry's interest. Despite the rise of green energy, their argument held that hydrocarbons would still be needed for decades to come. Teamed with his party's control of the Ministry for Energy and Environment, and with Littlemore in charge at the Home Office, 'Blue Horizon's control of the fracking industry would be complete.

The opportunity to send Olwyn to investigate a death at a site in Sussex had presented a chance to peer into the murky world that 'Blue Horizon' had created to discourage close scrutiny. To Jerry's surprise she had made unexpected progress, and her report made a start in prising open a locked door. With the prospect of Littlemore's imminent promotion, the implications necessitated getting Olwyn back in one piece to find out what she had left unwritten from her report.

Olwyn decided she would ignore Jerry until he rang to apologise. She looked a wreck. Staring at herself in the mirrors of a public toilet at Waterloo station, her hair looked as though it hadn't seen a brush in a week and her clothes, largely courtesy of Angela, aged her appearance by at least twenty years.

All of her personal belongings had been abandoned in the hotel room. She had left with only her purse and phone. Retrieving her things was another condition she would impose on Jerry when he eventually condescended to contact her.

Tired to her very core, Olwyn spent the last of her cash on a taxi. The driver filled the entire journey with mindless conversation. At least he was happy with her monosyllabic replies. Huddled in a parka several sizes too large, she sat in the back, lost in reflective thought, wondering what would become of Marius and Angela.

Distracted, she shook her head. A visit which began with the intention of identifying a nameless man in a satellite photo, had expanded out of all proportion. There was little to be amused about, though Olwyn wondered when Homer would return 'Scorpio' to her owner and smiled at the scene that played in her imagination.

Beyond the windows of the taxi, a languid drizzle had turned white snow to grey slush in the tired streets she passed. Part of her was relieved to be away from the turbulence that had filled the past few days. How on earth could the extraction of barrels of oil and gas turn into such a cat and mouse game?

Unless, as Grace had alluded, that was only part of the story. Hidden behind the veil of secrecy, concealed from public scrutiny, were things someone was determined to keep quiet. Much of the time, Olwyn had been seriously out of her depth, untrained and ill-equipped to deal with the consequences her presence had provoked.

Fortunately, the people she had met had made up for her shortcomings; the enigmatic and unpredictable Homer, the sanctuary that Angela provided, an intriguing relationship with Allison, and the unexpected appearance of Marius, surprisingly alluring for his age. Like Olwyn, he was ill-equipped for the game that had erupted around them.

As she neared her flat, Olwyn realised she had left out Grace from her appraisal. The woman puzzled her, more from what was left unsaid; a physical presence that hid behind a shadowy 'zeitgeist'. Marius, acting as an interface, had eased the tension between them but if Homer trusted Grace, that seemed good enough for him.

At Homer's request, Olwyn had shared her findings on her interviews with the fracking site operatives, including the note clandestinely passed to her. Did the claim of radiation sickness constitute evidence? She suspected Jerry would be dismissive without verification.

Yet Grace's claim, that groundwater samples she had taken from the immediate vicinity of the site, disclosed higher radiation levels than could be considered as normal. Without hard evidence, her claims were merely hearsay, invalid until hard facts were produced.

Most of the information she had obtained was subjective at best. And now Grace had left, disappearing into the ether, taking her findings with her.

Olwyn felt a pang of guilt. More precisely, Grace had been careless, and Jerry conniving. Installed on the phone he had given her at the start was an innocent looking app. Innocent until activated. When Grace had used her phone to make a copy of the note that had been passed to Olwyn, the app had promptly copied Grace's SIM card.

CHAPTER 38
A SEAT IN THE STAND

Distracted by her conversation with Marius, Angela almost missed the red warning light. Wailes had parked his police car on the road, preferring a surprise approach to her cottage on foot, something he had begun to regret as he slipped and faltered on the icy surface.

Angela was enjoying her time with Marius. He already held radical views on climate change and how his generation would shock the world into accepting their plans to save the planet. His almost total rejection of materialism would sound naïve in the extreme had he not expressed his views in precise detail with eye-watering clarity. With a wry smile, Angela could only speculate that the world would be unrecognisable in almost every aspect when, and if, Marius and his generation succeeded in their revolutionary ambitions.

For Angela's security, Homer had installed a sensor, but she missed the flashing red warning light on her wrist under her sweater. It was left to Joss to emit her signature warning grumble.

A quick glance through the kitchen window revealed the waddling figure of Wailes approaching the cottage. At least he appeared to be alone. Angela had turned the lock on the door by the time he arrived; he could knock and wait for her to open it.

"Say nothing," she said firmly to Marius.

"Stay at the table and appear to be working." Angela nodded towards his laptop.

"Leave the talking to me."

She waited until Wailes had knocked a third time before she opened it to the heavy-breathing policeman, balloons of cold mist forming around his head. Dark stains on inadequate shoes proved they were already soaked through, freezing his feet.

"To what do I owe the pleasure?" she asked with a note of sarcasm.

She intended to keep him waiting outside in the snow until he asked to enter.

"I was passing. I thought I'd pay a courtesy call ... in view of the weather," he added as an afterthought with fake concern.

She eyed him warily, knowing only too well that Wailes seldom behaved without an ulterior motive. She balanced her thoughts for many long seconds before standing aside to let him enter.

"Ah, I see you already have visitors?"

Wailes's statement asked a question as he shot a suspicious glance in the direction of Marius and headed for the Aga to warm himself.

"I doubt you've come all the way out here in this weather just for a cosy social chat," Angela said, closing the door.

She positioned herself against the opposite wall facing the range.

"There's coffee in the pot on the hotplate. Help yourself."

Despite her intense dislike of Wailes she had long since learned not to overdo the provocation.

Wailes filled a mug. "And you are?" He fired the curt question at Marius.

"My godson," Angela said, before Marius could open his mouth. The faint hint of a smile passed on his lips as he considered their sudden new relationship. "From up north."

She wanted to deflect Wailes, avoid any chance he would hear the boy's Australian accent. She crossed her fingers, hoping Marius would embrace his new role.

Wailes gave Marius a long hard stare. His coloured skin had obviously piqued his interest.

"There was a policewoman injured not far from here. Someone found her and applied a serious amount of first aid before taking her to hospital. Wondered if you might know anything about it?" Wailes looked at Angela with suspicion.

"What with all your herbal skills and black arts remedies," he added as a put down intended to intimidate her.

Angela felt a sudden spike of alarm. With all of his questions, as with the scorpion used against Olwyn, the sting was always in the tail. Did he know more than he was letting on or was he simply fishing for clues, probing for an incriminating slip.

"Was it a road accident?" Angela asked, watching Wailes's facial expression for a clue, at the same time avoiding his question.

Wailes smiled. "Someone injured her with a shotgun. It could have been deliberate." He sounded disinterested.

Angela disliked everything about this man, aware that encouraging her contempt was part of his act. If people loathe you enough, disdain will induce rash words and actions, and from the smug expression on his face he suspected something he couldn't yet prove.

She shrugged, hoping he wouldn't ask to inspect her van in case some shred of evidence had been left behind after taking Allison to the hospital.

"Living here in the forest we hear a lot of shotguns being used. Especially by the men from the fracking site; they seem to spend a lot of their spare time shooting the innocent creatures of the woods," she ventured.

Did he know, or was he just speculating that she was involved? Whatever his motive, he moved on without pursuing that particular vein any further.

"Anyone see a young woman? A stranger to these parts; early twenties, pretty, nice figure?"

Wailes leered in Marius's direction, baiting the boy.

Angela saw Marius's face tighten.

"The only sighting we have of her is in the company of Homer in a café in town." Wailes let the statement hang before adding, "Seen much of him lately?"

Wailes was staring hard at Marius as he asked the question. Had he seen something of a likeness in the boy, or was he just signalling contempt for the colour of his skin to provoke him?

"We don't see many people out here. Not exactly much passing traffic."

Angela tried to regain Wailes's attention in an attempt to distract him from Marius. But he was an old hand at the game, not easy to distract once he got his teeth into someone.

"Strange don't you think; woodland hermit like Homer with some high-heeled city tart?"

Had Wailes seen Marius stiffen when he described Olwyn? And this from the man who had most probably released a scorpion into her bed.

"Is the boy mute or just deaf?"

Angela managed an icy smile, silently praying Marius wouldn't retaliate.

"Neither. Like most teenagers, he doesn't think much of the police. I can't think why?"

Despite the warmth from the Aga, a silent hostility settled on the kitchen. Where was Wailes taking this impromptu interrogation?

"When did you last see your reclusive friend Homer?"

"A few days ago, when he dropped in a couple of rabbits."

A tell-tale aroma of rabbit stew wafted from the Aga.

"Poaching."

Angela shrugged. "Home reared for all I know. They all taste the same."

Wailes turned and placed his coffee mug in the sink, mentally counting plates and cups on the drying rack, searching for something that betrayed the presence in the cottage of more than two people. There was nothing obvious, which further darkened his mood.

He had expected to find Angela alone. The old hag was supposed to be as much of a recluse as Homer. Annoyingly, the presence of the boy prevented him from applying extra pressure upon her. If he tried a touch of cage rattling as he had intended, it would just be his luck this boy would record him. He crossed the kitchen and paused, hand on the door latch.

"A word of warning."

His words were directed at Marius. "Make sure you keep out of trouble. People in these parts take a dim view of strangers, especially ones who poke their noses into our business."

Wailes left the door open as he left.

"Such a vulgar man," Angela hissed, quietly closing the door.

Marius languidly unfurled himself with feline grace from his chair, shrugged and gave her a wry smile.

"I think the time is long overdue for Homer to return that scorpion to her rightful owner, don't you?"

I received an encrypted message enclosing an e-ticket. It carried neither name nor message, just a seat number in a stand at the Emirates football stadium in north London. I'm no fan of football, but then, that wasn't the intended purpose of the ticket.

For the sake of security we seldom met, and then only occasionally, when the need arose. Football aside, for a short period came the promise to relax, hidden amidst the anonymity of thousands of football-mad fans in an excited crowd.

I left taking my seat until just before the match kicked-off. At the same time, a muffled figure approached the seat beside me from the opposite direction. It was bitterly cold; no one looked twice at two late arrivals. We acknowledged one another only with our eyes as we took our seats.

My report was already stapled between the pages of my programme. No risk of online interception for me; exchange would take place during the melee when one side scored; we would be hidden in a sea of arms raised in the exuberance of celebration or protest.

"I was concerned about you."

His words were muted through a home supporters' scarf wound to cover his lower face and nose. With the visor of a peaked cap lowered to shadow his face, all I could see were his eyes, his identification confirmed by the subtle whiff of his trademark expensive aftershave.

"I saw the 'Wanted' poster. You've been careless," he said with intended criticism.

I nodded. "Someone I trusted. It happens. I understand it's been dealt with."

"Trust no one. How many times do I have to warn you people," he scolded.

Rebuked, I could only accept the reprimand. This was not the place or time for excuses.

"Any luck with drone insertion?"

I could barely hear his words above the clamour. It was more a statement of failure than a question, implying he already knew it hadn't taken place.

"It's difficult. I'm still working on it. The awful weather doesn't help." Even to me, my excuse sounded flabby and inadequate.

While our attention was distracted, the home side must have scored and the whole stadium erupted. In a split second, we too were standing and joining in the celebrations, as our match programmes were exchanged.

In the aftermath of the goal, we resumed our seats and the match continued. For a while, the noise around us clamoured ever more loudly and animated than before.

My companion leaned closer. "Time doesn't stand still. We need results."

I guessed he meant the prospects of promotion for 'Blue Horizon'. Their elevation in the government would make a worrying game changer.

"How long do we have?"

"Days. A week perhaps, two at the most," he said, pretending to be absorbed by the match.

"And there's nothing you can do to give us more time?"

"Above my pay scale. Even the Prime Minister seems helpless to stop it from happening."

"He could call a general election," I mooted, playing for time.

"And hand the entire government to 'Blue Horizon'?"

There seemed to be a note of fear in his voice. A recent survey had shown 'Blue Horizon' to be several points ahead in the public opinion.

Suddenly, the crowd roared loudly as the referee made an unpopular decision, filling the air around us with abusive opinions about the referee.

"But we need time to gain the evidence you need. Only then can we stop them in their tracks," I said with a certainty I didn't totally believe.

My companion was silent for several minutes. While I waited, I watched the match with only partial interest whilst checking the location of CCTV cameras on the roof around us. Even here, systems often used facial recognition. The 'Wanted' poster confirmed that 'Blue Horizon' had me on their priority list. Any slip on my part would signal my presence in minutes.

"There is an idea. It's audacious and risky, and will take precise timing. It's a one-off, all or nothing. The outline of the plan is in the programme."

He paused to allow his words to sink in. In front of us, the match proceeded at a furious pace, absorbing the attention of the crowd. I noticed several cameras had turned to focus on our section of the stadium.

"I can give you a week to set it up, the same to implement it. If Littlemore takes over the Home Office we can obscure things for a short time; blocking meetings, losing files, make his job tiresome, like walking through treacle. You just need to make that plan happen," he gestured to the programme in my hands. "If you can pull it off, you can leave the rest to us."

"How risky?" Self-preservation made me ask.

"Very." He smiled as he said the word, which alarmed me further. "But I'm sure you can make it work. After all, for you it's personal."

He turned to stare at me as if to emphasize the point. Not that I needed it. That was one fact I would never need to be reminded of.

I rolled the match programme into a tube, mimicking the vocal supporters around me. It suddenly felt toxic, as though the contents might explode at any moment. I ached to open the pages and read the plan hidden inside, but instead a sixth sense made me count the number of stewards in hi-vis jackets in our section of the stadium.

Perhaps it was because we were close to seats reserved for 'away' fans; more stewards seemed to have arrived while we were talking. I momentarily dismissed it; weren't local matches supposed to be highly competitive affairs? As half-time approached, emotions often spill over.

I watched the stewards carefully and re-counted, now certain there were more than just a short time before. Most wore headsets, several holding animated conversations while they stood with their backs to the match, searching faces in the crowd. It could have been my imagination, but the coincidence was too great. Two CCTV cameras seemed to be pointing directly at our row of seats.

I was saved by another goal. Intuition took over immediately. In the melee, I swapped my cap for a beanie, reversed my jacket and donned glasses, all with the speed of a conjurer, and as the half-time whistle blew, I leaned against the nameless man beside me.

"My cover's blown. They're targeting me. Time to go," I hissed in his ear and pushed past him, caught in the tide of moving bodies hastily making for the bars and toilets while the whistle still echoed around the stadium.

One of the advantages of being small and slight is that you very quickly become invisible in a crowd.

CHAPTER 39
THE COLOUR OF LITMUS

The following morning, Olwyn was surprised to find everything she had abandoned in the hotel room now sitting outside her flat, a rose tied to the handle of her suitcase with a coloured ribbon. Though not much of an apology, it was at least a gesture that went someway to assuage her anger at Jerry Houseman.

An hour later, Jerry's friend, Fabian, knocked on her door. It was the first time Olwyn had met him, a tall, waif-like figure with fine, fair hair and a beardless face making him look probably ten years younger than his actual age.

"Ten minutes," he said.

She noticed an effeminate lilt to his words.

"He's waiting in the park, somewhere near the fountain." Having delivered the instruction, Fabian left before she could protest.

'I'll ignore him,' Olwyn determined as she showered. Three days with little more than a face wash had left her smelling like the woodsman she had left behind.

Perhaps it was the needles of hot water that changed her mind. At least meeting Jerry face-to-face would provide the opportunity to vent her spleen, remind him of his callous disregard for her safety and watch him squirm amidst her torrent of home truths. At least, that was her plan.

As Fabian had directed, she found Jerry Houseman on a seat beneath a leafless chestnut tree. He wore a camel wool coat with a velvet collar and held a cardboard tray with two takeaway coffees. He stood as Olwyn approached, stooping to kiss her cheek.

"Ravishing as ever," he said, offering the gift of hot coffee on a freezing morning.

"Don't patronise. I look a total mess and it's entirely your fault. Bastard."

Despite her best intentions, Olwyn's last word sounded more of a compliment than a rebuke.

"You simply have to forgive me, dear girl; I'm totally lost without you," he replied in a tone that pretended contrition.

"I'm not sure what's worse, the casual disregard you have for the lives of others or the fact that you're a heartless manipulator."

Olwyn's attempt at anger wasn't surviving very well.

"And now you've brought me here you can add pneumonia to your list of crimes. It's freezing, Jerry, or hadn't you noticed."

As if aware of the snow for the first time, he tapped one immaculate hand-made shoe against the other. Olwyn hoped his feet were turning to blocks of ice.

"Alas, you can't come to the office if we want to maintain the fiction that you're dead."

With his customary urbane smile he sat down on the seat, patting the space beside him. "Come, we'll cuddle up while we chat and drink coffee."

Attempting to look unmoved, Olwyn glowered in his direction as she sat down.

"Had you any idea of the danger you were exposing me to when you so carelessly despatched me to that nest of vipers in Sussex?"

Jerry looked thoughtful for a moment.

"Perhaps. Though I assumed your delightful presence would merely rattle their cage. In that event you proved amazingly successful."

"Jer-ry." She pronounced his name with great emphasis on the final syllable. "They made two attempts to kill me."

"Both of which were unsuccessful, I might point out."

"One badly injured a female police officer, the other, a scorpion of all things."

"Yes, well, the scorpion was a bit of a surprise, I must admit. One has to admire their originality."

Olwyn failed to appreciate his attempt at making light of her experience. She shook her head, feigning mock disgust.

"You really are something else, Jerry. You're even worse than the idiot our woodsman says you are; you're callous too, which in my book makes you dangerous."

Jerry took on a pained look at the venom in her words.

"It wasn't a complete coincidence that your hunky woodsman came to your rescue purely by chance."

Infuriatingly, he spired his fingers, peering at Olwyn over the tips.

"Mr Reluctant, you mean?"

Jerry gave her a lopsided smile, still uncertain of her mood.

She sighed in resignation. "You could have forewarned me," she said in a grumpy tone.

"It all works on a need to know basis, dear heart," Jerry said, almost sounding patronising.

"And after all, it was Homer who notified us of the body in the woods in the first place and set this little escapade in motion. From an operational perspective, it's far more effective when a local gives help."

Jerry was silent for a moment. "Besides, when the people you seem to have upset catch up with you, the least you know, the less you can tell."

"Catch who?" Olwyn sounded as if a raw nerve had been jarred.

"Well, as you've made such an unexpected success of the operation so far, I was hoping you could help me out with a tiny extension to your mission."

Olwyn stood up in alarm at his words. He just managed to duck from the snowball she threw at his head.

As she stormed away down the path Jerry just caught the words, "… manipulative bastard."

"That's the second one this morning," Marius announced.

The tremor made the glasses dance on the drying rack and the ceiling lamp swung like a syncopated pendulum.

"They're becoming more frequent, and stronger," Angela said, concentrating on her needlework, her owl kite almost complete.

Without warning, the kitchen door swung open as Homer arrived, a pair of gleaming rainbow trout balanced over his shoulder, and Joss restrained on a length of baler twine. He laid the trout in the sink and turned on the cold tap.

"Bloody quakes, terrify the life out of the dog," he said, looking in concern at Joss.

"Keeps setting her off, careering around in circles, whining and moaning, making a general nuisance."

He snipped the improvised twine leash, leaving Joss to slink away to find her bed in front of the stove. As he stripped off his jacket, Homer noted a display of yellow paper flowers in a white vase. He didn't need to ask where they had come from.

"Do you know how to clean and fillet fish?" Homer asked.

Marius gave him an uncertain look. "Maybe."

Homer beckoned him to the sink and sharpened his knife.

"Watch. You never know when it might come in useful."

When the knife edge was to his satisfaction he slit the trout from head to tail, butterflied the body and emptied the guts into a bag.

"You can even cook the guts and feed it to the dog," he said.

He flushed the insides with water then twisted the knife to ease out the spinal cord and the bony skeleton. In seconds, the fish were filleted and cleaned.

Marius looked surprised. "As quick as that?"

"You don't need to stand on ceremony; the fish are already dead. They won't feel anything."

Homer hooked up the fish to drain; thin, bloody liquid staining pink the white porcelain of the sink. Behind Marius, he saw Angela wince as she eased herself into a chair beside the range, her hand fondling the damp coat of the dog beside her.

"At least we're rid of the two women and the troubles they bring with them," Homer said, washing his hands, relief at their departure etched in his words.

"I found their presence quite enlightening," Angela said to counterbalance his negativity.

She noticed Marius stiffen at the insensitivity of his father's words and leave the kitchen without another word.

"What's eating him?" Homer asked after his departing back.

Angela sighed then smiled. "You never change. If you bothered to pay attention you would have noticed the spark of attraction between Marius and Olwyn."

"But he's ten years younger than her," he said incredulously.

"Four, to be precise," she corrected.

Homer laughed with disdain. "Ridiculous. He's only a boy."

"He's nineteen," she reminded him. "And if you look, you'll see he's already growing a beard to look older."

"Nonsense. Besides, she's light years above his social class."

"Since when did that matter?" she responded in exasperation.

"Besides, he's a very good looking young man. I sincerely doubt age has got anything to do with the attraction he might have for her."

Homer had a squinty look on his face. The surprise news about his son suddenly made him look carefully at his friend. The concern in her words drew his attention to the lines now deeply etched by pain into her face. He noticed that her skin had the appearance and texture of parchment.

"Are you okay?"

Angela flashed him another pained expression in reply.

Homer nodded. "I know; nothing a good dose of chemo wouldn't cure. Which you refuse to take."

"I prefer my natural remedies."

She sounded tired, and he had increasingly imposed on her in recent days, the realisation leaving him with a belated feeling of guilt.

"We'll leave you in peace. Marius can come back to the cottage with me."

"Actually, I like having him around. He distracts me. I know people think I'm a recluse, but I've enjoyed having young people in the house. Their energy invigorates me."

"What, even the two troublemakers I dumped on you?" He couldn't resist a note of incredulity in his voice.

"Yes," Angela said, tucking a blanket around her legs despite the warmth of the kitchen.

"Though Grace is a mystery. Something about her seems to stay eclipsed, withheld. Eco-activist is only part of the story. I sense there's something she's concealing."

Homer shrugged. Intuition, especially the female variety, held little interest to him. He preferred facts to be clearly defined, etched in black and white; which took him back to the pain sculpturing itself into the face of his friend.

"We've skirted around this before. Don't you think it's time to come down off your ivory tower and let modern medicine fix the problem."

Angela sighed, with a weak smile on her face.

"Not my style. I'll stick to 'snake-oil'," her words a flippant reminder of how most people dismissed her herbal concoctions.

Homer realised he was pushing against a closed door. Angela had lived with the shadow of cancer for several years, never destined to end her life's journey in a hospital bed.

"Well, if you're sure, I'll leave Marius here with you, just in case that nosey police sergeant pays you another visit."

When Homer had returned to Angela's cottage through the woods he had seen Wailes leave. Intent on a phone call, Wailes hadn't noticed Homer shadowing him, just close enough to catch the occasional word of his conversation, enough to implicate his involvement with Bremer.

"Explain!"

Olwyn barked the command into the phone when Jerry rang a few hours later.

"Ah, explanations. Always a sticky subject in this game. Can't we just put it down to 'all in the line of duty'."

"Jerry!"

The edge in her voice almost cut itself.

"I'm a bloody clerk, not James Bond."

"Which is exactly why we sent you, dear girl."

His tone suggested a smile of self-satisfaction.

"Rather a case that I never thought they would take you seriously. I never dreamt you might be in harm's way."

Olwyn paused before replying, lowering her voice when she spoke.

"You knew full well what the people running the fracking site are like. With the local police in their pockets, it makes them reckless and dangerous. So where was my protection supposed to come from?"

"Steady on, old girl. There was that policewoman to help in an emergency."

"Yes. And she almost got her head blown off in the process."

"True. I did rather think our woodland friend could have been more proactive there."

"'Proactive? I've never met someone more reluctant to help a fellow human being."

"That sounds like our man. Always comes up trumps in the end though. The fact you're still alive is proof of that."

"That doesn't stop someone almost killing me," Olwyn reminded him.

"Ah, but the essential word is almost. Very important in this game. Sending you there was something of a litmus test; to see how vigorously they would react. Given the circumstances, I think you did rather well."

Jerry paused. "Which is why I need you to go back."

There, it was said. In the silence that followed Olwyn could hear a ticking clock in the background.

"No," she replied firmly.

"Before you decide, there will be no need to get up close and personal with these people. Matters are developing rapidly and I need you there as the coordinating link between this office and the consequence of action at the fracking site."

"The answer is still no. Why not get a warrant and go and arrest them. You must have more than enough evidence by now."

Jerry sighed. "Won't work. They'll hide everything long before we even get through the doors. Besides, with Littlemore as Home Secretary, he will never grant a warrant and we will have shown our hand with very unpleasant consequences."

"So what's the alternative?"

"I can't tell you the detail, best not to know. But you've made a success of your contact with your jolly little group in Sussex. They obviously trust you, so it's paramount to continue. Your task will be to make sure that what transpires is relayed to me personally, without anyone intercepting and manipulating the evidence."

The emphasis on the word 'manipulating' struck a chord with Olwyn. For once, Jerry sounded desperately serious.

"Oh, I've upgraded your status and pay to that of field operative," he added almost as an afterthought.

"Promotion? And there was me thinking I was only litmus paper. When do these supposed events start to happen?"

"A week; no more than two."

"I'll think about it." She paused. "Jerry?"

"Yes?" he replied with a note of caution. Olwyn hadn't exactly said she would do it.

"Can I have a gun this time?"

The line went dead without an answer.

CHAPTER 40
IN MEMORIAM

If my family had ever taken me seriously, I often wonder how things might have turned out. My Dad was the only one who had a suspicion that my dreams might be more than childhood ramblings. If he had, he kept them well hidden, well away from the opinions of my mother.

In the summer of 2001 he was sent to New York on secondment to Cantor Fitzgerald, then starting their association with the bank he worked for in London. Without doubt, it was the career opportunity of a lifetime and I can still clearly remember the family's excitement in the days leading up to his departure. For a few brief weeks he showered us with spectacular photos of New York, along with breathtaking panoramic views from his office windows.

It must have been at that point while he was away that my dreams returned. On many occasions, I awoke, agitated and disturbed, my head full of images of crashing aircraft and smoking buildings. Still in my early teens, there was nothing in the location of my dreams that I recognised. If I had paid more attention, or had someone to confide in, I might have been able to translate things more clearly.

It was at the start of his last day in New York that Dad rang my mobile. I was in class at school and when he called it went to answerphone. He was due to fly home that evening and was so looking forward to seeing us all again.

Would it, could it, have made any difference if we had spoken directly to one another? After all, he was the only one in the family who had ever paid attention to my dreams. Perhaps he even took them seriously.

But that's all history. When Dad rang, he had just arrived at his office at Cantor Fitzgerald. It was around eight o'clock New York time. He was calling from the 105th floor of the North Tower of the World Trade Centre, marvelling at the spectacular view on such a fabulous, clear, sunny day.

It was the 11th September 2001.

CHAPTER 41
THE PRICE OF BOOTS

Homer collected Marius and they drove into town with the intention of buying waterproof boots.

"I suppose waterproof is not really a priority in Australia." Homer cast a jaundiced eye at the boy's flimsy trainers.

"When it rains, we just get wet," Marius replied with a shrug.

Homer grunted. "Try that too many times here and you'll end up with pneumonia."

They drove in silence for a while before Marius asked, "What's wrong with Angela?"

Homer hesitated. "Tired bones. A life spent helping others has worn her out."

He omitted to tell him about her cancer. "I think you could stay a while longer with her; keep an eye on things."

"What was that nosey policeman after?"

Homer chose caution again. "Snooping for information. I suspect he would have tried to be more persuasive if you hadn't been there."

"Why was he interested in Olwyn? And you, for that matter?"

How much to tell him? The question stalled Homer's answer for a moment.

"Your friend Olwyn has been sent to gather information about the activities of a fracking site near here. Such places are off-limits, sensitive; it tends to cause trouble to poke your nose in their affairs. Trouble is, her boss doesn't care about consequences. He has a habit of getting people hurt."

"And how does that include you?"

"I've met her boss before. From my experience, he spells trouble. Not that he cares."

"Does he know you live here? Is that why he sent Olwyn?"

'Smart thinking,' Homer thought. The boy was working things out quickly.

Homer trod carefully. "Possibly."

"How does that involve Angela?"

"That's a long time ago. Best left alone," Homer said, a warning tone in his voice.

"But how can I understand things if you just leave me guessing? I've lived my life in a world of half truths because of you."

The accusation bit hard; it was intended to.

"And now I find you're surrounded by people being threatened and injured. What's going on? I have a right to know."

Homer turned into a side street, reluctant to answer, parking his Landrover where they couldn't easily be seen.

"One thing at a time. Let's make sure you have dry feet first. I promise you I'll explain more, but not here and not now."

"That had better be soon. Any more lies and I'll go and start asking people myself."

The years were catching up with Homer. They had just left the Landrover when a sleet squall swept over them and made him shiver. A sign for a public toilet reminded him of a pressing need for it.

"Wait here in the bus shelter. I'll just be a moment," Homer said as he hastily disappeared.

Returning a few minutes later, things had abruptly changed. He found Marius, not in the bus shelter but in the open, surrounded by a circle of four young men. From their mocking taunts it didn't take a second for Homer to realise the situation.

One of them, undoubtedly the ring leader, Homer recognised immediately. A short, slight boy, well dressed, with the same spiteful expression of his father, Miller, Bremer's chief fixer. Marius had backed away from the bus shelter and was standing against a litter bin, watching with a troubled look in his eyes.

Separated from his son, Homer heard the provocative slurs they were throwing at Marius, mainly focused on the colour of his skin.

"Okay, boys, I'll deal with this."

He tried to sound firm but non-confrontational as he approached the circle.

"Keep out of this old man," the Miller boy warned, his accentuated public school voice barely concealing a crude upbringing.

Homer sighed; he'd seen it all too many times before. It seldom ended well. With casual pretence, he searched his pocket for his bluetooth camera and clipped it to the front of his jacket. A tiny red light showed him it was recording to his mobile.

"Just move aside, boys, and we can say none of this ever happened."

Homer drew slightly closer to the ring leader, his eyes locked on the boy's right hand, pinched into a fist at his side. If there was a knife, that's where it was concealed.

"Look, you don't want to try anything stupid that makes me call the police."

The Miller boy laughed with contempt.

"I wouldn't try doing that if I were you. I can't see anyone paying much attention to some down and out old hermit that lives by himself in the woods. Might bring a whole heap of trouble down on your head, old man," he said, spitting his words with scorn.

The options were limited. Homer surmised two of the boys would be mere followers, but the fourth was probably armed with a knife as well and had moved closer to Marius, narrowed eyes scrutinising his prey. Homer felt confident he could deal with the Miller boy, but that left Marius exposed to deal with the other three until he could get to them.

Homer fired a quick glance at Marius. The boy looked nervous, but not transfixed by panic. Bizarrely, his right hand rested inside the litter bin.

"I wouldn't ..." said Homer, his stare locked on the Miller boy, making a half step back, palms raised and feigning retreat.

The Miller boy smiled. Homer heard the sound of a spring released blade as the boy advanced, stepping forward, lured into the gap. He realised, too late, that Homer was already airborne.

Homer's lunging boot missed its target, but caught the boy's thigh with enough force to send him sprawling sideways into the second boy, who, caught unawares, grabbed hold of the Miller boy as he fell to the ground.

Age had robbed Homer of some of his agility and he hit the ground hard, staggering, rather than springing, to his feet, but he scooped up the fallen knife, closed the blade and pocketed the evil device, while moving towards Marius.

Unintentionally, he stamped hard on the Miller boy's outstretched hand as he moved. Without stopping, he body-checked the third boy, now standing mesmerised, and in mid-stride kicked both legs from under him.

Driven by anxiety for his son, Homer seemed to cover the few yards separating them in slow motion, and as he did so the scene before him was confusing. Marius squatted, legs apart, his face disfigured in a wild, angry mask.

He was gripping a can tightly in his right hand, his jacket ripped open at the shoulder, blood already staining the material. In front of him, his attacker gyrated on the spot, clawing at his face, now stained vibrant cobalt blue. Behind him, on a wall, blue graffiti shouted in protest against fracking. In the litter bin, Marius had found the artist's discarded spray can.

"Marius, it's me, Dad." Homer had to shout in his ear to get through to him. "Let's get you away from here. That knife wound needs attention."

Marius hesitated, then ducking underneath Homer's arm, and with crazed eyes, he charged at his principal assailant. Mid-stride he kicked the Miller boy squarely between the legs.

"So much for the monkey chants," Marius hissed as the boy lay groaning on the ground.

Homer pulled his son away. They left town without buying Marius his much-needed boots.

Angela's face had a look of concern as she stood back to check her handiwork. It had taken a dozen stitches to seal the gash in Marius's shoulder.

"You realise there will be hell to pay from Miller for this?"

"Inevitable," Homer said with a grunt.

"Confrontation will always happen when we have to share the world with cobras like Bremer and his band of thugs."

Angela had given Marius one of her herbal remedies to make him drowsy while she stitched his arm. He now slept peacefully, a cocktail from the drink Angela had given him and the kickback from adrenalin.

"The boy who stabbed him intended to cause serious harm. It's lucky he found that spray paint can in the waste bin. It must have been left by whoever is painting the protest graffiti around the town. Without it ..." Angela's words trailed off, better left unsaid.

Homer briefly smiled. "At least Marius used his brain and didn't freeze like a frightened rabbit. He might not be up to anything physical, but those boys who attacked him won't forget the consequences for a long time."

"What about the Miller boy? His father is bound to have been told a version of events that cast you and Marius in a different light."

Homer had a wolf-like smile. "I thought about that."

He held up his mobile phone. "I set it recording the moment I saw what was happening. It includes the final shot of Miller's son coming towards me with the blade of his knife extended."

"And?" Angela said, shocked, her hand over her mouth.

"I sent a copy to Miller suggesting he wouldn't want to force me to post the video on social media."

"Do you think that will work? Miller can be very hot-headed?" Angela looked worried. "You know he really won't like that."

"Probably not. But it might make him think twice before he reacts."

Homer drew up a chair and sat down beside his sleeping son.

"But the reality is that we're only buying time. I think it best that Marius stays here with you until his arm heals and we see how things work out. Meanwhile, instinct tells me we haven't seen the last of our unwanted guests; if those women turn up again and Bremer suspects they're here, the gloves will well and truly come off."

For a moment, Homer and Angela were silent, filling the void with memories of a shared experience. It was Angela who broke the silence.

"You know, we spend a lifetime trying to stay out of trouble. But it always seems to come and seek us out."

Homer gave her a smile of encouragement, but then Marius distracted him, seeming to wake up, mumbling,

"In future, we'll buy boots online."

He wriggled into a more comfortable position and was fast asleep in a moment.

The photo caused a sharp intake of breath. A row of neat stitches held the wound together, the surrounding flesh angry and bright red at the violation. In an unguarded moment, Olwyn had shared her private number with Marius. He obviously liked her and the feeling was mutual.

What was it about men that, despite bad experiences, she was continually drawn to them, as though searching for one who wouldn't just take advantage of her? But something about Marius seemed different from the others, though didn't she always think that at the start?

Okay, he was younger than her, though not that much, with a maturity that bridged the gap. Coupled with dark looks that promised a mysterious side, any resolutions she might have made with regard to future relationships with men, wilted in the look of his dark eyes.

It was strange how the world turns. She gazed at her early morning reflection in the mirror. She looked a wreck, a payback of the events of the past week. She wondered if Marius would still find her attractive when he saw her like this.

And then there was the issue of his father. Marius had little of his father's looks. Growing up with an absent father had obviously been tempered with a degree of self-sufficiency, enough to make him stand against Homer when he disagreed with him; which was often.

So here she was, sworn to be done with men and their exploitative habits, mooning at the picture of yet another intruding into her life.

'*How? It looks nasty,*' Olwyn wrote.

'*A group of bone-headed racists decided to take on me and Dad.*' The answer flashed back in seconds. Marius was obviously waiting for her response.

Olwyn sent an emoticon for a horrified expression. '*How many?*'

'*Four. I think they came off second best.*'

Olwyn was impressed. '*Sounds heroic.*'

'*It was survival. I was terrified.*'

'*What caused it?*' Olwyn knew that Homer could be provocative.

'*Er … try the colour of my skin.*' Marius added a black-faced emoticon.

'*But knives?*' Olwyn replied.

'*Seems knives as the weapon of choice aren't just restricted to city life.*'

'*I wouldn't have guessed you carried one.*'

'*I don't. Just a spray paint can.*'

Now that did surprise Olwyn. '*?????? Paint?!*'

'*Yeah. Idiot that attacked me got a face-full.*'

Perhaps not heroic, but definitely resourceful. The antithesis of his father. Olwyn felt 'impressed' change to 'captivated'.

'*Paint. Where?*'

'*In a waste bin. Chucked away by a local graffiti artist.*'

'*Hoorah for graffiti artists.*'

'*And some.*'

Olwyn stared at the screen on her phone. What would Homer say if he knew what was being shared between them?

On impulse, she typed a line of kisses.

A smiling face emoticon flew back immediately. 'Meaning?'

Olwyn smiled. *'You'll have to wait until the next time I see you to find out.'*

She felt a surprisingly warm glow inside her as she closed the connection. At least she had a justification for returning that had nothing to do with manipulative Jerry Houseman.

"Anyone would think you don't trust me."

Milo lit a cigarette as both men waited in silence for Joss to complete her scan of the area surrounding the disused woodcutter's cabin that Homer had chosen for their meeting.

Homer didn't reply but just gave a look that said, 'Draw your own conclusions.'

Joss was back inside three minutes, taking sentry duty on the covered stoop just outside the door.

Homer opened his rucksack and produced a cloth bag, the sound of stones knocking together as he offered it casually in his hand.

"You've no doubt completed your trade with the first consignment I gave you." Homer held back the bag with one hand, the other extended, awaiting payment.

Milo took an intake of breath. "I had out of pocket expenses to pay. It's not an easy trade to break in to." The roll of bank notes had a miserly diameter.

Homer held an impassive expression, hand unwavering, still extended. "And the rest."

Milo had a wolfish grin. "Cosmo warned me about you."

"My man has mouths to feed."

"Ah, the mysterious clergyman."

"Imam to be correct, not that it makes any difference." Homer's hand was still extended.

Reluctantly, Milo dropped another, fatter, roll of bank notes onto the extended palm. "You'll bleed us dry."

"My heart breaks for you." Homer's fingers snapped shut, like a clam, ensnaring the money which disappeared as if by magic into thin air.

Homer laid the bag of uncut stones on the floor between them. "What's the word about the women?"

"You want intel included in the price as well?" Milo did his best to sound incredulous.

Homer said nothing. He wanted to add, 'You were the one who betrayed us,' but thought better of it and just stood waiting, his foot moving the bag of stones further from the other man as a signal.

Milo sighed. "The word is that Bremer is pissed off because he can't find hide nor hair of the eco-nut. Wailes is equally unhappy because the body of a woman from MI5 seems to have disappeared into thin air. His paymasters wanted her removed, but won't be happy until they see evidence of a body."

He paused and drew heavily on his black-stemmed Turkish cigarette, deliberately blowing grey smoke into the space between them. "And Miller is seething about something, but I guess you know all about that."

Homer looked impassive. "Anything else?" He pushed the bag of stones a few inches in Milo's direction.

For a moment, Milo stared through the single, opaque window, its glass obscured by decades of cobwebs and grime. He looked uncomfortable.

"There are questions being asked by people I try to steer well clear of. They pay big money for information, but that's like making a handshake with the devil." Milo shuddered. Homer didn't think he was acting.

"About what?" he asked.

"Seems the presence of some black kid has ruffled feathers in certain quarters."

"Coloured, actually. The kid has coloured skin, not much darker than you," Homer added pointedly.

Milo spread his palms. "It's all the same to me. I'm just warning you. I'd be scared if these people were asking questions about me. They're not enquiring to send a Christmas card or something."

"And we're not talking about Bremer or his people here?"

The question didn't need asking, but Homer wanted confirmation nevertheless.

"Nope," Milo answered in a measured tone.

On this matter, he showed clear signs of wanting to be elsewhere, as though fearing being tarred by association.

Homer pushed the bag towards him, likewise keen to be gone.

"In the interest of business, keep me posted on what you hear."

Milo nodded and bent to pick up the bag. "We might not like each other much, but I'd hate you to fall foul of these people."

He extended his hand. "Keep safe. I'll tell you if I hear anything more."

A simple handshake can be a great healer. Milo hadn't told him anything Homer hadn't already guessed, though hearing it spoken by the other man brought little comfort. The wild horses were dragging fate in his direction. And there was little he could do to stop them.

CHAPTER 42
TRAVEL IN HASTE

London, for so long my hideaway refuge, was now no longer safe. I guessed it was the latest generation of facial recognition that had tipped the scales. After my experience at the football stadium, intuition told me I was being followed.

I tried all the tricks; swapping disguises in tube trains and on buses, never repeating the same route or time schedules. But you could only do so much. I had made a mistake at some point, allowing my guard to drop. Now, short of plastic surgery, the capital had become my no-go area.

Using a new SIM card in my phone and an encrypted messaging system, I made urgent contact with my handlers. My presence known, it was essential that I left London immediately. The thing I most needed now was a safe house.

It took me less than ten minutes to pack all my worldly possessions. I scoured my lonely room, my temporary home overlooking a busy railway line south of the river, desperate to leave no trace, not even a hair for DNA profiling. Nights of sleeping rough in an alley near Kings Cross railway station beckoned. At least drunks and junkies never ask questions.

After several nights in a sleeping bag, an offer arrived. I was to join a new team in an area of fracking I had not visited before. They were in the final stages of planning a break-in and needed someone with experience. At least the operation would be some distance from the site in Sussex, well away from Bremer's sphere of influence.

The team had made recent progress, concocting a plan to gain access to the inside of a fracking site with the collusion of an anxious contact who worked at the site. Whether by blackmail, or sympathy with our cause, that pipedream had never worked before. I could only hope; there was always a first time.

Assuming the role of priority sub-contractors, once inside the site, the plan was to disguise our cameras to film real time and gain undisputable evidence of the contents of the mysterious containers that arrived each night, and its purpose.

Risky, but the operation planners had convinced themselves we could pull it off. Impressed by my latest skills, they decided I would make an invaluable member of the team.

The challenge was less on gaining access, more about evading detection when filming was complete. With all mobile internet blocked from within the site, the only secure route for releasing the truth to public scrutiny was for someone to escape with the physical evidence.

It sounded straightforward, but then the people planning our operations had a habit of underestimating site security. And, as ever there was the added pressure of time.

The appointment of Hugh Littlemore as Home Secretary was expected imminently. If that happened, the very existence of 'Terra Mater' could become precarious. Driven by our future prospects, the operation had been brought forward in a hurry. Our planners thought that inserting someone with my experience into the team would almost guarantee their chances of success.

Alas, things planned in haste seldom go well. As Homer would undoubtedly remind me, I should have known better.

Olwyn had never imagined the Serpentine as a frozen lake. Jerry had chosen the location; somewhere that briefing his supposedly dead field operative might go unnoticed. As if anyone would bother to place the dusty, neglected office above the launderette under surveillance; Jerry Houseman was becoming paranoid in his advancing years.

Predictably, he was late, leaving Olwyn to complete several circuits of the lake, amused by ducks whose webbed feet served them poorly on the frozen surface. Breathing clouds of white condensation that resembled a labouring steam locomotive, Jerry eventually appeared and fell in step beside her.

"Traffic heavy?" Olwyn quoted his often used excuse even before he tried to make it.

Jerry shook his head. "No. I had to walk for the last half-hour. Someone was tailing me."

He spoke as if it was an everyday occurrence.

Instinctively, Olwyn turned and glanced behind them. Some distance back, a woman and a toddler were feeding bread to skating ducks. They hardly looked candidates for counter intelligence spooks in the employ of 'Blue Horizon'.

"Shall we walk."

Jerry set off at a brisk pace along the path that shadowed the side of the frozen lake.

The Lido had tall plate glass windows with a panoramic view of the Serpentine. It wasn't very much a 'Jerry' sort of place, but his London clubs were too conspicuous for meeting a supposed corpse. They chose a side table, a row back from the windows where their conversation would be camouflaged by the gabble of voices around them.

They started with their usual bantering shadow-boxing talk; they were on their second pot of tea when Olwyn asked her question.

"You obviously have shared history with Homer. The man has a low opinion of your motivations. So why didn't he get Angela out of Iraq before the ISIS net closed around them? I want the truth, Jerry; don't start playing games with me."

For long seconds Jerry studied her in silence. Clever, the girl had been busy. His dilemma was what to tell her.

"Because loyal and sentimental Angela wouldn't leave her local aid workers behind to be killed by extremist Jihadists."

Was he being sarcastic or trying to be ironic? Olwyn couldn't decide.

"There was plenty of evidence of ISIS ideas of summary justice already circulating on social media. Homer had been sent to Iraq to get Angela and her staff to safety. Just the Europeans amongst them; there was no plan to include the locals. To take them all needed helicopters, and the only people in the area with those sort of assets were the Americans."

Olwyn drank her tea, trying to imagine the drama of the situation Jerry had just described to her.

"And so you organised such a deal."

She was guessing that Homer couldn't make these arrangements on his own.

Jerry regarded her over the rim of his cup.

"I did. But Uncle Sam doesn't lift a finger for charity, even for the special relationship; particularly when there aren't any Americans involved."

"And the price?"

For a moment, Jerry had a look of uncertainty. She was more perceptive than he had expected.

"It's difficult. In the smoke of battle, mistakes happen."

"Meaning?" Olwyn knew he was trying to be evasive.

"The Americans knew a senior ISIS leader was at hand to witness the capture of western aid workers."

"Albeit an NGO charity bringing humanitarian aid."

Jerry shrugged. "It makes no difference to ISIS; anyone from the west is a target."

"And the deal?"

He drew a deep breath.

"The deal was, if Homer identified the vehicle carrying the ISIS leader, the Americans would destroy it and helicopters would magically arrive to evacuate all of Angela's aid workers in the chaos of the aftermath. QED."

"But that's not what happened."

"Not quite." Jerry paused, drawing circles in spilt tea on the table top.

"Homer did his bit; lit up the target, a stolen Red Cross SUV with darkened windows, and boom, a nasty missile arrives seconds later. Cue helicopters, and within a few minutes, forty terrified staff are lifted to safety."

"So what went wrong?"

"Not much. Except, Homer picked what turned out to be the wrong target. Instead of eliminating a vicious ISIS warlord," Jerry hesitated, "he targeted the vehicle carrying his wife and children instead."

Olwyn was silent, imagining the consequence of a powerful missile striking a vehicle containing women and children. She shuddered; it would matter little that it was quick.

"Who gave Homer the target information? Amidst all the chaos I can't imagine he managed that by himself."

"He had a squad of four with him and that left them seriously outnumbered. It was my job to avoid a PR disaster and fix the deal for their evacuation. In exchange, the Americans passed the identification of the vehicle through to me."

"Did they know they had given you the wrong target?" Olwyn asked suspiciously.

Her question surprised him. She was brighter than he gave her credit.

"Possibly. One could imagine a scenario where killing an ISIS leader's family, rather than the man himself, could be seen as payback."

Olwyn stared at him. "At the time, did you know?"

Her glare and the question made Jerry feel uncomfortable. When he spoke, his tone had hardened.

"Just remember who you work for, Olwyn. You signed the Official Secrets Act when you accepted your post? There are things you're asking me that come within that. Reveal anything I might tell you, or start playing games with me, and you'll go to prison for a long time."

Gone was the image of the camp buffoon. His words had bite, leaving Olwyn in little doubt he meant every word.

She nodded. "I understand. In return, don't take me for a fool. If you're expecting me to play things your way, I intend to make my own judgement on what kind of man you really are."

Measuring her words, Jerry hesitated.

"So what if I did suspect the Americans' intentions? Turning away would have resulted in many innocent deaths, including, I would remind you, Angela and Homer, who would never abandon the people they had been sent to protect. Should we spare the family of a merciless terrorist for the lives of forty well-meaning innocents?"

He rocked backwards in his chair, regarding Olwyn with a hard, uncompromising stare.

"You insisted on knowing the truth, now you know. Welcome to the real world, Olwyn."

She shook her head. "You're forgetting one thing, Jerry. You were supposed to eliminate an ISIS warlord, not women and children. The real world is the one you've left Homer to carry alone, one consumed by the guilt for the blood of innocents and the shadow of ISIS hell-bent on revenge against his family."

Jerry leaned forwards and poured himself another cup from the pot.

"Try not to be too judgemental, darling."

He directed his gaze across the Serpentine towards a group of young children enjoying a snowball fight.

"Protecting the innocents of this world is not an exact science. But when it comes to making split second decisions, I know whose side my conscience is with."

Olwyn wasn't sure if Jerry's words were directed to her or to the children playing across the lake.

Wailes disliked fishing in cold weather. Miller had insisted they meet at the lake, as if indulging in some masochistic act of male bonding. The snow around the ponds had softened with a rising sun, and an area of clear water, lit by the low arc of the sun, lay still without a covering of ice.

"They'll be hungry."

"I thought fish were dormant in cold weather."

With frozen feet, Wailes was unhappy at the thought of spending hours sitting amongst the dead reeds in the marshy edge of the carp pond.

"The water here is fed by the overspill from the fracking site and that's bound to keep the fish warm. Not that the locals are aware of course," Miller announced with a note of irony.

"Anyway, we're here to catch more than just fish," he continued, surveying the surrounding banks with binoculars.

Miller had gone to considerable lengths to camouflage and conceal themselves. Wailes had assumed it was all part of the country pursuits for which Miller, city born and bred, had developed such a penchant. He cast the man beside him a puzzled glance.

"Meaning?"

"My son, Adam, had an altercation with our hermit woodsman."

Miller scanned the banks of tall reeds for some clue of a presence. "As a result, my boy ended up with several broken fingers."

"Why not file a complaint for assault? I could bring him in for a cosy chat at the station." Wailes shivered as the cold seeped up his legs.

Miller lowered the binoculars, staring at some point on the opposite bank.

"He's too crafty for that game." He gazed at the cold clear sky canopy above them. "Might generate a few unpleasant counter allegations."

"Such as?"

Miller turned his head away as a flock of crows rose in a cloud above the trees, cawing loudly.

"Seems my Adam and his pals took exception to our friend's son."

He returned his hawk-like gaze on Wailes. "The boy is of a coloured persuasion."

Miller paused to let his words sink in.

"A type not especially popular in these parts. As you know, youngsters can be rather primeval in their views and actions. They were, after all, only trying to defend their patch, but for the moment, their actions … shall we say, bent certain laws."

The binoculars returned to Miller's eyes. He momentarily suspended their conversation, leaving Wailes to follow the drift of his words.

"That will all change very quickly once Littlemore takes up the role of Home Secretary?"

"Indeed. But until then, I intend to seek justice without troubling the law. Just think of all the paperwork it will save you."

He laughed with an edge that increased the chill Wailes already felt in his body.

"Rumour has it that our friend, Homer, often poaches from this pond." Miller paused as a message suddenly flashed to the mobile clipped to his belt.

"It appears we may have a visitor," he said, laying his rod onto its rest amongst the reeds.

He turned towards Wailes. "I left a few of my employees nearby. Let's see if we can get a bite."

His smile disconcerted Wailes as he insisted he follow.

"Come on, hurry up," he chided, sensing the policeman's reluctance. "We don't want to miss the fun. You're here to earn your money as witness to our poaching friend resisting arrest."

"So, you'll return to Sussex?"

"Don't push your luck." Olwyn wasn't joking.

They had left the warmth of the Lido and as though to underscore his point, Jerry deliberately led them along a path in the direction of the snowballing children.

"Why not send one of your trained spooks, or better still, go yourself?"

"Ah, but you know the ground and have contacts with local people who you can trust."

"What? One psychologically disturbed hermit and a maimed policewoman?"

Jerry sighed.

"They've intervened to protect you on at least two occasions," he reminded her. "And I hear the policewoman is a valuable inside source even if she has been injured."

"Who almost got herself killed," Olwyn reminded him.

He halted, cocooned in a cloud of sparkling ice-breath crystals.

"The coming events will happen with or without your involvement," he said tersely. "I fear your friends will be drawn in to what will unfold. Whether or not they wish to will be irrelevant."

They walked in silence.

"Perhaps with my support, your presence might help to keep them safe."

"Blackmailer," Olwyn threw back at him.

She felt it was the same trick he had pulled on Homer and look where that had got him.

"You knew I would return all along. You've shown yourself as a duplicitous bastard. In my book, that makes you dangerous as well as manipulative. So, Official Secrets Act or not, I'll make the final call on what I tell these people or let them do."

Olwyn turned to stare at him. "That way, if things go wrong, it will be around your neck, not mine."

She walked away, ducking beneath snowballs, without a backwards glance.

CHAPTER 43
CONVERSATIONS WITH A RODENT

Leaving town in the back of a refuse lorry is seldom a good omen. Still, after three uncomfortable nights sleeping rough in an alley, the smell inside the lorry wasn't too much of a shock.

That my intuitions had been right brought a little comfort in the days following my exit from the stadium. I found out later that four men had kicked in the front door to my solitary bedsit and weren't best pleased to find that their prey had flown. 'Blue Horizon' were drawing their net ever closer. Inevitably, they would catch up with me; no longer a case of if, but when.

The smell aside, my journey offered at least some degree of comfort, my tired body supported on a mattress of black waste bags. I was kept company by two enormous rats. We eyed one another warily, bemused equals, though I'm not sure the rats saw it quite that way. After all, this was their territory, I was the interloper.

I tried not to dwell on my circumstances too much, but amidst the refuse, it was sobering to think how my life had descended to such a level. When the lorry ran over potholes, I bounced on a bed of other peoples' garbage, and it occurred to me that the rubbish beneath me could belong to the very people who were hunting for me.

'Escaped on a magic carpet made of trash.' That would be poetic justice indeed. I began to laugh; too hysterically for my own comfort, or for the rats for that matter, who eye-balled the accompanying mad woman with yellow-toothed mouths.

As my hysteria subsided, the larger of my two companions fixed me with a long stare. Locked inside a smelly box, neither of us was going anywhere in a hurry, so to pass the journey, I chose to strike up a conversation.

With a captive audience, I could share the dark secrets of my life and be certain the rats weren't going to tell anyone.

Perhaps it was the smell of methane, slowly permeating from my bed, which caused a slightly hallucinogenic state. I had spent too many months beating at the locked door that hid the terrible evidence of our future. Either way, I began to share my story. As it turned out, the rats were a good audience and didn't interrupt my tale.

When the driver dropped me off a mile from the landfill site, I was rather sad to bid farewell to my travelling companions. My rodent friends had listened with great patience to my rambling story. I thought to warn the driver they were in the back of his lorry, but decided the rats probably deserved their anonymity too.

I was now in desperate need of a bath. One of the first casualties of becoming a fugitive is personal hygiene; I'd be lucky to see anything resembling a bathroom for some time to come.

Left to trudge several miles to my pick up point, I was constantly sprayed by icy slush from convoys of passing lorries, my mood only marginally lifted by the thought of my step-father's self-righteous indignation if he ever discovered my current plight.

In the eighteen years since my father's death, my family life had changed beyond all recognition. At least while Dad was alive, I had an ally, the only one in the family who never dismissed my dreams as wild ramblings. My mother was far too much a pragmatist to ever give credence to my stories. Following Dad's death she used the excuse of her bereavement to withdraw even further from the wild ravings of her daughter. My brothers, anxious to protect their mother, followed suit, ignoring and isolating me from family matters. As a consequence, my step-father appeared in our lives without anyone consulting my opinion.

Would it have made any difference if they had? I doubted my mother re-married for love? She was still an attractive woman and not short of admirers, and you could say she celebrated her widowhood by embracing the aura of tragic celebrity at every opportunity. I believe it was his wealth and security that drew her to the man that I came to fear and detest as much as he hated me.

Lost in such thoughts, I missed the thundering truck that swerved into a roadside pond of ice and slush, aiming to drench me with a wave of spray, the mocking blast of its horns left to ring in my ears. Perhaps I could be forgiven for indulging in a measure of self-pity.

My personal struggle to save the planet felt pointless in the face of the family ridicule heaped upon me, orchestrated by my mother's new husband. From the moment they married, I never saw him any other way than the man who stole my father's legacy.

Olwyn was startled when her phone rang. Absorbed in thought from her meeting with Jerry, she looked at the name of the caller and began to wonder if her phone had been 'listening' the entire time.

"Hello, Allison. How are you?"

Despite her suspicions of the antics of her phone, Olwyn felt genuinely relieved to hear from her.

"Home from hospital. But scarred for life, so no modelling career for me," Allison quipped. "But at least I'm alive. It's a good job that front door was made from thick oak boards."

"Have the police accepted the story about how you were shot?" Olwyn asked anxiously.

Allison laughed.

"Hook, line and sinker. In the light of my performance, I think I'll seek a job on the stage. It was almost worth the pain just to see Sergeant Wailes's face. Perplexed confusion would be an understatement, though I suspect a measure of guilt prevented him from probing too deeply into my story."

The lightness in her voice only just avoided the vulnerability of her situation.

"I was wondering," Allison continued. "In a few days' time, I'm coming to London. I've an appointment at St Mary's hospital to start specialist treatment on my left arm and shoulder. Could we meet up?"

Olwyn hesitated, trying to think of somewhere they would be unobserved. "Lunch would be nice."

It wasn't that she didn't trust Allison, more concerned that Wailes might have her followed.

Brightly she added, "I'll meet you outside the hospital when you've finished your treatment." It would make it easier to check that she wasn't being followed. "We can decide where to go then."

It seemed the least she could do for someone who had put her life and career on the line for her. It never occurred to Olwyn that it could be interpreted in a different way.

Life is full of 'if's. 'If' Homer had brought Joss with him rather than leave her at the cottage with Angela and Marius, or more to the point, had he applied his usual instincts and scouted his route as he walked through the woods to the carp ponds, he might not have walked into their trap.

Without warning, a tripwire set across the path between trees, hooked around his ankles, while at the same moment, someone barged powerfully between his shoulder blades. Homer fell, spreadeagled, face down into the snow.

Winded, he instinctively tried to roll sideways, away from the force of the blow in his back. Ten years younger he might have been more agile and reacted faster. Instead, he found himself pinned, one large assailant kneeling on his spine, the other standing with both feet on an outstretched arm.

"Keep still or we'll break your arm," a voice threatened in his ear.

Homer noticed how badly the man's breath smelt; he instantly knew they had met before. Face pressed into a mattress of snow and pine needles, he didn't have long to wait for the purpose of the ambush.

"So, Homer, we meet again."

Miller's voice arrived with a pair of leather boots that stood just on the edge of his vision.

Homer could just make out the presence of two other men with him. Another man lingered a short distance farther back. The numbers weren't on his side; resistance would serve no purpose.

"We have business to discuss." Miller's voice held a sharp, precise edge, each word pronounced like a verbal stiletto.

"I don't trade with people like you, Miller." Speaking was difficult, a foot now pressed hard on the back of his head, forcing his face into the ground.

"We have an account to settle. It concerns my son."

"If it's about the video I sent, your son provoked the attack on my boy." Homer fought to draw breath. "I protected him, as would any decent parent." He made the implications clearly obvious in his words. "I'm not pursuing charges; there's nothing more to be said."

"Ah, you seem to have missed the point. My son, Adam, was merely exercising his civic duty, challenging an unknown stranger in the midst of our community."

"Four against one? Doesn't sound a fair challenge." Homer just managed to expel the words through a mouthful of snow and black soil. "Plus, your son and his cronies had knives; try explaining that to a court judge."

Miller was silent for a moment.

"I doubt any judge would place much credibility on the word of a vagrant poacher." He kicked aside the fishing bag and rod that had fallen into the snow beside him.

"But that's not only why we're here is it? You've been meddling in our affairs, Homer. You're clever, I'll grant you, but I know it's you. So this is by way of your last warning; if you know what's good for you, stay out of things that don't concern you."

The sole of his boot came down with full force on Homer's outstretched hand. Only the soft ground showed any mercy for his fingers.

"Consider that a down payment for my son."

Suddenly released, Homer coiled like a spring from the agony of his damaged hand, instinctively adopting a foetal position, anticipating what would follow.

It was little enough to protect him. The kick arrived with full force, aimed low into his solar plexus. At least it missed his ribs.

As he lay in the snow, he knew his judgement was slipping. 'If' he had applied his usual rules, he might not have ended up exposed and vulnerable.

'If'; such a small word with such powerful implications. Equally, 'if' Miller hadn't left with the air of a smug, contemptuous bully, Homer might not have seen the back of the figure who had stood apart from what had happened; a lone spectator to the attack on an innocent man.

As Homer struggled painfully to his feet, he decided Sergeant Wailes was long overdue a visit.

CHAPTER 44
IN THE COMPANY OF LICE

My new home was a threadbare mattress in a damp caravan, shared with other pickers, on an organic fruit and veg farm. I had been given a false identity and work CV, I spoke little and hid my home counties accent. With little experience, I was set to work in the packing shed where noise from the machines eclipsed most conversation. That left me alone with my own thoughts for much of the time. Avoiding socialising wasn't a problem; on that account I had logged plenty of practice in recent years.

There was another woman in my caravan called Rosetta. I doubted that was her real name when I discovered that she had only recently joined 'Terra Mater'. Although new to the organisation, she had been given the role of organising the imminent operation to infiltrate the nearby fracking site.

A considerable amount of planning had been made in advance, but exposing the secret workings of a site wasn't a task for the faint-hearted, as I knew to my cost. I read the operational plan with a feeling of growing trepidation, 'wishful thinking' being a key principle for success. It seemed to glibly dismiss the Bremers of this world, ignoring their cunning in hiding dark secrets of what was happening within their security fences.

I knew from first-hand experience that their attention to detail on security matters posed a serious challenge, something our organisation had so far failed to overcome. Homer was right when he called us amateurs; there was no excuse; we should have known better.

At least for a few brief days my time was consumed packing endless streams of cabbages into boxes. I was paid for mindless hours at the conveyor belt, something of a rare event in itself, while my spare time was absorbed by trying to persuade Rosetta, my co-conspirator, from being over-optimistic with her plans.

She was a pleasant girl, but her lack of experience held little regard for the task in hand, confidently predicting that site security were no more than 'gooks' or 'dead-brains'. Presented with such an assessment, Homer would have walked away in an instant.

So should I if I had any sense, feeling isolated and alone with growing unease. Withdrawn from the rest of my group, the only friends I made were bed lice. My mattress was infested by a colony who, despite my best intentions, happily migrated from my bed to my clothes.

Marius looked shocked by Homer's injuries. Despite their estrangement, he had always imagined him as indomitable, someone who could always cope with the unexpected. Now he had to watch Homer bent double from pain, blood and bile staining his beard and clothing, while Angela tried to clean his mangled hand.

"Drink this," she instructed. "It will ease things and settle your stomach."

Homer pulled a face. "Witch's brew," he grumbled, reluctantly accepting the mug she offered him.

She made no reply, waiting for him to drink her cocktail.

"We'll give it five minutes," she said brusquely. "Then I'll start work on straightening things out."

She nodded towards her ancient freezer.

"Bring me another ice pack," she asked Marius, carefully examining Homer's broken and twisted fingers, several projecting at odd angles. It was a mess.

"At least it wasn't your right hand."

"I suppose that's something," Homer muttered, sounding unconvinced. He tried to smile at Marius.

"Perhaps I should have used one of your spray cans. That was a neat trick, though I doubt it could have held off all of them."

Marius shrugged. "A back-up plan might have."

"Meaning?" Homer sounded doubtful.

Marius searched his pocket and produced a lighter. He pressed the flint, holding the valve open as he did so. The flame extended impressively.

"The spray can contents are highly flammable. You'd be surprised by the effect if you add a lit flame."

"Clever. Providing you don't blow yourself up."

"It's all down to timing," Marius said with a smile. "It might have made them think twice and could have spared you a broken hand."

Homer didn't look convinced. "I should never have walked into their trap in the first place," he grumbled.

Ignoring their banter, Angela stated the obvious.

"You do realise this will need an x-ray and setting properly."

"Not in any local hospital it won't." Homer winced as Angela examined his hand.

"So what? Do you intend to pay privately somewhere else?"

"If you can't manage it, tell me what's broken and I'll get it fixed," he said with a tone of ingratitude.

"What's broken? Try three fingers and several metacarpals in the hand. Oh, and add to that a few lower ribs while you're at it."

Angela turned to Marius with a smile.

"It's always the same. He's a dreadful patient."

Listening intently, Joss chose that moment to include herself, thrusting her nose beneath Homer's uninjured hand, demanding attention, her simple gesture a reminder of his black mood brought on by self-reproach. Reprimanded, he gave them all a tired smile and slumped in his chair, submitting to Angela's probing hands beneath the anesthetising balm of her potion.

She worked quickly. Marius looked on, fascinated by her assured skill. Fingers were broken, metacarpals dislocated; all needing to be eased back with careful manipulation. Within minutes she had his hand cleaned and straightened, adding splints and bindings.

Nothing could be done for his ribs, his lower chest already painted with every possible shade of yellow and purple. She listened intently with her stethoscope. Seemingly satisfied, she unhooked the earpieces and gave them to Marius to hear for himself.

"He's bruised, but no serious internal damage despite the force of the kick. This is what clear airways should sound like."

Homer was asleep by the time they had finished. They had to roll him from the chair to the battered kitchen sofa. He didn't stir, proving the power of Angela's so-called witch's brew.

"So, with no Homer for protection, it's down to you to protect us tonight," Angela said to the room in general.

Marius wasn't certain if she was addressing him, or Joss.

Allison decided to walk from St Mary's hospital to the Serpentine. Despite the snow, a weak sun shone and the air carried the sharp, metallic tang of winter. Absorbed by the cold beauty of the day and ice coated pavements, she never thought to look behind her. Had she done so, she wouldn't have recognised the woman who followed her, simply disguised in dark wig and sunglasses.

Olwyn was walking a short distance behind her, a simple act to see if Wailes had anyone tailing her. She had chosen the Lido deliberately; at short notice it felt safer than choosing somewhere new. They had arranged to meet in front of the café, overlooking the lake.

When Allison arrived, Olwyn held back amongst the trees, observing, with little chance of being seen. Allison stood casually, waiting. In the bright sunlight, she cut a solitary figure, alone against a backdrop of empty chairs and tables waiting for summer to return. No one else appeared to show any interest.

After a few minutes, Allison took the phone from her bag, inducing a momentary pang of apprehension, despatched a few seconds later when Olwyn's phone rang. She really had to learn to trust her.

"I'm here," Allison announced with a bright note of expectancy.

"Two minutes," Olwyn replied.

She backed away through the trees. She would take the longer path and approach from the opposite direction. Wailes was conniving, but she doubted even his reach extended into the heart of London.

Olwyn was greeted with a kiss that lingered just long enough to suggest some hidden, wished for intention.

"You look well, under the circumstances."

Olwyn stood back to scrutinise her friend. Allison's face, miraculously unmarked by the shotgun blast, had lost the previous ghost white colouring, her left arm wrapped in an elaborate blue bandage, supported in a sling.

Olwyn led the way into the warmth of the Lido café, guiding them to a table set back from the panoramic windows. As on her previous visit with Jerry, it afforded a clear view of anyone approaching, whilst conveniently positioned for escape through a fire exit. She had to smile to herself; she was becoming another of Jerry's paranoid spooks.

They ordered, and began chatting while waiting for lunch to arrive.

"I wanted to thank you in person. You put yourself at risk visiting while I was in hospital. It could have aroused Wailes's curiosity if anyone had recognised you."

Olwyn shrugged. "It was searching for me after my night in the hotel room that led to you getting shot. You mustn't put yourself in danger for me again. That's twice now, we don't want to risk a third time," she said with genuine concern.

"Has Wailes created any false leads to a suspect yet?" she asked.

"He seems mystified. I think he knows the truth but can't prove anything. If your suspicions are correct, Miller would have told him they set the trap. At the moment, the story being spun is the usual; they're following leads, with gypsies or travellers the fall-back suspects. Or poachers, if that line fails," Allison said with a thin smile that suggested she wasn't disappointed by his confusion.

"How's the scorpion?" she asked mischievously.

"Last seen serving time in a plastic box while Homer decides what to do with her."

"Ah, your mysterious hermit. Do you think it's just possible he could have set the booby trap? It was his cottage after all?"

"Not his style. He wouldn't even kill the scorpion when I was freaking out in the hotel bedroom. I suspect it's the other way around; someone from the fracking site set the trap to be rid of Homer; shooting you was an unforeseen accident."

Allison looked at Olwyn quizzically. "Homer, or the mystery woman, Grace, I think I heard you call her?"

That was the first time that thought had occurred to Olwyn, leaving her to wonder what Allison knew of Homer's house guest.

For a moment, Olwyn was thoughtful, uncertain with what to share. Much of what she knew or suspected was classified. Allison was a policewoman and had almost certainly suffered life threatening injury at the hands of the fracking security, undoubtedly with the knowledge of her boss. The mention of Grace was interesting. Even without compelling evidence, Allison had a right to be included, if for no other reason than her own self-protection.

Over lunch, Olwyn explained the basics of what she knew. This simple act of inclusion, when added to the risks in taking Allison to hospital, bound their friendship in shared experience. But there was something beyond friendship in her eyes, occasional glances that hid unspoken emotions.

Olwyn wisely avoided wine, keen to deflect an invitation she might find difficult to refuse. Across the narrow landscape of the table she saw Allison as an intelligent woman, attractive, awkward in a self-conscious way, shadowed by an unspoken sense of loneliness. Olwyn sensed she was used to rebuttal and didn't want to add to her disappointment.

"With luck, Wailes might have been arrested on suspicion of corruption," Allison said brightly. She really didn't like the man.

They were jousting about splitting a desert when Allison's phone interrupted them with a news flash from her police website. Despite leave to convalesce, curiosity prevailed. With an air of expectation, she opened the news page.

"So, we have a new Home Secretary," she said, turning the phone so that Olwyn could see the photograph.

"My new boss," she added with a note of irony. "Unusual to post a family photo don't you think? One wonders what PR purpose he could have intended?"

Olwyn gave the photo a cursory glance. 'A kitsch family line-up,' she thought, then read the caption.

The new Home Secretary, party leader of 'Blue Horizon', Hugh Littlemore, with his new wife on their wedding day a few years earlier, joined by their respective families.

Nothing particularly out of the ordinary at first glance, beyond a distasteful attempt by an extreme right wing politician to play the illusion of happy families from his playlist. Except …

In the photo, two tall young men stood to the right of their mother, obviously her sons. To her left was her new husband, the now Home Secretary Littlemore with a girl and her older brother. All smiled at the camera with fixed expressions, practiced and polished for the occasion. At first glance, it was all unremarkable, a flagrant attempt to bolster political respectability. Alarm bells were clamouring in her brain before Olwyn was aware of the reason.

It was the last figure, isolated at the end of the line-up. Standing detached, to the left of the two young men, was their younger sister, according to the photo caption. She was staring with a cold, expressionless face, though her eyes signalled a different story. Younger in the photo, she squinted angrily at the camera, a picture of confrontation.

Unmistakeable; unless a zeitgeist existed. It was the same woman she had escaped with in Homer's borrowed police van just a few days before.

Grace; Littlemore's step-daughter.

CHAPTER 45
IMPLICATED BY A PRESS RELEASE

If Allison was disappointed, she hid it well. As she left Olwyn, she had to be satisfied with a kiss on the cheek and the promise to contact her as soon as her future plans were decided.

The photograph of Grace had rattled Olwyn more than she wanted to admit, and she struggled to hide a rising sense of alarm. It seemed unlikely that Homer or Angela would have seen the photo accompanying the press release, the prospect of an imposter amongst them raising all sorts of alarming implications.

So it was with barely concealed distraction that she walked with Allison to hail a taxi and bid her farewell to return to her London hotel for the night before returning to Sussex. As Allison's taxi drove away, Olwyn fired a message to Jerry, demanding he call her at the first opportunity. Predictably, her message remained unopened.

Warning Homer became her next urgent priority. But where to start? The number she had used on the night the scorpion shared her bed had mysteriously evaporated. Homer obviously preferred to assume the guise of a 'digital invisible man'. Any online search for him disappeared into the vacuum of anonymity.

So that left Marius. She had no doubt he would be keen to help, but anything beyond innocent flirting carried the risk of drawing him into a web of subterfuge that she couldn't begin to understand. She knew the phone Jerry had given her was under surveillance; Jerry had admitted as much when he had claimed to be protecting her best interests.

That meant the prospect of returning to Sussex was a matter of urgency. Despite Jerry's justifications, she still felt reluctant to do his bidding. She had been way out of her depth on the first visit and it seemed utter madness to return again so soon.

But the knowledge that Homer and Angela had welcomed an informer was an undeniable game changer. Added to which, she had a growing suspicion that Wailes might yet devise a plan to deal with Allison. If she tried to uncover his corrupt involvement with the fracking site, he was quite capable of creating another 'accident' to silence her. Permanently.

So with a renewed sense of purpose, Olwyn set off to find a particular back street shop she knew in Soho, the type that are casual when it came to matters of identity. What did the Americans call them? Burner phones?

She found the slip in her bag with Jerry's credit card number. With his permission, she had used it to pay for the hotel in Sussex. With a smile, Olwyn went shopping.

As Homer awoke, the pain returned to his hand and chest. He tried to lever himself upright, resembling a beetle rolled onto its back. Joss regarded Homer's plight with a curious eye.

"Fat lot of help you've been," Homer grumbled to the dog as he gained his feet.

Joss felt reassured; all must be well in the world if Homer was complaining.

Loud music, of a style he didn't recognise, permeated through the floorboard ceiling, confirming that Marius must have woken. Muttering to the dog, Homer shambled over to the kitchen sink, ran the tap and immersed his face in ice cold spring water. Whatever Angela had mixed into her potion to ease the pain had left him lethargic and blurred his vision. The water's arctic chill soon dealt with that.

"I heard you moving around."

Angela entered the kitchen behind him, riddled the Aga and set the kettle on a hotplate.

"How are you feeling?"

Homer scowled.

"Like I've been kicked by a mule," he replied ungraciously. "What did you put in that witch's brew you gave me?"

"Just something to stop you complaining all the time," Angela said with a smile. "How's the hand?"

"Hurts." Homer held up his bandaged hand. It would be several weeks before he regained the use of it.

"You should have it x-rayed. I can't vouch for setting the bones properly. Same for the ribs."

"I'll take my chances," Homer retorted. "Do you need a written disclaimer?"

"No. But I'll settle for you at least listening to my advice once in a while."

The smile was gone, a sense of gravitas in its place.

"You know, if this campaign Grace has brought upon us continues, it's likely to end very seriously. For all of us."

Angela spoke while watching the early dawn paint the eastern sky through a skeleton of leafless trees, indigo making its transit through the spectrum to blood red.

"Prophetic don't you think," she said, turning to Homer. "I remember a dawn just like it rising beyond the mountains in the deserts of Iraq."

For a moment Homer didn't respond, his thoughts roaming to a distant time and place of shared memories. Eventually he nodded in agreement.

"Let's hope that it isn't an omen for a similar outcome."

He turned his back on the rising dawn, something Angela had seen before when he sought to conceal his feelings. Above them, the music rose in crescendo, slowly diminishing as a voice sang along with the words.

"We ought to send Marius somewhere safer." Angela left the idea to hang.

"You mentioned that Olwyn did something in MI5? He wouldn't need persuading to go and join her. Whatever she does, he's bound to be safer with her than here."

Angela watched as Homer processed her suggestion.

"Your hand and ribs are the clear proof that not even you can spare us every time. You can't protect everyone, Homer. Yesterday was evidence of that."

Before Homer could answer, Marius interrupted them, yawning as he entered the room. In his hands he held a slender paper stem, its head folded and cut to resemble a frilled, yellow flower head.

"I found this lying under my bed when I pulled out my rucksack. Did you make it?"

Obviously impressed, he directed his question to Angela.

She smiled as he placed it in her hand.

"It's an origami dandelion. Our friend Grace leaves them behind as a token of her thanks."

"It's cut and folded from a single piece," Marius said in appreciation. "Amazing skill."

"Less of the platitudes," Homer said, turning from checking the control panel for sensors he had set up around the cottage.

"From my experience, it's a reminder that she intends to return." He flicked a worried glance in Angela's direction.

"We don't need two guesses to know what that will mean."

One of the few skills Jerry had shared with Olwyn was the art of tracking a mobile phone. She lost her phone with alarming regularity so the App he installed for her had often proved invaluable.

She charged the phone she had bought with Jerry's credit card, installed a SIM card bearing a false ID and cloned the App and the details she had copied from Grace's phone from her original phone. She couldn't easily explain what had provoked her to behave so deviously; after all, with the help of Marius, they had got on well enough. A spontaneous act; perhaps it was no more than intuition.

With her new phone prepared, Olwyn embarked on her search for the mysterious Grace. That her phone was switched off wasn't a complete surprise. Fortunately, the App Jerry had given her could trace a phone even when it was asleep. But not when it was shielded.

She left her phone tracking whilst she travelled home. Grace might switch her phone on at some point and when that happened, the App would fix her location and alert

Olwyn who, having cloned her SIM card, could download all her contacts.

While the underground train rattled through the maze of tunnels, she evaluated Littlemore's wedding photo. Allison hadn't questioned her when she had asked for a copy. There was a possibility she was jumping to the wrong conclusion. There was always a chance it wasn't Grace, who crafted her looks for anonymity; a neutral choice of hairstyle and clothing that blended into any crowd. Reluctantly, she would have to find better evidence before sharing her suspicions with Jerry.

But the tendrils of coincidence remained, unwilling to be ignored. The photo wasn't recent; according to the caption it had been taken several years earlier. If it was Grace in the family line-up, it meant Hugh Littlemore, the new, controversial Home Secretary, was her step-father. In the modern world, what did that prove? Olwyn was herself estranged from her own blood relatives.

From what little she had learned from Grace, the fact sounded preposterous. Everything she claimed to stand for was opposed to what 'Blue Horizon' represented. Was her hard, unremitting expression in the photo intended to convey a message? Anger hides in many guises.

Grace had conscripted a reluctant Homer to help in her fight against the fracking industry, the centrepiece of Littlemore's party's energy policy. If that was so, how was it possible that his step-daughter appeared to be conspiring against such a key policy? Perhaps that was the point; 'against' was just a cover to infiltrate the opposition and pass information directly to Littlemore at cosy family gatherings?

For a moment, Olwyn felt shocked by this line of her thinking. There could of course be just the simple answer of mistaken identity. But if not, what were the consequences?

Her imagination refused to be ignored. Was it all just a very clever act of betrayal and Grace really was the informer? If her fears were correct, then Homer, Angela and Marius were in great danger, unaware of the imposter.

It was a danger that would embrace her as well if ever Allison let slip that Olwyn was still alive. Distracted by her thoughts, she missed her station.

Hidden from public scrutiny was the innocent fact that all fracking sites included powerful concrete pumps in their equipment manifests. Something, in itself, that seemed unremarkable. Except, the pumps in question worked at ultra-high pressure and were all built by secret military supply sub-contractors.

With the help of gravity, their task was to force thick, cementitious slurry huge distances through an enclosed shaft. It was nothing particularly outstanding in civil engineering terms beyond the primary unanswered question; what was in the material they were so secretly disposing? Every site had one, irrespective of the volume of gas it produced, leaving a gaping question mark in the hidden narrative around fracking.

From the beginning, 'Terra Mater' had embarked upon a mission to expose the extent and consequence of fracking. In principle, it happened in clear contravention of stated government policy, being undertaken in secret at a host of supposed test sites. But, given that most politicians spoke with duplicitous intentions, it left exposure of what was happening down to us.

What we urgently required was evidence, on film or video, that couldn't be dismissed as fake or distortion. So far, much of what we had came in grainy fragments, a string of events tied together by speculation that lacked substance and was easily dismissed as fabrication and manipulation. After all, weren't we just a group of activists with an agenda to distort the facts.

So that brings me to the purpose of our next operation, due to take place in a few days' time. In principle, it was disarmingly simple. I don't know why no one had thought of it before?

That's probably why I felt so perturbed. When it came to duping the security net surrounding a fracking site, it never pays to underestimate people; something my fellow activists singularly failed to appreciate. Even someone with the guile and skill of Homer found it hard enough to combat the likes of Miller and his mercenaries. The men employed weren't particularly sophisticated. But what they lacked in intelligence, they made up for with cunning and a ruthless application of force.

As the operation approached, I could be forgiven for feeling a sense of deep foreboding.

Homer devised a technique for using a shotgun. Supported on the leg of a monopod, he could support and swivel the gun while using only his right hand. His aim was pretty haphazard by his standards, but it made the recoil bearable. Though he wasted several cartridges, he still managed a few pigeons for Joss to retrieve.

Despite their disagreement, Homer needed Cosmo if he were to slip Marius out of the area unnoticed. An update on their account was long overdue. When dusk fell, he would visit a fast running trout stream clear of ice and snow, and try to add to the day's tally to tempt Cosmo to cooperate.

Moving cautiously this time, and using Joss to scour the ground ahead, Homer made his way to his cottage to dress the birds. He lit the Aga; the milder weather had been short lived, the temperature now dropping as the wind backed to the east.

Another consignment of stones had arrived, hidden in a vegetable box concealed in his barn; another link in the veil of subterfuge operated by the Imam in repayment to those with lives damaged trying to help his refugees. Homer smiled to himself; the inclusion of hot chillies was a request for urgent payment.

The silent house felt cold and empty. He shook his head; he was getting far too used to having people around him. The moniker, 'Hermit Homer', was something he had previously cast off with a shrug, always ignoring the consequence of solitude. But a man cannot hide from his destiny, no matter how hard he may try.

He heard Joss scamper down the ladder from the roof, her claws click-clacking on the wooden treads. She arrived beside him, a yellow origami flower between her teeth.

"Are you trying to remind me of someone?"

It was almost as though the dog had read his mind.

Joss dropped the paper flower on the floor in front of him and gently panted, smiling as only a dog can, while she waited for Homer to pick it up.

"Is this supposed to make me feel better?"

The good thing about a conversation with a dog is that they never contradict you. Instead, Joss turned her head to one side, with a look in her eyes which said, 'it certainly couldn't do any harm'.

Homer smiled, fondling the soft fur on the back of her neck. He wondered where on earth she had found the flower; he had searched the attic from top to bottom to ensure no evidence remained of Grace's presence. He gathered the origami offering, inserting it into a jug along with the other tokens she had left him.

Homer was at the sink, cleaning and de-feathering the pigeons with his one good hand. Six birds for ten cartridges; a poor harvest for the effort, the poverty of the catch a reminder he was making too many poor decisions.

Now, the future safety of Angela and Marius would rest on what came next. The continued cold weather prevented any attempt to fly Angela's owl kite. That left unfinished business and Homer was certain Grace would feel compelled to return. Despite the problems she carried in her wake, the thought of her coming back created a mellow feeling inside him, but also brought with it a threat to the security of Marius and Angela.

Jerry Houseman might promise protection, but what value could he attach to his words? Homer had little doubt some blackmailed mole in MI5 had already alerted his ISIS paymaster that Marius had arrived in the country. The confrontation with Miller's son had only served to highlight the fact. ISIS had a long memory and a fatwa to fulfil. The clock was ticking. It was only a matter of time before they were found.

Reluctantly, he would have to call upon Cosmo once again to smuggle Marius out of the area, Angela too, if she would leave, which he doubted. But where would be safe to send them? If asked to leave, Marius would more than likely go and stay with the dizzy-headed woman, Olwyn. So what to do?

Racked by these thoughts, Homer decided to go fishing to clear his mind. His favourite rod had been broken by Miller's boot, so he had salvaged the brass ferrules and repaired the reel. A search in the woods found a clump of hazel whips for the rod, with reeds and a bottle cork for a float. Perhaps the answer would come beside the cold clear waters of the trout stream.

With a whistle to Joss, they set off. Man and dog, a well-worn team, each a mutual support to the other. With his shotgun over his shoulder, this time he would take precautions.

CHAPTER 46
THE INDISCRETION OF BACCHUS

The message was plain and simple in several ways. Sergeant Wailes found the semi-conscious body curled up on the front steps of the police station. PC James wasn't drunk, though the smell of alcohol emanating from his filthy tunic was eye-watering.

Whilst not a single bone was broken, there wasn't a part of his body that wasn't blue with bruises. It had been a professional job, applied with a sand filled rubber hose during an interrogation the previous night. It had Miller's trademark all over it, a blunt warning of what befell policemen who disobeyed their paymasters.

As the ambulance took PC James away to hospital, Wailes was more concerned about how he could present his excuses than PC James' medical condition. To lose one police officer to an 'accidental' shooting tested plausibility. Rapidly followed by an accident to a second officer, it raised more questions than Wailes was prepared to answer.

Instead, James would make a statement that he had accidentally walked into the path of a passing lorry which had caught him a glancing blow. If he had any sense, James would be persuaded to sign the version written for him. Ever the expert in wording falsified accounts, Wailes would ensure that it disappeared, lost forever in the dusty annals of police records. The alternative didn't bear thinking about.

Yet that still left a troubling doubt hanging over him. Allison Markham was too enthusiastic for his taste and had a habit of seeking out the truth. It was time to take control and make sure she behaved.

The hotel room appeared bland and nondescript in the dim half light of morning. When Olwyn awoke, her head felt dull and foggy, clouded by the memory of a wine glass or three too many the previous evening. Propped on one elbow, her hand searched the other side of the empty bed;

it was still warm. The sound of running water emanated from the shower room.

"Oh god."

Olwyn collapsed onto her pillows, memories of a night's indiscretion flooding back to her.

Troubled by what she had discovered about Grace, and frustrated in equal measure by her ignored calls to Jerry, she had wandered into a wine bar. At some point after the third glass she had remembered that Allison was still in London. In need of company she had phoned her, only too aware that it could be a serious mistake.

Yawning, her memory of the previous evening was fuzzy, to say the least. Olwyn could vaguely recall it had been fun, in a flirtatious sort of way, and her skin smelt of another woman's perfume.

Before she could collect her thoughts, the door to the bathroom opened and Allison appeared, wearing a silk wrap, wet hair bound in a towel turban.

"Morning, sleepy. I didn't expect to see you awake before I left."

One sleeve of the wrap hung empty; her bandaged arm concealed inside.

"The wonders of clingfilm," Allison added with a laugh, unwinding the waterproof covering with her free hand.

"Was I drunk last night?" An unnecessary question; Olwyn's head hurt in the way of too many glasses.

"Enough to make you deliciously sociable." Allison gave her an impish smile. "Don't worry. I took advantage of you. Though I have to say you seemed to need consoling."

For a fleeting moment, Olwyn feared her friend would climb back into bed again to continue the night's activities.

"Don't look scared." Allison must have read her mind. "I've a train to catch in less than an hour, so you're safe to recover here on your own. There's coffee and aspirin. Take your time and drop the key at reception when you leave."

She quickly dressed in front of Olwyn, asking for help with her bra and shirt buttons. Suddenly self-conscious that she was naked, Olwyn wound the bedsheet around her.

Allison lingered for a parting kiss.

"The least that can be said is that it spared you from sharing a bed with a scorpion." Mischief coloured her words as she gathered her jacket and bag. "Don't forget to leave the key."

The door closed behind Allison, and Olwyn instinctively withdrew her legs from the lower reaches of the bed. She had to admit that Allison had a point.

We spent the weekend before the operation practising the procedure until it could be performed in our sleep. All that we now awaited was the call to say the control panel on the pump in the fracking site had broken down and we were needed with a new unit within a matter of a few hours.

At the last minute an older man, who none of us knew, joined our small group. He was a silent, withdrawn individual, an experienced electrician, and thought to be invaluable if the repair turned out to be more complicated than we anticipated.

I'm always nervous when someone new joins a team at the last minute; it disrupts the highly tuned balance that comes from living and training together. Given the precarious nature of what we were about to attempt, my instinct was to go with the original group of five.

Rosetta, our short-tempered and impulsive team leader, thought differently and my misgivings were disregarded. After all, hadn't I been a late inclusion to their team? We would go with six of us, including one member no one knew anything about.

While we waited for the call, I fretted, and almost decided to try and contact Homer to get his sway on how best to handle my reservations. Instead, I worked extra shifts, burying my fears beneath mountains of sprouts and carrots, grateful for the distraction and the cash it provided.

At this rate I'd be able to treat myself to something new rather than charity shop hand-me-downs.

In what spare time remained, I checked and re-checked my equipment; the camera concealed in the company hard hat I had to wear, continually charging batteries, and testing the link to the memory card cunningly concealed in the watch on my wrist.

In my few optimistic moments, I actually believed we might pull this off and obtain the evidence we so desperately needed. I so wanted to contact Homer. But I could hear his caustic comments ringing in my ears, and pride prevented me.

It is often a truism that pride comes before a fall. As it was to turn out, I'd have done better to listen to the proverbs.

Wailes had been drinking, which was probably what provoked him to phone Allison Markham. He spent his life gathering hidden secrets, skeletons in the cupboard, about those around him. You never knew what necessity might demand their use.

The beating PC James had received had been a warning; a clear message that he could be next if he didn't please his paymasters soon. With compliant PC James recovering in hospital, Wailes urgently needed progress to ingratiate him in Bremer's favour.

Wailes suspected that Allison Markham disliked him. Not a difficult conclusion to draw when he knew what she tried to hide. He had uncovered her secret life almost by accident. Now it was time to play his card; a threat of exposure should be enough to bring her to heel. Given her father's position as a senior bishop, an ultra-conservative with strong views against female ordination and gay marriage, the mere threat to release certain photos he possessed to a tabloid newspaper would bend Allison to his bidding.

Dealing with Allison was one thing; Wailes's instinct told him that the epicentre of his problems lay with Homer.

The beating he had witnessed at the carp pond had been unpleasant and achieved nothing to improve his own standing. The fact that he had provided details of the secret location for Homer's poaching was overlooked and gained him little breathing space. The truth was that Bremer wanted the entire troublesome group cleared away, once and for all.

From the start, the plan to incriminate Homer and Angela with the body of the man, who had died in the course of questioning by Miller, had badly backfired. Could they have predicted the arrival of the meddling Olwyn Wright-Smith? Her disappearance continued to puzzle him, tendrils of doubt growing from the coincidental failure of many CCTV cameras simultaneously.

His ordered world was continually disrupted by troublemaking women. It was high time he took the gloves off. What he needed was an obedient Allison Markham to make a social visit to Angela.

Over the years Wailes had sequestrated enough heroin to form a 'rainy day' reserve. With Homer's prints all over it, Allison would be instructed to hide a sufficient quantity in mad Angela's cottage. The search warrant would already be signed and would follow within hours of Allison's visit. Given Angela's reputation and Homer's police record, the courts would do the rest. Wailes had the cash ready to guarantee it.

And the boy, Homer's son? Wailes knew Miller's vindictive mind; there was still a vendetta to conclude. Allison would also plant a knife during her visit, one that could be identified as the murder weapon in a recent unresolved attack. Covered in the boy's prints, it would be sufficient to put the boy in prison for life.

It was all so simple. A single act, with Allison Markham's willing cooperation, and Wailes would get his paymaster off his back. With luck, when it all fell into place, he could expect a much needed financial bonus.

Olwyn needed to move matters forward. Frustrated by Jerry's prolonged silence, she decided a visit to his home address was needed. She wore a wig, glasses and a coat bought from a charity shop. The disguise was effective; Jerry didn't recognise her when he first opened the door.

"My, my, how my protégé has developed," he exclaimed, stepping back in surprise.

Though late on a weekend morning, he had come to the door from bed, wearing a Japanese styled gown, embossed with vibrantly coloured cranes.

"No thanks to you," Olwyn quipped with a stern face. "The coat smells of moth balls."

She followed as he led her to the kitchen. Jerry flipped the switch on the kettle. He laid out three cups; Florian must be upstairs somewhere. To her surprise, he was actually making coffee for her for once. How times change.

"How did you find me here?" He didn't sound too happy.

"Simple. I tracked your phone using the App you gave me."

Any look of annoyance turned to genuine surprise.

"And the purpose for this unexpected visit?"

"As you don't answer my calls, I'm left with no alternative."

"Ah. I thought it best to give you space. To consider your options."

"If I did that, I'd walk out and find another job."

"But you won't."

"Your lucky day, Jerry. I'm returning to see my friends in Sussex."

His smile broadened. "Excellent. We need to brief you and bring you up to speed. We can …"

Olwyn held up her hand.

"Not so fast. I return on my terms. I'll rely on people I trust."

She walked around the island unit and stood beside him as he filled the cups. Open on the worktop, a scribble pad showed a sketched cartoon image of the new Home Secretary, his hawkish features strongly caricatured.

"Our new lord and master," Olwyn nodded expressionless towards the sketch.

"So he would have us believe. Unless …"

Olwyn frowned. "Unless?"

"Put quite simply, my dear, you need to return to Sussex to pass back the evidence by which 'Blue Horizon' obtain their ill-gotten fortunes."

"So no problem there then," Olwyn said, her words creased with irony. "Remind me, how many activists have already 'disappeared' trying to achieve this?"

Jerry turned to face her, his eyes looking towards the ceiling, pretending to count.

"Twelve, that we know about."

"And you think I'll be successful where they have failed?"

"You won't be on your own, dear heart. Your role will be to support a local group of activists. Besides, you'll have your heroic woodsman to protect you."

Olwyn stared at him, momentarily tempted to tell him about the link between Grace and Littlemore. Intuition stayed her hand.

"We simply need you there to coordinate things," Jerry continued. "Their aim is to obtain video footage for streaming on a major social media platform."

Olwyn raised an eyebrow. "Sounds risky."

"Not as risky as letting our new master continue unopposed."

Jerry turned on his phone so that she could read the latest 'breaking news' bannerline.

"Seems the purge has already begun," he muttered.

The announcement confirmed the head of MI5 was to be replaced immediately.

"Soon we'll have another of Littlemore's acolytes to lead us. You won't need two guesses to tell you what that means."

For a moment, Olwyn and Jerry were silent. Imagination filled the vacuum.

"I must take a gun this time," Olwyn said.

"Not a chance, dear girl," Jerry said, reaching for his shoulder bag.

"Guns are nasty things that result in innocent people getting hurt. Besides, anyone seeing you waving a gun around would simply laugh, or kill you on the spot."

"Don't tell me to rely on Homer for protection," Olwyn snapped.

"Wouldn't dream of it," Jerry responded, opening his hand with a flourish, like a conjurer.

"This should do the trick." He narrowly omitted uttering words of magic.

"And that's supposed to protect me?" Olwyn picked up the cardboard tube.

"A tampon and what looks like my granny's plastic rain hat?"

Jerry rolled his eyes. "Patience."

He turned the cardboard tube around to reveal the cord protruding from one end.

"The so called plastic rain hat is a gas hood. Pop it over your head and pull this cord. You've got ninety seconds before you run out of air."

"The tampon, as you so delicately put it, is in fact a disguised CS gas canister. Tug the cord and run, preferably with the hood already over your head."

"Just be sure not to wear heels; if you have to use it, run very fast because everyone else is going to be extremely pissed off with you once the air has cleared."

Olwyn wasn't sure if that brought her comfort or not.

Allison Markham was enjoying her rail journey despite her injured arm and left side still ached when she exerted herself. The previous night, unexpectedly spent with Olwyn, hadn't helped, but was a pain well worth bearing. She had no illusion that an affair would develop between them; Olwyn was too expansive in her tastes for that to be a prospect. But, it was enough to know that Olwyn cared for her and it served to lessen the lonely void in her life.

Her carriage was largely empty for most of her journey from Waterloo, and with a spare seat beside her, Allison could watch the world pass by, lost in a fantasy world she could dream of but doubted would ever happen. Eyes closed, her thoughts drifted, lulled by the motion of the train. Her memories of the previous night would be a panacea for insomnia in long, lonely nights of wakefulness.

She had drifted into a light, peaceful doze, only to be rudely awakened by the angry vibration from her phone. It was Wailes, spitefully dismantling her fantasies.

The coffee shop, dressed in the vernacular of the times, was an unusual setting for Homer to choose. Popular and noisy, no one paid particular attention to the two men who entered, despite their rural, homespun appearance.

"A bit gentile for my taste," Milo said, offering an exaggerated wink to a passing waitress.

"I'm trying to introduce you to civilisation," Homer replied. "I'm bored with pubs and transport cafes."

Despite sore ribs and the use of only one hand, he managed to smile as he ordered tea and sourdough muffins for them both.

"From where I'm sitting, it looks as though some of your friends could do with a lesson in manners."

"Just an argument over fishing rights," Homer said dismissively. "There's trout, a carp and pheasant in the cold box." He paused. "On account."

"What are you after?" Milo leaned back in his chair to allow the waitress space to place a teapot and china cups on their table.

For a brief moment, Homer saw a flash of mischief in the younger man's eyes, half anticipating he'd smack her bottom as she bent over him in a tight skirt. As the waitress left, Milo read his expression.

"There was a day," he said with a grin. "Not any more. Too much political correctness for any fun and games now. Though I suspect she might be disappointed that I restrained myself."

He gazed after the young woman's departing back with a wistful expression.

"I doubt it."

"So, on account? What are you after?" Milo regained himself, watching Homer splash the scrubbed table top as he tried to pour tea single handed.

Homer was thoughtful for a moment. "What mood music are you hearing on the grapevine?"

"More tetchy and agitated than usual," Milo replied, struggling to hold a delicate cup with fingers the size of sausages.

"You'd almost think someone was rattling their cage." He stared deliberately at Homer's maimed hand, then downed the contents of the small cup in one go.

"Then again, it could be down to the loss of my drugs supply. I think their new dealer has turned out to be a dead loss." He poured himself another cup.

"By the look of your hand, I might yet have to return to the market to calm things down." Milo filled the room with laughter at his own joke.

Spooning sugar into the cup, he leaned forward, conspiratorially.

"Seems your friends in the fracking industry have taken to beating up coppers, just to make sure they toe the line."

He grinned. "Personally, I've got no problem with that, the bastards deserve some of their own medicine, but it's either a sign they have friends in high places or are getting desperate."

"Probably both," Homer responded, eyes intently watching a woman who had just entered the shop. There was something about her he recognised. "Any word about the eco-activists who are such a thorn in their sides?"

"The usual. Whispers and rumours. But given the level of agitation, if you're still in touch with that woman, you'd do everyone a favour if you warn her off. And delete her number permanently, if you know what's good for you."

Homer nodded thoughtfully, still watching the woman, who now sat on a stool at the counter with her back to them, studying her phone.

"Anything else?"

Milo thought for a moment, unsure what to say.

"Someone is making enquiries. Cosmo thinks it could be in connection with the arrival of your son, Marius."

"Anyone we know. Is it from London?"

Milo shook his head. "Midlands, probably Birmingham."

"What sort of questions?"

"There's a photo on social media; grainy, taken from a CCTV camera, with the caption, 'Missing from home; anyone seen this teenager'. Looks dodgy to me; I think someone is fishing for an ID."

"Have you got a copy of the photo?"

Milo opened his phone, skimmed through several photos and turned it around for Homer to view.

A low quality, black and white image. Despite the cap, he could just make out Marius, towing a suitcase, rucksack on his back, leaving airport arrivals.

"I think you'd have to know who it was to identify him," Milo ventured encouragingly.

But Homer didn't need a second glance. Whoever had posted the photo knew only too well who the boy in the photo was. He was certain the search wasn't just for Marius; it was also for him.

"Take my keys and leave," he said, still watching the woman at the counter. He passed them to Milo beneath the table.

"If I don't join you in a couple of minutes, leave in my Landrover. Keep your wits about you; you might be followed."

Milo followed his gaze and slightly nodded. "Do you need any help?"

The woman was watching them in the reflection of her phone screen.

"No, I think I know who that is."

"And there was me hoping for a quick pick up," he said in mock disappointment.

Milo helped himself to several muffins, deftly sliding them into his pocket.

Homer muttered, "There's a tradesman's door in the kitchen. You can leave unnoticed. If I don't follow shortly,

I'll collect my Landrover later when I've dealt with the woman."

As he spoke, the waitress who had served their table disappeared into the kitchen, attracting Milo's interest. Milo rose and moved away; from the smile on his face his mind was on other things. Ten minutes later, Homer paid the bill and left.

For a moment, he considered his options. Milo's SUV waited in the car park. He weighed the prospect that walking home through the woods might be safer, but even across country it was a good ten miles to his cottage. Normally, he wouldn't have hesitated, but rain fell in slanting showers of cold sleet and his ribs ached. He waited.

Behind him, the door opened and banged shut. He didn't need to turn around. The woman from the counter came and stood beside him.

"Do you need a lift?" he asked, aware of an injured arm, carefully concealed by her coat.

"Please," she nodded. "I need to talk with you."

She followed as he led her to Milo's SUV. The lights flashed as the doors unlocked. With only two good arms between them, Homer was relieved it had an automatic gearbox.

CHAPTER 47
THE IDES OF COMPLACENCY

Beneath the façade of a hot temper, Rosetta, our group leader, hid a measure of commonsense. Whilst she had made it plain she didn't share my reservations about the late arrival of the sixth member of our team, it didn't prevent her from taking steps to leave him behind. She chose a sedative, added to his coffee mug, to make sure he wasn't awake when we came to leave.

In the early hours of the morning, someone had disabled the pump control panel. Desperate to keep working, the night shift at the fracking site rang the first number on their call out list. Us. Clad in company overalls and hard hats and with a borrowed van and logo to match, we set off as soon as the call was received.

Between the five of us, we felt well prepared for most situations. The two men in our group could replace the control panel with their eyes closed. I wore a company hard hat complete with concealed camera, while Rosetta had a recording chip bluetoothed to my camera operating in her watch. The girl who had little to say for herself carried a back-up camera built in to a flashlight and another recording device in her asthma inhaler.

We felt we had thought of everything. We estimated it would take less than an hour to replace the control panel. Once fixed we could stand back to let the site operatives perform a test run with the pump. As it emptied the contents of the container, a geiger counter hidden in a toolbox would record radiation levels through the pipework feeding into the drilled fracking well.

All I had to remember was to open the toolbox and record the geiger counter readings as they happened. Simple. What could possibly go wrong?

Hindsight is a wonderful thing. I should have paid less attention to our sedated mystery man, and more to the girl in our team whose name no one could remember. Including anyone who is more or less invisible should raise questions. Homer would never let that go unchallenged.

'Amateurs. Bloody amateurs.' His often repeated words rang hollow in my ears.

Angela was curious. Marius had spent half an hour texting on his phone, a broad smile warming his face, oblivious to anything else happening around him. Even Joss failed to gain his attention.

Messaging complete, Marius asked if there was sufficient hot water for a bath and left the kitchen, whistling in high spirits.

Angela arched an eyebrow in the direction of a puzzled Joss.

"Seems we have a competitor for his affections."

Normally, his phone was none of her business. But these were far from normal times and the stab wound in his shoulder was enough for Angela to keep a protective eye on Marius. Without moving the phone from the table, she switched it on.

Fortunately, Marius didn't use fingerprint recognition. His birthday was two days before hers; it took only two failed attempts to find the correct entry pin.

Marius had left open the Snapchat page he had been using. Since he had left for his bath, other messages had arrived. Surrounded by emoticons of hearts and kisses was written,

So I'll come to Angela's cottage then. Can't wait to see you again. Leave you to clear it with her?

Guiltily, Angela closed the page.

"My, my. I wonder what happened to that policewoman who was badly injured?" she said to Joss. "I thought Olwyn was rather fond of her."

Unsurprisingly, on that matter, Joss didn't have an opinion.

"I need to talk to you," was all the woman said as she closed the car door.

Previously, Homer had only seen Allison Markham in the aftermath of being shot. It was only by intuition that he now recognised her in the café. He waited for the engine to warm, pondering how she could have followed him there without him realising.

"You really are losing your grip," he muttered in self-recrimination as he tried to engage the drive lever with his damaged hand. Allison leaned over and did it for him.

Homer gave her a puzzled frown. They made an unlikely pair, each with only a usable right hand.

"And how did you get here?"

"Taxi. Your Landrover was easy to follow."

He grunted in reply. Another mistake to add to his list.

"I needed to speak to you and I've been trying to find the moment. I have something of an issue with visiting your cottage."

She gestured to her injured arm to make a statement.

"It looks like we have something in common," Allison continued, looking pointedly at his broken hand. "I guess we must be keeping the same company?"

"Why all this subterfuge if you only need to speak to me?"

"You're not an easy man to pin down. Plus, I suspect I'm being watched."

"Who by?"

"You don't need two guesses on that. I thought the café might be a safe place and until the other man arrived I was going to offer to buy you coffee."

It seemed plausible.

"Okay, but what do you want?"

Homer turned at a junction, taking the forest road back towards town. As sleet patterned the windscreen, he flapped ineffectively at the wiper stalk with his maimed hand until Allison intervened. In different circumstances, it would have been quite amusing.

She glanced at him uncertainly, weighing her next step, suddenly not sure how much she could trust this gruff, scruffy man. She felt a natural sense of distrust with most men, though Homer had the endorsement of having already saved her life on two occasions.

"The scorpion, the one that attacked Olwyn …"

"And then thought better of it …"

"Do you still have it?"

"It is a 'her'. Obviously a fickle creature, so most likely female." Homer paused. "But yes, I do still have her. Why?"

Allison bit her lip. "Let's say, I need to return her to her owner."

Homer laughed, an ironic, hollow sound. "Why, is he missing her?"

Before answering, she looked at Homer pensively, eyes glistening as she struggled to hold back tears.

"Quite possibly. But that's not the reason. He's trying to blackmail me."

Milo's note on the driver's seat read,

You should keep better company

Milo obviously hadn't been impressed by his hasty departure through the service entrance of the café. Perhaps the waitress had declined his advances.

Homer found his Landrover in the town's only multistorey car park. He had stopped in a recess of shadows, concealed from the gaze of sharp eyed cameras, to allow Allison to get out before parking Milo's SUV on the upper deck of the car park.

His Landrover was on the lower deck, keys hidden on top of a filthy front tyre. There was no sign of Milo. He waited ten minutes, watching the comings and goings of other cars, but no one paid any attention to his much battered vehicle.

Before leaving town, Homer made a rare visit to a supermarket. He hadn't given Milo all the fish he had caught and intended to cook his speciality for Angela and Marius as a rare treat that evening.

Sometimes life's path can pivot on such trivial matters. The front of the supermarket had tinted glass. Homer suddenly stopped, mid-stride, shielded by the shadow of the glass. It was an intuitive thing, learnt across years spent in Kabul, Mosal or Baghdad, a sixth sense for the aura that surrounded certain men.

Homer saw the man as he crossed the busy car park. It wasn't a matter of colour, race or ethnicity, perhaps more the way the air moved around him, as though shrinking away before someone intent on a mission. As if by magic, a delivery lorry passed in front of the man and he disappeared from sight, leaving the impression of a conjurer's illusion.

On another day, Homer might have dismissed it as a trick of the mind, no more than a mirage of the imagination. But now, he knew they were searching.

He felt his senses tighten. Too many recent mistakes were exhausting his quotient of luck; it was like playing chess with a grand master where the stakes were life and death.

Olwyn felt a distinct pang of guilt as she looked at her phone. Marius was sending her regular messages; not the suffocating, emotional variety she found so common with infatuated young men, but curiously tinged with self-deprecating humour.

He was obviously very taken with her, which nagged at her conscience when considering her previous night with Allison. If their relationship developed, Olwyn hoped he possessed the maturity to accept her occasional foibles. She read again his last message.

Told A you need somewhere to stay. She seems OK with you being here. When?

Olwyn thought for a moment. At their final meeting, Jerry had given her a credit card and driver's licence in a false name. All standard issue for spooks, she guessed. On the strength of that she had hired a car (no 'Gladys' this time) and booked a room in an inconspicuous hotel just outside the fiefdom of Wailes and his paymasters.

Better to keep well clear of their tentacles until she could establish contact with the operation she had been sent to coordinate. Also, she decided she wanted somewhere private, away from the prying eyes of Angela and Homer.

Making arrangements. I'll message when sorted. Suggest we meet somewhere private.

With her message suggestively graced with emoticons, Olwyn awaited his reply with interest.

More importantly there remained the issue of Grace. Olwyn had forensically trawled social media for evidence. The woman was invisible, though her search uncovered more about Hugh Littlemore who, a few years before, had married the widow of a man tragically killed on 9/11 in the attack on the twin towers.

Beyond the family photo on their wedding day, there was nothing linking Grace to the new Home Secretary. Eventually, Olwyn's diligence bore fruit. She found a report in a local newspaper displaying the photo.

The marriage of the beautiful widow, Maria Williams, and her charismatic lawyer Hugh Littlemore, who had previously won her substantial compensation for the tragic loss of her heroic husband.

Olwyn stared at the photo, trying to evaluate emotions from the black and white faces.

It was hard to read without bias; too much of Littlemore's reputation went before him. The bride looked sublime as all brides do on their wedding day; her sons had the look of expectation for what their new step-father's influence might bring them. Littlemore's children shared their father's hawk-like facial countenance, with the same narrow eyes that surveyed the world from the perspective of a bird of prey.

Only Grace, if it really was Grace, looked totally out of place, at the end of the line-up, half a step detached from her blood relatives. Olwyn's first thoughts were that Grace looked impassive, underwhelmed by the day.

The quality of the photo was surprisingly good, so she expanded the detail of the face and saw the mouth set hard, expressionless. It was left to her eyes to betray what was unsaid, squinting not from the sun, but a furrowed brow that flagged an unspoken message to the observer.

'*Anywhere but here*'

The signal was unmistakeable.

With the timing of a metronome, Olwyn beat her pencil against her pad.

"So, Grace, who are you? More to the point, what are you up to?"

As she studied Littlemore's unsmiling, raptor-lined face in the photograph, the unspoken answer of Grace's stepfather made Olwyn shiver.

CHAPTER 48
IF YOU PLAY WITH MATCHES

By the early hours of the morning, the security guards were tired and bored. The delay caused by the sabotaged control board on the pump had extended their shift by several hours. They were more interested in saving time than their normal protocols.

Once clear of the double-locked gate system, I tried to absorb my surroundings. After months of vain attempts, I was finally inside a high security fracking site. The operation occupied an area probably not much larger than a football pitch and was filled with equipment, pipes, valves, and an assortment of buildings.

The installation was lit to a surprisingly subdued level, the huge camouflage net above us undulating in the darkness like a living organism. Amongst the spaghetti of pipework, a constant monotone sound played from the pumps, generators and winches, some of which fed into the well heads. Perhaps because of the hour of night there were few people about, though lights burned in most windows of the surrounding buildings, stacked like Lego bricks, one on top of another.

We prepared to work fast. Only one of the security team stayed with us and even he seemed bored and disinterested.

"Get it fixed as fast as possible," was the only comment thrown in our direction by the night staff departing to find the all-night canteen.

The guard left to oversee our work was understandably fed-up as his colleagues left him. He looked as though he would welcome distraction. While unloading our equipment, one of our team passed around a hip flask, with the instruction to avoid allowing the fiery liquid to more than touch our lips, though it needed little encouragement for our lonely supervisor to imbibe generously in compensation for the mundane job he had been left to carry out.

As it turned out, that was both a good and bad idea.

Maybe it was the lateness of the hour or the poor level of lighting, but I ran into problems from the outset. Frustratingly, I couldn't get the button, concealed on the side of my helmet, to switch on the camera.

This wasn't an immediate problem; I had no need to film the procedure of replacing the control panel. But it had to be working in time to capture the pumping process from the row of containers parked beside the well head and I also needed to make a video record of the geiger counter readings once the pumping operations resumed.

After several minutes trying in vain to get the camera to work, suspecting a loose connection, I slipped away from the others to find privacy in a washroom. There were no separate facilities for women, the site intended to be operated solely by men. Locked in a cubicle, with my hard hat and camera dismantled, the sound of male voices filled my ears. No one spoke English.

I soon found that a wire linking the switch to the head camera had become detached. Re-attaching it was simple enough, made more difficult by fingers that trembled with cold and nervous apprehension. I tested it and re-made the connection with my old-fashioned dial faced watch in which the recording device had been concealed.

I returned the hard hat to my head, straining ears for a pause in the male voices outside the cubicle. A toilet flushed, a door slammed closed and loud voices in a Slavic dialect died away as the outer door closed.

It seemed getting into the fracking site had been the easy bit; moving around within its security fencing was starting to prove far more difficult. So, with my face hidden by the scarf and helmet, I pressed the flush handle and stepped into the main area of the washroom.

A man was standing at a urinal with his back to me. I hadn't expected to find him still there. He muttered something I didn't understand, heading quickly for the door before he turned around. I mumbled a reply in a deep voice.

Just as my hand touched the exit door, it swung open and another man entered. Blood pounded in my ears; this was becoming far more stressful than I had imagined but with a grunt he passed with no more than a casual glance.

Once outside, the cold night air helped dispel a rising feeling of panic. Standing in a pool of unlit darkness, I felt relief slowly well up inside me. So far, so good. Pausing only to regain my breath, I scurried off to hide amongst the rest of the team.

Perhaps relief allowed my guard to drop. My thoughts must have been somewhere else as I approached our position at the broken pump.

Surprisingly, they had all stopped work, but at first nothing seemed to be out of place. Even the fact that Tom now stood with palms raised, staring at the nameless girl in our group who was standing with her back to me.

Mid-stride, I was in the act of removing the box holding the geiger counter from my shoulder, its strap having tangled in the collar of my overalls. Half hidden, Rosetta stood, eyes wide and staring, semaphoring alarm in my direction.

Following her gaze, despite the gloom, my vision came to rest on a gun, held extended in both hands by the girl with her back to me. She who had been so vague on the matter of her name and background.

The gun was pointing directly at the other three.

Homer has a theory; 'never start something you're not prepared to carry through.' That's especially true with guns. What followed can best be described as a comedy of errors. With almost tragic results. I acted without thinking; if I was wrong, apologies could come later.

I swung the box, and its precious instrument, on its strap like some medieval ball and chain. Instinctively improvising, I mistimed the arc of swing and missed the girl's head, instead striking her right shoulder. The geiger counter was heavy and she spilled sideways from the blow, dropping the gun as her hands spread on impulse to break her fall.

The gun skittered on the hard, wet ground, arriving at Rosetta's feet. She would have done better to have left it alone or at least just kicked it away. Instead, with shaking hands, she hastily bent and picked it up, unaware the safety catch had been released.

How she came to pull the trigger, no one knew, least of all Rosetta. A single shot, fired at random. Only fate could have decided that the aimless bullet would pierce the kneecap of our guard.

We might have still got away with it. The report of a single gunshot, amidst the cacophony of sound from pumps and generators, might just have gone unnoticed. But our solitary guard had his finger resting in the trigger of his gun. As the wounded man crumpled like a stringless puppet, in a reflex reaction he must have pulled the trigger and emptied the best part of a complete magazine into the night sky.

There's always a chance you might miss a single shot. But a dozen rounds from an AK47? Not a chance. In the dying echo of the shots, even the machinery seemed to pause in surprise. For a moment, the world held its breath in anticipation until, almost by the flick of a switch, all hell broke loose.

Ignoring the girl spreadeagled on the wet ground, I grabbed the transfixed Rosetta by her overalls. Only one word now had any purpose.

"Run."

The entry gates were currently open to allow a convoy of containers to be hauled into the compound.

Rosetta hesitated. "The filming?"

"No," I shouted. "The van. Quickly, before it's too late."

The sound of alarms began to wail their baleful song, and the gates automatically started to close. Stumbling as I dragged a terrified Rosetta, I ran the short distance to our van, followed by Tom and Gerry, hauling the other girl by the scruff of the neck.

With relief, the van started first try and I had it moving before the other four had even closed the rear doors. To say my driving was erratic would be a major understatement. As we careered across the compound, I could see that the entry gates were closing quickly and within seconds we would be trapped.

A group of men sprang from nowhere in the darkness in an attempt to block our path. I thought I saw someone carrying a 'stinger', which if released, would puncture our tyres. We were committed. With pedal flat to the floor, I held my breath, determined not to stop.

Would it have made any difference? If we were caught, there would be no negotiating with these people; no rule of law or court to protect us.

Men disappeared in all directions like bowling skittles as I charged onwards remorselessly. In an instant we were through the gates, the van weaving frantically from side to side as I fought for control on the loose cambered surface of the track. The van slewed violently as the first bend approached. Just a few more seconds and we would be out of sight, the first hurdle of our escape overcome.

I'm certain Homer would have guessed. They must have had a night patrol outside the perimeter fence. Concentrating on my driving, I didn't see anyone in the darkness. In shocked surprise, they must have let us pass before they could react. What if I had switched off the lights and cloaked our speeding departure in darkness? If only I had thought of that.

The first thing I knew was when three holes, fringed by a maze of spider cracks, appeared in the side and windscreen. The 'Genie' was well and truly out of the bottle; someone was shooting at us, their reports hidden beneath the roar of the engine. Several dull thuds followed, accompanied by a sound from within the van I almost missed; more a sigh than a cry.

It was Tom's desperate shout that followed that changed everything in an instant.

"Oh, my god. Rosetta's been shot."

CHAPTER 49
THINGS THAT GO BUMP IN THE NIGHT

Olwyn was a last minute person; she had decided to leave packing her bags until the following morning. In consequence, a phone call from Jerry in the early hours did not portend well.

"Jerry!"

Irritated, Olwyn didn't need to pretend to sound petulant.

"Sorry, darling; needs must. Circumstances demand. I must have you on the road immediately."

"It's three o'clock! In the morning."

It was dark; that fact hardly needed stating.

"You've hired your car, I hope?"

"What? Yes," Olwyn snapped.

"Good. So nothing to stop you tootling off forthwith." He sounded far too bright for the hour of the day.

"Why? What's so bloody urgent it can't wait for a civilised hour of the day?"

"Switch on 'Twenty-four-hour news'. It seems things have gone awry on a fracking site in rural Sussex. We need you down there to keep an eye on things. Immediately."

"Jerry, define awry." Olwyn was fumbling for her television remote.

"More blundering disaster. You need to observe and keep me informed."

Olwyn scrolled the channels. The news channel was live from outside the site. The bannerline said it all.

Terrorists caught in an attack on fracking installation, several innocent security guards seriously injured. Suspects have escaped and are currently being sought.

"Oh," Olwyn exclaimed. "Er, who am I there to observe?"

"I suspect if you call upon your heroic woodsman, you'll find out soon enough."

Jerry's tone switched from jocular to serious in the space of a sentence.

"Jerry, what's going on?"

Her eyes were fixed on a scrolling bannerline repeating incendiary points about an armed attack and life threatening injuries to site staff.

"Events, dear girl," he replied with a sigh. "Life has a habit of creating its own agenda." Jerry paused. "We're off script here, Olwyn."

There was warning in his words. He seldom used her name, only when he was cross or worried.

"It seems fate has decided to change our timeline. Let's just say, things have gone a bit wrong, as is the way of even the best laid plans. We need your eyes on the ground immediately, Olwyn. I don't need to remind you that if this turns out badly and Littlemore finds it leads in our direction ... well, just be careful."

Jerry finished the call without a farewell.

Olwyn packed in a hurry, thoughtlessly throwing things into a case, listening to the news stream with most of her attention.

A female reporter, her back to the lights of a distant fracking compound, was obviously reading from a well-prepared script, which from the tone of her delivery, she hadn't written.

The mention of Hugh Littlemore, the Home Secretary, brought Olwyn's packing to an abrupt halt, his unsmiling face interrupting the strained and nervous reporter.

He didn't wait to be introduced.

"This government has brought in powers to protect you from these wanton acts of violence."

Hugh Littlemore's voice spoke with an assurance that carried an edge so sharp it almost dissected his words as he uttered them.

"This latest attack, organised by a group of radical anarchists, is intended to deny your right to light and heat your homes. Rest assured, they will be hunted down and treated to such justice as provided by the new laws to protect you and your children."

Littlemore placed great emphasis on his last word.

"This blatant act of terrorism will not go unpunished. The perpetrators, and their supporters, will be brought to justice to protect you, the innocent law-abiding citizens of this great country of ours!"

As if to emphasise this final point, his hawk-like expression remained fixed on the camera long after he had finished speaking.

"Bollocks." Olwyn swore at the screen. "What fascist handbook did you plagiarise that clever phrase from?"

In disgust, she switched off the television. How could the media make any objective reports when someone like Littlemore prevented access to their site operations? All to protect 'you', the poor, innocent public, he purported, a narrative that reminded Olwyn of a certain US President's play book.

Momentarily she slumped onto the bed, riding a wave of nausea. Perhaps it was the early hour of the morning, but as she stood and snapped shut the clasp on her suitcase, it was more likely the groping tendrils of fear that had started to grow inside her.

"How bad is the bleeding?"

White-knuckled, Grace clung to the steering wheel, forcing the speeding van through the bends.

"Take it easy," Tom shouted above the roar of the wind through broken windows.

"There's a lot of blood. We're struggling to stop it."

"Is she still conscious?" Grace had to fight back the panic from her voice.

"Sort of, in and out," he replied, his voice trembling. "We need to find a hospital, fast."

Grace shook her head; that meant switching on their phones for directions, and that would lead to the police and fracking security tracking their route within seconds. Even if they could avoid capture, arriving at hospital with a serious gunshot wound was as good as handing Rosetta to them at the first road block they encountered.

Ahead, their headlight beam picked out a long stretch of tree lined road that Grace vaguely recognised. Encouraged, she pressed the accelerator even harder to the floor, the protesting engine screaming loudly in reply. Only action would keep her brain from surrendering to wild panic.

She forced her mind to focus on the girl who had betrayed them. Almost without thinking they had bound and gagged her and had pushed her into a corner of the van. There had been little option; left behind, she would have disclosed all she knew and made any chance of escape next to impossible.

"What's the plan?"

Tom's abrupt voice cut across her thoughts, his tone implying he held Grace responsible for their situation.

"We need a hospital. She might die if we don't."

Vainly trying to shield Rosetta, he hissed urgent words in her ear.

"She'll bleed to death if you don't find somewhere soon."

Fear easily translates into anger; he was very close to losing control.

The only person who could help Rosetta was Angela, and Grace had only a vague idea how to find her. Communication in their dire circumstances was difficult; there was simply no time to stop for a detailed discussion.

"I know people; not too far from here. They'll help us. It will be quicker and safer than hospital."

Grace threw her words over her shoulder, trying to shout above the cacophony of noise as the van oversteered violently through another bend. The gearbox crunched and grated, metal tearing metal, as she strove to find more power.

Driving purely on intuition, she would have to find Angela. Ahead, her eyes desperately sought some detail that she might recognise. There had to be something soon. It was either that, or she was completely lost.

Homer found Angela, wrapped in her eiderdown, dozing in her usual chair in the kitchen. He had been woken by Joss, pacing the bedroom, arousing him with a sound between a whine and a whimper.

"I've tried offering her the door," Homer grumbled. "She doesn't want to go out."

Angela sat with her eyes closed. Homer knelt beside her, fondling Joss as he checked her over; nose wet and shiny, eyes bright. Man and dog made eye contact.

"Something's up," Homer said.

"Guess we'll find out soon enough," Angela said, her voice coloured by strain.

Homer glanced at her face. "Pain bad?"

"It comes and goes."

Though she tried to sound dismissive, it was obvious it 'came' more than it 'went'.

Beside them, the Aga glowed a dull cherry red, so Homer riddled the fire bed and added several dry logs. Dancing flames immediately lit the room.

"The doctor could help," he said, guessing her response.

With a thin smile, Angela answered without the need for words.

Homer had stayed the night; if her illness progressed it was something he knew he would have to do more often. He filled a kettle and placed it on the hotplate. When words serve little purpose, you can always resort to a pot of tea.

"I think Marius is in touch with Olwyn," Angela said, almost in passing, as though just a natural everyday event.

Homer snorted in disapproval. "Much good that will do them."

"Don't comment. They're young. Let it take its course."

He huffed dismissively. It was the only acknowledgement Angela was going to get. The kettle sang a song in agreement.

For a while they sat in mutual silence, massaging steaming mugs; Angela chasing the illusion of sleep, while Homer counted the precious moments of peace on her painful journey. Above them, despite the early hour, the treads on the stairs creaked as Marius descended to join them, while unnoticed, Joss had moved to sit at attention by the back door.

Olwyn drove, reading the 'Breaking News' bannerlines from her phone, flashed onto the dashboard screen. Even at a fleeting glance, it didn't make comfortable reading. Things were different. Someone in authority must have decided a line had been crossed; the words of the kickback had a ruthless edge.

Despite avoiding main roads, Olwyn still encountered several checkpoints. She was amazed by the speed with which they had sprung into operation; the supposed attack on the fracking site had happened less than an hour before.

Ominously it suggested a degree of organisation that had preceded the drama of the night. Twice her security pass had been checked and dismissed. Whoever they were looking for it wasn't her; not yet, at least. But what seriously disconcerted Olwyn was that the checkpoints were staffed by armed men, most of whom had a poor command of English, without any sign of the police.

'How did such numbers appear so quickly?' Olwyn mused as she drove through dark empty streets. The answer was obvious. 'Blue Horizon' had mobilised their private security staff hours before, preparing a net in waiting for the perpetrators of the so-claimed terrorist attack. It was almost as if they had known in advance.

Shocked, she braked and stopped the car. If 'Blue Horizon' knew about the operation, there was one person who could be responsible. Littlemore's step-daughter; Grace.

Olwyn had never expected to have to contact Allison so soon. She stopped briefly at an all-night service station and posted a message, the need for caffeine and the bathroom necessitating the risk of a stop.

Fortunately, she had discovered an App that detected active CCTV cameras, and with this switched on Olwyn avoided several in the car park and more inside the building. Beyond that, a cap and hoodie helped to conceal her identity.

Her message must have woken Allison. A reply returned within seconds; question marks and a heart. Olwyn groaned inwardly, suddenly worried that Allison would arrive at the wrong idea. Too late to turn back, it was a gamble she would have to take. She needed to avoid Wailes at all costs, and for that she needed Allison to watch her back, even if it risked encouraging her hopes.

Returning to her car, Olwyn noticed a pale stain in the eastern sky. Dawn was approaching; if she could find an early opening convenience store, she could call on Allison with breakfast and dissuade her from the temptations of the bedroom.

Something's up. Joss won't settle.

Several streets from the address Allison had given her, Olwyn parked her car just as the early morning message from Marius arrived on her phone. She had no idea what he meant, but the next part of his message gave her a pang of conscience.

Miss you. When will you be back?

An assortment of emoticons left little doubt about his feelings.

Like most of Olwyn's affairs, this was starting to become complicated, more by circumstance than conscious choice. It was the first time that she had a man and a woman playing for her emotions simultaneously. Conflicted, it promised to make things difficult.

Olwyn sent Marius a holding message, aware of the dangers of drawing both him and Allison into a situation she didn't fully understand. As she drank a cup of indifferent coffee, she felt aware she might be playing both of them as camouflage for another of Jerry Houseman's dangerous operations.

Hunt for terrorists. Net closes.
It was almost as if the news bannerline had read her mind.

"For god's sake, find a hospital!"

Tom leaned over the seat, screaming in her ear. He was on the verge of hysteria.

"Rosetta's bleeding to death in the back here and all you can do is drive aimlessly around the countryside."

Grace had no answer, desperate to recognise any road that might lead to Angela, while at the same time avoiding the checkpoints that had sprung up to block their path. At one point, she caught sight of the lights of a drone searching a main road parallel with the lanes they were following. Grace drove the next few miles without lights, wishing for a pair of Homer's night-sight goggles.

She was on the edge of admitting defeat and switching on her phone to alert the nearest hospital. It might save Rosetta in the short term, but Grace had no illusions that there would be a reception team waiting at the hospital for when they arrived.

She was reaching for her phone when they passed a bus shelter. Tired and emotionally drained, it triggered a memory, and without thinking she slowed and took the next turn. They hit ruts and bumps far too fast, the complaining van bouncing violently on its springs, but never had a potholed track felt so good. From the back, the two men hurled abuse.

"Stop shouting. We're there," Grace shouted back, offering a silent prayer in hope that Angela was at home.

As they slid to a halt on the loose gravel in front of the outline of the cottage, she felt a swell of relief when the black and white form of Joss darted through the beam of her lights to welcome her.

CHAPTER 50
A BIASED ROLL OF DICE

In the grey light of approaching dawn, the headlight beam pitched and rolled along the track. Joss changed from pacing and whining to frantically clawing at the door. Homer knew his dog; he reached for his shotgun and released the gouged door. The dog disappeared in a blur of black and white.

The van approached too fast, bucking alarmingly across the rutted surface. Waiting, Homer stood in the shadow of the porch, aware, with a measure of misgiving, that the shotgun wasn't loaded.

At full speed, Joss ran circles around the van, the fanfare of her barks attenuating the sound of its protesting engine. Homer couldn't see the driver, his eyes drawn to round holes in the windscreen and the web of tiny cracks that spiralled across the glass.

Sweeping abruptly side on, the van shuddered to a halt and stalled, exposing a stitchwork of holes along its dented flank. Involuntarily Homer's hand gripped the barrel of the shotgun beside him; the driver's door flying open before the van had stopped.

There are times when a man of few words is exactly what is called for. I was trying to control the rising tide of panic, suddenly overtaken by an overwhelming feeling of relief. By some miracle, I had found Angela's cottage.

"A girl's badly injured," I blurted out, for once even ignoring Joss's excited welcome.

"Shot; lots of blood; she's in a bad way."

I was trying to make sense, only succeeding in making a mess of things.

"She needs help. Urgently."

My stuttering, breathless delivery made it a dramatic arrival.

Homer merely grunted in reply.

At the precise moment I needed speed and action, time seemed to stand still. At first he was motionless, processing my outburst before slowly turning and replacing his shotgun inside the door just as Angela, thin and pale, appeared in the doorway beside Marius.

'Thank god,' I thought. 'At least she's here.'

Without waiting, I ran to open the rear doors of the van. Instead of following me, Homer turned towards Angela. I saw her speak briefly to Marius who hastily disappeared into the cottage without a word.

"Leave her in the van," Angela said, her voice strained yet her words direct.

Marius returned carrying a medical bag, supporting Angela's arm as she walked to the van. I opened the doors, glancing briefly inside.

The problem with blood is that when spilt, even a little looks like a lot. The inside of the van resembled an abattoir. For a moment, Angela hesitated, appraising the scene inside before accepting Tom's blood stained hand and climbing inside.

Abruptly, Homer pushed me aside. Angela must have said something I didn't catch and, moving swiftly for the first time, Homer ran into the cottage, returning moments later with a battered green box bearing a red cross in a white circle.

It was Marius who interrupted my shocked state of mind.

"Come and help me."

He tugged my arm in the direction of the cottage. In the kitchen, we set to work clearing the large wooden table. As I swept it down, Marius disappeared, returning with armfuls of sheets.

Kettles and pans were filled with water and placed on the Aga to boil and Marius produced two brooms, stretching one of the sheets between them to fashion a stretcher. It took less than a minute to bind it with lassoes of tape around the broom handles; all without a word passing between us.

Unnoticed, Tom had stumbled into the kitchen, looking in an even worse condition than I felt. He silently crossed the room and slumped into a chair, leaning forward, holding his shocked, pale face between his hands.

So this was the consequence of the risks we were taking, unforgivingly brought home, hard and viscerally.

Joss thrust her nose against my hand, reminding me of her needs, her eyes alive, questioning. The smell of human blood must have disturbed her.

In a brief moment as I stroked her head, I found my scarf still looped around her collar where I had left it. Homer's cantankerous exterior must have hidden an element of the sentimental somewhere inside him to leave the scarf there.

Despite the early hour, Allison had already dressed. She could tell by the way Olwyn entered her flat that this surprise visit had a more professional purpose than a desire for romance. Allison brushed Olwyn's hand as she gave her a bag of pastries from the early morning baker. Slowly removing her hand, Olwyn got straight to the point.

"Sorry, Ally." She hoped the adoption of her sobriquet would soften the disappointment. "I'm here on business, I'm afraid."

"What sort of business?" Allison asked guardedly as she started searching for plates and mugs from a cupboard.

Olwyn watched what she laid out; crockery often gave insight into personality. To her surprise, Allison produced an assortment of Turkish or Arabic designs; no two pieces the same, and collectively it suggested a hidden taste for the exotic in this outwardly austere policewoman.

"My boss has got wind of an operation being carried out by a group of activists against a local fracking site."

Olwyn paused, wondering if Allison had heard the overnight news. "He needs me here to keep an eye on developments."

"Has this anything to do with the dead man you discovered?"

"I'm not sure. I'm only given information on a need to know basis. I suppose you could say I'm here to 'shake the trees' and see what falls out. If I don't know what to expect, I won't embellish what happens with pre-conceived ideas."

She looked fleetingly at Allison's injured arm and slightly regretted her words.

"So, this time I get shot in the other arm to make a matching pair," Allison said with a light note of humour in her voice.

"Ah, I've brought a bulletproof vest for you to wear instead," Olwyn quipped.

They both laughed at the ridiculous drama their lives had succumbed to.

"Who would have thought it," Allison said ruefully. "What do you need from me?"

Olwyn looked thoughtful. How much should she share?

"Your boss, Wailes, thinks I'm dead."

"Ah, our friend, 'Scorpio'."

Olwyn nodded.

"If he finds out I'm still alive and wandering around his patch again, well, let's say there's one bedtime experience I don't want to repeat. Look, I know you're on sick leave, but if you could tell me if, or most likely when, Wailes discovers I'm in the area, it would help to make my plans."

Olwyn shuddered involuntarily.

"I'm not in a hurry to make an acquaintanceship with another specimen from his insect menagerie."

Allison filled their coffee mugs and shared out pastries from the bag Olwyn had brought.

"That won't be easy," she said, turning her back to her friend.

She didn't want Olwyn to read the troubled expression on her face.

"Wailes might be ignorant and manipulative but he's far from stupid. He makes an art form from investigating the lives of others for his own ends. He keeps a book of their 'skeletons in the cupboard' to produce when he wants to get his way."

She stood at the window, watching the grey morning come alive.

"He's got a sixth sense for investigation," Allison continued, turning to face Olwyn.

"I often think he can almost smell a situation and knows instinctively when someone is lying or covering up. As long as you're around here, you'll never be safe. He's vindictive, especially if you've outwitted him before. Never forget, dealing with Wailes will be as unpredictable as handling 'Scorpio'. Promise me you'll be careful if your paths cross."

Olwyn watched her face as she spoke. Allison held a frown she hadn't previously seen, forming a cloud, concealing something. She wondered what demons lay hidden within.

"Stretcher." Homer barked from the kitchen doorway.

Marius gathered up the hastily prepared stretcher and followed his father, an expression of foreboding on his young face. They returned a few minutes later, carrying Rosetta on the stretcher between them. Under Angela's guidance, they gently transferred her to the table.

Something of a miracle had been performed in the confines of the back of the van. Angela had staunched the blood flow and, for the moment at least, Rosetta had been stabilised.

"Who's blood group 'O' positive?" she called, checking Rosetta's dog-tag and began sterilising a transfer tube and needles.

Tom, silent and pale, struggling to contain his shock, raised his hand. Angela held up a length of plastic tubing.

"I need a couple of pints from you, now." Her tone left no space for disagreement.

For the next few minutes, with only occasional words of instruction and direction, Angela ran her improvised 'triage' kitchen, one eye constantly fixed upon unconscious Rosetta.

Leaving Marius and Tom to assist her, Homer took Grace by the arm and led her aside.

"What happened? Give me the short version."

Grace shrugged. "A good plan; went wrong because of her." She gestured to the girl, bound and gagged, now seated on the floor in the corner.

"Explain."

"We managed to get into a fracking site under the disguise of repairing a broken slurry pump. Just when we were preparing to get the video of what they are doing, she," Grace nodded in the direction of the nameless girl, "our 'supposed' team member, ruined everything by turning a gun on her friends."

"Who is she? More to the point, who's she working for?"

"We don't know anything about her."

"A team member, and you know nothing about her?" Homer said with obvious scepticism in his voice.

"'Terra Mater' runs on single person cells, just in case one of us is caught, they can't give away the identity of the others …"

"Which leaves the door wide open to imposters." Homer shook his head wearily, walking towards the silent girl on the floor.

"Did she shoot her?" He gestured towards Rosetta.

"No. It happened as we escaped. There must have been a security team outside the site. In the darkness, I didn't see them. They fired shots as we passed and by sheer bad luck they hit Rosetta."

"And a healthy dose of incompetence." Homer couldn't resist scorn in his words.

Having overheard their conversation, the girl looked nervous as Homer approached. He lifted an edge of the duck-tape that gagged her mouth and removed it with an unceremonious tug.

"Get her something to drink," he said, barking at Grace.

"Come with me," he said to the girl, cutting the plastic ties that bound her ankles and helping her to her feet.

Pushing her ahead of him, he led her to another room and directed her to a chair farthest from the door.

"Don't even think of trying to escape. You're in enough trouble already and it will only make things worse."

"Are you going to hurt me?" The girl tried to keep her voice steady, her darting eyes betrayed her.

"Not my style," Homer said cryptically. "Though I can't speak for the others."

Grace appeared with a steaming mug. Homer took a taster's sip before handing it to the frightened girl. He left her to drink for a few minutes, allowing time and space for her to consider her position while Grace stood beside him. He leaned against the wall, arms folded.

"First question; your name? I don't like to talk to anonymous people."

The girl cradled the mug in her hands, perhaps its warmth brought her comfort as she weighed his question.

"You can call me Alice."

"Good. That's a start, Alice."

He turned to Grace. "Actually, a mug of coffee for me would be good. And get something for Alice to eat while you're at it."

Grace gave him a dark look, but decided against refusing.

"So, Alice, we're alone," Homer continued. "Before she comes back, how about telling me who you work for, though I have a suspicion I already know."

Alice sipped her coffee and nervously licked her lips. "I can't tell you that."

"Why? If you're covering for someone, they're not here to help you now. From where I'm standing, the only person who can save you from the wrath of your ex-friends is me. And that can only continue if you cooperate with me."

Homer paused. "You've got about thirty seconds before she returns."

Alice shook her head. "I can't tell you because I don't know his name."

"So you work for what, a nameless boss and a nameless organisation?"

"I'm frightened what would happen to me if I told you."

"From my perspective, I'd be more frightened of the people who you've just betrayed than some supposedly nameless organisation who will disown you the moment they find out you've been caught."

Homer fixed her with a hard stare.

"Last chance, Alice; let me make it easier for you."

He opened his phone, risking a rare internet connection. Occasionally, rumours filtered through to an encrypted site he shared with the few surviving members of his unit, warning of developments and people hunting for them. A 'rogues gallery' of faces stare back, male and female, caught in secret or from interviews.

Homer had a suspicion and fast-forwarded to a group at the end, mainly young faces, of men in their early twenties.

"Recognise any of these?"

He held the phone so that Alice could view the images as he scrolled. A dozen faces flicked past with no more than a shake of her head, until one caused her to hesitate before shaking her head again.

"Are you sure?"

Alice nodded, uncertain.

Homer moved on to several more before returning to the photo that had brought her reaction. He stared, not at the image, but at the girl's eyes.

After a moment, Alice shook her head again, as if the act of shaking erased the photo. Her eyes betrayed the lie.

He had seen enough and closed his phone, leaving her to stare into space where the photos had been. He knew the game, had seen it too many times before. She now sat, lost in thought, reliving the threats she had to endure from those who controlled her.

Behind them, a board creaked in the hallway as Grace returned. Alice sighed, not tired, more a cry for redemption.

"Will she live?" Alice asked.

"I don't know. My friend is doing her best."

He could tell from her face that his words brought little comfort.

As I handed Homer his mug of coffee, I sensed a change in the room, as though the air had stilled, confrontation transformed into something closer to compassion.

The girl, Alice, if indeed that was her real name, still sat in the chair, the earlier look of defiance altered to something closer to anguish. I looked at Homer with a silent, questioning expression.

"How is Angela coping?" he asked in an unusually soft voice.

"She's organised a transfusion, directly out of Tom's arm. It seems to have stabilised things for the moment. But Angela's quieter than usual, which is worrying. She seems to be fretting about what more she can do."

I gave my last sentence with a note of caution but if Homer sensed my warning, he gave no sign.

"Did she tell you who put her up to this act of betrayal?" I nodded towards Alice.

Homer slightly shook his head. "Not in as many words, but she gave herself away when I showed her a photograph."

"Who?"

Did I already half suspect the answer to my question? He opened his phone and showed me the photo the girl had identified. It was Hugh Littlemore's son.

"A nastier piece of work than you would ever want to meet."

Homer studied my face as he spoke. I could only hope my eyes didn't betray me.

A few moments later, Angela, tired and strained, joined us in the quiet of the room. She was drying her hands, leaving blood to stain the front of her shirt and jeans.

"Rosetta's comfortable for the moment. I've stemmed the worst of the bleeding and given her something for shock and pain. Tom's transferring blood as we speak."

She paused, looking hard at Homer.

"But he can't give enough." Angela hesitated, anticipating the unasked question.

"She'll die soon, if we don't get her to hospital."

Homer shook his head.

"You know that's impossible. 'Blue Horizon' will know we're there before we can leave the hospital. Pulling off that stunt was one thing with the policewoman, but now there's a countrywide alert in place thanks to the botched operation by Grace and her friends."

It was the first time that night I detected rancour in his words, but in honesty, I couldn't blame him.

"Then you'll have to make that call," Angela said in a firm voice, taking the phone from his hands. "Or I will. I won't stand by and watch this girl die."

Homer pushed back. "I'll not ring that bastard and ask him for help, even if my life depended on it."

"But it's not your life is it? He owes you, both of us in fact. No time for pride, Homer. Call him and make him save Rosetta. Now!"

Angela held out the phone, waiting for him to take it. He looked at the phone with utter disdain and contempt, though he knew he was beaten; Rosetta's death would hang on his conscience if he continued to obstinately refuse.

With a scowl, Homer snatched back his phone and pushed past us, heading outside.

In the stillness that followed I asked, "Who will he call?"

Angela turned to me. "It's time to call in a debt. From Olwyn's boss; Jerry Houseman."

The motorbike startled Olwyn as it sped past in a mist of spray. While at Allison's flat, she had received a message from Marius asking to meet her at the bus shelter on the forest road. Presumably he wanted to greet her away from the prying eyes of Homer and Angela, though she was puzzled by the tight phrasing of his message and the absence of emoticons.

The bus shelter was empty when Olwyn arrived so she drew clear of the road a short distance beyond. From there, she could watch the deserted road in her mirrors, leaving the engine running, as much from the need for warmth as a quick departure.

The night had been long; the time for sleep cut short by Jerry's early phone call. A mixture of fatigue and the warmth from the heater made her drowsy. She might have dozed for longer than it felt, jumping with a start as Marius opened the passenger door, breathless from running most of the way from the cottage.

"Someone's been shot," he gasped, struggling to catch his breath. "One of Grace's friends. Their break-in at a fracking site has gone badly wrong."

Olwyn pressed her finger against his lips in an effort to still his words.

"Catch your breath, take your time." Despite the obvious drama, she still wanted a moment together.

"I've missed you," she said, moving to kiss him, but stopped with a sudden intake of breath.

Beneath his jacket his clothes were covered in blood.

"It's bad," Marius said, aware of her alarm.

"Angela said she thought the girl might die if she doesn't get immediate hospital attention. Homer has made a phone call to someone. He obviously isn't very happy about it, but a medic arrived on a motorbike just as I was leaving, so it must have brought about the right reaction. Hopefully, an ambulance will be here soon."

Homer making a phone call puzzled Olwyn. She knew how reluctant he was to use a mobile phone, so who had he taken the risk to call?

"How did Grace get here?" she asked.

"After they escaped from the fracking site, they drove here with the injured girl in their van. It seems that one of the group betrayed them."

Olwyn was stilled by his final sentence. "Who betrayed them?"

"One of the women. She tried holding the others at gunpoint when they were about to start filming. They were actually inside the fracking site and it was the crucial evidence they needed to prove what's really going on."

His words came in an avalanche now that the pressure of the immediate situation had been lifted. Without hesitating, Olwyn put the car in gear and sped off in the direction of Angela's cottage.

In his relief at seeing Olwyn, Marius had omitted to tell her he suspected that one of the group still had the gun in their possession.

The only thing the man in black removed was his helmet. Just his eyes were visible above a black balaclava. He remained impassive, spoke little and then only to question or instruct Angela.

Within moments he had connected Rosetta to a monitor and equipment brought in the panniers of the motorbike. A plasma drip was arranged and a quick appraisal made of her wounds.

The visit was brief; leaving filled syringes and a few brief words of instruction. He left as Olwyn's car passed by, a cloud of spray and slush marking his path down the rutted, water filled track.

I was surprised when Marius entered the kitchen with Olwyn. Perhaps the urgent need to save Rosetta's life had distracted me so that I hadn't noticed Marius was missing. Either way, the glance that Olwyn gave me when she entered the room also passed my notice.

We were waiting for the arrival of the ambulance. Homer's call had achieved results but hadn't improved his mood. Until help arrived, the room held its breath, all of us listening to the metronomic bleep of the monitor tracing Rosetta's fight for survival.

Homer touched my shoulder, drawing aside from the others.

"I'm going to the hospital with the injured girl. I need to be sure she arrives safely; alive." He put particular emphasis on his last word.

"I'll take the other two men from your team with me in the ambulance and drop them as far away from here as possible. They're a liability to us while they remain here. Do you want to leave at the same time?" he asked bluntly.

I shook my head. I no longer had anywhere else safe to hide. 'Blue Horizon' had targeted me nationwide on facial recognition. Every CCTV camera was now hunting for my face. Not a fact I needed to remind Homer, he had already guessed as much.

At a silent nod from Homer, Marius left the cottage and returned to the end of the track to flag down the ambulance when it arrived. Even the wonders of sat-nav were unlikely to find our isolated spot, and time was critical for Rosetta.

After Marius had gone, I was suddenly conscious of Olwyn talking to Homer in hushed terms. For a moment, they both glanced in my direction. Was there suspicion in their eyes? Or was that just the strain of events taking their toll on my growing feeling of paranoia?

The ambulance arrived just as Rosetta's pulse began to weaken. Two men in military fatigues got out of an olive green Landrover with a red cross stencilled in a white circle.

Despite his diffident manner, Jerry Houseman could pull 'the rabbit from the hat' when the need arose. Whatever he and Homer had agreed had at least provided an ambulance for poor Rosetta, not from the NHS but removing her from the clutches of 'Blue Horizon'.

The room was suddenly busy as the two paramedics, well-trained for situations such as this, set to work on Rosetta.

With a firm hold, Homer caught my arm.

"We need a talk when I get back. It seems you've got some explaining to do."

He didn't wait for a reply, but he shot a barely concealed glance in Olwyn's direction.

Within minutes, the paramedics had Rosetta prepared for her journey to hospital. Homer pushed the two men from my team into the ambulance, and took the spare front seat. The ambulance disappeared, hidden in a squall of driving sleet, before anyone could bid farewell.

A silence followed. The world felt closed in and we all slumped, exhausted, around the kitchen table where a life and death struggle had just played out. It was probably why no one, not even Homer, thought to look to the sky above the cottage.

Had we done so, someone may just have made out the grey shape of a whisper drone. And the world to come might have been a very different place.

CHAPTER 51
WIRES SOMETIMES GET CROSSED

In the steamy railway station café, Milo distractedly helped himself to a second mug of tea. Two men, each dark, bearded, and swarthy aroused his interest to an extent that he had opted for the inconvenience of a later train. Both dressed to be inconspicuous; yet one held a haughty, demanding expression, while his younger companion looked flushed and edgy, occasionally mopping his anxious face with a handkerchief.

The description 'tripwire' sprang to mind. Milo had messaged the gem cutter in the east end of London to warn he would be late for their meeting. With the latest bag of uncut stones weighing heavily in his coat pocket, he would be relieved to pass them on. But instincts intervened, something about the two men jarred a nerve, demanding attention, and he wouldn't leave without satisfying his curiosity.

Two of his brothers sat at a table on the opposite side of the café. With a nod, he beckoned Jude, the elder of the pair, to join him.

"Take a trip to the loo. Nudge 'rat features' in the back as you pass. He's sitting at a table next to the entrance to the Gents. Take an indirect path so he can't easily see you coming. I want to see how he reacts when you surprise him. And tell Luca to get a photo of them both without being seen."

Jude was the tallest of his brothers, a slow giant of a man, someone you always wanted on your side if it ever came to a fight. Thankfully, there had been few occasions when that had been put to the test.

Jude grinned and walked back to join his younger brother, pausing only to exchange a few words before continuing towards the toilet door.

Jude must have kicked a chair leg as he lumbered past. Milo saw the 'rat face' man jump in his seat, his hand instinctively flashing to his jacket pocket. In a split second, he spun around, his eyes aflame with ignited anger while opposite, the younger man leaned back in his seat, his face twisted in alarm.

It was over in a second. Milo had to admit 'rat face' was a professional, dowsing anger the moment he saw Jude's looming bulk behind him, the large maws of his hands already spread wide in apology, the hint of a tempting, sardonic smile just perceptible on his fat lips.

Jude held the situation for a few seconds, feigned laughing for just long enough to gain the measure of this man while Luca took the photographs he needed. As the wide back of Jude disappeared through the toilet door, Milo was already messaging on his phone.

There could be several reasons for the man's over-reaction, though none that would ease his suspicions.

"Homer, my friend," Milo muttered quietly to himself. "Unless I'm mistaken, you could have a serious problem on your hands."

As if Homer didn't already have enough to contend with.

So what had passed between them? Homer's departing words inferred questions about the conversation he and Olwyn had shared before he left. It created a chilled front, some sort of invisible barrier that floated between us in the aftermath of the departure of the ambulance. In the narrow confines of the cottage, we avoided one another, speaking only when necessary in monosyllables.

Angela's face, scored by pain, with skin the colour of yellowing parchment, was a clear indicator that she was unwell, that even resting in her favourite chair couldn't disguise. I felt deeply shocked by the change in her in such a short period of time.

Marius, ever attentive to Angela's needs, fussed around in anxious distraction, attuned to the frosty atmosphere that permeated the kitchen, keenly aware that whenever Olwyn and I passed close by, her stony glare conveyed an unspoken message. I would have normally drawn matters into the open, but out of respect for Angela, we settled for the silence of avoidance. Inevitably, it all became too much.

"How did you allow this to happen?" Olwyn suddenly blurted the pointed accusation as we jointly scrubbed the kitchen table, stained red by Rosetta's blood.

When I replied I chose to ignore the intended jibe.

"When we escaped in the van we must have passed a security squad hidden in the dark. I didn't know they were there until shots were fired at the van. Rosetta was hit by random chance."

My words had a defensive ring I hadn't intended, but then, I wasn't the one who had been shot.

"And the girl who you claim started things?"

"I found her holding the others at gunpoint." My defensive tone continued.

"How convenient that she waited for you to disappear before acting." Olwyn's implied accusations were still apparent.

"My camera wouldn't work. I had to take it apart and remake the connections. She obviously chose a moment when the odds were on her side."

Olwyn gave me a look that implied disbelief. I let it pass; the last thing Angela needed at that moment was a cat fight in her own kitchen. Besides, I was weary and not prepared to argue my case when the culprit, Alice, was kept locked in the lounge. It was for her own safety while Homer was away, he obviously didn't trust me as he had taken the key with him.

"Two men, Arabic extraction, one alpha, the other younger, deferential. I've mailed photos."

From a payphone, Milo's words were tight. The call lasted only seconds and he was gone.

Using the hospital wi-fi, Homer downloaded the images. Several photos; two men in a café, bearded, dressed in black. A sharp-featured man snarling, unwisely, at Milo's goliath of a brother standing behind his chair. Anonymous. Dangerous.

Tom entered the room behind Homer, disturbing his thoughts.

"They're taking Rosetta down to surgery now. I'd like to stay until she's out of danger, just to be certain."

"If you must," Homer said. "Just don't linger too long and arouse anyone's interest. Even here, there will be someone prepared to sell their soul for the bounty money that's been placed on your heads."

"I'm more worried about my friend. The guy seems to have completely lost it," Tom replied.

"If you want my advice, buy fake passports and get out of the country as soon as possible. You'll both be caught if you stay here."

Homer glanced at the photo of the two bearded men on his phone. He might be wise to take his own advice.

Behind them, a nurse appeared in the doorway. "Is there a Greek man here?"

Her question took a second to strike a chord; there was only one person Homer knew who would use that term.

"Who's asking?"

"He didn't say," the nurse replied. "But he has some sort of official pass. He's waiting in a car outside."

Homer turned to leave. "Make sure you're gone the moment Rosetta is out of surgery," he tersely said to Tom.

"What about Alice? You can throw her to the wolves for all I care, but just make sure she doesn't finger the rest of us."

Clearly, self-preservation was still foremost in Tom's mind.

"I'll deal with her when I'm good and ready. Make sure you and your friend disappear. You won't last long when 'Blue Horizon' get their hands on you."

Homer held up his damaged left hand, broken fingers still bound and taped. He watched the colour drain from the other man's face. Reality can provide a harsh awakening.

A green vintage Jaguar sat outside in a corner of the hospital car park. Homer had seen the car before. He needed no telling who awaited him. A young man, definitely not your typical chauffer, sat behind the wheel, engine gently idling to keep the passenger warm in the back of the car.

"Fabian, darling, nip outside and have a quick fag." The voice from the back seat placed amused emphasis on the last word.

Homer slid into the front passenger seat as Fabian left. Inside the car, the smell of waxed leather traded places with cigar smoke.

"You've got a bloody nerve, Houseman."

"A thank you would be more appropriate, don't you think."

Though they hadn't met face-to-face for several years, nothing much had changed. Prompted by Homer's phone call, Jerry Houseman had arranged for Rosetta to be treated in a military hospital. It wasn't an entirely altruistic gesture; keeping her and the rest of her team away from 'Blue Horizon's clutches was more likely an act of self-protection to keep 'fingerprints' from the failed operation leading back to him.

"You only organised this," Homer gestured to the buildings around them, "because this cock-up of a so-called operation has the hallmarks of your meddling stencilled all over it. Otherwise …" He left the sentence to answer itself. "Why are you here? To gloat?"

"Always so judgemental," Houseman sighed, feigning offence. "Actually, apart from making sure the poor injured girl will be safe from 'Blue Horizon', I'm here to give you a warning."

He waited, trying to read Homer's reaction.

"It has been brought to my attention that a certain undesirable individual has recently been gaily waved through immigration without a second glance."

He handed Homer a grainy photograph of a man of middle Eastern extraction, exiting at Heathrow.

"With the express permission from none other than our esteemed Home Secretary, Hugh Littlemore."

He smiled satirically. "And they didn't even check his passport."

Homer studied the photo in silence, weighing his options. The likeness to the image Milo had sent him was unmistakeable.

"Who is he?"

"Pick a name. He has more aliases than we can count. Suffice to know he's an ISIS coordinator, a Mr Fix-it of considerable skill and reputation. You don't need my help to join the dots."

"Why let someone like that into the UK?"

"Simple. Political quid pro quo. Payback to ISIS for favours and services rendered in the murky depths into which 'Blue Horizon' delves."

"Presumably you're keeping tabs on him?"

"Ah," Houseman sighed the little word, with immense significance.

"So? Littlemore may have let him into the country but that doesn't stop you watching this man."

"In normal times I would agree. But away from the overview of parliament, our friend, Littlemore, has begun a purge of MI5, rather in the manner of Hercules and 'the cleaning of the Augean stables', flushing out the filth that dares to question his plans or hint at exposing what 'Blue Horizon' might really be up to."

"So you've lost him."

For a moment, Houseman didn't answer.

"Rather worse than that I'm afraid. I'm somewhat on the run myself. By chance I found I was on Littlemore's list of undesirables. So Fabian and I are heading north, to lose ourselves on the grouse moors of the Scottish Highlands for an extended vacation until, one way or another, all this dies down. I thought it only right to give you the tip-off before I go."

"Does your agent, Olwyn Wright-Smith, know you're leaving her in the lurch?"

Houseman shook his head. "Best not to tell her; it will only create panic and spoil her judgement for what is about to unfold."

"So you abandon her and the rest of us while you and your boyfriend Fabian run for cover in the wilds of the Scottish Highlands?"

"A rather harsh description I feel, if in a general sense correct." Houseman smiled; it wasn't a pleasant expression.

"Still, someone has to be around when this is all over to pick up the pieces, so it might as well be me."

"And what is coming? Don't try and tell me you don't know, you manipulative bastard," Homer said angrily.

"Alas, I'm afraid there you have got me. I can only say the dice have been rolled; all any of us can do now is sit back and wait to see how the numbers fall."

The driver's door opened and Fabian returned, fag, or whatever, complete.

"Time to go." Houseman took back the photo from Homer.

"Toodle-pip, my old duck. Take care of everyone in my absence." He gave a supercilious smile.

"If you give Fabian your address, I'll send a brace of grouse."

As the Jaguar departed, Homer felt a foul taste in his mouth that wasn't caused by its exhaust smoke.

CHAPTER 52
THE PRICE OF A PHONE CALL

The row was inevitable. Grace and Olwyn spent most of the morning in separate orbits, trying to avoid one another in Angela's presence. In the end it was Joss who unintentionally acted as the catalyst. When it became obvious that she was pacing the room, agitated and whining, it was too late.

"For god's sake, will someone do something about that dog," Olwyn snapped as Grace entered the kitchen.

"Don't take your annoyance with me out on the dog," Grace replied, coming to Joss's defence.

She tried to make her words non-confrontational, and failed. Somehow, either the act or the words crossed the truce line.

"And why, do you suppose, I should be annoyed with you?" The question hit Grace with the force of a punch.

"I haven't the first idea," Grace reasoned, trying to deflect the issue.

A response wasn't slow in coming.

"Why not try the act of betrayal."

Olwyn suddenly flipped, opening her bag, her hand searching for what; incriminating evidence of her supposed crime?

"Betrayal?"

"Let's say it seems a strange coincidence that every operation you're involved with turns into a fiasco. It's almost as if someone forewarns the fracking sites before you arrive."

Grace looked uncertain, trying to measure where Olwyn was taking her accusations.

"The only betrayal I can see has been perpetrated by the woman Homer has locked in the room next door."

"I wonder," Olwyn said, feigning amusement. "Are you possibly related to her as well?"

For a moment, the question hung in the air between them, only to be interrupted by Marius who, feeling flummoxed, intervened to remove Joss from the 'no man's land' that stood between the two women. The dog dug her heels in, reluctant to be moved, incredulous that no one understood the urgent warning she was trying to signal. At times, humans could be incredibly dim.

"Related?" Grace repeated, while noticing the odd behaviour of Joss, and that Marius had to use her leash to remove her from the confrontation of the room.

"You know the sort of thing. Family groups in cosy photos. Have you appeared in any lately, Grace? If that's really your name? Strange, you never use your surname. Now why would that be, do you think?"

Such was the intensity of the atmosphere between them that, even speaking in terse hissed tones, they managed to disturb Angela from her hard won doze. Suddenly aroused, she watched as Joss, agitated and complaining, was forcefully removed from the room. Distracted, even she missed the obvious until suddenly the kitchen was illuminated by an approaching stroboscopic pulse of blue light.

The price of a phone call when you don't look to the sky above.

Alice had seen the light the moment it turned onto the track that led to the cottage. Bored by waiting for Homer to return, she had dozed in an armchair. Even with her eyes closed, the blue light still penetrated.

She snapped out of her half asleep state in an instant. Only a single ambulance had been needed for Rosetta and being a military vehicle, it hadn't broadcast its presence. Even if the ambulance returned, it wouldn't use its light to approach the cottage. Which meant …

"Let me out. There's someone coming," Alice shouted through the door.

The muffled whine of the dog and a man's voice replied from the hallway.

She repeated her warning, this time shouting and hammering with her fists on the solid wood of the door.

"There are lights outside, blue lights. It can't be good. Let me out, don't leave me trapped in here."

A key rattled in the lock. Marius had been given the key by Homer. 'Just in case. Keep it hidden and don't let either of these women know you've got it. I don't want any summary justice carried out on the girl while I'm gone.'

Marius opened the door an inch.

"What's all the fuss about …?"

He kept his foot braced against the door. Through the narrow gap, the blue light began to bounce off the walls of the hallway. He didn't wait for a reply. Whatever purpose the light held, he doubted it was good news.

Entering the room, he took Alice by the arm and pushed her towards the window.

"Friends of yours?" he asked in accusation.

Alice shook her head, a pale ghostly face in the blue light.

"Nothing to do with me. Did you call anyone?"

Marius was silent. He drew Alice to the shadows of the drapes at the window.

Outside, an ambulance abruptly slewed across the drive. Two men dressed in high-vis jackets left the cab and moved quickly towards the front door of the cottage.

Mesmerised by the strobe light, Marius was about to speak when the rear doors of the ambulance opened, disgorging four black figures, all of which appeared armed.

As the men dispersed, more headlights swung into view. It didn't require much imagination to see that this wasn't a social call. Without pausing to think, he pressed Joss's leash into Alice's hand.

"Whatever you've done to get yourself into this mess, I'm going to have trust you. Take Joss and hide in the woods until these men have left. They'll hurt her if she tries to intervene to protect us. Go out the back door, quickly, before the place is surrounded."

Hastily, he pushed Alice out of the room.

"Go, now. And don't let her bark."

"What are you going to do?" Alice asked over her shoulder as she moved away.

"Not much I can do," Marius replied. "But hopefully enough to stop anyone from getting hurt."

Angela recognised the man now standing in her doorway. It had been quite some while since she had last set eyes on him. Dressed in a grey, wool coat with black velvet lapels, he removed what looked like dog hairs from the arm of his coat.

"Angela? We have met before, I think."

His voice reeked of false charm, his manners as immaculate as his dress.

"Do you mind if we come in?"

She stared back, her expression fixed, impassive. Of course she minded. But refusing would only make matters worse. Her glance flicked to behind the man, counting fleeting shadows that moved in the darkness beyond the light from the kitchen.

"What's going on here?" The tall frame of Marius edged beside her.

"It's alright. I know this gentleman." Her final word was tinged with contempt.

She placed a reassuring hand on Marius's arm, afraid he might try and act the hero.

She stepped back, allowing the man to enter. It was the first time Bremer had crossed her threshold.

Reluctantly, I had agreed to allow Angela to open the door. Despite her frail appearance she had insisted, and the first man to enter I didn't recognise, though I sensed Angela knew him. He was tall, spare-framed and dressed as though he had just left a dinner party, and the tone of their conversation soon made it pretty obvious it was Bremer.

He was followed by Miller, who I recognised from an earlier visit to Homer's cottage with a retinue of bodyguards dressed in black. A florid police sergeant was the last to enter, his eyes darting nervously around the room. With relief, I noted that Marius had the presence of mind to have hidden Joss.

Despite their balaclavas, I recognised one of the men; a large man with bad breath who Joss had bitten on a previous visit. I suspected things would not go well for Joss on a second acquaintanceship. Why were they here, including the top man himself?

Holding a spasm of pain in her eyes, Angela eased herself into her chair beside the range.

"So, Mr Bremer, to what do we owe the pleasure of a visit at this time of night?"

Angela's question emphasised this wasn't a normal event. There could only be one reason for such a high-level visit; with a hollow feeling in the pit of my stomach, I knew it would involve me.

I watched Miller's eyes searching every face in the room and made a step backwards while Olwyn moved closer to Marius, blocking me from Miller's view.

Behind me, the door to the hallway was slightly ajar. With all the attention focused on Angela, I slid behind the half open door and moved quickly through the hallway, pausing momentarily when I saw the door wide open to the room containing Alice.

There was no time to balance my options; Miller was bound to notice I had left, and the margin to escape was narrowing every second. Thankfully, the back door wasn't locked and someone, most probably Homer, had oiled the hinges.

Soundlessly, I opened the door and I held my breath. I didn't have a plan beyond run and escape. The rest I would have to make up when I was clear of the house.

A stream of thoughts bannerlined through my brain. I wasn't sure I accepted Homer's assessment of Alice as just another victim. Do victims produce a loaded gun to use against others who are defenceless? Alice had known we couldn't protect ourselves. Plus, the arrival of Bremer and his entourage more than suggested a further leak of our plans in which I suspected Alice had a role. Chillingly, what had been the purpose of including an ambulance on the night's visit?

Too many questions for a precarious situation. I should have listened to my intuition.

I crossed the rear yard, with the only light coming from a few stars in the sky above the surrounding trees. It took a few moments for my eyes to adjust.

From the barn to my left a dark figure moved and a soft whimper kissed the air. Was that a warning my ears alerted to that my eyes couldn't detect?

"Grace?"

"Alice?"

Had she taken the dog and was waiting for me?

Perhaps, if she had rescued Joss, my judgement of her was too harsh. Instead of heading away from the waiting figure, I walked forwards.

A female Judas had just called my name and my world dissolved into total blackness.

CHAPTER 53
THE CURRENCY OF JUDAS

Cosmo arranged the meeting with Homer as a matter of urgency. They met in a layby some miles from the travellers' camp. For the first time Homer could recall, Cosmo arrived with three of his sons. Things were serious if he felt the need for bodyguards. He didn't explain his reasons and Homer didn't ask.

"So, my friend."

Cosmo spoke quickly as Homer joined him in the back seat of the car.

"It seems the moment is approaching. What are your intentions?"

Homer was quiet, staring forwards, avoiding meeting the eyes of his friend. "I'll wait for them."

"Which ones? Seems there's a list of people interested in your whereabouts, and the woman, for that matter."

Cosmo laughed ironically. "More a question of who finds you first I suspect. Unless …?"

Homer ignored the question. "This time I'll wait for them," he said again, and turned away from his friend to stare out at the snowscape beyond the layby.

"Whatever happens, get Marius to safety. For old time's sake if nothing else."

"Four hundred and thirty days in a prison cell together and we come to this," Cosmo said wistfully.

"It's got to be worth something."

"You could always run? It's served you well up to now."

Homer shook his head. "I'm tired of running and tired of hiding from my destiny. Just look after Marius. You'll need to get him out of the country if it comes to …"

He suddenly gripped Cosmo by the hand. "Promise me."

Cosmo nodded, his eyes closed. As if to confirm what Homer had already known, he squeezed his friend's hand and leaned forward, kissing Homer deliberately on both cheeks, slowly, one by one, the absolution of a gypsy who knew the future.

Without another word, Homer left the car. What more was there to say? He knew the delivery of the message had cost his friend dearly. The net was closing around him; he sensed that this time it couldn't be avoided.

As he watched his friend walk slowly away across the snow, Cosmo closed his eyes, concealing his tears from his waiting sons.

Olwyn watched Sergeant Wailes. For a moment, the smirk on his face eclipsed the fear and discomfort that shadowed his eyes.

"So what do you want here, Bremer?" Angela asked.

"My dear." Bremer's voice assumed a kind, homely timbre, a sly and corrupting serpent in reply to her question.

"I'm informed that you've been aiding and abetting a nest of terrorists in your little cottage. You well know the laws on national security, yet you either choose to be complicit, or perhaps just look the other way. Now I might just be able to use my influence to overlook your role in this regrettable display of disobedience," Bremer waved a metaphorical finger of rebuke at Angela, "but the same can't be said for your new friends, some of whom seem to be ... missing, if my eyes don't deceive me."

No sooner had he finished speaking than the outside door swung open, emitting a flurry of snow as two men entered, dragging the body of Grace between them. They were followed by a third man, accompanying Alice, an empty dog leash twisted in her hand. One of the men went directly to the sink, washing a bleeding hand in a cold stream of water.

"Bloody dog," he muttered, cursing under his breath.

"So, who have we here?" Bremer asked with an air of amused indifference.

"Unless my eyes deceive me, it looks like the prize we're seeking."

He nodded to Miller. "Seems like your boys have been a trifle rough. Bring her round."

Before Miller could move, Angela had already left her chair and filled a bowl with cold water. Taking a sponge, she began bathing Grace's face. On her left temple, the imprint of a rifle butt was already clearly visible. She spoke to Marius.

"Ice pack from the freezer."

Before Marius could move, the man with the bitten hand had blocked his path.

"No ice. Her future accommodation will be cold enough."

Miller gestured to another of his men who took the bowl of water from Angela and tipped it over Grace's head; the shock of the cold did the trick.

With a force that was harder than necessary, he pushed Angela in the direction of her chair. Marius moved with surprising speed, just managing to catch her before she fell to the floor.

"So you're here to beat up old women," Marius shouted in a frustrated outburst as he helped Angela to her chair.

Smiling, Bremer leaned back against the sink, watching everything happening in the kitchen.

"Sergeant Wailes," his voice filled the room. "It would seem you have grounds to detain for resisting arrest."

Wailes jumped in surprise, discomforted by the scene in which he was little more than a bit-part player.

He nodded. "I already have warrants made out to detain them."

'How convenient,' Olwyn thought. 'He knew we were here before he had left the police station.'

Wailes held out a plastic wallet containing paperwork that no one would have the time or opportunity to read.

The man with the bitten hand secured Grace's wrists together with a plastic zip tie. He took the laces from her shoes and removed her belt. A line of blood had appeared in her hairline, diluted and spreading by the soaking over her head.

"And who do we have here?" Bremer gestured in Olwyn's direction?"

"An imposter, I think you'll find," Wailes responded, suddenly animated, feigning to examine the pass still hanging on a ribbon around Olwyn's neck.

"It says she's Field Agent Wright-Smith from MI5. But that can't be true; she's already dead."

Wailes paused, a smug grin on his face. "I think we have sufficient grounds for taking this charlatan in for questioning."

He snapped the pass from around her neck, discarding it with a flick of his wrist into the glowing flames of the Aga.

"It would seem our imposter has no identity," he chuckled, and nodded towards the man who had just secured Grace.

"No," Marius shouted, as the man withdrew another zip tie and moved towards Olwyn.

No one saw Miller produce the taser, but the effect on Marius was instantaneous.

"Impeding arrest, I think," Miller stated, watching Marius writhing on the tiled floor, his face contorted in shock and pain.

"Now, I did enjoy that," he said, and bent down to remove the electrode.

"Payback for humiliating my son," he hissed with a note of sardonic satisfaction.

Marius showed no reaction. Though most of his remaining faculties were concentrated on trying to ride the spasms that rendered merely breathing difficult, the memory of the spite in that final sentence would last a lifetime.

It took less than a minute. Short of breath and shocked by what was happening, Angela watched impotently as Marius and the two women were secured. Duck-tape was used to silence Marius. He was lucky; a slit was cut in the front and a straw pushed between his teeth so he could breathe.

Before her hands were tied, while attention was on Marius, Olwyn removed the contents of her bag into her pocket. She had briefly contemplated releasing the gas canister, but with so many armed men around she had second thoughts.

No, however this developed, Olwyn decided it was necessary to wait for a better opportunity to escape, guessing that if she was searched, no man would delve into a woman's sanitary protection.

"Where are you taking us?" Olwyn demanded as they secured her wrists, ignoring Wailes and directing her question to Miller.

"Overnight accommodation," he replied with a smile. "Someone wants to interview her in the morning." Miller pointed towards Grace who sat slumped in a chair, her eyes closed.

"Accommodation she's been trying so hard to gain access to for months. As a treat, you both get to enjoy the experience free of charge."

Four men appeared and partly dragged and carried the two women towards the door. When Olwyn tried to resist, someone kicked her in the back of the knees. After that, she was little more than a puppet.

"Don't you dare hurt them, Bremer?" Tired voice or not, the threat was implicit in Angela's words.

Bremer stopped and turned in the doorway.

"That choice is in their hands. With regards to their future safety, they'll have to seriously consider their options after the cosy chat tomorrow."

"And us?" Angela said with a worried look in the direction of Marius who lay eyes closed, breathing heavily on the floor.

"Miller and his men will stay with you and await the return of Homer, so you can all look forward to a jolly little reunion."

Bremer stood aside as a man pushed Alice out of the door. Willing accomplice or reluctant Judas? Angela noted that her hands hadn't been bound.

CHAPTER 54
CURIOSITY CONTAINED

Joss watched the tableau unfold, cloaked by the darkness amongst the surrounding trees. The wound in her neck had stopped bleeding, leaving her coat matted with blood that she couldn't reach and clean with her tongue.

She saw Grace and Olwyn stumble to the open doors at the rear of the ambulance. Two men pushed them roughly inside, slammed the doors shut and climbed into the cab. They drove away, blue light strobing onto the surrounding trees, hastily followed by an SUV, leaving the cottage with the light still shining from the kitchen window.

Cautiously, Joss moved from the trees to the shelter of a log store closer to the house. From there she saw another man, the one she had seen strike Grace with the butt of his rifle, come outside to light a cigarette while he peed against the wall. It was the same man who had attacked Joss while the girl held her tight on her leash. Joss had bitten him hard in the hand as he tried to stab her with his knife.

It was a stunned Grace who had somehow managed to release Joss from her leash. Driven by her urgent command, "Away, Joss", whilst reluctant to abandon Grace, she had sought refuge in the woods.

The man discarded his cigarette and returned to the kitchen. It was almost as if he knew the missing dog was nearby. Joss hadn't seen anything of Angela or Marius, and stood panting, anxious to know what had become of them.

Part of the answer was provided a few minutes later, when three men escorted Angela to another waiting SUV. Even in the darkness she looked frail and tired, something her guards seemed oblivious to as they bundled her into a rear seat. Bright headlights pierced the night and the SUV left in a spray of mud and slush, ignoring the ruts and potholes left unfilled in the track.

Joss was curious, and hungry; she had missed her dinner. The wound in her neck ached in concert with her empty belly. On another night, she might have sought a meal in the woods, but now she was tired and wet and mystified by what remained in the unlit cottage.

Warily, the dog left the security of the log store and approached the kitchen door. It wasn't locked. If she stood on her hind legs, she could just reach the latch with her paw. Stretching, she felt the warning crack of dried blood that closed her wound. It took several attempts to lower the latch lever. Fortunately, the door opened inwards and her weight pushed it open.

They had left Marius coiled on the floor. Miller had been unable to resist leaving the boy without a hard kick in the stomach as he left. It was only the breathing tube that had spared him from suffocating on his own vomit.

Joss heard a primeval grunt as Marius became aware of her presence. With difficulty, he had moved his bound wrists from behind his back, beneath his legs, to his front. His eyes lit up as the dog approached, snuffling and licking his face in affection. Groaning, he held out his wrists with their conspicuous zip tie.

It was asking a lot of the dog, and for a few moments she failed to get the message, so Marius risked spitting out his breathing tube and imitated trying to bite the plastic tie that bound his hands together. It took a few attempts to get the dog's attention, but once she had grasped what he meant it took only seconds for her sharp teeth to cut through the plastic.

Released, Marius tore off the tape that gagged him, staggering to the sink to empty the contents of his stomach. For a while he could do little beyond rinsing his mouth and face. It was fresh blood, seeping from the cut in Joss's neck that regained his focus.

"Where do you think they're taking us?"

I shrugged. Despite our circumstances, Olwyn wasn't someone with whom I wanted to share a conversation at that particular moment.

"If we've been arrested, it should be a cell at the police station," I said with a weary sigh.

Why did everything have to be explained to this woman?

"A cell would be good," Olwyn replied with what I considered was a bizarre thing to say. "Allison will soon hear if we're taken there."

"Allison?"

"The policewoman who was shot at Homer's place."

I let the comment pass. Dealing with Olwyn took more than I had energy for at that moment.

We had both been handcuffed to grab handles in the ambulance, which, combined with the zip ties, made the ride difficult and uncomfortable. My temple was sore and swollen; whoever had hit me left an imprint of the butt of his gun on my head.

"Bremer's boss? Is he your father, then?" Olwyn asked the direct question I was in no fit state of mind to address.

"My father died on the 108th floor of north tower on 9/11," I snapped. "If you're referring to Hugh Littlemore, he has nothing whatsoever to do with me. I despise him; the feeling is mutual."

"But he is your stepfather?" She emphasised the word '*is*'.

"If it's any of your business, he can legally claim to be my stepfather; no blood tie, not even a shared name. I'm my father's daughter; period."

It was difficult to contain the rage I felt. If we carried on with this conversation, the contempt I held for Littlemore would boil over to consume the woman who sat opposite me.

"But your mother is married to him?"

God, this woman was pushing her luck. Perhaps it was best we were chained apart at that moment.

Before I could answer, the ambulance braked to a halt, mercifully sparing our conversation from a physical conclusion. The doors were opened and we were greeted by a breeze with 'Arctic' printed in its character.

Above us, an enormous camouflage net hushed as it undulated on the cold air currents. Wherever we were, this was definitely not a police station. Someone threw me a set of keys.

"Unlock bitch's handcuffs, tell her release you." His English was poor, overlain with a heavy accent.

They'd be lucky; from the way I felt about Olwyn and her accusations at that moment, I could have happily left her locked in the ambulance. But, commonsense prevailed, and with some difficulty we released the metal handcuffs that had restrained our ankles, and stumbled, blinking, into the night.

Pale, subdued lights hid much around us. Someway off, a generator grumbled and high pressure pumps pulsed and throbbed. I didn't need two guesses to know where we had been taken.

For what good it would do, Olwyn chose to go into attack against our captors.

"If we've been arrested, where are the police?"

Confused, she looked around her, seeing the machinery and drilling rigs.

"Otherwise, release us immediately."

The only response was a laugh that circled like a Mexican wave amongst the group of men who surrounded us, accompanied by a firm push in the back towards a line of steel containers that arrived at most fracking sites on a nightly rota to await connection to the high pressure pumps positioned beside the drilling rigs.

"Police; you see in morning. Tonight you sleep here. Special arrangement for man who want to speak you tomorrow," the heavily accented English continued.

"You spend long time trying to break into restricted site. Now you get you wish; is dream come true. All up close and personal."

Fleetingly, the thought of escape crossed my mind. Would they shoot us if we tried to break out? Probably.

Besides, the double gate system was closed and the fence, fringed with razor wire, was too high for any chance of climbing.

With firm hands we were led towards a metal container that stood apart from the others. A ladder led to the roof where a hatch was propped open.

"Up. You climb."

The large man gestured with his automatic pistol. Close up, the container was painted azure blue. How appropriate I thought in a moment of irony. I had a disconcerting idea what this meant.

Climbing a ladder with tied wrists is an interesting experience. Twice, Olwyn, poorly dressed for this little adventure, slipped and almost fell, much to the amusement of our watching guards, two of whom had already climbed ahead of us.

On the roof, we shivered in the wind. An intimate body search took place for all to see. No doubt they were enjoying this.

"Now you climb down ladder in hatch. It is you hotel for night."

Someone tapped the swollen bruise on the side of my head with his rifle butt.

"Climb or fall, is no difference to us."

Beside me, Olwyn stood frozen to the spot. If we didn't move, I had a feeling this wouldn't end well. But if someone wanted to speak to me the following morning, they weren't likely to seriously harm us before the said 'interview' took place.

Instinctively, afraid of where we were being forced to enter, I resisted. A sharp punch in the face that split my bottom lip changed my mind.

"Move now or serious rough stuff," the large man shouted from below.

'Interview' or not, their brief didn't seem to exclude beating us up if they had to.

At the hatch, someone cut the plastic zip ties that bound our wrists and pushed us onto the ladder that descended into the ominous darkness of the container. I went first, Olwyn followed. Behind us, someone threw down two thin blankets and a tatty plastic bag.

"Torch good for two hours," were the last words we heard as the hatch was slammed closed above our heads with a harsh sound of rasping metal.

In the darkness we fumbled to find the torch in the plastic bag. Its weak beam illuminated the hard metal ribs of the inside of the container. Hostilities suspended between us, my first priority was to stop us both from shivering.

In our hasty departure from Angela's cottage, I had been allowed to grab one of Homer's old parkas. Many sizes too big, there was room for us both to share it, opposite arms in each sleeve, bodies pressed tightly together. I tied the two blankets around us.

There were two small foam pads in the bag. I placed them both across the metal ribs so that we could sit side by side on the floor. Without the torch, it was total blackness, a breeding ground for every nightmare you could imagine. To keep our demons at bay, we agreed to ration the torch to five minute periods, three or four times an hour. It took some time for Olwyn to stop shivering.

If you struck the walls of our prison, the dull tone confirmed they were metal, coated in some smooth, ceramic material. It was during our second period of pitch darkness that Olwyn posed the obvious question we had both been trying to avoid.

"Please tell me this hasn't been used to store what I think might have been inside it?"

If we hadn't been arguing, would we have seen the lights before they arrived outside the cottage? Who knows, we were both to blame. Now there was no point in continuing our quarrel; I could hear the fear in her voice. Under the blankets, I gave her a hug.

"Well, if our hair has all fallen out by morning, I guess we will both know the answer to that question."

CHAPTER 55
IMPRISONED BY DARKNESS

The older man performed the ceremony of absolution. The fact it was a sham was something his young acolyte, Yousef, never realised.

Bewitched by his mentor, he believed his soul had been freed to travel to paradise; the joss sticks, impregnated with marijuana and the subliminal background tones of prayer, did the rest. For many months he had been well tutored for his approaching role. Now, the pseudo-religious atmosphere, laced with a drug-induced cocktail, made irrelevance of any fear or resistance to his onward journey.

Unhappy at home, the boy's conversion into extreme fundamentalism had begun at school. Through a subtle dripfeed, his mentor, a teacher, selected and converted his young followers, in plain sight. His reward? An MBE for the integration of mixed community education, coupled with high profile roles on influential committees, were his cloak of anonymity. Beneath a smoke screen of decency, no one thought to question his motives. No hint of online radicalisation, no trail to alert MI5, the police, family members or community watchdogs, his pupil was ready to fulfil his final act as 'the sword of vengeance'.

Yousef was largely ignorant on matters of the Quran. His brain, fogged by fear, adrenalin and psychotic drugs, would believe any nonsense he was promised. Chanting, the mentor sprayed 'supposedly' holy water and blessings over his young disciple; the body tight waistcoat lay set out on the bed.

"You are promised entrance through the doors of paradise," the mentor reassured Yousef, kissing him on each cheek as he theatrically lifted the waistcoat, laced with wires, detonators and several kilos of high explosive over the young boy's head.

No amateur job this, all had been professionally made; slim and close fitting, suitable to be worn beneath a loose shirt on a summer's day, without revealing its true purpose. All that was needed was the location or a trackable mobile phone number, all conveniently provided by the gypsy, sold for a 'Judas' bag of gold.

The boy gave no sign as the waistcoat rested on his shoulders. Neither did he react as the rear straps were laced into a position he couldn't reach in the unlikely event he might change his mind. Within seconds, connections were snapped in place, tiny red lights confirming all circuits were live.

From a cupboard, the mentor removed a thick woollen jumper and a worn, green jacket. With boots and a poacher's bag, the boy looked the part. The teacher stood back to admire his workmanship, positioning the boy in front of a white wall, draped in a black and white ISIS banner, stained red-brown with blood. Around Yousef's neck, he hung a board, inscribed with an Arabic message the boy wouldn't understand. The mentor told Yousef the message simply read

A Holy Brother of Islam

He smiled to himself as he stepped back to start the video. In reality, the message said

No matter where you hide, our vengeance will
always find you

He prided himself on a satisfying day's work. The headteacher at the school he used for recruitment would be well pleased.

It was the early hours of the morning before Marius could move his head without feeling nauseous. He washed the taste of bile from his mouth, aware all the joints in his body ached from the shock of the taser, while his stomach and ribs were sore from Miller's parting kick.

On the table sat his shattered phone, a bootprint clearly visible on what remained of the screen. The cottage was empty. In the silence he set about cleaning the wound in Joss's neck. It seemed to help, deflecting the feeling of futility that had swept over him.

Homer had left Angela in his care and he had failed to protect her, and he'd been unable to prevent Bremer from taking Olwyn. From the mist of pain on the floor he heard no clues of where they had taken her and Grace, though he was pretty certain someone had mentioned Homer's cottage as a destination for Angela; bait in the trap set to entice Homer's return.

It was Joss who discovered Olwyn's phone. Her bowl made an unusual rocking motion with her dinner in it. By accident or design, beneath her bowl was Olwyn's phone, which Marius discovered when Joss knocked the bowl over to attract his attention.

He stared at the screen. It provided the breakthrough and he needed to call for help, but who to trust? Certainly not the police; it was the sergeant who had been in the cottage and just stood aside while Bremer's men did their work. Marius guessed he had also supplied the taser used to prevent him from intervening.

Without success, he spent ten minutes trying to decipher Olwyn's pin code. The screen stared back at him, blank, unresponsive. Musing abstractedly, he picked at the protective case. It resisted obstinately, then reluctantly surrendered to his fingers.

Simple really, on the back of the phone, in coloured nail varnish, was a six digit code. For the first time since Bremer had walked into the cottage, Marius found himself smiling. Trust Olwyn, prone to forget things, to think of a basic solution.

Within seconds, he was scrolling through her list of contacts, half expecting to discover a long list of ex-boyfriends and lovers. The list was surprisingly thin; the only male name, apart from his own, being someone called JH. There was no contact for Homer, not that it would have helped; he seldom switched on his phone.

But one name he did recognise was that of the injured policewoman, Allison Markham. Marius knew Olwyn trusted Allison and there had been something in the cast of her eye that suggested she was fond of Olwyn. Was that enough to trust the woman? After all, she was a policewoman.

With few viable alternatives and desperate to discover where Olwyn and Grace had been taken, Marius pressed the call button. As Allison Markham's phone began to ring, he only then remembered it was two in the morning.

Homer decided to walk the six miles to Angela's cottage. The meeting with Cosmo had a feel of a 'last supper' experience, one in which Cosmo's conscience had decided that in this departing act, he would warn his friend he had betrayed him. So, that was it. Easy in its way; forewarned is forearmed.

On foot, Homer was in his element, though his broken hand was a reminder that not even he could anticipate every trap. With no more than his compass and occasional stars, he tracked across country; alone, but not lonely, though he missed the company of faithful Joss. Light of foot, Homer moved quickly, stopping regularly, ears fine-tuned to the noises of the night, a 'radar' searching for anything out of place.

He half expected to be followed, noting with perverse disappointment that he wasn't, an absurdity when considering that he was unarmed and had no means to call for help. Yet that was no excuse to lower his vigilance. He avoided tracks and paths with an intuitive skill honed over decades, often when survival relied upon outwitting opponents.

A soft winged owl shadowed his passage, occasionally calling his signature warning as he crossed the territory of others. Without his dog, Homer took comfort from the laser eyed presence of his feathered companion.

After a while, he began to recognise the feel of the landscape, even in darkness. Nearer to Angela's cottage, he recognised the contours of the ground and the sculpture of the surrounding trees. The owl bid farewell, planing above his head, departing with a soft double call, an unspoken token of companionship between man and his feathered accomplice.

The trees thinned as Homer approached the cottage. All seemed in darkness, except a yellow glow against the kitchen window. He paused behind the fringe of the trees. The car Olwyn had arrived in was still in the same spot. Beside it was parked another, a small white car that he recognised. Someone was visiting in his absence.

In their steel prison, Grace and Olwyn sat in dark silence. It was some time before Olwyn brought up the subject that was forefront in both their minds.

"So this is what I think it is," she said in a tone as bleak as their surroundings.

"Yes, I think this is what they transport their radioactive waste in," Grace slowly replied.

Olwyn perceptibly shuddered at her words and switched on the torch, shining its beam around the glassy sheen of the interior.

"I suppose the least you could say is it's been cleaned," Grace offered with a hint of irony in her voice.

"Oh, that's alright then." Olwyn's words were laced with dark humour.

"What the hell are they doing? I thought this was a gas extraction site by fracking?" she asked incredulously.

"Which it is."

"So this is …?" Olwyn used her head to nod to the surrounding metal container.

"The source of 'Blue Horizon's ill-gotten party funds. They use a ring of shell companies to process nuclear waste and ship it to fracking sites where it's pumped underground to fill the voids left by the fracking process."

"Is that legal?"

"It is if you fabricate the law to make it so. I doubt the environment will think much of its legality though."

Olwyn was silent for a moment.

"Okay, so it might be dodgy, but even I know the storage of nuclear waste is an ever growing problem. Surely, pumping it hundreds of metres underground is a better solution than leaving it in the open, stored in drums at power stations?"

Grace considered her point. 'If I start telling her about my dreams,' she thought, 'she might think she's locked in a metal box with a mad woman. I've had enough experience of that from my mother.'

Grace cleared her throat.

"The thing is, it might just be a solution if it just stayed there, deep underground. The problem is, radioactivity being what it is tends to have a mind of its own, even when mixed into a concrete slurry and pumped underground."

"But how can you be certain that's what's happening? I thought there is always a natural background level of radiation," Olwyn said.

"It's always been a problem to prove it. Fracking site security go to extreme lengths to stop anyone finding out what they're up to. We've got evidence of high radiation levels in groundwater surrounding the sites. It's patchy, but the problem is only just starting. In the decades to come the problem will probably magnify a hundred times."

"But surely, if it's as serious as that, can't we just stop them; shut the process down?"

Grace laughed involuntarily.

"This is 'Blue Horizon' we're talking about. We don't have a chance until we have a proven trail of evidence to connect the radioactivity to what's inside these containers they so considerately haul into their sites at the dead of night."

She paused, overwhelmed by a flood of emotion.

"And remember, so far at least five members of my organisation have disappeared without trace trying to expose the truth."

Olwyn switched off the torch to save the battery. Even after their eyes had adjusted, they still stared into a black abyss of darkness.

"Is it everywhere? On every site?"

Grace nodded, forgetting that act was futile.

"Every site we've visited. Potentially hundreds of tons of radioactive slurry, pumped down hundreds of wells in sites all around the country. And trust me, it makes 'Blue Horizon' tens of millions of pounds from the licence payments they obscure and filter through the shell companies that organise the process throughout the world."

"And this whole nightmare is run by 'Blue Horizon', which if rumours of a pending general election are true, are headed by the man who will become our next prime minister?" Olwyn asked.

The implications of that nightmare scenario loomed like a spectre in the darkness around them.

"Correct. And before you ask," Grace's words caught in her throat as she tried to admit to the truth, "against my wishes, my mother is married to him."

She refused to use the word 'stepfather' for a man she loathed and rejected with every fibre in her body. Her real father was dead, his body ground to dust in the pyre of 9/11. You didn't need to be a neutral outsider to feel the mutual power of loathing and contempt that existed between Hugh Littlemore and Grace, his unwanted stepdaughter.

CHAPTER 56
A FAMILY APPOINTMENT

Ice had formed on the inside of the cottage windows. Whether by conscience for Angela or more likely concern for his own comfort, Miller had the stove lit in Homer's kitchen. He appeared indifferent to her frailty, ignoring her obvious spasms of pain and tiredness. He had only one purpose; drawing Homer into his net; mere bait on a hook.

"When Homer finds her missing, he's bound to come and search here. When he turns up, make sure she greets him at the door and doesn't try to forewarn him," Miller instructed his men.

To Angela's surprise, one of his men took pity on her and positioned a chair beside the warm glow of the stove. The irony of her situation wasn't lost on her, though not for the reasons Miller could ever have imagined. With her eyes closed, she sat on a rollercoaster of pain, occasionally a thin smile on her lips. Fate held the reigns, not Bremer, Miller, or anyone else for that matter.

No doubt Miller's words were spoken for her to hear, but Angela couldn't rouse herself to open her eyes, unwilling to grace him with even the merest stare, too tired to care.

Alone, she slept, dreaming fitfully. In scenes of the past, she could make out the figure of a young man; perhaps Homer many years earlier, dressed as a woodsman, a worn waxed jacket and a sack tied across his chest for a nightly harvest. In sleep space, Angela could live an alternative world, one where things were as they might have been had they met in the decades before life's journey took her toll.

She must have called out his name in her sleep. The bearded man, who had arranged her chair, woke Angela with a gentle shake, a look of concern on his face, a glass of water and painkillers in his open palm. She took the glass, declined the tablets. Angela would travel the rest of her journey alone.

It was predictable that Joss would forewarn of Homer's approach. She was agitated and pacing the room before he had even left the cover of the trees.

Homer wasn't particularly surprised when Allison Markham opened the door to release her; he had recognised the car as that of the policewoman who had asked to borrow 'Scorpio'. He guessed her motive was to return the scorpion to Wailes.

As he tried to contain the excited dog, he wondered what Allison wanted now. He hadn't given her the scorpion yet; surely she wouldn't have come to the cottage at this ungodly hour just to repeat her request?

Homer settled Joss and examined the wound in her neck where the fur had been shaved. It hadn't been there when he had left earlier in the night. In the kitchen, he found Marius asleep on the old sofa. Allison noticed Homer's questioning glance.

"You've had an exalted visitor. None other than Bremer, in person." She paused.

"Miller used a taser to silence Marius. He's okay, just badly shaken up and sore all over. I made him rest when I arrived."

"How did you come to be here?" Homer couldn't exclude a note of suspicion from his words.

"Marius rang me from Olwyn's phone. Mine was the only name he recognised," she replied, continuing before he could ask.

"They've taken Grace and Olwyn away with them. Marius doesn't know where, but as Sergeant Wailes was involved, I guess they'll end up at the police station. Eventually." Concern was imprinted on her final word.

"I passed the station as I came here; it was in darkness, so my guess is they weren't taken straight there. If they're lucky, they'll be charged in the morning, when Bremer has finished questioning them.

"And Angela?"

"Marius overheard Miller say he was taking her to your cottage as a bargaining counter while he awaits your return. It doesn't sound as if he wants to negotiate."

She raised a sceptical eyebrow.

"Seems even Miller doesn't trust meeting you face-to-face without a winning card to play."

She looked deliberately at his injured hand.

Homer didn't reply. Instead, he left the kitchen, moving from room to room, looking for something, anything that might give a clue as to where Grace and Olwyn had been taken.

Perhaps Marius had heard another comment, no matter how insignificant? For the moment, Homer decided to let the boy sleep. There would be time enough when he woke. Besides, he had matters to conclude with Miller before he started looking for the other two.

It was dawn when someone opened the hatch and lowered the ladder.

"Out," the voice demanded.

With muscles stiff and cramping, climbing out was harder than entering. On the roof of the container, the air tasted unbelievably clean and fresh after the hard, chlorinated reek of their night's prison.

In the growing daylight, an armed man led the two women to a ladder to ground level. As she stepped from the bottom rung, Olwyn folded at the waist, retching against an empty stomach.

Fear or early signs of radiation sickness? Either way, their guard showed little sympathy, pushing her roughly towards the paling lights of a site cabin.

"You wash here. Eat later."

He brusquely frisked them, before turning to the door.

"Be ready, five minutes."

He locked the door behind him as he left.

Olwyn rinsed her mouth, filling the basin with cold water and sluicing her face.

"Where do you think they'll be taking us?" She tried to sound brave and failed.

Grace shrugged. The wound on the side of her head had bled in the night, and blood from her split lip had smeared in a red gash across her chin like lipstick applied by a drunk. She had no intention to wash; it served her purpose to look like this for what she guessed was coming in the interview.

"If law still has due process, we should be taken to a police station to be charged and questioned and given access to a lawyer."

"Surely they can't hold us without grounds or allowing us to make a phone call to someone."

Grace couldn't avoid a hollow laugh.

"Remember who we're talking about here. Merely by applying the Anti-Terrorism Act they can hold us without charge for fourteen days. As for legal representation, 'Blue Horizon' removed that entitlement when they changed the law defining terrorists. My guess is that's how they intend to treat us."

Suddenly unbearably weary, Olwyn slumped into the only chair in the room. This wasn't how things were supposed to play out.

In her plan, there was always time and space to do her job under Homer's protective umbrella and relying on Jerry to come 'riding over the hill' in her moment of need. She had a feeling she was going to be disappointed on both counts.

"So where does that leave us?" she asked, aware Grace had more experience in handling these people.

"And please don't tell me any more lurid stories about the pig farms; I'm frightened enough as it is."

Grace was staring out of a dirty window, hatched by a chequerboard of steel mesh.

"They're keeping us alive because they want to talk. That implies they need something from us."

"Does that interview include me?" Olwyn asked nervously.

Grace shook her head. "Not initially. There's only one person I know of who would want to talk to me and that will exclude you," she said, more sharply than she intended.

"Well that's okay then. Just don't leave me out if you make any deals to save your own skin," Olwyn replied.

Grace looked at her with eyes that held genuine concern.

"I'm afraid the person I expect to share the interview with won't want to discuss matters like our freedom. The point of view of others doesn't exactly figure in his view of the world."

The key rattled in the lock. The door opened and the man who had released them from the container gestured for them to leave. Outside was a black SUV with darkened windows, the engine running. There were already two men inside as they were pushed into the rear seats.

As the door slammed hard behind them, Olwyn offered a prayer in the hope that Marius had found the phone she had hidden beneath Joss's bowl.

Homer checked his watch as he eased the shotgun from its locked case in Angela's pantry. The gun was there as a spare for his occasional hunting trips he made from her cottage, though it had often been a shared joke that their days might end re-enacting a finale of a famous western film, running into a golden sunset, guns blazing. Somehow, that no longer seemed so ridiculous.

"So, we're agreed. I'll return to my cottage with Joss and find out what Miller wants with Angela. You take Marius."

Now awake, Marius looked decidedly groggy and disorientated, trying to make sense of the world.

"Take your car and go to the police station and see if you can discover what has happened to Grace and Olwyn. Keep it casual, no more than passing interest. Make some excuse for being in town for some other purpose," he suggested, feeling better now they had the outline of a plan.

Allison's arm, though still bandaged above the elbow, was at least free of its sling. Though naturally undramatic by nature, her thoughts tipped precariously close to panic if she tried to consider what might have become of Olwyn.

"See what you can discover at the police station and join me at my cottage."

He gave Allison an encouraging grin.

"You can remember where that is? Park some distance away and approach through the woods. Wait in the trees and send a signal to my phone. I'll send Joss to find you when it's safe to approach the cottage."

Almost as an afterthought, he handed Allison the plastic box with its angry tenant.

"Treat her carefully. She seems to be one extremely unhappy scorpion."

He left without waiting to ask about her intentions for the disagreeable *Arachnida*. Homer whistled for Joss and set off into the early morning shadows of the woods.

It's curious how the world turns.

If he hadn't been so hasty, he might have heard Marius call out that Angela had taken Homer's phone when Miller had abducted her.

Allison had just arrived when four men brought Olwyn and Grace into the police station. Despite the early hour, Wailes was ready to receive them, taking over from the four 'special constables' as he loosely termed the armed guards from the fracking site.

Grace looked a mess, blood conspicuous under the bandage at her temple and from a swollen, split lip. Allison wasn't surprised; she had expected Grace to resist arrest. But the state of Olwyn shocked her; she looked wrecked, carrying a conspicuous bruise on her cheek and ochre stains down the front of her shirt and trousers. She seemed to have gathered her composure but her eyes looked nervous.

Allison held an impassive expression, but as her friends were led past to separate interview rooms, she made eye contact with them when Wailes had his back to her. It was little, but she could only hope it might offer comfort enough.

"What are they here for, Sarge?" For Wailes benefit, she would play the naive card.

Startled by her presence, Wailes stared at Allison warily, suspicion clouding his eyes. He hesitated, animal cunning weighing the situation.

"Someone high up wants to talk to the scrawny one; very high-up, I shouldn't wonder."

The smirk on his face gave the clear impression he thought Grace would be just her type.

"We'll need to have a legal paper trail to hold them," Allison said, ignoring his innuendo.

"Just to keep the records straight, Sarge," she reminded him. "That's why I came in; I thought you might be a bit stretched."

She offered her best act at sincerity. Wailes nodded; suspicion temporarily parked.

"Waste of time if you ask me."

Paperwork bored him at the best of times. He didn't need second asking if someone else volunteered to do it.

"They're only here for an interview. When that's finished, we can either charge them or hand them back to Miller and his boys to play with. They can do what they like with them and save us the trouble."

As the cell doors slammed shut behind the two women, Wailes didn't elaborate on what that might involve.

Homer had to steel himself against the adrenalin that pulsed in his bloodstream. The drug could be both friend and enemy. Recently, he had made more mistakes than usual, often succumbing to the seductive power of his body's natural instincts.

"You're getting old," he muttered to himself.

Joss looked sideways at him; for once she seemed to agree with him.

With the exception of a doze in a hard chair in the hospital waiting room, Homer had foregone a night's sleep. Despite his fitness, his legs and arms had a leaden feel about them, his tired mind was numb and inclined to wander. Although he knew the woodland tracks like the back of his hand, he needed Joss to guide him back to the path on several occasions. It hardly bode well for a confrontation with his local nemesis.

Homer checked his watch. It was only just daylight, still time for a few hours of sleep before trying to release

Angela from Miller's grasp. Using her as bait, a trap had been set to ensnare him; they knew he would have to react. The question wasn't if, but when, he would play his hand.

Well, so be it. If he was to offer the plan he had in mind he would need a clear head. A few hours rest could make a lot of difference if he could clear the fatigue that was fogging his brain.

He was standing in a shelter for drying logs on the rising ground amongst the trees overlooking his cottage below. An SUV was parked to one side of the barn, partially concealed from view. A single vehicle suggested no more than four or five men.

Homer instructed Joss to stay while he tracked down a cleft in the hillside to pay the SUV a visit, wedging long steel nails behind the tread of the front tyres. If anyone tried to drive away they wouldn't get far. Not good odds, but better than nothing.

"Well, they're not going anywhere fast," Homer said yawning, when he returned to the waiting Joss. "At least not until we've paid them a visit."

Man and dog squirmed into a narrow space under an assortment of logs and drying brushwood. Homer set the alarm on his watch and resting his head on his rucksack, he was asleep in seconds. If anyone made a move in his direction, he felt certain Joss would be sure to wake him.

They were careless in their search, too intent on allowing groping hands to wander. No one thought to check the improvised bandage I had tied around my head, or to take the watch from my wrist. Both were essential in what was to follow, their purpose the only reason I had agreed to an interview.

I was led into a sparsely furnished room; just a table, chair and large computer monitor. A single central light added anaemic, ghostly shadows to my tired, strained face.

Before the interview commenced, I had been offered the bathroom to clean up. I declined. The only make-up I intended to wear was the blood from cuts and abrasions smeared across my face.

"Filthy bitch," was the only comment from the supervising police sergeant as I was subjected to yet another search.

They were too busy making derogatory remarks to do a thorough job.

So, here I was, waiting for the screen in front of me to come to life. Hidden eyes watched, stirring the silence. I looked for a switch. Was I supposed to start things, turn on the screen to start the interview?

Casually I removed my blood stained bandana as I rubbed my swollen temple, fiddling with my watch, pretending to count the passing minutes, perhaps my last in this life? I acted as they expected, nervously glancing around the room; the epitome of the nervous female.

Well, let's see. After all, I had seen the future.

CHAPTER 57
MEMORIES ARE MADE OF THIS

Angela awoke with an abrupt start. Sleep had been fitful, dream-laced. The images of illusion were slow to dissipate, hovering in her mind's eye, their clarity slowly evaporated like mist on a spring morning.

Memories in which Angela had seen herself picking mushrooms with her father decades earlier, a simple act they had often enjoyed together even after she had grown out of childhood. Around her, lazy sheep grazed, their soft, woolly bodies nudging her legs as she plucked mushrooms before they trod them down. The memory of such joy had been profound in her dream, interrupted by a call and a wave from a distant figure across the sunlit meadows.

Homer.

The only man she had ever really loved. They had met too late in life to embrace the excitement of young lovers, yet somehow that never seemed to matter. It was as if he had always been there, invisible, protecting and shadowing her risk strewn life with the wand of a guardian angel.

On dream legs, she cast off her basket and made towards him, yet the faster she ran, the farther away he appeared to become. As she moved away, her father called, his voice diminishing, fading as the words spanned the distance between them. He waved as she turned. Torn between father and the man she loved, Angela waved back but when she turned, in the blink of an eye, her father had disappeared.

Disconsolate, Angela felt sheep push against her leg. She turned again, searching for Homer, but he too was no longer there, leaving just the horizon, empty, save for the rising ball of a sun eclipsing slowly behind purple clouds.

I must have sat there for several minutes before realising the screen was already switched on. Behind the black rectangle was a faint, ghostly image.

"*I wondered when you would wake up.*"

The voice spoke from the dark screen, words with a sharp, satirical edge.

Involuntarily, I jumped.

With a slow, dawning effect, the ghost became real. Hugh Littlemore, my mother's husband, metamorphosed into life. He was sitting, cross-legged, in my father's study, in what had been his favourite leather chair. His pose set the tone for what was to follow.

"So, Grace, how was your night's accommodation? Any signs of sickness yet?"

Littlemore smiled at his own question.

I ignored his feigned, smug concern. "If you're enquiring about the radioactive box in which you imprisoned us, it's clear that trick won't fool any coroner and never escape an autopsy."

Littlemore shrugged and waved a dismissive hand.

"That's the nice thing about pigs, they're not fussy eaters and don't expect their food to have been the subject of an autopsy."

I returned his stony glare; mutual loathing avoids any need for false civility.

"What you're doing will become public knowledge. It won't matter how many of us you kill. Your act of poisoning the countryside," I paused, "in the pursuit of absolute control will bring you down. The question is, can you be broken before you leave your stain of an eternal legacy?"

Littlemore smiled at my outrage and shook his head. It was unusual to see him casually dressed. For once he looked almost human, yet still a usurper in my family home, a stain on my father's legacy.

"Sadly, delusion seems to be a family trait."

I felt a sensation of even deeper chill surge through me.

"Where's mother?"

"Away. Resting."

Why was it that he only seemed to smile when discussing something unpleasant?

"Your behaviour in recent months, now so plainly in the public domain, has caused her even greater anxiety and trauma. Caroline needs care and attention to help her recover."

In an instant, the smile was eclipsed. "As, so obviously, do you."

'So,' I thought. 'We're starting to get to the point.'

"Personally, Grace, it matters little to me whether you live or kill yourself by your misguided actions."

A hand appeared at his side, placing a steaming mug of coffee at his elbow. Momentarily, his son, a second ghost in the shadows, appeared at the edge of the camera. Father and son, one the apprentice of the other.

For a moment, Littlemore turned his attention away. Nervous, I flicked a tentative glance at my watch, feeling a sense of relief when a tiny blue light winked back at me from behind the sweep of the second hand.

Littlemore picked up his mug and gestured provocatively in my direction, guessing at my unquenched raging thirst.

"Frankly, Grace," he even made my name sound an obscenity. "We're only having this cosy little chat for the sake of your mother. I'm indifferent to your fate. But, I offer you a way out."

He paused to drink, the eyes of a hawk, no, a vulture, regarding me over the rim of the mug as he made great play of enjoying his coffee.

"You have a choice to make. You can make a public disclaimer for the folly of your actions, disclose all you know of the terrorist organisation for which you work and commit yourself," (he made great importance on the word 'commit'), "to a course of indefinite, corrective therapy."

"Or?" I needed him to clearly spell out his alternative.

"Or?" He paused to affect a look to the heavens as if for inspiration. "Like all subversives, you have to be removed *from the public domain. The people of this country expect to be protected. We can't leave terrorists to freely wander the streets."*

"Presumably I'm entitled to a trial, even if it's merely for show?"

"Quite so. But so very few of your kind live long enough for the courts to get around to trying them."

"Ah. That explains the radioactive boxes you use to store the hot poisonous material you use to pollute the countryside. Why not hold me on remand, in prison, like all others awaiting trial?"

"Because people like you are subversives, you pollute the minds of others under the cover of the myth of saving the planet."

Ever so slightly, Littlemore's voice rose in the octave. Talking with me was, as always, starting to irritate him.

"So you murder people like me by imprisoning us in the storage containers with which you perpetrate your crimes."

"Such emotive language. But you're missing the point. The people you claim you represent don't care. What they do want is civil obedience, law and order, and the preservation of their well-fed, peaceful lives. That means keeping jobs, the lights switched on and affordable warmth in their homes; the exact opposite of all that you offer them. Frankly, Grace, they don't care what happens to terrorists like you so long as it doesn't upset the status quo."

I laughed cynically.

"Fine words, but I don't recall that you've asked them for their opinion."

His smile broadened.

"That's precisely why we're holding a snap general election. My mandate will be to rid the population of anarchistic influences such as those you represent. You're dangerous, Grace, like a rabid dog loose amongst us, and like all rabid animals, we need to be rid of you."

"While you steal the next election and reduce vast tracts of this country to radioactive wastelands and pocket the profits."

It was my turn to show anger, spitting out the words laced in venom.

"My, my, such hysteria. Even if you are right, what are a few dozen square miles of fenced off radiated wasteland compared with the benefit of cheap energy and our nuclear power stations free from the scourge of radioactive waste."

For a moment, we glowered at one another like a pair of pitbulls, circling in a cage.

I sighed loudly.

"It would seem that you think you have the upper hand. The options you offer are that I either sanction your crimes, allow you to continue, and submit myself to a brain lobotomy, or die slowly from radiation sickness waiting for you to bring me to a trial that will never happen."

"So succinctly put. Accept that you and your dangerous cohort have lost the argument, Grace. Submit to the will of the people. They don't care what happens to you. They do care about being returned to the stone age, which is the consequence of your lunatic fringe ideas."

I had achieved little, but enough.

His face held the look of a smug bully, rejoicing in his own version of triumph. He thought he had won the argument. All he needed to do now was arrange his victory in the upcoming election, into which he intended to induce my complicity.

He must have seen the distraught look on my face and interpreted it as the look of defeat. Inside, I glowed. Hidden behind the bruised, bloody mask of my face was the conviction that it just might not be as straightforward as he planned.

CHAPTER 58
THE PATH OF FATE

"We'll charge them together," Wailes said. "That way they can hold hands."

The smug grin that followed was a deliberate homophobic slight. Allison could have happily rammed it down his throat.

"Patience," she whispered to herself. "Patience. Just wait." Swallowing hard, she forced a grin.

"Good idea, Sarge. But we'll still need two sets of paperwork, not one."

It was all against procedure, but who was to know or care, for that matter.

Grace and Olwyn were taken to the interview room, shadowed by a pair of Wailes 'special constables' borrowed from Miller for extra-ordinary duties at the instruction of the Home Office on the pretext of dealing with the manpower shortage. At least these two could speak English. Allison suspected they were armed, though they had the sense to keep their weapons concealed.

They followed them into a room far too small for six people. Apprehensive, Olwyn fired an anxious glance in Allison's direction as she was pushed into the room. It was overcrowded; there were only four chairs and a small table.

Allison noticed zip ties had been reapplied to the wrists of both women. She nodded towards the nylon restraints.

"Don't think we need the heavies to stay in here, Sarge." The very act of talking to Wailes stuck in her throat.

Wailes looked thoughtful for a moment before gesturing to the two men to leave. Reluctant to obey, one of the men questioned his decision, causing a distraction.

Allison grasped her opportunity, urgently signalling to Olwyn with her eyes, 'Be ready. Follow my lead.' An unspoken message of encouragement she hoped that Olwyn or Grace understood. She was going to have to pull off a convincing act in the next few minutes if there was to be any hope of setting them free.

After some heated words, the men left. Wailes locked the door behind them, sliding the key into his jacket pocket.

"Why are we still here?" Olwyn began with a challenge, glaring hard at both of them.

"I'm not prepared to listen to anything you have to say without a lawyer present."

Wailes flipped open a file on the desk in front of him and found a directive on Home Office headed paper. He held it up for them to see.

"Your rights under the latest emergency Anti-Terrorist legislation. Seems we don't have to provide you with legal representation until after we've charged you."

With a flippant gesture, he slid the paper across the table to make his point.

Allison intervened.

"We can come to that in a minute, Sarge. Just need to get the formalities out of the way first. The charge forms are in the drawer in front of you."

This would be the risky bit. She had deliberately chosen the right-hand chair. For this to work, she had to make sure Wailes was sitting on her left side. At first he seemed puzzled, instinctively objecting in principle to any instruction given by a woman.

Time held its breath. Allison looked down at the table, desperate to avoid eye contact with anyone. For a moment she thought he would refuse and override the tedious unnecessary paperwork in his keenness to be rid of the two women, handing them in to the 'care' of his paymasters as soon as possible.

"Best get the paperwork right, in case anyone comes looking for them. We might need to wash our hands of any involvement in their disappearance."

Wailes nodded; truculence trumped by an instinct to avoid blame. Now seated at the desk, he unlocked the drawer with his key, smirked at the two women opposite him and slid his hand into the drawer to take out the forms that Allison was so tiresomely insistent about.

It was no more than the lip of a plastic box peeking from Allison's shoulder bag, draped across the back of her chair, which jarred an alarm bell in his brain. Too late, he knew he should have checked the drawer before putting his hand inside.

Wailes flew backwards in the manner of a man stabbed. An apt description, simple statement of fact.

After weeks imprisoned in her box, 'Scorpio' took her revenge on the wrist of her keeper, pumping all the venom she could muster into the carelessly proffered vein.

Eclipsed by horror, time stopped.

As Wailes fell to the floor, Grace and Olwyn jumped to their feet, knocking over chairs, backing away from the table, shocked by what was happening, oblivious as Allison hastily cut their wrist ties.

"Be ready to leave when I say," Allison said in a low voice. "There are armed men outside the door and we have to deal with things here first."

The initial shock of the sting was beginning to wear off. Wailes was trying to scrabble to his feet, groping frantically for his jacket and the key to the door. He needed the anti-venom he always carried, essential for any collector of poisonous *Arachnida*.

But before he could raise himself from the floor, Allison placed a foot and all her weight on his wrist, already swelling painfully as the venom raced through his bloodstream to do its work.

"Looking for something, Sarge?"

Her words were painted with contempt. Her fingers held the key as she threw his jacket to the floor.

She had come prepared; the prospect of a vengeful scorpion loose in the small room filled her with dread. She opened her bag and withdrew the glove and tongs given to her by Homer and removed an agitated 'Scorpio' still hiding in the desk drawer.

Allison turned, twisting her foot and painfully pinning Wailes's outstretched arm as his spare hand tore frantically at her leg. Was this murder? She didn't think so. After all, an animal can only behave as its instinct directs.

How many times can a scorpion sting its victim? Allison wasn't certain, but there was no harm in being sure.

Without more ado, she leaned forward and dropped the scorpion inside Wailes's open shirt front. With his medication flushed down the toilet, she felt certain that chronic heart disease would do the rest.

Within a minute, Wailes was too weak to move.

"Have you still got that 'tampon' your boss gave you?" Allison spoke, an urgent note in her voice.

Rendered speechless by what had just happened, Olwyn could only nod.

"Right, give it to me and prepare yourself for when I use it. There are 'special constables' on the other side of this door and it will appear less suspicious if I go out first."

Allison took the gas hood from Olwyn's bag.

"It's the only way we're going to get out of here. Remove your socks, tie them together and make a mask around your mouth. When you leave this room, grab hold of me and keep your eyes tight shut. I'll lead you outside, but remember, the men might recover quickly, so we must move quickly."

She paused briefly while the two women removed their socks. Olwyn pulled a face at the thought of how they were to be used.

"It will be worse without them," Allison said, reading her mind.

"Quickly. Ready?"

They both nodded.

The young man was totally flummoxed when Allison opened the door and handed him the cardboard tube. Though it carried no brand name, he was certain he knew what it was.

"The cord has got stuck. Can you pull it out?"

Mortified as much as confused, he hesitated, thought to question her, but wanted to get rid of the embarrassment she had thrust into his hands. These odd British women certainly made strange requests on their men. He grasped the errant cord between his fingers.

Had he thought to look up before pulling on the cord, he might have seen Allison placing the gas hood over her head. To his surprise, the cord came free with ease and for the briefest moment he thought he had broken something as the entire room around him was enveloped in a cloud of choking, white gas.

Coughing and stumbling, even with the protection of the gas hood, Allison's eyes streamed and her breath snagged in her throat. The three women escaped the police station through the fire exit before the canister had finished ejecting its contents. They left a building filled with the shouts and curses of the men caught inside.

"My white car at the end of the car park. Marius is waiting for us. He'll drive," Allison said, suddenly remembering she hadn't asked if he could drive.

Grace and Olwyn couldn't answer, fighting for breath from the effects of gas. Whoever had prepared the device hadn't stinted on its potency.

Allison was threading a route through a cluster of parked cars. It was slow progress but she reasoned it made them less conspicuous. Halfway across the car park Grace tripped and fell, costing them precious seconds.

They had just cleared the parked cars when Olwyn stopped, bent double, fighting a violent bout of retching. A lung-full of CS gas on top of the night in the container was a toxic cocktail.

"Don't stop," Allison pleaded.

Fifty yards away, Marius had positioned her car, doors open, for a hasty departure.

Perhaps they had been too slow, or one of Wailes's men had been less affected by the gas, but suddenly several shots rang out. Nearby a windscreen shattered, bullets ricocheted from the tarmac. Spiked by alarm, they increased their pace.

Breathless, they pushed Olwyn into the rear seat, accompanied by the sound of more shots. In less than a minute they would be speeding out of the car park; maybe luck was now on their side.

As Allison made her way to the other side of the car she suddenly stumbled, her injured left arm clutching her right shoulder where a ballooning red rose of blood was already staining her white shirt.

"Oh, no, not again." Allison gasped, the words a sigh of frustration, as she collapsed into the car on top of Olwyn.

Homer woke with a jolt. Lying against him, Joss stirred, a barely audible grumble vibrating her body. Something was up.

Homer blinked his eyes, misted by sleep.

"What is it, girl?"

Joss grumbled again, the note so low and deep it was almost subliminal. She half stood, adopting the crouching stance she used to challenge errant sheep.

Homer rubbed his eyes. Were precious seconds forfeited while he struggled to come to his senses? Could it have made a difference?

He knelt up on his haunches to the side of the dog, following the direction of her gaze. In the grey light, he could see nothing out of the ordinary until a slender, almost transparent figure, crossed his line of vision between the trunks of the trees.

Angela? In the dawn light she was walking slowly down the track from his cottage, coatless in the morning chill, with arms extended in greeting as though towards a long absent acquaintance.

At first the woodland scrub obscured Homer's sight. Too late he saw him. A figure, clad in a worn, green jacket, with boots and a poacher's bag, walked towards Angela with fixed arms, shoulders pinned by the message he carried. A cap hid the features of the stranger Homer had always anticipated.

But Homer didn't need recognition; he knew in the way of the hunted confronted by those who seek him. His legs were running before his brain had time to react.

Behind Angela, in her wake, five men had fanned out to form a crescent, matching her pace, anticipating the approach of the man they sought.

Sliding on the leaf litter, Homer and Joss plunged down the slope towards the catastrophe developing in front of them. From Bagdad to Erbil, Homer had seen this appalling tableau unfold before, could recognise what was about to happen.

He wanted to shout in warning, but the words choked in his throat as he ran. He wanted to shoot, but the distance was too great, and anyway, there wasn't time to load the cartridges.

Inescapably, fate had decided the outcome as Angela reached out to embrace the mirage of the man she loved.

Miller was confused. Unexpectedly, Angela had slipped out of the door before any of his tired men could react. She hadn't even looked out of the window, instinctively aware that Homer was approaching.

They followed her; her head start mattered little. His men fanned out to either side, while he shadowed Angela's footsteps. He was banking that Homer, no matter the odds, wouldn't abandon her. Coatless, with arms extended, she moved forward to greet him.

This would be easy; soon Miller would have his captive and redeem his reputation in the eyes of Bremer, tarnished by weeks of disruption orchestrated by Homer's guiding hand.

As the gap between them closed, he could see the approaching figure more clearly. Was he blinded by the prospect of such simple success? Everything about the man seemed to fit, yet somewhere, in the deep recesses of his mind, an alarm bell began to ring.

Miller slowed, hesitated. Something felt wrong. The coat, the profile, the figure, all resembled Homer, but something wasn't right. His arms? Why did they …?

The last thing he heard was Angela call out a name.

"Homer."

A warning, or the whisper of devotion?

CHAPTER 59
THE PROTECTION OF LOVE

Even from fifty yards, the shockwave lifted Homer off his feet. He fell hard on his back, covered in debris, as the echo of the explosion reverberated painfully in his ears.

Miraculously, Joss was unscathed. She had been running, her profile low to the ground, protected from the worst of the blast by a fallen tree trunk. Almost without breaking stride, she circled back, tail between her legs, racing away from the scene of the detonation.

Searching for Homer, Joss found him struggling to collect himself, covered in snow, debris and fallen branches. He was winded, cut and bruised, and in pain, having fallen on his broken hand, which was twisted painfully beneath his body. With difficulty, Homer prised himself into an upright position.

Around them, a cloud of grey smoke slowly cleared. On the track, a scorched blast circle described a radius in which seven figures had played a scene Homer had been helpless to prevent. Above them, a gallery of crows screamed raucously as they spiralled in an unruly gaggle above the tree tops, evaluating repairs to their damaged nests.

Where seven figures had stood, random dark shapes now littered the ground in a loose circle. A smouldering depression in the track now existed from which the tendrils of grey smoke drifted in veins into the cold daylight.

Without even a glance, Homer knew what had happened. He had been here before, witness to the aftermath of a similar scene in a busy market place in Mosul, which had left the same landscape of pathetic human flotsam in its aftermath. Explosions leave their own smell. A mixture of raw, hard, burnt chemicals and burnt human flesh. This was no different.

He expected Joss to keep well clear, but instead she flew like an arrow towards one pathetic shape, the smallest in the cluster. Homer knew without looking.

The air fell silent, the rooks and crows returned and slowly began to settle, leaving a void filled by a piercing, primeval cry to echo through the listening trees.

Breathing and seeing have to be re-learnt when lungs and eyes have been seared by tear gas. In the back seat of the car, I had just begun that journey when the car lurched and Allison Markham fell on top of me. The smell of warm blood on my face stifled any protest before I had time to utter it.

It was hard to make sense of what had happened. Distracted by the effects of gas, the sound of gunshots went unnoticed. But Allison was bleeding from a nasty wound in the top of her chest. In a state of shock, she was gabbling, making little sense.

"It's really too much; that's both arms now."

The car bounced and lurched; no one had thought to ask Marius if he knew how to drive. In fairness, he just got on with it, but as we careered down the High Street, the broken wing mirrors of parked cars suggested he had little idea. Once the road opened up, it seemed that he could at least hold direction with the car, even if he couldn't change gear.

Less affected by the gas, Olwyn climbed over from the front seat to join me, leaving Marius to do his best. It took her only a few seconds to realise Allison had been seriously hurt. I felt Olwyn's hands grip me, pulling me forward, releasing the back of the seat. With the seat laid flat, she pushed me out of the way and rolled Allison sideways, her feet in the boot.

"Hospital?" I asked.

"No, too dangerous. We need Angela," was her immediate decision.

Olwyn did well to take charge of the situation. She ripped open Allison's shirt revealing a gaping hole that welled blood, just below her right collarbone.

"Exit wound," I heard her mutter, snatching the discarded balled socks, a legacy of our improvised gas masks.

"Take over from Marius," she directed, pressing a sock ball firmly against the gaping wound.

"I'll look after Allison. Get us to Homer's place as fast as you can."

Marius actually seemed disappointed when I came to take over. As we shuddered to a stalled halt, I suspected he had been rather enjoying himself.

I drew away and flicked a glance in Olwyn's direction. She had used the balled socks front and back, bound in place with a torn scarf with knotted ends. Wrapped around Allison, it held our smelly socks in compression against her wounds; hardly hygienic, but an emergency stop gap until we found Homer and Angela.

Using Olwyn's phone, Marius gave directions which took us away from main roads, warming to his new role as navigator. In the back, Olwyn sat with Allison's head on her lap, an almost empty water bottle held to her lips.

This all had the feeling of deja-vu. Though I tried to push my fears to one side, I felt an unnerving sensation tremble through me. I had dreamt this all before. The outcome had left a feeling of dread. I could only hope that for once my dreams might be wrong.

They found Homer, cross-legged on the track in the midst of a scene of devastation. Horrified by what she saw, Grace slowed the car to a halt. The radius of damage created a wide circle of burnt vegetation and shattered trees, littered with the remains of corpses.

Grace sat stunned, holding the steering wheel, appalled to be found right yet again. She didn't need to get out of the car to know what had happened.

"Where does this end?"

Her unanswered question was full of self-reproach, as though what she dreamt became reality; a self-fulfilling prophecy.

"Stay here," Grace said softly to the others as she left the car.

Slowly, she walked towards Homer. He was sitting with his back to her, cradling a wrapped white sheet stained with blood, the discordant notes of a sad lament drifting from his lips.

Beyond, the world looked normal; the cottage door was open, curtains drawn at the windows. Bright sunlight sparkled through the trees. A few metres away a blackened depression bridged the track revealing bare, raw earth, its edges burnt and scoured.

"Homer," she touched his shoulder.

She felt him flinch. Grace didn't need an explanation of the scene around her; she already knew.

It made what came next easier to handle.

"So they came for him." Marius suddenly appeared beside me.

"Yes."

"He always said that would happen. Except …"

"… Angela intercepted them. She gave her life to spare Homer."

Beside me, Marius made a sound, a sigh that ended in a sob.

"Poor Angela."

I shook my head. "She would have been happy in her way. She cheated cancer and re-paid her debt to Homer in the process. Perhaps fate always intended it that way."

Together, we stood in shared grief, until interrupted by a plaintive call from Olwyn.

"Can someone help me here? I can't keep Allison awake."

Reality returned, making abrupt demands for the living.

"Homer."

His spoken name implied direction and compassion in equal measure.

"We can't stay here. There's nothing you can do for Angela. We need to leave this place. Quickly."

Homer gestured with his free hand, swatting Grace away like some irritating fly.

With her broken body wrapped in a sheet, Angela's face looked surprisingly serene and unmarked, released from the pain that had haunted her.

Grace was thinking quickly. There was much to be done. She turned quickly to Marius.

"Find Homer's driving licence. Anything that identifies him."

Leaving him bemused, she moved to check the other victims. She found what was left of Miller. Directly behind Angela, he had taken the full force of the explosion. Of the other four, two were still alive, but unlikely to survive the wait for an ambulance.

She returned to Olwyn in the car; the engine was still running.

"Two minutes. Allison's phone must be in her jacket. Find the nearest hospital. We'll have to risk taking her straight there."

Grace paused, adding an explanation.

"They're all dead, including Angela. It was a suicide bomber that had been sent for Homer. She must have intercepted him."

Marius arrived at her side, Homer's driving licence and bank card in his hand. Grace dropped them on the ground and stamped hard. She didn't explain.

"See if you can persuade Homer to move. We can't stay here."

In a discarded rucksack she found zip ties. One badly disfigured body fitted her plan, head and face burnt black by the full force of the blast. It was a macabre task; she zip tied the lifeless, broken hands together, checked for existing ID and inserted Homer's in their place.

Marius caught up with me as I hurried back to the car where Olwyn and Allison waited.

"I've persuaded Homer to move. He says there's a disused woodcutter's cabin a few miles away, deeper into

the woods. It should be safe for a few hours while Bremer gets his act together. It's the best I can do."

Marius looked at me uncertainly. "How long do you think we have before someone comes looking?"

"Hours. Not long. The police will be in turmoil; Bremer will re-group after what's happened, so we need to move quickly."

I hesitated, handing Marius my watch.

"You'll find a video file on this. It's something I made in the police station. Unbelievably, no one noticed. It's essential it's uploaded to an email address as soon as possible."

"Does it need editing?"

"No. Just send it raw, as it is. The recipient will know what to do with it. But it's urgent. There won't be much time."

I snatched a pen from my pocket and scribbled the email address on his hand.

"Don't lose it. Wash your hands when you've sent the file."

I only just remembered to say, "And send me the location of the refuge so we can find you. It's risky, but that's a chance we'll have to take."

Grace almost overlooked their watchman. Detached and alone, Joss sat removed from the scene of human carnage. For a moment, their eyes met. She gazed back at Grace with deep, fathomless eyes, reflecting wells of incomprehension.

"Joss," Grace whispered in her ear. "Stay with Homer until I get back."

It seemed a forlorn request, but as Grace accelerated the car down the track, Joss took up guard beside Homer and Marius as they bore Angela away through the trees.

It was only later that Grace realised she had forgotten to tell Marius that she was using Allison's phone.

Using a rear services entrance, we entered the hospital grounds. With the help of Homer's hip flask, we had managed to revive Allison. Her loss of blood had eased, but her breathing had become more laboured.

"Do you think they'll track her phone?" Olwyn asked nervously, glancing at the sat-nav signal used to locate the hospital.

I could only shrug; it was a risk we would have to take.

In the back of the car Olwyn was performing an admirable job in keeping Allison conscious, but medical attention was becoming ever more pressing.

I drove cautiously to the rear of the hospital, aware of the watching eyes of the cameras, wishing I had thought to ask Homer for his jamming device. Too late for that now.

By chance, we found a waste bin containing dirty laundry waiting for collection. Two sets of used blue scrubs were easy to find. With no one about, we hastily donned the soiled coveralls. A single CCTV camera overlooked the area and didn't track or follow us. Perhaps, optimistically, I took that as an encouraging sign.

Olwyn hastily rehearsed the script with a breathless Allison, painfully aware that her injured friend was being asked to disguise their presence for a second time. I left them fine-tuning the cover story while I went in search of a trolley.

Accident and emergency was thronged with activity. One man's misfortune can be a blessing to another. A road accident, involving a coach party on the nearby bypass, had inadvertently come to our rescue. Most were cases of minor injuries; cuts, abrasions and shock. Amidst the throng of stroboscopic blue lights and shouting voices, slipping away with a trolley was easily overlooked. Everyone seemed focused on the coach casualties; wheeling the rattling stretcher back to the service area went unchallenged.

Together, we lifted Allison onto the trolley. What the nurses would make of our improvised sock and bandage, I couldn't begin to imagine.

"We need to move quickly while they're busy in there. Once they're quieter, someone will start asking awkward questions."

I wheeled the trolley, Olwyn held Allison's hand. In normal circumstances, even two medical staff without passes, arriving with a badly injured patient, would have been cause for comment. We even managed to queue jump, pleading serious injury, without anyone questioning our presence.

It was barely moments before we made our brief farewells and slipped away, leaving a nurse and harassed doctor making a detailed examination of Allison's condition.

As they parted, Olwyn paused to plant a parting kiss on the lips of her friend. Disappearing into the crowded reception area, we left a smile on Allison's face that somehow made our act of abandonment more tolerable.

CHAPTER 60
SURVIVORS

It took several hours to find the cabin. Distracted by his burden, Homer missed a significant turning point, adding an extra mile to carry Angela's broken body. On several occasions, Marius thought of asking if he should, could, share the sad load. One look at Homer's face answered his unasked question.

The cabin had been deserted for years. Hidden away, there were few, if any, passers-by and it had survived with only the woods to protect the weathered exterior. Close by, the remains of a small wood store offered dry logs. Marius had the forethought to hastily salvage a few basics from Homer's cottage before they had left. He lit the rusted pot-belly stove and swept out the worst of the mice droppings.

They spoke little; what was there to say? Together, they found several discarded wooden pallets and laid Angela's body on the slatted bed, the once white shroud now dyed deep red with her blood.

While Marius set water to boil, he watched Homer dig a shallow pit under the watchful eye of Joss. The cabin had been well sited. On high ground, beneath the canopy of trees, the ground was dry loam mixed with pine needles, and the pit was soon dug.

"I'm off to collect wood," Homer said as Marius pushed a mug of coffee into his hands stained black by dried blood and pine needles.

"There's logs." Marius nodded to the wood store.

Homer shook his head. "I need brushwood, dead branches, hardwood that will burn hot and quickly. There isn't much time."

His hooded eyes searched an unseen distant horizon; a raised brow answered an unasked question. In a minute Homer was gone, faithful Joss trailing in his wake, ever watchful, forever vigilant.

Left alone, Marius examined the watch Grace had given him. At first glance, it appeared just a copy of an antique, its face aged and crazed, a second-hand slowly describing the arc of passing time.

Marius frowned. She had said there was a file in her watch? Puzzled, he examined the case. Apart from the maker's name and the number of jewels in its action, it told him little. But Grace had been insistent; there was a file stored inside it and she had made great emphasis that it should be sent to the address hastily written on his hand.

The watch hands showed the wrong time, so Marius eased out the adjustment wheel and re-set the time. Pressing the wheel back into place coincided with an alert signal from his phone. The watch had made a bluetooth connection.

"Clever," Marius whispered to himself while he unfolded the blood soaked bandana Grace had thrust into his hand along with the watch.

So that's how she had pulled it off. She had worn the bandana to seal the gash at her temple when they had been overpowered in Angela's cottage. Amazingly, no one had thought to check either her watch or the bandage; why should they? She was little more than a threadbare amateur in their eyes; just another hopelessly misguided eco-terrorist, causing ripples in the pond of global politics where she didn't belong.

Marius smiled to himself. Grace had broken into the fracking site on the ill-fated mission that had resulted in the girl, Rosetta, being shot. Somehow she had salvaged the micro camera hidden in her hard hat. It had been a simple job to insert it in her blood stained bandage. After that, her decoy watch did the rest.

The video file easily downloaded onto his phone. Enthralled, he watched the interview between Grace and Littlemore. She must have removed the filthy bandana and placed it on the desk in front of the screen.

He was shocked by the raw, visceral mutual contempt they projected, one for the other. Though he had a sketchy knowledge of politics at best, there was no avoiding the toxic nature of the interview; it was obvious Grace intended the contents for a wider public platform.

"Clever," he repeated, impressed by the simple audacity of her scam.

The email address Grace had scribbled on his hand seemed nothing out of the ordinary. He stared at the address, at first thinking he must have misread it. Yet she had been emphatic. Even allowing for the carnage of the scene that had surrounded them she wouldn't have made a mistake. But why send such an important file to an obscure whisky distillery in the Highlands of Scotland?

With a sigh, he wrote the address Grace had written on his hand into the message box of his phone.

jmh5@glenmoraymalts.gov.uk

At the swipe of his finger, from a penniless woodcutter's cabin in the middle of nowhere, Marius unwittingly initiated a political earthquake.

"Is this the real thing between you and Allison?" I asked Olwyn the question as much for distraction as curiosity.

We were lost, though I was trying hard not to admit the fact. Our success at having delivered Allison and escaped from the hospital without being questioned caused an initial bubble of euphoria. That quickly evaporated with the realisation we had no clear idea where Homer had gone and no means of contacting him.

We abandoned the car in a concealed spot about a mile from Homer's cottage and hiked to the spot still littered with the remains of Miller and his men. They were all dead. The bomber had fulfilled his task to a degree he could never have imagined.

This was the point Homer and Marius had set out from as we sped away to find a hospital. I estimated a two-mile radius and risked looking at a Google satellite view on Allison's phone, searching for anything that might resemble a woodland cabin. There was a strong probability that Bremer would see the signal and despatch a drone, but that was a risk we had to take.

Luck was on our side. The image had been taken in winter, but I was still uncertain when I spotted something that could be the cabin. I took a compass bearing and switched off the phone in case it was being tracked, and we started walking with nothing more than a compass and a step counter.

We were filthy and tired; it was expecting a lot. It should have taken around five thousand steps, but after an hour it was obvious we were lost. I considered the risk of using the phone again to locate our position, but the dangers of doing that outweighed the suspicion that we could be going around in circles.

"I thought Marius had made it plainly obvious he was smitten with you?" I continued, noticing a large Scots pine I was sure we were passing for the second time.

She could have easily told me to mind my own business but that wasn't Olwyn's style.

"It's the story of my life. I seem to have the looks that attract both men and women; often at the same time."

"I bet that makes life interesting," I replied.

We had passed the tree and I paused to take a bearing and check the step counter, at least making a show of knowing what I was doing.

My tired brain was consumed by the anxiety that Marius might have forgotten to send the video. 'Blue Horizon' would be thrown by what happened at the police station and Homer's cottage, but Bremer would soon recover and had access to deep resources. He would already know we had slipped the net. The events at Homer's cottage would cause confusion for a while, but a search wouldn't be long in coming. Time, like the sand in an hourglass, was slipping away fast.

"So," I continued, trying to mentally re-calibrate our position. "Who do you choose; one, both, or neither?"

I'll say one thing for Olwyn, she's disarmingly open when it comes to personal matters.

"Allison is lonely. She's attracted to me, I like her a lot, but it's not a reciprocal feeling, not in the way it is for her."

Olwyn looked around her, as though the answer to her dilemmas might be found hidden amongst the trees.

"I'm generous with Allison, but she knows my future lies in a relationship with a man."

"Marius? He's obviously very keen on you."

She looked at me incredulously.

"You really think that either of us will survive for long enough to have future relationships?"

Without even needing to think, I knew the path my destiny held. But Olwyn didn't feature in that window; there was a chance that fate would offer her a future. I gave her a comforting smile. I had no reason to deceive her.

We must have chased the subject of relationships for at least another half-hour. Despite my best endeavours, we seemed to be approaching the Scots pine for a third occasion and this time Olwyn was bound to notice. Very soon, darkness would descend and the chill of the night would settle an icy hand on our shoulders.

The prospect of using our solitary phone beckoned, its signal a talisman to a searching drone. We might find our way to Homer, but it would most likely bring Bremer and his cohorts hard on our heels.

Yet, with nothing to drink or eat, and a generous dose of radiation in our bodies, a hard, cold night under a clear star-filled sky offered an ominous portent.

The lesser of two evils?

My finger hovered just above the 'on' button when a slender black and white apparition suddenly appeared on the path in front of us.

The glow from the burning pyre bathed the surrounding trees with an ethereal orange light as Grace and Olwyn approached. It was dark when they arrived. Without Joss, even with the help of sat-nav, they doubted ever finding the cabin. Overgrown from years of neglect, it would have gone unnoticed by even the closest passer-by.

A look of relief lit up Marius's face as they entered. The hug of welcome he gave to both women told its own story.

On a gas ring, a pan of soup gently simmered; packet soup, woodland herbs and stale bread hastily gathered from Homer's cottage as they departed. It wasn't much, but to an empty stomach, it smelt like a meal for a king.

"We'd have never found this place without Joss," Grace announced, slumping wearily into a broken chair with missing spindles.

"Where's Homer?"

"Saying farewell to Angela." Marius nodded towards the pyre's reflected flames on the window.

"He won't leave her until it's finished," he said with a note of finality.

Battling with his own emotions, he held Olwyn close, kissing the top of her head.

"And my video?" Grace asked.

Marius grinned.

"Sent. To say it has stirred up a whole lot of trouble is an understatement. Whoever you sent it to has flooded social media on multiple platforms. It caught live newsfeed just a short time ago. Seems someone took exception. It's all been shut down now and the news channels have had to post an apology. 'Fake news'. But not before there were hundreds of downloads."

"So they silenced us?" Olwyn asked with a look. "What does that amount to?"

Marius cocked an eye in the direction of Grace.

"Over-reaction. Given the manner in which the Home Office has responded, no one is going to believe your video."

He paused, thoughtful for a moment.

"Aided by the fact that the price on your head has increased enormously."

He held up his phone screen for the two of them to see. A manipulated version of Grace's face stared back, distorted to give her a wild, half crazed appearance.

Olwyn whistled softly.

"A million pounds. For that, I think I'm tempted to turn you in myself," she said with an attempt at humour.

"Join the queue," Marius added, their laughter providing a note of brevity as the flames outside suddenly reached high into the air, lifting tiny cinders like fireflies into the night.

"So, how long have we got before they track us down? For that amount, every would-be bounty hunter in the country will be searching for you."

Grace turned away, not answering at first, and washed her hands in the bucket beside the door. Drying her hands on a torn cloth, she turned to face them, an unsmiling face with unblinking eyes.

"That's exactly what I'm looking for."

The finality in her words implied that she knew the future. There was nothing she could do to alter that.

Despite her hunger, Grace shared a meagre supper with Joss. The dog thanked her with her eyes. How she had found them was a mystery, as was so often the case with Joss.

For a while, Grace warmed herself by the stove. Outside, the glow of the fire slowly subsided so she decided to leave Olwyn and Marius together and left with Joss to find Homer.

She found him cross-legged beside the fire pit, feeding the last of the brushwood into the flames. Without asking, Grace sat beside him, feeling the pressure of his body ease against her, in a silent request for support.

With a smouldering branch he prodded the bed of red hot embers, encouraging a sudden flare of white flames and cinders to spiral into the darkness.

"Some think the flames carry the spirit into the afterlife," he said, quietly.

"And you?"

"I'll settle for that. Though I'm not sure I buy the thought of an afterlife."

It wasn't the moment for a philosophical discussion, so Grace asked the obvious question that had been troubling her.

"How long … for everything to be consumed?"

He took a deep breath. "Three, four hours. I need another hour to be sure."

Feeling left out, Joss squirmed in between them; nose, shoulders, body. Instinctively, they parted and made room; Angela was as much her friend as theirs.

"In the morning, very early, there's one last thing I have to do," Grace said quietly.

Homer laughed softly at her words. "And that is?"

"I need to post another video; live stream. It will be risky. Littlemore will be on to us the moment we start transmitting."

"Your extremely pissed-off step-father."

Grace shook her head. "No, my mother's husband. My father died."

Homer nodded. It was no time for semantics.

"Either way," she continued, "there isn't room for the two of us in this world. So …"

"Last man standing."

Grace tried to smile. "Something like that, though you're beginning to sound like Clint Eastwood."

They both laughed at the thought.

"I need only a few minutes. Marius will video and transmit live. Will you be able to hold them off if they try to intervene to stop me? I'll understand if you can't."

Her words made an offer her voice didn't want him to accept. Homer sighed in resignation.

"What?" Grace asked.

"Seems Angela was right after all," he said. "Just a shame we're not in Bolivia."

It was almost midnight by the time the five of us, including Joss, settled down to sleep in the meagre confines of the cabin. Marius was briefed, phone charged and prepared, my contact prompted in readiness.

So, my star role approached; the sequel to the now silenced opening salvo of earlier in the day. This time, 'Blue Horizon' would be ready and waiting.

I could only hope that encrypted alerts had been sent to all those who had watched and downloaded the first video, now relegated in the mainstream to a crime of fake news perpetrated by a dangerous wanted terrorist.

Now I needed thousands of silent activists, ordinary people worried for their future, and their children's, to see events that would validate the crimes being perpetuated by the clique now ruling our government.

"Well, let's see about that," I muttered distractedly to the sleeping room.

Only Joss, eyes bright, heard my words. Perhaps she had shared my dreams of the morrow.

CHAPTER 61
THE PRICE OF PENITENCE

I lay awake most of the night, Joss pressed against my side for mutual warmth and support. Eventually I must have dozed for a while until awoken by the whistle of the kettle on the gas ring.

Soft-footed, Homer made tea, a ghost-like apparition in the darkened cabin. Marius and Olwyn were entwined in a sleeping bag, oblivious of the arrival of the new day. With a heavy heart, I thought; no Angela.

Homer handed me a chipped mug.

"There's only dried milk, no sugar, no breakfast," he whispered. "Sunrise will be in ten minutes, half an hour until it rises above the trees."

He looked tired, black rings around his bloodshot eyes.

I had heard him moving in the night, occasionally going outside to check Angela's pyre where he had witnessed a clear, starry, night sky, wondering if somewhere amongst them her spirit now roamed free.

The dawn was blessed by a glorious sunrise, promising a cold clear morning.

Intent on warming stiff limbs, Homer and Joss led off through the woods at a brisk pace, keen to place distance from the cabin, suspecting Bremer would soon be hard on their heels.

Homer had left the remains of the pyre still glowing, even though it advertised their presence at the cabin; he couldn't bear to extinguish the passing of his friend. In his rucksack rested a solitary jar of ash, the only physical evidence that Angela had ever existed. It would be cast to the winds, sharing her with the very woods she loved so much.

"Have you checked passwords?" Grace anxiously asked Marius for the second time, her words etched with concern.

Their contact had changed addresses overnight, new passwords altered with it. The sites were encrypted, hidden in a space 'sub-dark net', knowing the eyes of 'Blue Horizon', caught by surprise the previous day, were watching, waiting, for the first glimmer of their digital presence.

Marius nodded. He had changed his own profile and ID several times, shadowing 'Blue Horizon's digital search.

"Once we start transmitting, keep things tight. You won't have long."

Short on breath, his words were clipped.

"Before they shut us down? How long do we have?" Grace asked.

"Anyone's guess. Five minutes could be optimistic."

Distraction arrived as Joss ran past, completing one of her many wide circuits, checking, searching, scanning their path, alert for ambush or patrol. Bremer would have recovered from the shock of the previous day; from first light, the woods would soon be combed for miles around. Marius predicted their transmission could be jammed in five minutes, their physical capture not far behind.

Grace left Marius with Olwyn and ran to catch up with Homer. He carried his loaded shotgun across the cradle of his arms. Comforting as an image, but it wouldn't be much help against a squad of Bremer's mercenaries.

"Is everyone clear on the rendezvous afterwards?" Grace asked, her voice fretting.

"Yes," Homer said with pained forbearance.

They had been over this countless times the previous evening.

"Though that pre-supposes we are going to get away with this."

His words were tinged with irony.

"Good," she replied in a breathless voice.

"Afterwards, get them to the car. Olwyn knows where we hid it. You are certain Marius can hot-wire another car when they need to change?"

Homer stopped, his faced creased by concern.

"What aren't you telling me, Grace? 'They' doesn't sound as though it includes you?"

She shook her head dismissively. "Just me being anxious." Then added, "Just get them to safety. All hell will break loose when we do this."

Homer tried to smile encouragingly.

"Try not to dramatize things. After all, who on earth is going to pay any attention to you, given that your current reputation provides ample qualification for a life sentence in a mental hospital. I'd have thought their best way to deal with you is to ignore you, dismiss you as a total irrelevance. Play the hysterical fake news card, you'll be forgotten inside a day. Given that scenario, I don't think you have anything to fear."

Considered from that perspective, what did she have to worry about?

Try asking wounded Rosetta, seven bodies on the track, and Angela's funeral pyre. They all served to confound his words.

The sun raised its golden orb above the trees, bathing the frosty mantle in the clearing in steamy, white light. I had chosen a rough pasture on a downhill slope, with drill heads of the fracking compound just visible in the distance above the crowns of surrounding trees.

I could stand with my back to these incriminating masts, my face clearly visible to the sun, hair matted, wounds blooded, bruises a pallet of purple and black.

Marius re-fixed my blood stained bandana.

"It's your badge of office," he joked.

"It even features on your 'Wanted' poster. No question that it's you with this on your head."

He might well be right, but it did little to ease my feeling of exposed anxiety.

"We need to start soon," he added, casting a worried glance at what might lurk in the trees around us.

As I prepared my thoughts, Joss arrived. She sniffed my outstretched hand, grasping my cuff with her teeth, trying to draw me back towards the trees.

"Soon, Joss," I said with as much confidence as I could. "I'll come with you soon."

I fondled her head. Such a bond had grown between us.

"We'll be together soon."

Homer called her. Undecided, she looked back at me as though she had already read my thoughts.

In front of me, Marius held his phone, Olwyn to one side with a microphone, Homer beyond them, feigning indifference, beneath a cloud of blue smoke from a lit pipe. I had no idea he smoked and couldn't decide if it was an act or if he actually needed to settle his nerves. I hoped it wouldn't induce another seizure.

Marius dropped his arm, the signal that he had started videoing on live feed.

"So, it's me again, 'Crazy Grace' according to the despot who runs 'Blue Horizon'."

"As you can see, I'm free of their clutches, despite their rough tactics and a night in one of their radioactive containers. I leave you," I paused, fighting rising anxiety, gulping air, "to draw your own conclusions on my guilt or my sanity. In making this video, undoubtedly my last, I leave you to make your own decisions on both counts."

Without thinking, I rubbed the dry, bloody clot on the side of my head.

"Either way, my body has been beaten and poisoned with radioactivity on the instruction of my mother's husband," (that was the closest he was going to get to an admission of family), "with the intention of shutting me up. Well, 'crazy' I might well be, but that doesn't alter the truth of the facts."

I had to stop for a second as a band of anxiety constricted my chest. Olwyn shot me a worried glance. I nodded and continued.

"Behind me, you can see the drill heads of fracking Site 17, to give it an official title. Despite the lies peddled, tainting me and my colleagues as perpetrators of anarchy, intent on returning you all to the stone age, the crime here is not of our actions, it's what is being hidden from you beneath the ground under those drill heads."

I paused to point an arm in the direction of the fracking site.

"If this were just about the practice of extracting oil and gas from below the ground, a method in itself that harms the environment, it would be bad enough. But that's not the crime we've discovered."

I had to take a breath. Or had something in the distance caught the corner of my eye? Joss made a barely perceptible grumble, performing that recognisable shuffle of impatience with her front feet. Had she sensed something?

Marius, one hand holding the mobile with which he was filming, gave a hurry-up signal with his spare hand. I continued.

"My friends and I have spent months finding out why 'Blue Horizon' wanted total control over the fracking industry. They ridicule investment in renewables and ignore all debate on ending burning fossil fuels. But to what end?"

"Where does the money come from that enables a political party to start from scratch and dominate our country in such a short period of time? Has no one ever asked themselves that question? When they have, what means have been used to silence them?"

"We have discovered that hidden behind an umbrella of shell companies and a veil of blackmail and murder, lies the crime this cabal is using to steal the levers of power in front of our very eyes. We're witnessing the rise of fascism in the guise of popularism, the ultimate 'wolf in sheep's clothing', stealing our democracy and committing a crime that will last thousands of years in the process."

I sensed I was starting to preach, but needed urgently to get to the point. Restless, Joss moved again in the corner of my vision. Homer didn't seem to notice, the bowl of his pipe glowing cherry red through a mist of blue smoke.

"If you don't believe me, go out, look for yourself. Check the groundwater around the fracking sites, check the surrounding meadows and fields where animals graze and your food crops grow. They're being poisoned by radioactivity far beyond what could be expected from natural sources."

"Why? Because 'Blue Horizon' trade in recycling radioactive waste. The world is awash with it. Countries are prepared to pay billions for someone else to take it off their hands. Which is where 'Blue Horizon' come into the picture. Hidden behind the facade of their shell companies, they take the waste and process it into cement paste that can be pumped. Where? Into the fracking voids deep underground amidst our countryside. Out of sight, out of mind. Invisible. A hidden crime."

"But not quite. The waste may eventually set into a solid, kilometres beneath the surface. But it is still radioactive, and by its very nature that radiation is leaking, seeping slowly to the surface, to poison and kill our world from beneath our very feet. And it's happening now, this very moment, on almost every site in our country, not for a few months but hundreds if not thousands of years."

"Only you can stop it. Not 'Nutty Grace' and her co-anarchists. 'Blue Horizon' have forced this coming general election onto our democratically elected government, to bribe you into voting them 'legally' into office. Ask *yourselves, if they can do this to our environment, leaving a poisonous legacy for hundreds of generations to come, then what else are they capable of doing?"*

Was I ranting, confirming that I was no more than all the lies that Littlemore was spreading on every digital platform he could to intimidate me and give him space? Without thinking, I shook my head, suddenly weary beyond words.

It was that moment I saw it. The imagining of dreams that come true? Too late to turn back. Time suddenly kicked into high gear, with wings on her feet.

"Only you can stop them," I rushed on, desperate to finish.

"The ballot box and the law are your only defence. Ask the questions, find the truth and destroy 'Blue Horizon' before …"

I never got to finish.

Joss was airborne, leaping from an almost impossible distance as we both hurtled towards our destiny.

The Breakfast television presenter sat dumbfounded, hand over her mouth. She had opened the unexpected sequence with an introduction.

"We break our normal schedule for an exclusive interview with the most wanted woman in Britain."

There hadn't been time to explain how her editor had arranged this sudden addition; it hadn't appeared on the morning's schedule or at her briefing. Even at short notice, she had expected a two-way question and answer slot.

Instead, she sat mesmerised as Grace's live transmit evolved, waiting for a pause to intervene. At last, after five uninterrupted minutes, the dishevelled woman on the screen seemed to hesitate, as though distracted.

It was as she leaned forward to use her microphone, that Grace was assassinated in front of her eyes, live, in the kitchens and living rooms of tens of thousands of early morning viewers.

The bullet pierced Joss, deflecting just enough as it shattered her sternum, so when it left her frail body and passed into Grace, it missed her heart by a mere hair's breadth.

A second shot missed, shrilling the morning air in its supersonic path, but the next hit Grace in the face, entering below her left eye, exiting below her ear as she fell backwards under the weight of her beloved Joss.

The air vibrated with the hard, double crack of the shotgun. The first missed, but the second maimed the assassin whisper drone, bringing it tumbling to the ground like a maimed pheasant.

The screen vibrated as the cameraman began to run, a woman's voice screaming, the words a confirmation of what had just taken place.

"Oh my god, they've killed her."

In the seconds that remained, four men forced entrance into the television studio and tore out the live transmission feed, leaving Grace's bloody body still clearly visible on the screen, embracing the slender black and white form of the dog she had come to love, who had tried so hard to save her.

CHAPTER 62
A GRACEFUL CODA

To be honest, Margarita was glad of the work. For many years she had cleaned and looked after the villa, tucked away amidst a profusion of olive and orange trees, on the edge of the village.

The previous owners, a Greek family who lived in Athens, had only visited for national holidays, while in summer there were occasional weekly rentals, but even they had tapered off in recent years. So when a Scandinavian couple bought the place and approached Margarita for her services, she was more than happy to welcome them to the village.

Christiansen, she never knew his first name, came over as a direct, taciturn man. Always polite, he seldom smiled and seemed a man of few words. He spoke little Greek, and while Margarita didn't even know which country in Scandinavia they came from, they managed to converse in English, of which she knew a few words.

Christiansen explained he needed her help with the house while his partner recuperated. That much was obvious. The woman had a livid scar on the left side of her face, and when she washed her hair Margarita noticed the lower half of her left ear was missing.

They had arrived with a wheelchair, though she had never seen it used, but even the slightest incline or flight of steps left the woman acutely breathless. They led a quiet, private existence; bought produce locally, but refrained from any form of socialising beyond passing the time of day.

The woman made a living as a potter. She made what Margarita thought were exquisite pieces, in white porcelain, veined with fine lines of coloured clay. Margarita's daughter had shown her pictures in a fashion magazine, an oriental style described as 'neriage'. Every month, a transit box was carefully packed and despatched by courier to an address in Copenhagen, which supported the local gossip that they were Danish.

The woman gained a degree of popularity amongst the local village women by distributing what she considered her seconds, or failed pieces, for free. Throughout the village, windows were adorned with her elegant vases, bowls and pots.

Christiansen was often seen wandering the hills and wooded valleys armed with a shepherd's crook and an air rifle, accompanied by a young black and white sheepdog in the early stages of training. Despite his withdrawn nature, he was known to share the odd pigeon, or partridge, in exchange for a jar of honey or bottle of local wine.

Over time, curiosity faded and they became part of the tapestry of village life. Margarita, with access to their private lives, kept their secrets. She shared little with the local gossips, so they soon became bored and plied her with fewer questions. There was much she saw, things she surmised but never imparted, even to her husband and daughter.

A few visitors came. The most frequent was a young couple; a blonde woman and a tall, raven haired man with skin the colour of pale coffee. They had a child, a young girl only just starting to walk, with her mother's skin colour and father's hair. An ease between the two men implied a family relationship, though no one said.

They visited perhaps twice a year, often in the company of a tall slender woman, a friend, not a relative. Curiously, she too had difficulty carrying her bags, and when you watched, you could tell her arm movements required thought. Yet there was an ease when they were all together, an aura seemed to surround them that, perhaps, implied a shared, private secret.

In their company, Margarita watched with interest, especially the interaction between the two younger women, for there was something in the gaze of the taller woman towards her blonde friend, a crossover between friendship and desire.

Occasionally, two different men appeared. The younger, Margarita heard, was called Fabian, while the older man, always dressed in a foppish sort of way, brought a serious air to the house for the duration of their stay. They shared a bedroom with a sea view; there was no secret to their relationship.

The only insight Margarita gained on their lives followed their visit when she found a discarded British newspaper in their bedroom. The front page, carried a headline,

'Blue Horizon' wiped out at the polls
Beneath the bannerline was a photograph of a new British Prime Minster, surrounded by his cabinet on the steps of 10 Downing Street. From the back row, the face of the older man stared smiling back at the camera.

People came and went; Margarita kept her counsel, told no secrets. Why? Well, perhaps there are some things you just sense and don't need to tell.

One morning, she had the house to herself. Christiansen had taken the van to the local town to collect supplies of clay and gas for the kiln. He offered to take the woman with him, promising lunch on the beach beside the sea. It was one of those days when the early morning air was like crystal, inducing a lightness in step, a brightness to the eye, and for once they left to the sound of shared laughter.

Two matching slender vases, of the style the woman created, sat at balanced ends of the oak beam above the fireplace. They framed a similar vase of exquisitely crafted origami dandelions. The lids of the vases were almost seamless, while their weight implied they contained something precious.

Gently, Margarita raised a lid. It was almost completely full of ash of the palest grey. The vase at the opposite end held the same.

The air stirred gently. Left by her owners on the promise of a hot day, the young dog had entered the room behind her and lay watching from the cool shadows of a corner. It was almost as if the dog nodded, reading her mind.

Every morning, Margarita had seen the woman kiss her hand and press it to the side of each vase, a long, far-away expression in her eyes. Margarita looked back at the dog, imagined asking for permission.

The vases were heavy, with no apparent markings apart from the coloured veins. Beautiful, she thought, as she turned each one carefully in her hands.

Written in black lettering on the base were the names,
Angela and *Joss*
Nodding to herself, Margarita returned her gaze to the young dog behind her. Her name, too, was Joss. And the little girl who came to stay? Well, she danced to the nickname Angie.

When Margarita looked again at the dog, she could swear the dog smiled back as she stood with a languid stretch. With her tail gently wagging, she left the room.

Nothing more need ever be said.

Printed in Great Britain
by Amazon

86901457R00284